Praise for Max Barry's *Syrup*

"Snappy . . . satisfyingly revenge-driven, full of scary marketing tips and fizzy as Fukk."
—*Los Angeles Times*

"There's something so nostalgic and right on the money about this novel . . . a ~~youth~~ joyous youth, where everything is poss~~ible~~ ~~universal~~, organizational skills, im~~ ~~s~~, it's possible to get whate~~

st

"A fast-paced tour through L.A., Hollywood, Madison Avenue and corporate America."
—*Chicago Sun-Times*

"Seductively hip . . . wickedly funny"
—*USA Today*

"A hilarious satirical novel . . . Barry has a deft ear for dialogue and a sharp-honed wit."
—*Chicago New City*

"Funny and fast . . . A rollicking debut about a cola marketing campaign that takes on Hollywood, Madison Avenue, and corporate America in one perfectly executed triple play."
—*Kirkus Reviews*

"A deft, satirical indictment of an industry that makes its living pushing satire."   —*Spin*

"[A] terrific comic novel . . . charming and hilarious."
—*Booklist*

PENGUIN BOOKS

SYRUP

Max Barry is the author of *Jennifer Government* (2003), *Company* (2006), and *Machine Man* (2011). His latest book is *Lexicon* (2013). He lives in Melbourne, Australia.

A Note
to the Reader

Syrup

MAX BARRY

A NOVEL

PENGUIN BOOKS

PENGUIN BOOKS
Published by the Penguin Group
Penguin Group (USA) Inc., 375 Hudson Street,
New York, New York 10014, USA

USA | Canada | UK | Ireland | Australia | New Zealand | India | South Africa | China
Penguin Books Ltd, Registered Offices: 80 Strand, London WC2R 0RL, England
For more information about the Penguin Group visit penguin.com

First published in the United States of America by Viking Penguin,
a member of Penguin Putnam Inc., 1999
Published in Penguin Books 2000
This edition published 2013

THE LIBRARY OF CONGRESS HAS CATALOGED
THE HARDCOVER EDITION AS FOLLOWS:
Barry, Max.
Syrup / Max Barry.
p. cm.
ISBN 978-0-670-88640-1 (hc.)
ISBN 978-0-14-312530-3 (pbk.)
I. Title.
PS3552.A7424S97   1999
813'.54—dc21   98-53485

Printed in the United States of America
1   3   5   7   9   10   8   6   4   2

Set in Adobe Garamond
Designed by Mark Melnick

For my beloved Jen, always

Acknowledgments

I'd like to gratefully acknowledge those who made especially important contributions to this book: the members of the Internet Writing Workshop, particularly Charles Thiesen, for their unique and invaluable advice; Carolyn Carlson and the team at Viking, for their unending enthusiasm and skill in bringing Syrup to the shelves; and Todd Keithley, for his confidence, support and that truly spectacular demonstration of buzzmaking.

Me, Me, Me

CHAPTER 000001

i have a dream

I want to be famous. Really famous.

I want to be so famous that movie stars hang out with me and talk about what a bummer their lives are. I want to beat up photographers who catch me in hotel lobbies with Winona Ryder. I want to be implicated in vicious rumors about Drew Barrymore's sex parties. And, finally, I want to be pronounced DOA in a small, tired LA hospital after doing speedballs with Matt Damon.

I want it all. I want the American dream.

fame

I realized a long time ago that the best way to get famous in this country is to become an actor. Unfortunately, I'm a terrible actor. I'm not even a mediocre actor, which rules out a second attractive path: marrying an actress (they inbreed, so you can't marry one unless you are one). For a while I thought about becoming a rock star, but for that you either have to be immensely talented or have sex with a studio executive, and somehow I just couldn't foresee either of those little scenarios in my immediate future.

So that really leaves just one option: to be very young, very cool and very, very rich. The great thing about this particular path to fame, *Oprah* and line jumping at nightclubs is that it's open to everyone. They say anyone can make it in this country, and it's true: you can make it all the way to the top and a vacuous, drink-slurred lunch with Madonna. All you have to do is find something you're good enough at to make a million dollars, and find it before you're twenty-five.

When I think about how simple it all is, I can't understand why kids my age are so pessimistic.

why you should be a millionaire

I read somewhere that the average adult has three million-dollar ideas per year. Three ideas a year that could make you a millionaire. I guess some people have more of these ideas and some people less, but it's reasonably safe to assume that even the most idiotic of us has to score at least one big idea during our lifetimes.

So everybody's got ideas. Ideas are cheap. What's unique is the conviction to follow through: to work at it until it pays off. That's what separates the person who thinks *I wonder why they can't just make shampoo and conditioner in one?* from the one who thinks *Now, should I get the Mercedes, or another BMW?*

Three million-dollar ideas per year. For a long time, I couldn't get this out of my head. And there was always the chance I could have an *above average* idea, because they've got to be out there, too. The ten-million-dollar ideas. The fifty-million-dollar ideas.

The billion-dollar ideas.

the idea

The interesting part of my life starts at ten past two in the morning of January 7th. At ten past two on January 7th, I am twenty-three years and six minutes old. I am just contemplating how similar this feeling is to being, say, twenty-two years and six minutes old, when it happens: I get an idea.

"Oh shit," I say. "Oh, *shit*." I get up and hunt around my room for paper and a pen, can't find either, and eventually raid the bedroom of the guy I share my apartment with. I scribble on the paper and get a beer from the fridge, and by the time I'm twenty-three years and four hours old, I've worked out how I'm going to make a million dollars.

now hold on there, smart guy

Okay. So how do I know this idea is so good?

a little explanation

When I was in my senior year of high school, the counselor said, "Now, Michael, about college . . ."

"Yeah?" I was distracted at the time by cheerleading practice outside his window. Or maybe I was just inattentive and daydreaming of cheerleaders. Not sure. "I'm doing pre-law."

This was my plan. I'd had it for years, and I was pretty proud of it, too. I mean, just having a plan was a big deal. When people (like my parents) asked, "And what are you going to do after high school?" I could say, "Pre-law," and they'd smile and raise their eyebrows and nod. It was much better than my previous answer, a shrug, which tended to attract frowns and comments about youth unemployment rates.

"Yes," the counselor said, and cleared his throat. Outside the window, or inside my mind, cute girls twirled red-and-white pom-poms. "I think it's time we looked at something . . . more realistic."

I blinked. "More . . . ?"

"Let's be honest, Michael," he said gently. He didn't have a particularly gentle face—it was kind of bitter and jaded—and the effort he made to twist it into something sympathetic was a little scary. "You don't have the grades for it, do you?"

"Well," I said, "maybe not, but . . ." And I stopped. Because there was no *but*. I didn't have the grades. My plan, perfect until this moment, was missing this small but crucial step: good grades. "Shit," I said.

backup

And weren't the parents pissed.

If I'd been fooling myself, I'd been fooling them worse. They were already picking me out a dorm at Harvard and talking about Stanford as a "backup." It was a little difficult for them when I broke the news that I was going to need a backup for my backup.

When the only school that would have me was Cal State, they moved to Iowa. I'm still not sure if that was coincidence.

college

I majored in marketing because I was late for registration.

I mean, suddenly I was in *college;* I was in a dorm and I was surrounded by college girls. There was a lot on my mind. Now, sure, there were upperclassmen and faculty advisers dedicated to making sure that freshmen like me didn't miss registration, but it wasn't hard to ditch them in favor of more horizon-broadening pursuits. My biggest mistake was making friends with a guy who had just transferred from Texas and was pre-enrolled: I forgot all about registration. I was scheduled between ten A.M. and eleven, and I turned up at four the following Thursday.

I was lucky anyone was still there, because by then enrollments had officially closed. When I tapped on the glass door, my choice of two first-year electives was reduced to three sad little tables: Programming in Visual Basic; Masculinity in the New Millennium; and Introductory Marketing.

Masculinity in the New Millennium was actually kind of interesting.

But Marketing was unbelievable.

mktg: a definition

Marketing (or *mktg*, which is what you write when you're taking lecture notes at two hundred words per minute) is the biggest industry in the world, and it's invisible. It's the planet's largest religion, but the billions who worship it don't know it. It's vast, insidious and completely corrupt.

Marketing is like LA. It's like a gorgeous, brainless model in LA. A gorgeous, brainless model on cocaine having sex drinking Perrier in LA. That's the best way I know how to describe it.

mktg case study #1: mktg perfume

TRIPLE YOUR PRICE. THIS GIVES CUSTOMERS THE IMPRESSION OF GREAT QUALITY. HELPS PROFITS, TOO.

welcome to reality

The first principle of marketing (okay, it's not the first, but it doesn't sound nearly as cool to say it's the third) is this: *Perception is reality.* You see, a long time ago, some academic came up with the idea that reality doesn't actually exist. Or at least, if it does, no one can agree what it is. Because of perception.

Perception is the filter through which we view the world, and most of the time it's a handy thing to have: it generalizes the world so we can deduce that a man who wears an Armani suit is rich, or that a man who wears an Armani suit and keeps saying "Isn't this some Armani suit" is a rich asshole. But perception is a faulty mechanism. Perception is unreliable and easily distracted, subject to a thousand miscues and misinformation . . . like marketing. If anyone found a way to actually distinguish perception from reality, the entire marketing industry would crumble into the sea overnight.

(Incidentally, this wouldn't be a good thing. The economy of every Western country would implode. Some of the biggest companies on the planet would never sell another product. The air would be thick with executives leaping out of windows and landing on BMWs.)

graduation

I ended up taking as many marketing classes as I could, and actually graduated from Cal State summa cum laude. If I'd just finished pre-law, I'd have settled into earnest conversation with the top law firms of the country, bandying about six-figure salaries, ninety-hour weeks and twenty-year career plans. Law seems very structured like that.

But marketing hates systems. Which is nice, in an idealistic, free-spirited sort of way, but it makes it a pain in the ass to get a job. To get a good job in marketing, you need to market yourself.

hello

My name is Scat.

I used to be Michael George Holloway, but I had no chance of getting into marketing with a name like that. My potential employers, who had names like Fysh, Siimon and Onion, didn't even think I was making an effort. The least I could do was echo their creative genius by choosing a wacky, zany, top-of-mind name myself.

For a while, I seriously toyed with the idea of calling myself Mr. Pretentious. But when sanity prevailed, I chose Scat. It sounded kind of fast-track.

career plan

So, armed with my new name, I was ready to hit the major corporations for a job. I was ready for the work week, tailored suits, corporate golf days, pension plans, Friday night drinks, frequent flyer programs and conservative values. I'd take it all.

But then I get my idea.

Fukk

CHAPTER 000002

great ideas

Of course, my great idea is a great *marketing* idea. And some of the best marketing ideas in the world haven't been that exciting. Take fridge magnets. Great idea. Somebody probably made a bundle out of that one, before larger corporations with better manufacturing economies ate him up. But nobody cares.

My idea is for a new cola. This is important, because the soda market is very big. It's so big that if a new product captures even a tiny percentage of the market, the revenues are into the millions of dollars. People tend to think of soda as little cans in fridges, without really understanding that the top two companies—Coca-Cola and PepsiCo—turn over about twenty billion dollars a year, and could, if they felt the urge, actually buy themselves a country.

So a *good* idea for a new cola is pretty exciting.

into the breach

At eight A.M., I'm sitting at the kitchen table with a beer, a pen, a scribbled-on piece of paper and a whopping headache. Unfortunately, after my initial burst of genius, I've stalled. It turns out that although I've come up with good ideas for the important stuff—the name, the concept and the target market—I'm short on the rest, like how it should taste. And, more important, I've realized that there's no way I can bring this product to market alone.

This is depressing.

Fortunately, Sneaky Pete arrives home.

sneaky pete

Sneaky Pete is the coolest person I've ever met. This is partially due to his amazingly snappy fashion sense, but mainly because he rarely says anything, which allows him to preserve a slightly mysterious air of smooth confidence. I met Sneaky Pete at a marketing function during my last semester at Cal State and we became friends—surprisingly easily, considering his lack of conversation. So it was logical that we should pool our resources to find an LA apartment, especially since Sneaky Pete's resources are much larger than mine.

If you happen to meet Sneaky Pete, maybe at some beach-house party, you'll be told he's from Tokyo, Japan. You won't be told by Sneaky Pete, of course, because he is far too cool to hold forth about his international travels, but it's a sure bet you'll find out from someone. They'll tell you in slightly awestruck tones that in Tokyo, Sneaky Pete was the wild child of marketing; that he moved from company to company and revived brand after brand; that in the end he had to come to America because the Japanese haven't learned the same absolute respect for marketing that we have and as such find it difficult to justify marketing salaries of more than a million dollars a year.

You will raise your eyebrows and look over at Sneaky Pete, and he'll be standing there with his deep shades and stunning cheekbones, and you will believe. If you are brazen or addled enough to ask "Why is he called Sneaky Pete?" you will receive a short, alarmed roll of the eyes. A roll that suggests you don't really want to know, and if you do, you should know you can't ask in public.

I have a lot of respect for Sneaky Pete, not least because he is actually a fresh marketing graduate from Singapore who has never worked in his life. His real name is Yuong Ang (I saw it on his passport), his most valuable possession is a crumpled little book called *Through American Eyes: The Asian Stereotype*, and he attended Guandong Technical School, where he managed bare passing grades.

sneaky pete helps

"Sneaky Pete!" I say, leaping up. "Man, I'm glad to see you." He may be pleased by this, or maybe not: it's kind of hard to tell through his shades. "I have a huge idea and I need your help."

He cocks a chiseled eyebrow at me, then pulls up a chair at our tacky kitchen table. I tell him all about my idea and he listens solemnly, nodding. I'm pretty relieved he doesn't shoot me down, because even though you need to back your own judgment on stuff like this, it's good to have other people believe in you, too.

"My *problem,* though," I say, "is that I don't know what to do now. I mean, I can't launch a cola product by myself. I'm stuck."

Sneaky Pete leans back in his chair, smirking.

"What?" I say. "I'm not stuck?"

He shakes his head.

"Hmm . . . hey, no! You mean I should sell this to one of the majors?"

Sneaky Pete's lips stretch into a grin.

"Okay." I think about this. "That would be good if I knew someone in the industry. But I don't. If I just walked in there, they'd chew me over and take my idea. I need a contact." I sigh. "I guess I need the name and number of the New Products Marketing Manager at Coke."

I snigger at this little fantasy. But Sneaky Pete doesn't share my joviality. He leans forward, and he's not smiling anymore. Sneaky Pete looks very serious.

"No," I say. "No way."

Then Sneaky Pete speaks. This is always a little thrill, both because it's so rare and because of his accent, which is strangely addictive.

"Yes way," Sneaky Pete says.

omen

It turns out that Sneaky Pete met this girl at a Malibu nightclub who has just been appointed New Products Marketing Manager at Coca-Cola. I am continually amazed by how many people Sneaky Pete manages to meet, given that as a general rule he doesn't talk.

I don't quite catch the girl's name, but Sneaky Pete waves his hand in a way that tells me he'll take care of everything. He pulls out his cellphone and goes into his room, and when he comes out he hands me a scrap of paper with a time—two hours from now—and an address.

"Sneaky Pete," I say earnestly, "thank you. I'll remember you when I'm rich and famous."

welcome to coca-cola

I am the only person in Los Angeles who doesn't own a car, so I catch the bus to Coca-Cola's downtown tower (they're technically based in Atlanta but have obviously realized they can't *really* operate out of anywhere but California). It's twenty minutes away from our East LA apartment, but the building is so mammoth that I spend another five gaping at it. It's huge, black and so much like a big glass of Coke it had to be accidental.

I take a deep breath, then stroll into reception, pausing only to dutifully admire the smattering of ancient Coke memorabilia. I note that as in all large corporations that loudly subscribe to equal opportunity and employment based solely on skill, the receptionist is young, female and gorgeous.

"Scat," I tell her. "To see the New Products Marketing Manager."

The receptionist fields this without looking up. Just when I'm about to introduce myself again, only louder, she says, "She'll be a few minutes, Mr. Scat. May I show you to a meeting room?"

"Yes you may," I say generously. She slides a VISITOR badge across the counter and leads me to a well-lit room with a mahogany desk, big red chairs and carpet thick enough to lose small children in. I throw my briefcase on the table and sink into a chair. "Thanks."

The receptionist sends me a truly insulting smile—only half her mouth even makes the effort—but I just put that down to her being gorgeous.

a spiel about gorgeous

Gorgeous women really annoy me.

Not all gorgeous women. Some gorgeous women I like a lot. Gorgeous women who like me, for example, I can't help but find attractive. Gorgeous smart women I like a lot. But the rest, I can't stand.

The problem, as I see it, is that a sad percentage of gorgeous women just settle for being gorgeous. They get to sixteen, go, "Well, I'm gorgeous, people like me, that's it," and just *stop*. I mean, they've got nothing on the girls who struggle onward with zits and bad dates, the girls who fight life every step of the way so by the time they're twenty they're funny and smart and cynical and utterly, utterly desirable.

That's what I like.

Which makes what happens next really ironic.

scat meets 6

The New Products Marketing Manager enters the room and I am stunned. I am flabbergasted. I want to grab her, fling her across the table and make love to her. For whole seconds I can do nothing but stare.

She's about my age, but she walks like an experienced nut-cracker. Her hair is shoulder-length, jet-black and sheer enough to deflect bullets. Her legs pop out of her heels and proudly strut their stuff all the way up to her miniskirt. Her eyebrows could cut steel. Her face is exquisitely cruel, and I can immediately tell she has never smiled in her whole life.

"Good afternoon, Mr. Scat," she says briskly, seating herself across from me. She is carrying a slim folder and she slips it onto the table. I am not watching the folder. "My name is 6."

A response is called for here. I realize this far too late.

"Mr. Scat," she says sternly, "for your information, I fuck girls. So take your eyes elsewhere."

"Sorry." To avoid embarrassing myself further by asking her to repeat her name, which sounded suspiciously like her dress size, I push a business card across to her. She returns the favor and I study her card. It confirms that her name is 6. I am impressed. I bet her real surname begins with *Z* and she got sick of always being last in line.

"Mr. Scat," she says. I am already in love with her lips. "Are you aware of how many unsolicited approaches our company receives from people like yourself?"

I consider taking a punt, but decide against it. "No."

"Actually, not that many," she says. "But the point is they're all crap. Without exception. We've never bought one." She leans forward. "I tell you this now so you don't become too disappointed at the rejection."

(Part of the problem with selling ideas to marketers is jealousy. Marketers are supposed to come up with their own ideas.)

"Thank you for setting my expectations," I say.

"You're welcome." She looks at her watch. It is expensive. "You have thirty seconds."

At this, I lose my cool a little. "Thirty seconds? I have an idea that could make your company millions and you want to hear it in thirty seconds?"

6 blinks. She seems genuinely surprised. "Mr. Scat, we have thirty seconds to sell our ideas to our customers. It's called advertising." She even looks a little hurt, and her pouting lips make me want to ravish her even more.

"You're right," I say, humbled. "Let me apologize." My eyes narrow cunningly. "Over dinner."

6 sighs deeply. "On my office wall, Mr. Scat, is a large, nude picture of Elle Macpherson. I have this picture to remind people such as yourself that my ideal lover is one without a penis."

"Fine," I say, as if this doesn't faze me in the slightest. In truth I am completely fazed. I'm so fazed I've forgotten what I'm here for.

"You have seven seconds left," 6 says.

"That's not fair," I protest.

"Four," she says, and she's actually looking at her watch.

I spill it. "New cola product. Black can. Called Fukk."

6 looks at me for a long time, expressionless. I am beginning to wonder if she has granted me bonus time and I should be expand-

ing my description, when she says, "Mr. Scat, I would be pleased to have dinner with you tonight. The Saville, seven o'clock."

but your honor

In self-defense, I would like to say that I wasn't taken in by her looks. I mean, sure, she was the type that would make shallow men in cars yell out things like, "Hey, *baby! Woo!*" but not me. I'm not like that.

What I'm trying to say is that, really, I was interested in her mind.

No, really.

peer to peer

See, you just have to respect someone who really markets themselves well.

Some of us change our names to something crazy, zany and/or wacky. Some favor crazy zany wacky fashion, like 1930s hats or purple baggy pants. Some use particular sayings over and over, creating their own bylines. Some just go off the edge and don't do anything at all.

When you go to all that effort, and you see other people making a lot of effort for pretty pathetic results, you have to admire someone who really pulls it off.

So you see, when you strip it down, what I really felt for 6 was professional respect for a colleague.

Plus, okay, a deep desire to get naked with her.

The Saville at seven is very much a Porsche occasion. It's disappointing, therefore, that I don't have a Porsche.

But this is no obstacle. The first thing I do when I get home is call a Porsche dealership. I tell them I've just arrived from Australia and am leaving tomorrow for England, but while I'm here I'd like to purchase a car for my father's birthday. Would it be at all possible for them to extend their hours for me? The man tells me, with the tone of someone who has just stumbled across a surprise commission on fifty thousand, that the dealership never closes for its valued clients. I commend them for their customer-friendly policy and tell them to expect me around six.

Then I find a nearby Mercedes-Benz dealership and deliver the same spiel. Then a SAAB dealer. Then finally a Ford dealer.

The thing is, you can't just rock up on foot and ask to take an expensive car like a Porsche for a spin. But you can test drive a Porsche if you turn up in a Mercedes, and you can test drive a Mercedes if you turn up in a SAAB, and you can test drive a SAAB if you turn up in a late-model Ford. I'm pretty sure I can sucker the Ford guys on foot.

My calls complete, I ask Sneaky Pete for wardrobe assistance. "Occasion?" he asks quietly.

"Seduction. Beautiful girl hiding her desire for me beneath a charade of lesbianism."

Sneaky Pete absorbs this silently. He stares into my closet, then rips out a jacket, a tie, pants and a shirt. I'm impressed, but he's just getting started. He wanders over to my desk and studies my accessories. Sadly, nothing there appears to take his fancy, and he disappears into his own room. When he returns, he is carrying a Rolex, sunglasses and a thin chain I'm not sure if I'm supposed to put on my wrist, my waist or around my neck.

"Thanks," I say gratefully. Sneaky Pete nods and silently withdraws.

When I'm showered, shaved and dressed, I catch a bus to

the Ford dealership. It's no problem to talk my way into a Ford, and from here the process goes smoothly all the way up, so when I slide my current-year Mercedes into the Porsche dealership, there is a small man with bright eyes helping me out of the car. The Porsche people are a little more strict about letting people take test drives on their own, but this doesn't slow me down for long, either. I drive around with the dealer in tow, admiring the car, and when we get back I pretend to call my father on my cellphone.

"Hey, Dad," I say loudly. I am trying very hard to let everyone hear me while appearing to be concerned that no one hears me. "Where are you, at the studio? . . . How's Geena? . . . And Uma? . . . Fantastic." I act so badly I make myself sick.

"So, Dad." The dealer is pretending to arrange a potted plant. He turns it left, surveys it critically, turns it back. His acting is far worse than mine. "I've got a surprise. No, just be out the front of One in twenty minutes. Okay? . . . Great. Love to you. Okay. Okay."

I turn to the dealer. "It's a done deal. Gimme the car."

He breaks out in smiles. I give him a big greasy helping of my own. We are both happy, smiling people. "You take American Express, right?"

"Of course," he says, mortally offended.

Inside, of course, I am astounded to discover that my American Express Gold Card is missing. I rifle through my wallet, spilling three hundred dollars in cash (my entire savings), my bogus American Film Institute card and my driver's license across the desk. "I can't believe this." The dealer proffers great sympathy. "Hey," I say, "you know who I am, right? You don't mind me fixing you up tomorrow?"

The dealer, who of course has never heard of me in his life, picks up my driver's license. I can see him considering whether he should know me or not.

"Look, tell you what," I say. "I'll leave that with you. As security."

He's doubtful, but it's amazing how flexible people can be

when they think there's a commission in it. He calls someone to check that I exist, and apparently I do. So I get the car.

Porsche's success is largely due to excellent marketing, but it's still a fuck of a good car. I put the foot down and eat up most of Los Angeles in twenty minutes.

mktg case study #2: mktg cola

NEVER, NEVER DISCUSS TASTE. TASTE IS 90 PERCENT PSYCHOLOGICAL AND IT DOESN'T SELL COLA; IT'S ROUGHLY A TENTH AS IMPORTANT AS IMAGE. THERE HAVE BEEN STUDIES.

an epic dinner with 6

The Saville is amazingly classy. I doubt I'd even be let inside a place like this unless I drove a Porsche, sunglasses or not.

By some beautiful stroke of fate, 6 is already inside and seated just behind the glass, so she sees me drive up. This is great luck, because it frees me from having to slip the Porsche into conversation somewhere. I grin to her as I toss the keys to the valet and she raises one killer eyebrow in return. She is so sexy I am in pain.

When I arrive at the table, I see that she's wearing a white dress, which is clinging to her so tightly I doubt she can breathe. Against her midnight hair, the effect is a little dizzying. "6," I say. "You look ravishing."

"Mr. Scat." She hesitates.

"Please," I say, sitting. "Just Scat."

"Scat." She presses long, elegant fingers together. Pianist fingers. Brain surgeon fingers. Except for the nails, which are half an inch long and painted black. "Let me jump right in."

"Please do," I say with real feeling.

18

"This Fukk Cola . . . it's intriguing. I think it may have potential."

"Thank you," I say, beginning to fiddle with my napkin. On some level I realize this is a giveaway of my nervousness at having a power dinner at the Saville, but I can't help myself. I try to twirl the napkin every so often to appear kind of bored and cool rather than manic-obsessive.

6 ignores my napkin performance to pick up a short stick of celery and slip it between her lips. "You were thinking, of course," she says, gently masticating the celery, "of the gwwfnnnfss hggnnyupp dmmnngffn."

6 is looking at me and I abruptly realize that I should quit concentrating so much on the way she slips food between her lips and start concentrating on what she is saying. "Pardon me?"

She frowns. "I asked if you were thinking of the gen-X, high-end yup demographic."

"Oh, of course," I say, recovering. "It'll be the drink of cynics."

6 is nodding her head wisely.

"Forgive my asking," I say, feeling abruptly bold. Perhaps it's the soft reassurance of the napkin. "But you seem pretty young to be a marketing manager in such a big company."

"I'm twenty-one," 6 says.

"No you're not," I say.

"Ah, no," she says. "I am."

"I'm sorry," I say, "but you can't be twenty-one."

"Mr. Scat," 6 says firmly. In the candlelight her eyes are very deep. "I'm twenty-one. Deal with it."

I can pretend to swallow the lesbian routine, but this is too much for me. "Hey, I'm sure it impresses them in your alumni, this young-marketing-genius-with-attitude deal. But I don't buy it."

"You seem to think I should care," 6 says.

"Look, 6," I say, trying to soothe, "I know where you're coming from. It's hard to get credibility without some sort of angle. But it is just an angle, right? You're not twenty-one and you're as homosexual as I am."

"It's interesting, what you're doing," 6 tells me. She leans forward and rests her chin on one immaculately manicured hand as if she is genuinely intrigued. "You obviously have an esteem problem with your sexuality, and can't accept that a beautiful woman isn't attracted to you." She sniffs. "I did some psych units."

"When?" I say scathingly. "Elementary school?"

"I went to Stanford," 6 says steadily. I curse silently, because I usually lie about having gone to Stanford and she's beaten me to it. "I graduated from high school at fifteen, courtesy of an advanced learning program. I did four years at UCLA, an M.B.A. at Stanford, and now, after six weeks at Coca-Cola, I am twenty-one years of age."

I want to argue, but she gets to me. I know what she's doing: that everything she tells me is to build this marketing image, but I can't resist it. I know Coke is one part faintly repulsive black syrup, seven parts water and forty-two parts marketing, but I still drink it. Perception is reality.

"Scat," she says, "you're a little screwed up, but I want to work with you."

I blink. A witty comment is called for here, but I don't have one. "Boy," I say.

6 pulls a large black folder out from I have no idea where. I cannot conceive of 6 carrying anything large enough to contain this folder. 6 is saying, "We're going to draw up a concept sketch here," but I am transfixed by this folder. I try to think how she can possibly lug this thing around and still appear cool, and I fail completely. I miss Sneaky Pete, who is at his best with puzzles like this.

"Scat?" 6 is staring at my napkin, and I look down to see that somehow I've managed to idly extract two feet of white string from the hem. I subtly push it and the two forks it has entangled into my lap. 6 clears her throat. "The concept sketch?"

My mind races back to my college days in search of what a concept sketch is. I'm pretty sure I skipped that class. "Good idea," I say heartily.

"I can req some people," 6 says. "We'll work it through to-morrow and have a presentation ready for Friday."

Today is Tuesday. "So long?"

6's eyes shift. "Let's allow some X-time."

I have no idea what X-time is, but it sounds like way too cool a concept to not know about. The part of my brain that got me through college quietly suggests that it may be time to allow for various screwups. "Good thinking."

"Thank you," she says, looking for the waiter. She manages to catch his attention with a raised eyebrow, and he is immediately by her side, handing out menus. She doesn't even need to look at them. "Six."

"Very good," the waiter says. I look at the menu, and amaz-ingly enough, there really are numbers beside the selections and it is possible to order a number six. I am immediately sure that 6 has searched the city for classy restaurants in which it is possible to do this, and I am stunned—again—by how cool 6 is. She is whipping my butt in the cool stakes. I need to execute a tremen-dously suave move to recover from here.

I toss the menu aside. "How about some big tortellini? Can you do that? Not those little tortellini, but really big ones. I just want four giant tortellini on a plate."

I sneak a glance at 6, and she is looking so nonchalant at my ordering off the menu that I must have scored. The waiter is frowning a little, but not so much that I think I need to worry about my food. "Shall we make that veal?" he asks. "With a funghi sauce?"

"Excellent," I say, thinking that eating cute young animals can't help but win me points here, too. The waiter nods and disappears.

6 flicks open her folder to reveal massive sheets of thick paper. "I'm thinking of a staggered distribution across the country, rather than simultaneous release. I want to create two waves of release, from LA and New York, to ride the WOM dispersion. Assuming the CTs green out, of course."

WOM is word of mouth, and every ad exec's worst nightmare.

21

If it wasn't so powerful, marketers would try to pretend it didn't exist. See, the problem with advertising is that lots of people tend not to believe it. You might think that after a company spends several million dollars on an advertising campaign, the least the general public could do in return is swallow the thing whole, but, unfortunately, this is not true. Instead, most people tend to place more credibility in the opinions of their friends. Horrible truths like this keep marketers awake at night.

CTs are Chicago Trials. Every major product released into the American market since the 1970s has been through a Chicago Trial. Basically, a CT is a scaled-down version of the planned national campaign, confined to the city of Chicago. Everyone does it, because in 1972 some guy released a research paper reporting that the population of Chicago was demographically very similar to that of the entire United States of America. It had almost the same percentages of people in each age bracket, same ethnic division, same income distribution, et cetera. So the guy strung up this theory that if a product works in Chicago, it will work throughout the nation. Sometime after 1972, but way, way before now, the demographic makeup of Chicago and the nation changed so they no longer resemble each other nearly as much as they used to, but CTs have become so ingrained in the marketing process that no one can get rid of them. Everyone does CTs.

6 is scribbling on her pad. I crane my neck and see she is drawing arrows and boxes and circles and graphs. I silently approve: it's much easier to be incomprehensible than intelligent, and most people can't spot the difference. "Sounds great. And international?"

"It will follow, of course," she says, not looking up. She is now drawing a huge spiraling thing that looks like a tornado. I think she's beginning to push it a bit far. "We have great design people. It's critical to get the look of the can right."

"Essential," I agree.

"And the aeration. We had a bad experience in Massachusetts with aeration."

"Really?" I ask, interested.

22

6 looks up at me uncertainly, obviously unsure if she should be telling me this, so I smile reassuringly at her. She looks even more nervous, so I immediately kill the smile. This seems to calm her and she goes back to her doodling. "The bottlers got it way too high. Three thousand people rang up to complain that their Cokes were tickling their noses."

"Wow," I say, because she seems to expect it.

6 nods and draws for another moment. She appears to be shading when she adds, "Then there was that exploding can fatality."

She looks up quickly to see if I react badly to this. It's important not to appear shocked, but I struggle for a moment and 6 realizes she's gone too far. "I don't want that comment interpreted to mean that any product of Coca-Cola has ever caused any personal injury to any of its customers," she says stiffly.

"I am under no impression whatsoever that your employer has ever caused any of its customers injury," I respond quickly. I didn't do business law for the fun of it.

6 studies me for a further moment. "Good," she says, going back to her shading.

I breathe a small sigh of relief and slap my hand, which has begun seeking out the napkin again.

"There," she says, tearing a bedsheet-sized paper from the pad and offering it to me. I pretend I don't understand she wants me to take it and instead slide my chair around the table to her. She looks momentarily disconcerted, but I hardly notice because suddenly her delicious, heady scent is trying very hard to knock me to the floor. I close my eyes for a second to regain control. When I open them, 6 is regarding me warily.

"Visualizing," I explain.

"Oh." Relief spreads across her features. At this range they are astounding. "What's your feedback?"

It's a real effort to tear my gaze away from her and down to the paper, but I manage it. I'm surprised to see that 6 has actually been doing something constructive, not doodling at all. What I mistook for a tornado is a soda can: deep black with the word

Fukk impressively rendered in Matura MT Script. It looks amazingly cool. I would drink this.

"Wow," I say. "6, this is great. You're very talented."

"Thank you," she says, as if people say this to her all the time. I don't doubt it. "I'm not in Design, but I have always liked to draw."

"Tell me about it," I suggest quietly, sensing the potential for a childhood story here; perhaps the baring of a small portion of 6's soul. I look deeply into her eyes.

"About what?" she says, crossing her arms. "I just draw, that's all."

"Oh," I say, embarrassed. I change the subject fast. "So tell me, why 6? Why not, say, 5?"

"What?" she says, looking puzzled.

"Your name. Why did you pick 6?"

When she answers, I almost kick myself for not expecting it. "I didn't choose it. It's my real name."

I look at her. She regards me coolly. "Oh, come *on*," I say. "Your parents did not name you 6. No parents ever gave their kid an unusual but cool name. There are only parent-given normal names and parent-given embarrassing names." I am thinking in particular about a boy I went to elementary school with named Petals.

"You've obviously spent some time on this, so I hate to kill your theory," 6 says, "but I was named 6 by my parents."

I search for a refutation but fail to come up with anything better than "Crap." I wisely decide against using it.

"Although," she adds, "not at first."

My mind reels. "Not at . . . ?"

"When I was born, I was named 0. On my first birthday, I was renamed 1. It was especially meaningful, having my new name as well as my age in frosty blue icing on my birthday cake."

"Oh, *please*," I say. 6's fantasy world is threatening to overwhelm me. Her lies are so obvious that I can't help but believe them a little. "Even if you could remember your first birthday, you're telling me that you were renamed to a new number every year?"

"That's right," she says.

There's an obvious flaw in this little story, and I wait for her to explain it. She doesn't, choosing instead to sip at her wine. I sit for a moment to see if I can ride out the urge to quiz her further, and, as it turns out, I can't. "Okay," I say. "What happened to 7?"

6 puts down her glass and looks at me. "My parents were killed in a plane crash. When I was six years old."

mktg case study #3: mktg shampoo

PICK A RANDOM CHEMICAL IN YOUR PRODUCT AND HEAVILY PRO-MOTE ITS PRESENCE. WHEN YOUR CUSTOMERS SEE "NOW WITH BENZOETHYLHYDRATES!" THEY WILL ASSUME THAT THIS IS A GOOD THING.

messages

Despite everything, by the time I'm driving back to the Porsche dealership *(Gee, you know, maybe I won't buy this after all)* I'm feeling pretty pleased with myself. 6 is very interested in my idea, and while she's less interested in me, I have survived a first date without humiliating myself. My biggest mistake was just hoe-ing into those tortellini when they arrived, because as the plates were being cleared I realized that I never saw 6 take a single bite of her meal. She either exquisitely orchestrated it so that I missed it all or slipped the whole meal into her folder. Either way, I'm impressed.

When I get home, there are four messages on my machine. The first three are from someone who likes calling answering ma-chines and hanging up without saying anything and the fourth is from Cindy. Cindy is a friend of mine from high school, and she's tall, cute and determined to marry Brad Pitt. I almost believe she can do it, too; when Cindy gets set on something, she's pretty hard to dissuade.

Cindy's message is something about meeting up for lunch, and since the dinner with 6 has left me with enough adrenaline to lift a truck, I call her.

"Hello?"

"Hi there."

"Scat," she says, pleased. "You just caught me. I'm off to Berlin tonight."

"Hey, great." Cindy is a flight attendant. "Another international flight. You must be doing well."

"The job sucks," she says. "On the last run from Paris, *three* guys tried to pinch my ass. I am *so* close to quitting, I swear. The second I catch a break with my modeling, I'm out of here."

"Well," I say. "You go, girl."

She laughs. "So, do you want to do lunch sometime?"

"Yeah, sure. I'll tell you about my get-rich-quick idea."

"Oh, Scat," she says, bemused, "you're such an upper in my life."

"Uh, thanks," I say.

"See ya."

"*Ciao,*" I say, and hang up.

prowlers

I'm still awake when Sneaky Pete comes home around two. Lying in bed, I hear him go through his regular routine: percolating some coffee, zapping through a dozen TV channels, flicking through a magazine. Our apartment doesn't have a hell of a lot of soundproofing and thus is no good for bringing home dates, but then it's also so dilapidated that no girl would want to sleep with either of us after seeing it, anyway. Hot beachfront apartments are nice for the image, but way, way out of my league.

I consider going out to him for some more advice but decide against it. Sneaky Pete has helped me enough. From here, I fight alone.

what a wonderful company

I call Wednesday morning and get 6's personal assistant. "I'm afraid Ms. 6 is very busy," the PA tells me. She sounds suspiciously like my mother, so much so that my mind spins with conspiracy theories. I am momentarily positive that my mother is sitting on a sofa with 6 and taking her through volumes of photos of me when I was four years old and much less inhibited.

"I could pass on a message," the PA offers, and now she doesn't sound so much like my mother after all. I get down to business.

"I need to talk to her. It's Scat."

This gives her pause. With a name like that, I may just be important.

"I'll check for you," the PA says. She can't resist adding, "But I must warn you, she's very busy."

"I'm warned."

Suddenly I'm listening to KPWR, which informs me that they are California's hippest music depot. As KPWR launches a techno version of *What a Wonderful World,* I wonder when radio stations became music depots and feel a brief sadness for KPWR's obvious self-deception about its musical prowess. The PA breaks in on them. "Ms. 6 will speak to you now," she tells me. There is deep disapproval in her voice, as if she has cautioned 6 again and again about speaking to me, but 6 is recklessly going ahead anyway.

"Grats," I say.

27

The PA turns into a click, a short but terrifying revisit to *What a Wonderful World*, then 6.

"Scat." She sounds thrilled to hear from me, as if she's been hoping all day that I would call. I wish this so much it is almost true.

"Hi," I say cheerfully. I'm about to say something more when I suddenly realize I can hear 6 breathing softly into my ear. It's so erotic that I just stand there in the kitchen and close my eyes.

Finally 6 says, "Yes?"

"Oh," I say, recovering. "I just wanted a status on Fukk. Are we green for Friday?"

"Yes," 6 says. She sounds as if she is trying to hide a slight irritation, but not very hard. "My team started work this morning and we're not going home tonight until it's done."

"Great!" I say. "Need any help?"

"No," she says. "Your role will come at the presentation. On Friday."

"Ah. Right."

6 waits.

"Well, I guess that's it then," I say.

"Fine."

"Bear my child, you great goddess of a woman," I say, although by then she has hung up.

scat clicks

There's a late-night Elvis movie on KCOP, and since I've got nothing better to do, I stay up to catch it. Just as Elvis is about to give a few disrespecting rednecks what-for, Sneaky Pete arrives home, dressed in a sleek black suit and smelling vaguely of aftershave and cigarettes.

"Hi," I say. "Hey, I met 6."

Sneaky Pete opens the fridge and studies its contents.

"She loved my idea. Pulled a team of people onto it straightaway. In *fact*"—I look at my watch—"they could still be working on it now. They weren't going home until it was done." I stretch, oh so casual. "We present to the board in a couple of days."

I risk a glance at Sneaky Pete to see if he's impressed. He is staring at me.

"What?" I say. "What's the matter?" In the face of his blank shades, I suddenly get defensive. "You're surprised 6 thought it was so good? Good enough to dedicate a team to working up a proposal the same day? Even though . . ." I falter. "Even though the board meeting isn't until . . ."

Sneaky Pete shakes his head slowly, almost sadly.

"Oh, *fuck*," I say.

scat gets serious

"I'm sorry," the receptionist says, "but Ms. 6 is unavailable."

"Where's the boardroom?" I demand aggressively. I am so aggressive I scare myself a little and step back. It's seven in the morning and I'm not really used to operating at this hour.

"What?"

"The boardroom," I say impatiently. "I know she's there. Where is it?"

The receptionist's mouth hangs open for a second. It's not particularly attractive, and I would gently tell her this if I wasn't being so overbearing. "You can't interrupt a *board* meeting," she whispers, horrified.

"Damn it," I shout, because it seems appropriate. "This is mission-critical!"

This is enough for her. She hurries down an oak-paneled corridor without looking to see if I am following. I have a nasty moment when I think she's going to dodge into the bathroom, then she stops at a giant set of double doors. They are huge. They are amazing. They are the sort of doors you expect someone very large to burst from, bellowing "Fee, fi, fo, fum." They are exactly what I would want if I could play with millions of dollars of other people's money.

Behind these doors, I am reasonably sure that 6 is betraying me.

I take a deep breath, and

through the looking glass

I throw the doors open and stride inside as if I know what I am doing. There is so much space in the boardroom that for a moment I think I must have wandered outside by mistake. Stuck in the center of this hall is a big oak table, and around it are a dozen big men. I can tell that obesity is a tradition here, rather than a passing fad, because the wall is lined with portraits of past, overweight board members. They're a bunch of irritable Santa Clauses with jowls instead of beards and cutter gray for fluffy red and white.

Standing in front of the table with a sheaf of papers and a flip chart is 6. The chart sports a delicious black rendition of a can of Fukk cola.

"Sorry I'm late," I tell the room. "Traffic was terrible."

There is a long pause as the twelve men, each undoubtedly worth many millions of dollars, grope for something to say.

6 beats them to it. She grasps the situation so quickly that I know she's planned for it. "I'm sorry," she tells the board, "allow me to introduce Mr. Scat." She turns to me, and her eyes are like black knives. "He's a consultant who worked with us on Fukk."

I'm also prepared, so I laugh. "Actually," I say—because a consultant is entitled to an hourly rate and zip of the profits—"I'm the *creator* of Fukk."

This sparks frowns and mutters from the board, and the atmosphere turns icy and disapproving. One of the men speaks up, and his voice is deep and rolling and pretty much what you'd expect to come parceled with the board member of a multinational company. "Ms. 6, we were under the impression that Fukk was developed internally." 6 shifts her weight slightly, but her expression doesn't change. "As I'm sure you're aware, there are numerous complications involved in marketing someone else's concept."

You bet there are. Complications like having to pay a tiny royalty on every can, which on Coca-Cola's scale works out to tens of millions of dollars per year. Suddenly I'm feeling very, very good.

"If that's the case," the man continues, "we simply can't proceed with this product."

All moisture in my mouth evaporates. I feel like somebody has given me a check for unlimited fame and fortune, then gone "Oh sorry, *that's* not for you; have this commemorative coffee mug instead." I am about to do something really stupid like beg or scream or call the board a fascist regime of assholes, when 6 steps forward. She is totally calm.

"My apologies again, Mr. Croft. I'm afraid my partner may have misled you."

Partner?

"Mr. Scat and I codeveloped Fukk," 6 says. She is so convincing that this statement slips easily into my brain and settles there for a second before I realize it's not true. "And he is prepared to relinquish his trademark rights for three million."

and they lived happily ever after

This is how the story goes after that:

Scat realizes he's being offered the choice between three million dollars and nothing, and although it's not a one cent royalty on every can of Fukk sold in the known universe, it's not exactly a slap in the face. It's enough to buy a huge house and clothes and a car and even start to get noticed by the right people. So Scat smiles and nods and agrees that, yes, he is prepared to sell his brilliant idea for three million dollars, and by the way, Ms. 6 did a super job and should be promoted, in his humble opinion. Smiles all around. There is paperwork to be signed, of course, but that's fulfilled over the next few days, and suddenly Scat is lighting cigarettes with hundred dollar bills and buying CD collectors packs just because he can and fielding investment agents with hard smiles who all have strong opinions about how to invest three million dollars.

So that's how the story goes.

Almost.

why scat should have studied pre-law

Of course, you can't sell ideas as such. You can sell patents, and you can sell copyright, and you can sell trademarks.

Which is why when 6 says, "And he is prepared to relinquish his trademark rights for three million," two thoughts simultaneously race through my brain. The first is like a high-pitched firecracker that screams into the night, and it goes:

Three miiiiiiiiillion dollars!

The second feels like remembering I promised to pick my mother up from the airport three hours ago, and that one goes:

Trademark?

contractual bliss

The board gets much happier upon hearing that they can acquire Fukk for a bargain basement three million, and I leave Coca-Cola on the crest of their radiant smiles and 6 promising to call me and a heap of paperwork with lots of blank spaces for "Scat" and "Fukk cola product."

There's a phone booth conveniently next to the bus stop, and I look up the address of the Los Angeles Patents and Intellectual Property Office. Defying all laws of nature, the first bus that comes along is headed toward it, and en route I stare out the window and wonder if I am a brilliant millionaire or a really big chump.

There is, of course, no reason why I can't go down right now and register Fukk. As long as I'm first, it's mine. If Coca-Cola assumes that no one would be stupid enough to forget to do that before trumpeting their genius to large corporations, then that's just lucky for me. I can slip down, fix my mistake and it will be like nothing ever went wrong.

The thing that bothers me, though, is that 6 doesn't strike me as the sort of person who would, in the midst of a three-million-dollar deal, make any sort of assumption like that at all.

nice one, einstein

I tear through the form, completing it in three minutes. At the desk, I ask the clerk how long I have to wait until I can find out if my application will be accepted.

"Four weeks," he says. He's roughly my age, but no more forgivable for this.

"Ah," I say. "You see, I was kind of hoping to find out a little sooner than that."

"Were you?" the clerk says, almost as if he is interested.

"Yeah," I say, smiling a little.

"Too bad, huh?" he says.

He is looking over my shoulder for the next customer, so I say whatever leaps into my head. This usually just gets me into trouble, but very occasionally pays off. The law of averages, I guess. "You know, you look a little like Einstein."

Amazingly, a huge smile breaks across his face. "A lot of people tell me that," he says. "And you know, working in the patent office and all . . ."

"Yeah, of course." I laugh. I have no idea what he is talking about.

"Hey, you know, about that application," he says, leaning forward. "If you just want to pick a particular field, I can run a check for duplications right now."

"Really?" I say, turning on the good-buddy charm. Einstein

33

and I could have played football together in high school, confided longings for senior girls in one another, hung out at pinball parlors. Except we didn't. I'm a marketing grad with three million dollars at stake and he's a pimply twerp in a dead-end job. "Hey, that'd be great. Can you just check for the name?"

" 'Fukk'? Sure thing. Hang on a sec." His fingers dance across the keyboard. Watching them, I feel a little lightheaded. This guy is about to tell me if I'm worth approximately three million dollars or exactly two hundred and eight.

His computer pipes up with a small *beep*. Einstein frowns at it disapprovingly. "Oh. Hey, sorry. You're going to have to pick a new name."

"New name?" I say faintly. There is a great roaring in my ears, which sounds, I imagine, a lot like three million dollars rushing past my face and heading for the toilet.

"Yeah," Einstein says. "There's already a registered cola product called Fukk. Just a new one, too."

So there it is. I've been screwed over. I'm going to be the poorest inventor of a billion-dollar product in history. Marketing textbooks will probably have my story in an amusing little box on page 122, with a heading like "Great Marketing Blunders #4."

Somehow I manage to spit out: "Who owns it?" For my own masochistic reasons, I need to hear him say "6."

"Oh," Einstein says. "Oh boy, that's a tough one. How do you pronounce that?" His forehead screws up. I wouldn't have thought there were too many variations, but I let Einstein struggle along at his own pace. "Well, there are two names. I mean, one person, known by two names."

Despite having just pissed three million dollars into the wind through sheer stupidity, the prospect of discovering 6's real name makes me perk up.

Until Einstein says:

"The first one is, um, Yuong Ang. But the other one is Sneaky Pete."

A Brief Interlude with Scat and Sneaky Pete

CHAPTER 000003

a no-holds-barred confrontation with sneaky pete

I expect him to be gone when I return home—the whole empty closet, raided fridge and stolen aftershave deal—but he's not. He's on the sofa, watching *Oprah*. Oprah is challenging a panel of extremely fat women to come up with one reason why they can't be beautiful, and Sneaky Pete is grinning at them as if he already knows the answer.

I shut the door behind me and he turns. He is wearing his indoor shades, which are less tinted and almost allow me to see his eyes. For some reason I find this unnerving.

"Hey," I say.

He nods at me, then picks up the remote and zaps Oprah and her fat women into oblivion.

I dump my briefcase on the table and walk over to the sofa. My suit is already rumpled so I just sit down beside him.

"I did the deal today."

He nods.

"6 was trying to go it alone, but I caught her in time. In the end, I sold the idea to Coke. One up-front payment. No royalties."

35

He nods again, slowly. I sit there and watch him for a minute. I'm finding it difficult to work out how he can be so calm. In the end, I can't take it. "Three million dollars."

A smile slowly spreads across his face. If I hadn't just come back from the patent office, I would be pleased that Sneaky Pete is so enthusiastic about my success. But I have just come back from the patent office, and I'm not enjoying that grin at all.

"The only thing is," I say, standing from the sofa, "I realized at the last moment that I never registered a trademark on this thing. In fact, I only thought about it after Coke agreed to buy Fukk. So I went down to the patent office this afternoon."

Sneaky Pete says, "But I beat you there."

I exhale. The last little flickering hope that maybe he would say *Yeah, you moron, here's your trademark* snuffs out.

"Sneaky Pete," I say, struggling a little. "That's my money."

He shrugs expressionlessly. He turns away, and for a second I think he's going to turn *Oprah* back on. Then he says, "That's business."

My jaw drops: I actually feel it go. "You—you would—" The thing that's really getting me here is that Sneaky Pete is the sort of guy who, if he was stuck at a nightclub with no money, would rather go thirsty than borrow from someone (well, Sneaky Pete isn't the sort of guy who would be stuck at a nightclub with no money, but if he was, that's what I think he would do). Up until three hours ago, I would have described him as the most honest person I had ever met. If, three hours ago, I had been forced to construct a list of the people most likely to steal three million dollars from me, Sneaky Pete would be flat against the bottom, right underneath my parents. "You're really doing this? You'll actually stab me in the back for money?"

He turns. In his shades, I see my own face reflected. "Scat," he says, looking vaguely disgusted, "I don't want money."

mktg ethics

On some level, I understand where he's coming from. But it's not a very high level and I don't think I can really articulate it.

The bottom line is that although Sneaky Pete would never screw me over for money, he will betray me for business. He leaves me little piles of the change I forget to take out of my dirty clothes because it would be heinous to take it, but he will sign the deal with Coca-Cola and bank my three-million-dollar check.

Somehow, this all makes sense within the moral system of Sneaky Pete. I can almost understand it.

But not quite. I throw Sneaky Pete out of the apartment, and when I find a pair of his sunglasses between the sofa cushions, I drop them on the floor and step on them.

take that

I feel vindicated, if not quite satisfied, about getting rid of him until the landlord calls me up and reminds me that the lease isn't in my name but Yuong Ang's. So, actually, I can't throw him out. I can only throw myself out.

So I do.

cindy

Which, of course, leaves me with nowhere to stay.

Life After Fukk

CHAPTER 000004

three months later

Cindy arrives home, still wearing her cute flight attendant uniform. The apartment is dark, so she wanders around switching on lights for a couple of minutes before spotting me on the living room floor.

"Scat." She studies me, pulling long, dangerous-looking clips out of her hair. "How are you?"

"I'm insane."

"Oh," she says happily. She leans down and gives me a tight hug. I'm too drained to return it. "That's *good*. Isn't it?"

"I'm not sure," I say, trying to keep my voice steady. "I've been sitting here for eight hours, trying to work out if insanity is an improvement on suicidal depression. I still can't tell."

"Oh," Cindy says, less enthusiastically. Her eyes narrow. "What are those? In your hands?"

My voice breaks a little. "My Calvins." I try to hide them under my buttocks.

"Oh, Scat. I'm sorry." She begins gently scratching my head. I can't help it: I feel better immediately. It's a weakness of mine. *"I* know what will make you feel better."

"Cindy," I protest, "I don't want any head scratchies. Really." I am lying through my teeth.

"Well, I've got something even *better*." Her voice makes me look up. She's smiling, like she's guarding some kind of secret. "What do you want most in all the world?"

I sigh. "Fame. Fortune. General adulation. I want my Fukk back. I want to be invited as guest speaker to Stanford to present on how I developed it. I want a short article in *Time* and a front-page feature in *Marketing*." This brings back just how badly I want these things. I feel it so desperately that I almost—almost—feel like getting up and entering the real world again. "I want to be invited to Microsoft premieres and Coca-Cola boat parties. I want to be *successful*."

Cindy is silent for a moment, so I guess her surprise is something smaller, like maybe a cheesecake. "What do you want if you can't have that?"

"Cindy, that's *all* I want. If I can't have that then I'm just going to sit here and go crazy and I'd appreciate being allowed to do it in peace."

Cindy squats down in front of me, pressing on relentlessly. "Would a visit from a special friend cheer you up?"

"Let's have sex," I say suddenly. I reach out to her imploringly.

"Scat," she says, getting exasperated. In a flash of insight, it occurs to me just how low I have sunk. Three months ago, I was pretty smug about how I'd never taken advantage of my friendship with Cindy. Now she's turning me down.

"Scat," Cindy says. "We don't have time. She'll be here any minute."

"Who?"

"Your *special friend*." Cindy stands up and regards me, hands on hips. "It's time you got back to your life."

"Who's my special friend, Cindy?"

"I mean," she says, walking into the kitchen, "it's not that easy to look after you, you know." She pours herself a glass of something, throws it back, pours another one. "Frankly, it's become a bore."

"Cindy," I say patiently, "I'm very grateful to you. I really am. But I do just need to change the subject back for a second, because if someone is visiting me, I really need to put some clothes on."

"Oh, sure!" she yells, really upset. "You just do what you want! Don't worry about me and *my* needs!"

The buzzer sounds. I sit there uncertainly for a moment, fingering my Calvins, but when Cindy says, "Yes, 6, come on up," I bolt for the bedroom.

a visit from 6

She is still stunning. This I cannot get over.

I mean, we all have our little fantasies, right? But they don't last. You see the object of your desire a year later and think: *Whoa, did I think that was cute?* It's a fleeting thing, is my point. A momentary deception of perception.

But 6 stands there in her blinding white miniskirt and smooth black business jacket with her hair like a cape of midnight, and she's captivating.

"Scat," she says. Reminders: dark eyes, lips like a rubber dinghy.

I am wearing pants, a shirt and a jacket that mismatch so badly I'm hoping 6 will mistake them for cool. I haven't had time to even attempt the shoes, but I have one sock on my right foot and am holding the other in my left hand.

"6, it's . . . stunning to see you again."

She shrugs this off, taking a brief appraisal of the apartment. "Can we go somewhere?"

"Take me away," I say, as if she hasn't already.

café revelations

"So," she says, looking me over. I suppress a shiver. "How have you been?"

I'm momentarily caught between lying and telling the truth, then berate myself. Three months ago, I wouldn't have hesitated. "Oh, fantastic. Losing Fukk was a blow, of course, but I try to look at it as a learning experience." I shrug. "I've got a couple more projects on the go; naturally Fukk was just one of many."

"Good." 6 looks relieved, sipping at her lattè. Perhaps she was worried I would tell the truth.

"And you?" I brace myself.

"Well," she says cautiously, "I'm frantic on Fukk, of course, working ninety hour weeks." She throws me a glance but I think I've managed to remain deadpan. "It's chaos to get this product on the market for summer."

She doesn't have to spell it out for me. I'm guessing they've changed her title to New Products Marketing and Operations Executive, raised her to $200,000 and asked her to please pick out a nice car and send them the bill.

I manage to say it. "And how's the launch going?"

"As expected," 6 says, still careful. I interpret this to mean: *I'm ahead of schedule, I've got a $10 million budget and I meet daily with the CEO.* "The CTs did . . . very well." Now 6 is saying: *I'm pretty sure we're going to make unbelievable amounts of money.*

"So." It's hard to keep the bitterness out of my voice. "I guess the board wasn't fazed by discovering that the guy who sold them Fukk wasn't the guy who owned it."

Almost tenderly, 6 says: "No."

I put down my lattè. "I see. So everything's going great. Everyone's happy. Coke is going to release the biggest hit soda of the decade, you're shimmying up the corporate ladder and Sneaky Pete is probably vacationing in Hawaii with my money." I gesture wildly at the upmarket café and clientele around me. "Then I guess the only reason you brought me here is to rub my nose in it." I actually stand up at this point, and though I can't say for sure, I think my eyes are blazing with righteous anger. "I think I'll leave before you stiff me with the check."

"Scat," 6 says, looking pained, "sit down."

I don't want to, but with 6 looking pained at me it's hard to resist. I decide to sit down only with a cutting remark, but then I can't think of one and end up just sitting.

Then something beautiful and astounding happens.

6 says, "Scat, I need you."

6 reveals all

"I've been shafted on Fukk. They'll probably take me off it before the end of the month."

I gape. "Shafted? How? Who?"

6's deadly eyebrows sharpen into a frown. I'm sure that if she turned these weapons onto whoever knifed her, she could slice him into little pieces. "Actually, it was your friend. Sneaky Pete."

"*What?*"

She only throws a tiny shrug, but it's enough to tell me she's furious. "I didn't even know he was in the game. I thought he screwed you for the money and vanished." She scowls at her latte. "A couple of months ago, I find out Coke has hired him to work alongside me on the launch. I protested, of course, took my complaint to the CEO. No good. He's their new golden boy."

"Bastard," I say wonderingly.

"Two weeks ago, I figured that for all practical purposes, he's doing my job. He's going to take full credit for the success of Fukk."

I almost choke. Not only does the guy get three million dollars for the rights, but he grabs a top marketing job in the best marketing company in the world and snares responsibility for launching a surefire hit. I can't help but admire that.

"I've been asked to work on something else," 6 says, disgusted. "The summer campaign for Classic Coke."

I blink. "That sounds like a promotion."

She shakes her head. "Our ad agency has already finished the design work. Coke wants me to . . . *implement.* Logistics. Space negotiations." Her face blanches.

"Oh." I think for a moment. "So . . . what exactly do you need me for?"

6 sips her coffee, watching me carefully. I get little shivers up my back.

"I'm not going to do what they want. I'm going to redesign the summer launch. With your help."

She sets down her coffee.

"You and I are going to produce the best ad in marketing history."

okaaay

. •. ° ° ● ●. : ● ° ● °. °° .° ● :° ● ° ●. ° ●° ° ●. ° °°

I stare at 6. She stares back at me, those dark eyes sizing me up.

"Are you offering me a job at Coke?"

"No," she says immediately. "I can't do that. No one at Coke can know about this until it's done."

"I see." I think about this. "So you're effectively against the company. If they find out you're trying to replace the campaign they've spent months developing, they'll can you."

6 hesitates, then nods.

"In fact, even if you do come up with something special, they could can you for pure insubordination."

"That's possible," 6 admits.

"And, given that summer begins in under two months, I guess you've got maybe four weeks, at most, to produce this thing."

"Actually," 6 says, "you'd be surprised at how far we work in advance."

I wait.

"The concept has to be finished this week."

Her eyes start to widen fetchingly so I look down at my coffee to steady myself. When I look up again, I'm ready.

"So," I say, "what you're telling me is that you want me to

work on a doomed project with an impossible deadline for no tangible reward." I give 6 what I hope is a sardonic smile.

6 says, "I need you, Scat."

"Okay," I say quickly.

the benefits of a tertiary education

It would be hard to tell, from this encounter, that I scored an A— in MKT 346: Business Negotiation.

a no-holds-barred confrontation with cindy

Cindy arrives home around three A.M. *"Hey,"* she says, sounding pleased.

I look up from my writing. "Hey."

"Dressed," she says approvingly. "Shaved. Even *active.*" She comes over and kisses me on the back of my neck. "You look dangerous, Scat."

"Uh, thanks," I say.

Cindy stands behind me silently for a minute. I've already sunk back into my world of Coke bylines when she says, "I knew we could do it, Scat. I knew we could pull you out of this one."

"Yeah," I say absently. I have started to wonder about the beach: about variations on a giant inflatable beach ball. I am thinking about this ball rolling through a major American city, with people running and screaming.

Cindy walks around the table to face me. There's a strange expression on her face, and it's so unfamiliar that it's a second before I recognize it. Then it dawns: Cindy is looking at me as if she is impressed.

"Cindy—"

"Scat," Cindy says, her eyes shining.

"Whoa, Cindy." I abruptly realize that this is going to turn very ugly very quickly. "I think . . . we need to talk."

"*I* think," Cindy says, smiling, "that it's past Scat's bedtime." She fingers the buttons on her uniform.

"Cindy—" I search for the words I need: words to tell her how much she's helped me, how much I appreciate everything she's done to rebuild me over the past three months, and how that means I don't need her anymore.

"Cindy," I say gently, "I'm back."

cindy rebuts

By the time I get downstairs, most of my stuff is already strewn over the lawn. I try to catch the remainder as it sails down from the second-floor apartment window.

"Son of a *whore!*" Cindy screams.

"I'm *sorry!*" I grab my jeans before they drop into the gutter. Somewhere in the night a dog barks happily.

"*Bastard!*"

I look up, but nothing else seems to be on its way. I collect as many of my clothes as I can and wrap them into a manageable bundle. When I look up again, I catch a glimpse of Cindy peering through the blinds.

"I'll call you!" I shout. It's pathetic, but I can't think of an alternative.

I'm halfway down the street and wondering where the hell I'm going when Cindy's reply drifts to me on the hot night breeze.

"Okay . . ."

6

So, once again, I am homeless.

Buy Now, Pay Later

CHAPTER 000005

mktg case study #4: mktg groceries [1]

SPREAD THE MOST POPULAR ITEMS (MILK, CEREAL, SODA) THROUGH-
OUT THE GROCERY STORE SO CUSTOMERS PASS BY AS LARGE A
RANGE OF GOODS AS POSSIBLE. SHIFT THE LOCATION OF GOODS
REGULARLY TO KEEP CUSTOMERS WANDERING.

saturday night in the big city

I realize very quickly that I'll have to call on 6's assistance for ac-
commodation. Since I happen to be doing her a tremendous favor at this time, I figure my chances should be pretty good.

However, since it's nearly four, I decide to wait until morning
to call her. I trudge around the backstreets of Santa Monica for
three hours, past countless alleys, doorways and small inviting
parks, all of which are already occupied by people with tight grips
on bundles of clothes even smaller than mine. At dawn, I'm so
exhausted and desperate for a shower that I can't wait any longer,
and I find a pay phone, dial 6's number and hope.

She picks up on the fourth ring. "Hello?" Her voice is like honey smeared across velvet pajamas.

"6! It's Scat. Gorgeous morning, huh?"

There is a pause. "Hello, Scat," she says cautiously.

"6, there are some things we need to discuss," I tell her importantly. "How about I come over?"

"You, come here?" 6 says, alarmed.

I quickly recheck my words in my head, to make sure they didn't come out: *Let's make mad passionate love.* I'm pretty sure they didn't. "Uh, yeah."

"No."

"Oh." This puts a dent in my plan: I had expected to get in the front door. I tremble briefly on the verge of asking her why I can't visit, then chicken out. "Oh. Then . . . somewhere else?" I look around. "How about a coffee on the beach? I'm at Watchers in Santa Monica."

"Fine," 6 says, and hangs up.

I put down the phone. "Okay," I tell myself. "Okay."

It feels good to be okay.

scat and 6 go to the beach

I decide to sit on the stone wall separating the sidewalk from the beach so I can see 6 drive up. I'm very interested in what sort of car she's driving because I think it will reveal some insight into her personality. After all, I don't have a car at all, and that reveals plenty about me.

However, when 6 arrives an hour later I'm surprised to see she's walking. She's also wearing cute white shorts and a thin black tank top so unnerving I have to grip the wall. She spots me and heads over.

"Hey," I say. "Walking?"

"I like to walk," she says shortly.

"How un-Californian of you," I offer daringly. 6 ignores me.

We sit down at a small cozy café looking out over the ocean and order lattès. 6 slings her impressive satchel, which has again simply materialized, over the back of her chair. "So?"

"Right," I say. "Well, I haven't come up with the most brilliant ad in the history of marketing overnight, if that's what you're wondering."

"Oh." For a fleeting microsecond, she actually looks dismayed. "No. Of course not."

"But I do want to talk about a couple of things. First, you have to get me inside Coke."

"Yes." 6 has obviously anticipated this. Almost every great ad ever written has come from research, and I'm certain she knows this.

"That's not a problem?"

"No."

"Oh. Of course not." I can't help myself; I'm homeless and I haven't slept in twenty-four hours. "Let me know when anything ever fazes you."

6 stares at me, utterly unfazed.

"I mean," I continue, a little hysterically, "when we've produced this amazing ad and you use it to destroy everyone who has ever threatened you, what are you going to do next? What could possibly turn you on?"

6 turns and looks out over the ocean. I abruptly realize how far I have stepped over the line of cool detachment and open my mouth to apologize. Then 6 says: "Success." She turns back to me. "Just like you, Scat."

scat confesses

During the second lattè, I begin my pitch to move in.

"You know . . ." I say mysteriously. "There are some things you should know about me."

6 raisès an eyebrow.

"I don't really have a Porsche," I confess. "I just borrowed one for the dinner."

"Oh," 6 says, genuinely surprised. Her other eyebrow shoots up to join its sister.

"Were you impressed?" I ask sneakingly.

"No."

"Just a little?"

"*No,*" she says, crossing her arms. "An expensive car doesn't mean anything."

"I'm glad to hear that," I say truthfully, "because actually, I don't have a car at all."

"Oh," 6 says, sounding a little depressed.

"In *fact,*" I say, "I don't have a place to live anymore. I'm homeless." I try 6's wide-eyed trick back on her, but she stares it down impassively. "So . . . if you have any ideas, I'm open to suggestions."

"Ideas?" she says, as if she doesn't understand what I'm talking about.

"For places to live. I need somewhere to live."

"Oh," she says, looking out at the sea again.

"Do you know anyone? Anyone who might want a boarder?"

"I don't think so," she says, as if the entire subject is vaguely distasteful.

"Anyone . . . such as yourself?"

6 turns back to me, her eyes wide and outraged. "Absolutely *not.*"

I reach out for her hand. She starts to move it but I snare her before she can get away. Her fingers are cool and smooth, and this would be a tremendously passionate moment if she wasn't twisting them in my grip. "6, I wouldn't ask if I wasn't desperate. You're my last hope in Los Angeles."

"*No.*" Her eyes shift. "I live with a girl."

"You'll hardly know I'm there."

"*No.*"

"6," I say. "If I can't find somewhere to live, I can't work with you at Coke." I suck in a breath. "I'll quit."

6's dark eyes scrutinize me. "No you won't."

I blink. I check to make sure I'm serious. I am. "6—"

She must see it in my eyes. "Don't you have *parents?*"

"Iowa," I explain quietly.

"Oh." Another look of distaste flits across her face.

I decide that this is a good time for a goofy, shit-happens grin, so I let one leak out.

"Oh, Christ," 6 says.

the arrangement

"This is how it will work," 6 says. "Today is Sunday. You can stay five nights, and *only* five nights, which will take you until Friday, when we complete the project. Then you're out."

"Okay."

"You won't get a bed. You'll sleep wherever suits me. You'll have whatever blankets and pillows I give you. It might not be comfortable."

"Right," I say, secure in the knowledge that anywhere in 6's apartment has to be more comfortable than a doorway in Santa Monica.

"You will assist in daily activities, including but not limited to cooking, cleaning and washing. You will make a proactive effort to ensure the harmony of the household."

"Sounds fair."

"Privacy," 6 says. "You will not intrude on my privacy. If I want you out of the apartment for a while, you'll take a walk. If I want to play loud music at two in the morning, I'll do it."

"Hmm," I say. "I guess."

"And," 6 says, eyeing me menacingly, "you'll leave the toilet seat *down.* I don't *ever* want to see the toilet seat up. If you leave the toilet seat up, our arrangement immediately terminates. Understood?"

"6," I protest, "that's an instinctive action. I may not be able to consciously control that."

"If the toilet seat is left up, you're out. Understood?"

"I can *try*," I concede.

"You can do it," 6 says.

I say nothing. If this ever becomes a problem, I'll protest that I never explicitly agreed.

"And Scat—"

"Yes?"

She hesitates. "There are some things you should know about me."

mktg case study #5: mktg cereal

BASE YOUR ADVERTISING AROUND THE INSINUATION RATHER THAN THE CLAIM THAT THE PRODUCT IS HEALTHY. HAVE SLICE-OF-LIFE ADVERTISEMENTS DEPICTING SLIM MODELS EXERCISING AND EATING THE PRODUCT. WHEN DONE PROPERLY, YOU DON'T EVEN HAVE TO LIE.

a vision of 6

6 quietly takes my arm and we stroll along the beach to where she is parked. It's a low-slung Ferrari—powerful and feminine— and I silently approve. I slip inside and we roar down the PCH. We have witty, sparkling conversation, and 6 smiles at my jokes all the way to her beachfront apartment in Malibu. I can tell from the outside that this is possibly the most stylish apartment I've ever seen, but when the elevator opens on to her floor I am stunned at how amazingly cool it really is. It is a huge, airy, open-plan shrine to taste, money and sheer funkiness. I voice my approval and 6 smiles demurely and offers me a scotch. That night, when we're both a little giggly, 6 looks into my eyes and says, "You know, Scat . . . you may as well bunk in with me tonight."

This is *so* not true.

6 confesses

6 is mostly silent on the bus to her apartment. There is an annoying child sitting behind me who keeps kicking the seat, so I'm quietly stewing, too. I keep my bundle of clothes on my lap, and 6 very successfully avoids looking at it the whole trip.

We disembark at Lincoln and Oak in north Venice. I look to 6 for directions, but she's staring at the ground.

"6," I say sensitively, "it's cool that you aren't rich. I'm not rich, either. I'm carrying my worldly possessions in my hands here."

6 takes a deep, slightly unsteady breath.

"I don't think less of you for this. I know it's important to look the part for the people we deal with, but it's not important to me. I'm a marketer, too." 6 abruptly starts walking, and I hurry to fall into step beside her. "You're very cool, and you don't need the image."

"I don't have an *image,*" 6 says.

"Well, 6," I say, a little startled. "Of course you do."

"No I don't."

"6," I say. "You have an image. The young, independent, hotshot lesbian—"

"I *am* a lesbian," 6 says. "I don't want to have to keep reminding you."

I'm about to say something stupid like, "Oh, crap," but 6 stops at an apartment block and I am stunned into silence.

the worst apartment in north venice

Take a small, stupid infant. Blindfold him. Make him draw a building.

Take the drawing and rip it in half. Give each half to a different construction company and don't let them talk to each other. Insist on materials that will crumble and accumulate vast quantities of mold.

Paint it a light putrid green, except the window trimmings, which may be done in a thick oppressive brown. Use paint so cheap that sunlight will peel it off in great slabs.

Don't let anyone repair it, maintain it, renovate it, *touch* it, for a good twenty years or so.

Then rent it out to college graduates.

fukk

"Well?" 6 says, a little aggressively.

"I'm just grateful for a roof over my head," I say, and, pathetically, it's true.

6 sighs and heads for the stairwell. I decide to trust her over my own impression of the stairs' safety and join her. By the time we reach her apartment on the third floor, I've plucked up the courage to say, "Well, this is kind of what I'm talking about. You didn't want me to see this, because it would ruin your image."

She shoots me a withering look of disdain. "I never said I was *rich*. I've been at Coke four months. And I have student loans to repay, too, you know."

I open my mouth to rebut, but, damn it, after the lesbian thing and the twenty-one-years-old thing and the being named 0 by her parents thing, I realize that this may be the one thing she's never lied to me about. "Oh."

6 opens the door and I follow her inside, still carrying my bundle. She's done very well with the place, and it actually looks pretty cool in a low-budget, college-student, movie-posters-on-the-wall kind of way. There's a tiny kitchen which opens onto the living room, complete with TV, video, stereo, sofa and framed degree. I immediately check out the degree and discover to my shock that 6 really did graduate from Stanford University. I don't contain this very well. "You actually went to *Stanford*?"

She doesn't even deign to reply.

"6, I'm sorry for doubting. That's really impressive."

"Thank you," she says tonelessly. She fetches a bottle of Pepsi from an ancient fridge. "Drink?"

I blink. "You drink Pepsi?"

6 shrugs. "Market research. I drink everything."

"What have you got in there?"

"Pepsi, Pepsi Max, Diet Pepsi, 7 UP, Fanta, Diet Fanta, Classic Coke, Diet Coke, Cherry Coke, White Coke—"

"*White* Coke?"

"It's a trial product."

"Wow, sounds cool. What does it taste like?"

"Coke," 6 says.

"Well, yeah," I say, "but how is it different to, say, Classic Coke?"

"It's in a different can," 6 says.

I wait, but 6 just looks at me. "What, that's it?"

"No," she says. "It will also cost twice as much." She pours herself a Pepsi. "We're after a more upmarket niche."

"You really expect people to pay double for a white can?" I ask, astounded. "When it tastes exactly the same?"

6 aims a chiseled frown at me. "I didn't say it *tastes* exactly the same. I said it *is* exactly the same." She sips at her Pepsi, waiting for me to catch up.

"The cans contain special chemicals?" I ask hopefully. "That affect the taste?"

"America's most popular range of pasta sauces are made by the same company responsible for the number one brand of dog food. Do you think they advertise this? Co-brand?"

"No," I hazard.

"Taste is *marketing*," 6 says with finality.

"Huh," I say.

"I also have Iridium, which is an independent we're going to buy out and bury soon, and Fukk."

I choke. "You have *Fukk?*"

"Of course," 6 says. "It's my product." Her sizzling eyebrows descend. "Or was."

I restrain myself from leaping at the fridge. "Can I see it? Is it a bottle or a can? What's the packaging like?"

6 gestures to the fridge. I walk into the kitchen as steadily as I can and lean down.

There is a truly awesome assortment of sodas in there, but Fukk stands out. Its deep black contours are like a splash of defiance against the bright reds and blues. It just sits there and says, *Fukk*.

I reach out a trembling hand and touch the can. It's refreshingly cool, it's sleek, but most of all it's *real*. I thought this up one night three months ago and now I'm holding it in my hand. It's an indescribable feeling.

"Take a sip," 6 urges.

I pop the top and it hisses angrily.

"Extra carbonation," 6 explains. "When you pop a Fukk, everybody around you knows it."

"*Very* good," I murmur, my eyes never leaving the can. Slowly, very slowly, I raise it to my mouth. The metal slips between my lips and then cold, liquid Fukk is sliding down my throat. It's much lighter than Coke or Pepsi, sitting somewhere between a mineral water and a cola. And it's perfect. Just perfect.

"You like?" 6 inquires.

"I love it," I manage to say. "You've done a fantastic job."

"Thank you," she says, and, amazingly, 6 actually sounds pleased.

tina

I'm so lost in my Fukk that I don't even hear the door open. Then 6 says, "Tina, this is Scat," and I suddenly realize that this must be 6's girl.

It's a shock. I'm expecting someone . . . well, someone like 6. Tina is not like 6.

6 says, "Tina's doing an arts degree."

"Oh?" I say, as if the eyebrow ring, blond hair with a streak of black and oppressive eye makeup hadn't tipped me off.

"Oh, let me guess," Tina says. "He's a *marketer*."

"Hi," I say.

Tina throws her hessian bag onto the sofa and stalks into the kitchen. She's very short, but the way she walks tells me it would be a very bad idea to point this out to her. "I hope they pay you well for strangling the youth of this country with cultural conformity." She opens the fridge and frowns at the sodas.

"Unfortunately, no," I admit. "I'm unemployed."

Tina pulls out the Pepsi and pours herself a glass. *"Really,"* she says, eyeing me suspiciously. Her eyes, beneath pints of mascara, are actually a deep, attractive green.

"Trust me," I say. "I wouldn't make that up to impress you."

Tina smirks. "I thought that was *all* marketers did."

I throw out a wild guess. "You don't like marketing?"

"Marketing is like being given joke dog shit for your birthday," Tina says. "It's useless, stupid *and* insulting."

"Ah," I say.

"Marketing is a leech on a turd," she continues. "Disgusting and unnecessary, sustaining itself on the bowels of society."

"Ugh."

"Marketing," she says, "is a pair of silicone tits. Superficially attractive, but secretly fucking up your life."

"And yet," I say, "you're drinking a Pepsi."

Tina frowns, wounded. "I just like the *taste*," she says.

tina, 6 and sexual preference

Tina offers to show me around the apartment, and I find out the most important thing first. "You and 6 have separate bedrooms?"

"Of course," Tina says.

My heart jumps. "I was under the impression that you and 6 were . . . romantically entangled."

Tina laughs. "Oh, right. Sure." She leads me into the bathroom, which is cluttered with more cosmetics than I knew existed. There's also an oddly placed window that would offer a pretty good view of the street to anyone standing in the shower.

"So that's not true?"

Tina says dryly, "I can assure you that 6 and I are not sleeping together."

"A-*ha*," I say. "I knew it."

"At this point in time," Tina adds, watching me carefully.

My brain struggles to assimilate, but I can't wait for it and let my mouth make the call instead. "You mean you *used* to be with 6?"

"Oh, I get it," Tina says, stepping closer to me. "You're one of those guys who pigeonhole everyone by their sexuality, right? Do you call gays 'fags'?"

I'm beginning to find Tina just a touch confrontational. "No! I—"

"Is someone's sexuality that important to you?"

"Usually, no—"

"Good."

"Tina, look," I say. "I'm not really interested in whether 6 is a lesbian or not. It's whether she lied to me about it."

Tina stares at me for a long moment. "Men," she says, and not in a good way. "I'm amazed that this patriarchal society even has a word for lesbianism. As far as men are concerned, it's just another word for *threesome*." She points at a closed door. "That's 6's bedroom. Don't go in there."

"Okay," I say, resolving to check it out as soon as possible.

"I mean, Christ," Tina says, her face twisting. "It's none of your business. It's no one's business but the *girl's*. She's still a person, that's what's *real*. But no, men want to know *all* about it. There's nothing more fascinating than a girl who won't have sex with you."

I am defeated, and I hold up my hands to show it. "Okay, okay."

Tina pauses. "At least, that's what 6 says."

bedtime

I do get the sofa.

After the fun and frivolity of last night, I'm totally bushed. 6, however, wants to stay up for *Letterman*. On the sofa, I snuggle into a pillow and a blanket, my feet nestling a few tantalizing inches from 6's bottom. For about five seconds I drown in a rush of stupid fantasies, then utter exhaustion claims me and I dream that

a brush with letterman

"Wow," Letterman says. "Hey! This is good!"

I smile modestly, and, since this is TV, give a little aw-shucks shrug for the camera.

"No, this is really good. I like it," Letterman says. He looks at me, still holding the can of Fukk. "Can I keep this? You mind if I just hang on to this?"

"Sure, Dave," I say.

"Tell you what," Letterman says. "I'll do an ad for you."

"Hey, you don't have to—"

"No, let me do an ad," Letterman says. "I can do it." He strikes a pose for camera two. "I've had a Fukk today—have you?" The audience goes crazy, and Letterman gives them all a big grin. "What do you think, Scat? You want to run with that? Huh? Huh?"

"You should write ads," suggests Pamela Anderson, who I

notice at this moment is sitting to my right in a fluffy white dressing gown.

I smile. "Actually, Dave, we had to be very careful with the advertising, because—"

"Because it's *Fukk*," Letterman says. "You can't say *Fukk* on a billboard! No! You can't do that! Can he do that?"

"Well, exactly." I frown intelligently into camera one. "We had to be careful. That's why all the advertising has just the word *Fukk*, nothing else. You see, if—"

"Hey, wait a minute, what's this?" Dave cuts in. I turn and see him frowning at the Fukk on his desk.

"What?"

"I can't pick up the can."

"What?" I say again, confused.

"I can't pick up the stupid *can*." He reaches for it, and his hand passes straight through it. The audience gasps. "What a stupid can," Dave says, looking at me accusingly. "I can't even pick it up."

"I don't understand . . ." I lean over and try to pick up the Fukk, but I grab thin air.

"It's not even *real*," Dave says contemptuously. "What a stupid soda."

Someone in the audience boos daringly.

"I don't understand," I say again.

"Well, boy," Letterman says. "You must be a dumb ass."

"Dave," I say, wounded.

"Why don't you just shut up," Letterman says, "you dumb ass." The audience screams with laughter.

I look around wildly for support. Pamela pouts sympathetically and reaches out a supportive hand. It passes straight through my shoulder. "Ooh," Pamela says.

"*Now* look what you've done," Letterman says, as if he just can't believe it. "Now *Pamela's* not real, either. What a dumb ass."

I open my mouth, but suddenly I'm sinking, starting to pass right through the sofa.

"Oh, boy," Letterman says, rolling his eyes. "He's disappearing into the sofa, now. Can't he even sit on the sofa?"

"*I'm* still on the sofa, Dave," Pamela says, smiling up at him.

"What amazing buoyancy," Letterman says. "Okay! What's next?"

"*Dave.*" Pamela giggles.

The floor is starting to dissolve underneath me and now I'm really panicking. "Dave? Can I get some help here? I need something to hold on to."

"Something *real,* maybe?"

"*Dave!*" I scream, and the floor actually lets me go and I'm falling into a deep, thick, cloying blackness. I flail my arms wildly but there's absolutely nothing to grab on to, and just as I'm sure I'm going to die, something bright and solid opens above my head and

the intangibility paradox

6 is leaning over me, dizzyingly close. My world is framed by her jet-black hair.

"6?" My voice is thick with sleep. 6 starts a little, a strange expression flitting across her face. I am suddenly sure that she has been watching me for a while. "6?"

Abruptly she stands and walks away. She doesn't even look at me when she says, "Tomorrow we go to Coke. I'll wake you."

She steps out of the room, closing the door behind her.

morning breaks

I'm woken by a dozen furious, hissing snakes crawling all over my body. I desperately grab at them for a few seconds before realizing that there are, in fact, no snakes, unless 6 is cooking them along with the bacon.

"Morning," I say, sitting up.

"Bacon and eggs?" 6 asks.

"You're *cooking* for me?"

6 sighs. She's wearing dark red silk pajamas that are just a little too sheer for me at this time of the morning, and her hair is hidden under a huge towel. "Why shouldn't I?"

I struggle out of the sofa and wander into the kitchen for a glass of water. "6, don't get me wrong, I really appreciate it. It's just I thought that you being . . . well, you, you wouldn't subscribe to stereotypical roles like cooking for a man."

6 stares at me from under her towel. "The sad thing is right now you think you're being nonsexist. You think if you just do everything the opposite of traditional gender stereotypes, you're progressive and sensitive. Right?"

I haven't been awake long enough to be having this conversation. "Uh, well, yeah, I guess."

"*Reversing* gender stereotypes doesn't *eliminate* them," 6 says, tossing the bacon. "You just create a whole new set of prejudices. The fact is, if you weren't sexist it wouldn't matter whether a man or a woman cooked you breakfast."

I try to think of a reply, but everything that springs to mind is inflammatory. While I stand there dumbly, 6 eyes me, waiting for my next conversational blunder.

"Can I make you a coffee?" I say.

a window

While I'm in the shower, I look out the tiny window and watch people going to work. It's fun and somehow liberating to be able to stand there naked and stare at people. I watch for about ten minutes, and then I realize that in their cars and business suits, everyone looks pretty much the same.

6 signs me in at Coke and I get a special CONTRACTOR badge. I spend most of the trip to the 14th trying to work out how to pin the badge onto my shirt before realizing it's meant to clip on to my tie.

The doors open and I'm hugely pleased to see that the first thing to greet me is a Coke machine. Around it, giant framed Coke ads litter the walls, so densely packed that some eager but misguided executive must have once said, "I want to see every ad we've ever done up there."

6 leads me down a corridor (red carpet) to a small dark office. It's bare apart from a desk, an ergonomic chair and a computer with a pile of instructions. I study it for a second, then look back at 6, who is standing in the doorway like a gunfighter surveying a saloon. "Good luck, Scat."

"Thanks, kid," I say, and if she hadn't closed the door so fast, I would have tipped her a wink.

MEMO TO S. BLACKLAND
RE: NEW COKE PROJECT

6/25/84

Hi Steve,

The latest results on New Coke are unbelievable! Can't wait until we get this one in front of the board.

We've completed the market research, where we let people compare Coke and the new strain (from unmarked cups, of course). I don't want to preempt the presentation, but it looks like FIVE OUT OF SEVEN prefer the new taste!

I think this is going to be big, Steve. It's going to blow Pepsi off the map.

JJ

MEMO TO S. BLACKLAND
RE: NEW COKE PROJECT [2]

1/12/85

Steve,

Thanks for your help on Friday. We have to wait for the final decision, of course, but I think you're right—the board's going to OK it.

I am concerned about Will's reaction. Sure, everyone's real attached to the brand, but Christ, when five out of seven prefer the taste of the new strain, we'd be crazy not to change the formula. I mean, taste is taste, right?

JJ

MEMO TO J. JACKSON
RE: REFERENCE

10/31/85

JJ,

I was certainly disappointed to hear of your resignation. Unfortunately, though, I would

prefer it if you didn't list me as a reference
on your CV.

You know how much we lost on New Coke, JJ, and
people want to know how we could have let it
happen. They want to know how our people could
forget what marketing was. I'm barely covering
my own ass here.

Hope there are no hard feelings. Best wishes for
the future.

Steven Blackland

day one

6 has some sandwiches sent to my office for lunch, which is disappointing because I was hoping she'd take me out somewhere,
plus I don't really like cucumber. But I guess she has power
lunches with important people to attend to.

She finally reappears at eight, long after I've become heartily
sick of browsing Coke research files and instead clocked the
fastest time for Minesweeper. When the door opens I surrepti-
tiously Alt-F4 it.

"How did you do?" 6 asks. Her voice is steady but her hand, I
notice, is gripping the door handle tightly.

So I tell her: I have sore eyes, a stiff back and no ideas for an ad.

the scat diaries

TUESDAY.

Woken up by Tina arriving home at 5 A.M. with boy. Tried to go back to sleep but distracted by noises from Tina's bedroom. Wondered what this means about 6's sexuality. Couldn't tell.

Locked in tiny office at Coke all day again. Developed pathological hatred of Minesweeper. No ideas for ads. 6 disappointed.

Worked late, got take-out. Fell asleep on sofa while 6 watched *Letterman*.

WEDNESDAY.

Discovered on computer that they once actually released Coke-flavored cigars. Spent an hour checking this, certain it must be a joke. It's not. They really did.

Highlight of day: 6 in huge fight with marketing guy outside my office. Peered through blinds and saw hysterical young guy in blue shirt and Mickey Mouse tie: apparently thinks 6 is leaving print runs too late for summer campaign. 6 controlled but dark eyes very scary. Quickly shut down Minesweeper and went back to work. Still no ideas.

THURSDAY.

Worked hard all morning, no ideas. Depressed, forced down cucumber sandwiches, played Minesweeper to relax. Played badly and deleted game from computer in rage. Regretted within hour.

People quiet in corridors at Coke, tight lips, grim expressions. Occasionally they peer in my window. Since no one's meant to know I'm here, I guess they're wondering who the hell I am.

"Scat," 6 says carefully. We're having Indian tonight, and it's arranged on the carpet in little plastic containers. "I can't help but feel that we aren't making much progress on the ad."

"Well, I've got one idea—"

6 sighs. "We're not going to have a giant beach ball crush New York. It's creative, but it's not going to sell product."

This is true. "Okay, okay."

"You must have found *something* in the files. There has to be *something*."

6 is thinking about Ogilvy. David Ogilvy wrote what many consider to be the best advertisement ever created, and it came from research. The client was Rolls-Royce, and Ogilvy found a line in an engineer's report that he stuck into the ad pretty much verbatim: "At sixty miles an hour the loudest noise in this Rolls-Royce comes from the electric clock." It's catchy, it's creative, and it's true. So it works. But it's damn hard to duplicate.

"6," I say steadily, "I've been through more Coke history than I knew existed. If anyone ever uses the phrase 'secret formula' within my earshot, I'm going to slap them. But there's nothing right for an ad."

6 looks at me silently for a moment. "I don't want to put any more pressure on you, Scat," she says, "but we have until five P.M. tomorrow to come up with something."

"Well you know," I say, a little exasperated, "I haven't exactly heard a wealth of great ideas from you."

"I'll be honest with you, Scat," she says, which immediately makes me suspicious. "Ideas aren't my strength. They're yours. My strengths are in development, negotiation and management. Which you don't have, or you'd be worth three million dollars right now."

I open my mouth but fail to fill it with a snappy reply. Poor management skills, perhaps.

6 says, "That's why I chose you, Scat. We have complementary skills."

"I see." I'm not sure whether to be flattered or insulted, so I settle for a little of each. "So you're relying on me to come up with the greatest ad in the history of marketing."

"Yes," 6 says, widening her eyes. I know by now that she does this just to suck me in, but I take a delicious moment to bathe in them, anyway.

"And unless I come up with this ad by close of business tomorrow, you have to go with the old campaign. Spend your next six months implementing other people's ideas." I allow myself a little smirk at this scenario, because, finally, I am in a power position over 6.

6 is silent for a long moment. "Actually," she says, "that's not quite true."

6 confesses [2]

* ° ° ° ● ° : ° ● ° ● ° ° ° ° ° ° ° : : ° ● ° ● ° ° ● ° ° ° ° ● ° ●

"The thing is, it's too late to go with the old campaign."

I blink. "Too late?"

"Yes." 6 bows her head, her midnight hair sweeping forward. "The campaign's design calls for some specialized graphic work, and I haven't hired anyone to do it. There's no way to get it ready for summer now."

"I see." I choose my words very carefully because it's important to get this right. "So are you telling me that unless I, Scat, come up with an ad by tomorrow afternoon, Coca-Cola isn't going to have a summer campaign?"

To her credit, 6 also spends a few moments checking through this. Because, like I said, it's important to understand our position. If Coke has no summer campaign, it will lose maybe 50, maybe 100 million dollars in sales, its stock will fall through the floor, the CEO will resign, PepsiCo will make millions, and television networks all over the world will lose one of their biggest customers. I'd guess that 6 doesn't particularly want to be remembered as responsible for that.

"I made a decision, Scat. I could begin implementing the campaign immediately, or I could take a risk on developing a new campaign from scratch." She shrugs fractionally. "I decided to take a risk."

"6," I say gently, "I don't want to be pessimistic here, but there is a chance I won't have anything by tomorrow afternoon. What happens then?"

6 takes a long sip from her 7 UP. "I place a call to the CEO to inform him of the situation and tender my resignation. Then I'm unemployed and no marketing manager in America will ever hire me again."

She looks at me with dark, surprisingly calm eyes. I try to think of something sympathetic and consoling to say, because suddenly I really feel bad for her.

Then 6 says, almost gently, "Or hire you."

snap

I have a deep, solid sleep so I wake completely refreshed Friday morning.

I keep repeating this statement over and over in my head, but it refuses to work. It's two in the morning and I can't sleep for nuts. It's amazing how mortal fear can do that to you.

At three, I get up and nuke myself a milk drink, watching my fingers shake as I push the buttons. I take it back to the sofa and drink it slowly, trying to avoid thinking about how my career could be over in fourteen hours. I realize very quickly that it's impossible to deliberately avoid thinking about something, so I cleverly try to avoid thinking about elephants instead. Unfortunately, my brain works out that the best way to avoid thinking about elephants is to think about how my career could be over in fourteen hours, and at 3:30 I still can't stop shaking.

The worst part is that now I'm standing with my foot in the bear trap, it's obvious. It's the biggest bear trap in the world. It wasn't even hidden; it practically had neon signs. 6 said, *"Scat, do you mind moving your foot so I can put this huge, neon-lit bear trap underneath it?"* and I said, *"Okay, sure thing, 6."*

I've been seen at Coke.

I can't believe I let that happen.

The textbooks wouldn't put this in a "Marketing Blunders" box: this will be reserved for "Marketing Catastrophes." Given that I'm currently fielding entries in both categories, I could be a shot for "All-Time Marketing Fuckwits," too: *After losing Fukk, Scat was apparently involved in the failure of Coca-Cola to launch a summer advertising campaign. Insiders at Coke say—*

Out of sheer exhaustion, I finally fall asleep around four. So I'm particularly distressed to be woken by a boy sitting on my head at 4:20.

"Whoa!" the boy says. "Sorry dude, didn't see you there!"

"*Tim*-othy," Tina chides from the kitchen, giggling. "Sorry, Scat."

Choking with rage, I spit, "God—damn—stupid—"

"Cool it, dude," Timothy tells me, backing off. Tina collects him and steers him toward her bedroom. "What's *his* problem?"

"He's a *marketer*," Tina explains as she shuts the door.

I'm so inflamed I can't even imagine sleeping. I get up and wander around the apartment for a while, swinging my arms and taking deep breaths. Gradually I feel myself returning to a state of calm, at which point Tina and Timothy begin a muffled giggle-fest. Then I get so mad I have to sit down fast.

At five, I'm seriously considering just getting the hell out. This is a particularly idiotic plan, given that it actually guarantees the ruin of my career, but I almost do it anyway.

Finally, at 5:20, just thirty minutes before I have to get up, I work out how to get to sleep. I march into the bathroom and flip up the toilet seat.

Just looking at it, I feel calmer. When I return to the sofa, I slip effortlessly into the deepest, most intense half hour's sleep of my life.

mktg case study #6: mktg cigarettes

FOR A PRODUCT THAT KILLS ITS CUSTOMERS, THIS IS PRETTY EASY. FOR ONE THING, YOU ONLY NEED TO CONVINCE PEOPLE TO START BUYING. BUT THE BEST PART IS THAT YOU GET TO DEFEND THE ACT OF SELLING A PRODUCT YOUR CUSTOMERS CAN'T STOP BUYING BY CLAIMING THEY HAVE FREEDOM OF CHOICE. BEFORE EACH MARKETING CAMPAIGN, PRACTICE THE LINE: "IT IS NOT THE POLICY OF OUR COMPANY TO DICTATE THE LIFESTYLE OF OUR CUSTOMERS."

hope

The bus ride to Coca-Cola is strained, but in the elevator 6 tries to give me a little pep talk. "Scat, if anyone can do this, you can. You need to look at this as a great opportunity."

"Sure," I mutter, frowning at the little glowing floor numbers. "A great opportunity to ruin my life."

"I'm sorry," 6 says, and maybe she does look a little contrite. "When I dragged you into this, I didn't stop to think how you would be affected. I haven't been fair with you."

It's hard to argue with someone who agrees with you, so I settle for a dark look.

6 takes a breath, then hits the EMERGENCY STOP button. The elevator stops so fast I almost hit the ceiling. Before I can recover, 6 is in my face, holding me by my lapels. Despite myself, I'm stunned by her proximity. I'm undone by the spice of her breath.

"You're talented, okay?" She actually looks angry. "You have real genius. I've never said that to anyone before." Her huge black eyes drill me. "You might be the best marketer I've ever met."

She kisses me.

the kiss

Hard. Fast. Devastating.

faith

6 breaks away, and I gasp for air. White spots come over and peer into my eyes to make sure I'm okay. My nerves leap around, saying, "What the fuck was *that?*" and for a second I'm sure 6 has taken the opportunity to punch me hard in the guts. When she starts the elevator again, I have to grab the wall to avoid falling to the floor.

The doors slide open but 6 doesn't move. She just says, "We can do this, Scat. We are going to do this."

I believe her.

the last stand

Three million-dollar ideas per year. Three.

I don't even switch on the computer. I search through the desk drawers until I find a sheaf of paper and a pen, and I start writing.

I write copy. I draw pictures. I write TV-spot scripts. I don't review anything, I don't edit anything, and I don't throw anything in the trash. I just churn through page after page, and I don't stop.

Three million-dollar ideas per year.

When 6 delivers my cucumber sandwiches at noon, I don't have time to talk to her; I just take the food with my left hand and keep writing with my right. 6 watches me for a moment, then withdraws.

I go nonstop until 4:30, when 6 visits me again. She looks as nervous as I've ever seen her. "Scat, it's time. Whatever you've got, we need it now."

I take a long, slow breath and flip to the start of my pad.

And I start reviewing.

why "calvin and hobbes" is so funny

"Calvin and Hobbes" is my favorite comic strip in the world.

I'm a bit of a fan of "Robotman," too, and I can't go past a "Dilbert," but neither of them can really match it with "Calvin and Hobbes." Because "Calvin and Hobbes" is true.

The strip has a great range, but my favorites are the cutting insights into the marketing industry and America's marketing culture. Bill Watterson, the creator of "Calvin and Hobbes," hates marketing. You don't need any more proof of this than the fact that he's never allowed any "Calvin and Hobbes" merchandise: no coffee cups, no lunch boxes, no T-shirts. He's deliberately turned his back on the opportunity to make a great deal of money in order to preserve the integrity of his strip. Now that's impressive.

Bill was also known for taking frequent sabbaticals from his work. It's difficult for a cartoonist with commitments to the daily papers to take a break, because the strip risks losing its spot in the papers, but Bill did it again and again.

I'm guessing, but I think Bill did it to keep his art honest. I think Bill couldn't stand the idea of having to submit a strip he's not completely happy with just to meet a deadline.

Because, sometimes, you just can't force it.

"Well?" 6 asks. Her voice is tight and strained. I look up and see her face is ashen.

"It's crap," I say dully. "It's all crap."

The word *crap* hangs in the air between us for a few seconds. 6 stares at me as if I have betrayed her.

"No," she says. "There must be something. There must—"

"6—" I throw the pad with all its pathetic ideas onto the desk with disgust. "I couldn't do it. I just couldn't do it."

6 hangs her head.

"I'm sorry," I say.

She looks up at me, and her face is absolutely white. "I need to make a call." She reaches over my desk and picks up the phone, dialing an extension from memory. She waits for a long time before speaking, so I guess she's got voice mail. "Mr. Jamieson, this is 6 at four-forty-five on Friday the Twenty-eighth. I would like to tender my resignation from Coca-Cola." She swallows and takes a long second before continuing. "I have failed to perform satisfactorily in managing the launch of the summer Classic Coke campaign, which will now be at least four weeks late. Through my mismanagement, I have endangered the profitability of the company. I have no excuse.

"Thank you for the opportunities you have shown me at Coca-Cola, and please accept my humblest apologies.

"Good-bye."

Life, Death and Coca-Cola

CHAPTER 000006

aftermath

We stand in the parking lot for a long time.

Well, I stand in the parking lot. 6 sits in the parking lot, paces the parking lot and stares at the parking lot.

"Uh, 6," I say again. "Maybe we should be going."

She stares at me expressionlessly. Then she turns back to the black Coke tower.

I clear my throat and look around nervously.

"I'm finished," 6 says suddenly. "I'm *over.*"

I sigh, which is apparently a bad reaction. 6 rounds on me, her eyes narrow slits. "*You,*" she spits. "I thought you had *ideas.*"

"Oh, Christ," I say, disgusted. There are a couple of business suits walking by, but I ignore them. "You might not have picked this up on your little self-obsession trip, but *you've* just screwed *me.* I sure didn't ask you to pull me down the toilet with you."

"You little shit," 6 says, as if this is a fact of great wonder. "You *loser.*"

I turn and walk away.

I'm pretty sure she's going to call after me, but even so I'm almost a hundred feet away before she does it. This gives me enough time to make mental bets on what I think she'll say, and I'm pretty confident about: *"Scat! Wait!"*

"Asshole!" 6 shouts.

and don't come back

That would be a pretty decent breakup, if all my clothes weren't still at 6's apartment.

scat comes back

I have to hold the buzzer down for about a minute before Tina picks up. "Hello, Scat," she says warily.

"Hi, Tina," I say, letting an edge of contrition leak into my voice. Given that they're my only worldly possessions right now, I really am pretty keen to get my clothes.

There is some scuffling, then another long pause. I suspect that Tina is holding her hand over the microphone and receiving instructions from 6. Eventually she says, "What do you want?"

"Just my things. I'll get them and get out."

More scuffles and pauses. "Maybe we don't want you in here."

I sigh heavily. Somewhere in 6's apartment a door closes. Then Tina whispers, "Come on up, Scat," and the security door clicks open.

Tina is waiting for me at the top of the stairs, mascara-and-eyebrow-ring-free. She's wearing an old tracksuit and, in all, looking disturbingly normal. "She's in the bathroom."

"Fine. She doesn't even need to know I'm here."

I start to walk inside but Tina grabs my arm. I look at her, surprised, and she gives me one of those *I-don't-believe-it's-this-stupid* looks. I seem to have a bit of a knack for attracting women who specialize in these looks: I could name a long list of teachers, ex-girlfriends and shop assistants.

"Scat," Tina says. "She's in the *bathroom.*"

I am obviously missing something. "Yes . . ."

Tina shifts her weight impatiently. "You have to *comfort* her."

"Whoa," I say, freeing my arm from Tina's grip. "I don't think you understand what happened at Coke today. We didn't part well."

"Whatever," Tina says. "Trust me on this. She needs you."

I can't help it: I laugh. It comes out just right—cynical, hardened and really pretty scathing. "Tina, I'm through with being needed by her. I don't know if you've noticed this yet, but being needed by 6 is not a good thing."

"Men," Tina says disgustedly, and pretty unfairly in my opinion. She stalks into the apartment and I follow her.

My clothes are neatly piled by the sofa, so I go over and scoop them up. "This is all I need. Nice to meet you, have a good degree, bye."

Tina lets me get to the front door. "Don't you want your razor?"

I stop.

"It's in the bathroom," she adds helpfully. "Seems like a nice one."

I take a few deep breaths and work up a seriously evil glare by the time I turn around.

"Oooh," Tina says.

"Tina," I say steadily, "will you please get my razor for me?"

"Hmm, let's see . . ." Tina says. "No."

"Okay." I dump my clothes in the doorway. "Fine." I march resolutely to the bathroom door, set my lips in a tight line, and rap three times. I don't knock, I rap. Firm, authoritative raps.

I'm braced for another *Asshole* or perhaps a *Fuck off*, and the long silence is something of a relief but also something of a concern. I resist a grimace as I try the handle.

It turns. The door swings open. 6 is sitting on the rim of the bath.

She looks fine, which stops me a little. I had expected red eyes, maybe disheveled clothes, at least an attractive sniffle. But she looks as composed and cool as if today had never happened.

"I just want my razor," I say.

"So get it," 6 says.

"I will." I sidle past her to the sink and pick up my razor, which looks a little lonely among the jungle of 6's and Tina's mysterious sprays and bottles.

Then there's a little pause, and in it I realize just how easy it is for me to walk out of here and never see 6 again. I only have to say, *Well, see you,* and she'll probably ignore me and I'll just walk out. And that'll be it. No more 6.

It's that simple.

I stand there and hold my razor.

I say, "You know, if you're not doing anything . . ."

a tender love scene with scat and 6

" 'Not doing anything'?" 6 says, her eyes narrowing. "You mean, like working?"

"Oh—no. I mean . . ." I sigh. "Come on, 6. We've spent a week working eighteen-hour days. We're both strung out. So let's . . . let's just go out somewhere."

She arches an eyebrow. I've noticed that 6 is very egalitarian with her eyebrows: sometimes the left gets to arch, sometimes the right. "You want to go out?"

"Yes," I say. "I think it would be good for us. Both of us."

6 lets long, silent seconds pass, as if this really is a judgment call. Could go either way. "Fine," she says.

mktg case study #7: mktg music

REVIVE A ROCK STAR FROM THE '60S AND APPEAL TO BABY BOOMER NOSTALGIA. NEVER FAILS.

billy ray

There's a southern-style restaurant called Billy Ray just two blocks down from 6's, and since I can see from the street that they have a well-stocked bar, I suggest we go in.

"Here?" 6 says, wrinkling her nose. "It's *southern*."

"Yeah," I say, thinking fast, "but it's secretly ironic."

"Really?" she says, suspicious.

"You bet," I say. "It was in *Vanity Fair*."

Inside, however, it quickly becomes obvious that Billy Ray is a big mistake. Their booths each represent a particular southern state, and the waitress leads us straight to Georgia. Squeezed among the pictures of Martin Luther King Jr. and someone I think is Jimmy Carter is a banner happily proclaiming "The Home of Coca-Cola!" and next to our table there's even a big Coke machine. "Uh," I say to the waitress. "Could we get another state? Louisiana, maybe? Or even Texas?"

"Sorry," the waitress says, with a truly frightening hybrid accent. "Georgia's all we got left. Texas always goes first, on account of the hats."

"Oh. Of course." I glance at 6. "I guess this is okay, then."

"Can I get y'all somethin' to drink?"

"Scotch and . . . water," I say, pulling out of a Coke reference just in time.

"A Bloody Mary," 6 says. "A tall one."

"Y'okay," the waitress says, which I think is pushing it. She scribbles this down on a little pad.

"6," I say carefully, "you should take it easy tonight." Then it occurs to me that maybe 6 shouldn't take it easy tonight: that, in fact, if 6 doesn't take it easy tonight, she might just hold forth about her childhood and all the shitty men she's ever known and end up in my arms attempting giggling, unsteady kisses. "Unless you feel you should. You know, to blow off all that crap at Coke."

"Coke is history," 6 says shortly. "I'm thinking of the future." She abruptly glances at the waitress, who is still hanging around. "Something you need?" 6 demands. The waitress blinks and snaps closed her little pad, then heads over to three men in Texas, who are demanding Lone Stars and making jokes about cowgirls. 6 turns back to me. "The smartest option now is consultancy."

I blink. "Really? With which firm?"

"With no firm." She shakes her head. "Scat, you need to realize that when the Coke story breaks, there will be no other option. It's self-employment or nothing."

"Oh," I say, feeling a little bleak. "Right."

"Obviously the soda industry is out. I'm thinking about entertainment. Maybe pop music."

"You, managing a rock band?" Somehow I find this a little difficult to imagine.

"*Packaging* a band," 6 says. "You buy a good, broke songwriter and match him to a group of sixteen-year-old boys with good skin. If you push them hard enough at the contract stage, the potential profits are enormous."

"Wow. You've got it all worked out."

"That's where most of the packagers screw up," 6 muses. I'm not even sure if she's talking to me anymore. "They don't twist the talents' arms hard enough at the start. If you give the actors a cut of the profits, they start thinking they're real musicians."

The waitress arrives with our drinks, dumping them indifferently on the table and heading off to Tennessee.

"Well," I say, holding up my glass, "to the future, then."

6 looks up, then nods. "To the future."

the future

"I guess we'll need an office," I say. "And for that we'll need a bank loan. I don't know about you, but my credit history isn't exactly—"

"Scat," 6 says, looking at me oddly. "This isn't something we can do together."

I stare at her. "What?"

"I'm sorry," she says. "You can't work with me."

I'm stunned into silence, and when I do manage to speak, my words come out high and whiny. "But why not? I thought—"

"Think about it, Scat. The only way to survive this catastrophe is to distance ourselves from it. And each other." She sips at her cocktail.

"But—6 . . ."

"I'm sorry," she says again, and this time her voice is harder. "This is the way it has to be."

I don't know what to do, so I stare at the table. I feel totally lost. Across the room, the Texans bray laughter. I reach for my scotch with unsteady hands, sip at it, then gulp the rest.

"You'll be all right," 6 says. "Even if you have to get out of marketing, you'll find something."

And that does it: suddenly I'm furious. I'm as furious as I've ever been in my life. Great, thick bubbles of rage burst inside me, spilling out everything I've kept pent up for the last week. "Oh. Well, gee thanks, 6. It's so nice to have your confidence in me, after you've destroyed my career. It's so great to know that after you've sucked me dry, you still think I can pick up a job flipping burgers at McDonald's."

"Scat," 6 says, faintly alarmed, "quiet down."

"Don't you tell me to quiet down!" I shout. I lurch to my feet, failing to make the best impression because I'm still wedged between the booth's fixed seat and table. "I'm through with listening to anything you've got to say! I can't even believe I'm here with you now!" I grind my fists against my forehead. "The only reason I asked you out was because Tina wanted me to, and I'm sitting here"—yet another injustice strikes me—"drinking *water* with my scotch because I don't want to offend you by drinking Coke! And you're—"

"Have Coke with your scotch," 6 says. "I don't care."

I stare at her, unable to believe she's really doing this. "I will! I'll drink all the goddamn Coke I want!" I pull out a fistful of change from my pants pocket and turn to the Coke machine.

A couple of the Texans have stood up to see what's going on. "You need any help, miss?" one of them asks 6.

White spots blaze before my eyes. "Don't give her any help!" I yell, shoving coins into the Coke machine's slot. "Help her and a week later you'll be wondering what the hell happened to your *life!*" I push the button for a Coke and a can rumbles toward the slot . . . then stops.

I bend down and peer into the slot. There is no can. "Oh, *great!*" I scream. I have now completely, utterly lost it. "This is just *perfect!*"

"Scat," 6 says from behind me. "Why don't you sit down?"

I wrap my arms around the Coke machine and start rocking it back and forth, grimacing with the effort. I'm just getting up some momentum when a strong hand falls on my shoulder. "Hey, buddy," a Texan says. "Why don't you leave the machine alone?"

"Yes, Scat, leave it," 6 says. "Those things are dangerous."

"*You're* dangerous! I'm getting my can!"

"Scat," she says, exasperated, "there have been fatalities. Don't mess with the machine."

In response, I say something like, *"Rrrrrrrrraaeegh!"* and push the Coke machine as hard as I can. It rocks backward, teeters on the edge of falling over, then swings back.

"Oh, shit," I say.

I try to get out of the way, but my legs tangle with the Texan's and the Coke machine crashes down onto us. It feels like catching a train with my spine.

I must black out for a few seconds, because I open my eyes without having any memory of closing them. 6 is standing over me, looking down. She even looks concerned. "Scat? Can you hear me?"

There is something stuck in my throat. "I . . ." I croak.

She leans closer. "What?"

"I . . ."

"Scat, are you all right?"

I abruptly realize what the thing in my throat is. It is the best ad in marketing history. "I . . . have an idea."

The Ad

CHAPTER 000007

a meeting with jamieson

So it's six A.M. Monday morning and we're pacing back and forth outside Coke.

"He'll be here any minute," 6 is muttering. I'm not sure if she's talking to me. "Always at six." 6 rose at three this morning and spent about two hours on her hair and makeup. I'm not sure if I'm more impressed by the length of time or the end result. "There," she says suddenly, and the headlights of a dark blue BMW sweep the lot. When the CEO of the Coca-Cola Company steps out, 6 and I are waiting for him.

"Mr. Jamieson," 6 says, as if it's a bit of a surprise to catch him. "Good morning."

Jamieson is relatively young, or else he has a damn good dermatologist. With his side part and natty glasses, he looks a little like an accountant done good. His dark eyes assess us quickly.

"Morning, 6," Jamieson says. "Coming to the gym with me?"

"It's a date," 6 says.

working it out

This is a very important conversation, so I try hard to concentrate. But it's hard with 6 in Lycra bike shorts and a crop top.

"So," 6 says, casually pumping what looks like a hundred pounds. "Did you get my voice mail?"

Jamieson takes a pause from the punching bag. There's a little Pepsi logo drawn on it, which is cute. "I don't check my own messages anymore. Don't have the time. Julie takes them down for me." He thumps the bag, one-two-three. "What was your message?"

"Oh, you know," 6 says vaguely. "Just updates."

a visit to julie

"*Hi*, Julie," 6 says. I'm amazed: she sounds really warm and friendly. For a moment I could believe that 6 and Julie are old friends.

"Oh," Julie says. She smiles warily. "Hello, 6." So I guess you don't get to be the CEO's personal assistant by being gullible.

6 walks around and sits on the corner of Julie's desk. Back in her business attire, she's the epitome of professionalism. I just stand in the doorway and try to not look out of place.

Julie looks up at 6.

"I need you," 6 says.

the seduction of julie

"I don't think so," Julie says.

"Julie—"

"I can't do that, 6. Mr. Jamieson's messages are private."

"I understand that policy, and it exists for a good reason," 6 says. "But this is a message *I* sent. I just want to retract my own message."

For a second Julie appears to be lost in 6's dark eyes. Then she blinks. "I'm sorry, but no. I can tell Mr. Jamieson that you wish to retract the message if you like, but I still have to show him—"

"Julie, the message is my resignation. If Mr. Jamieson gets that message, I'm through."

Julie is silent for a long moment. 6's eyes never leave her.

"Nevertheless," Julie begins.

plan b

"Stupid *bitch*," 6 snarls, stalking through the corridors like a wildcat. "Goddamned bureaucratic *idiot*."

I am prudently silent.

"It doesn't matter," 6 says brusquely. "I'll tell Jamieson I was drunk." She opens the door to her office, which, incidentally, I haven't seen before. It's huge. You could raise a family in here. There's a forest of indoor fernery, neatly offsetting the solid oak desk and dark patent leather chairs. 6's personal coffee machine sits on its own table underneath a massive framed Coke ad from 1962. One wall is completely glass, which, since this is the four-teenth floor, is a little scary. But most impressive is the flanking poster of Elle Macpherson, who is smiling brightly and very, very naked.

I take a chair, trying not to look at the Elle. That really is a nude picture. "So—"

"So," 6 says, "we go ahead and present your idea this afternoon."

"The presentation," I say. "Right."

We spent the whole weekend preparing for this, but I still feel nervous and unprepared. It's Fukk all over again.

It's even the same room, with the same giant wooden doors. The only real difference is the audience: we don't get to present to the board, who only meet once a month, but to the SMT: the senior management team. These are the guys responsible for actually running the company, as opposed to making grand decisions about strategic direction. They're thinner, too.

There's a very different atmosphere among these folk than the board, and we enter to uproarious laughter. A short, bald guy is telling a story, surrounded by a dozen colleagues in pants and ties (no jackets, no women). Jamieson is at the back, smiling.

"Then the call girl goes," the bald man is saying, " 'Wait a minute, wait a minute. Are you *sure* you're Gary?' " The group explodes into laughter again, and 6 takes the opportunity to thread between them.

"Hi, Jim," she says. "You ready for us?"

"Sure." He raises his voice as the men begin a half dozen private conversations. "Let's settle down, fellows."

They drift into seats around the massive oak table, and I'm amazed at how casual they all are. These men are responsible for the biggest brand in the world, and they're just ordinary people. I even spot a half-slung tie. I can't decide if this is really cool or sacrilegious. I think maybe it's a little of each.

As arranged, I check the overhead projector, then slip a transparency—covered, for now—onto it.

This is my ad.

6 nods at me, then turns to the SMT. "You're expecting an update on the Classic Coke campaign. You're expecting a tedious half-hour brief on advertising coverage and reach statistics. Everything you've seen before. Right?"

These twelve men must be smart: none of them says anything.

"That's not what I'm giving you. I'll explain why. Most of you know that until recently, I was in New Products. And if you know that, you know why I'm not there today.

"But, gentlemen, I'm a creative person. And I'm an ambitious person. I had some trouble confining myself to my new job spec. I'm afraid I went outside it a little."

6's eyes rake the room.

"Mr. Scat and I have redesigned the summer Classic Coke campaign."

Again, I'm impressed by the SMT: almost no one betrays surprise.

Almost. Jim leaps from his seat, spitting outrage. "You *what?* You did *what?*"

6 regards him coolly.

"Do you know how much work went into that campaign?" he demands. "How much *money?*"

Jamieson interrupts him. He speaks softly, but Jim's mouth shuts like it's on springs. "Excuse me . . . when you say 're-designed,' you mean—"

"I mean I threw the old one out," 6 says. "It's history."

Jamieson digests this for a second. Finally, he says, "This is unacceptable."

"It's *outrageous,*" Jim seconds. "6, if I have to explain to you how important this campaign is to our company's continued success, you don't belong here. You can't *touch* that campaign. We spent six months developing and market testing that thing, and it was *perfect.*"

"It was boring." 6's tone is gentle, as if she is presenting an accepted truth that Jim hasn't quite grasped yet. "It was obvious. It was exactly like last year's campaign."

Jim flushes a fairly unattractive red. "Last year's campaign was a success, in case you've forgotten."

6 tilts her head thoughtfully. "Why do you think that, Jim?"

"We increased sales by six percent," he says through his teeth.

I notice no one else is buying into this debate: they're waiting to see whether 6 or Jim falls first.

"You know, Jim, I don't think that's very much," 6 says. She pauses, just long enough for Jim to think of a retort but not long enough for him to get it out. "I can get six percent at my bank. I think maybe we should be thinking about increasing sales by fifteen percent. What do you think about that, Jim?"

Jim opens his mouth, then wisely closes it. There is no good answer to this question.

"And you don't do that with last year's campaign. Beaches and bikinis don't work anymore. We need something different. Something radical." Her gaze sweeps the room, and, amazingly, Jim wilts back into his chair under it. "Something that people will see and remember, tell their friends about. Memorable and identifiable."

This is the battle of the advertising copywriter: to be both memorable, so the market recognizes your product, and identifiable, so they like it. It's pretty easy to be one or the other: for example, you could make a very memorable ad by saying, "This product sucks bad. Only losers buy it." But you have to wonder how many customers would identify with that.

"We want to be hip. We want to be controversial. We want to be cynical." 6 tilts her head. "Basically, we want to be just like our customers. Don't we?"

Silence, but I catch two slow, thoughtful nods.

6 says, "Gentlemen, welcome to fifteen percent growth."

On cue, I whip off the cover sheet, and my ad springs on to the wall.

the new classic coke summer campaign

Last year, 12 Americans lost their lives while
attempting to steal from a Coke machine.

[Picture of a railway station at night, with a Coke machine fallen on its side. There's a guy's arm sticking out from underneath it.]

Wouldn't you die for a Coke?

moving on up

There is quite a heated debate, led by the stalwart Jim, who advances the theory that the ad will turn off the significant proportion of Coke customers who aren't young, hip and cynical. In response, 6 accuses Jim of losing touch with what Coke is all about, and Jim comes, I think, very close to punching her.

So it's a pretty interesting meeting.

We break at five, when one of the catering staff wheels in a huge tray of drinks. Jim looks grateful for the respite.

While I'm popping myself a beer, a tall, tanned man hands me his business card. "Great concept," he tells me. "Very special. I can find a lot of work for you. Stay in touch, all right?"

"Okay," I say. I look at the card and see that this guy is GARY BRENNAN, VICE PRESIDENT, MARKETING. After a brief moment when everything goes white, I look up, but Gary is already gone. Three or four other men are moving toward me, broad smiles on their faces.

I think: *This is where it starts.*

Measurement

CHAPTER 000008

mktg case study #8: mktg groceries [2]

USE LARGE SPECIAL! TAGS ON GOODS WITHOUT REDUCING THEIR PRICE. PRACTICE THE LINE: "OUR COMPANY FEELS THAT THE WORD SPECIAL IN NO WAY IMPLIES A CONNECTION WITH PRICE."

scat and 6 retire to a local bar

"This is unbelievable," I say. I take a sip at my scotch and Coke, then decide I should just throw it back and order another one, so I do. After all, whatever debt I rack up on my credit card today is sure to be covered by my impending financial rewards from Coke. "I can't believe it's happening."

6 rests her elbows on the bar beside me, expressionlessly nursing a tall Serial Killer.

"What, aren't you excited? Isn't this what we've been working for?"

6 sighs. "Scat, you really don't understand how business works. It's not over yet."

"What do you mean? You blew them away in that meeting. They're going to run our campaign. You're a *hero*. What more is there?" My all-new scotch conveniently arrives on the scene and I chug that one, too.

6 sniffs. "If I was a man, I'd be a hero. If I was a man, half the SMT would be taking me out for drinks tonight, instead of just you." She drains the rest of her cocktail.

"Uh," I say, not sure if I want to be getting into this, "so why aren't they?"

"Because I'm a woman in a dick-measuring contest," 6 says. "Business is a man's game, and they don't like me playing. Opening my mouth is a challenge to their masculinity."

I'm starting to feel a little challenged myself, so I say, "6, you can't tell me that every man in business can't handle working with a woman."

"That's exactly what I'm telling you," 6 says, gesturing for another drink.

I take a moment to think about this. "That's paranoid."

6 shrugs. "You can afford to believe that. I've seen every woman who showed a glimpse of femininity fall out of the dick-measuring contest."

"So, what—you're still in there?"

"Yes," 6 says. "Like everyone else, I go around trying to convince everyone that my dick is the biggest."

I stare at her. "But—"

"Perception is reality," 6 says.

scat proposes a hypothesis

"So you're telling me that they'll try to take the campaign away from us?"

"Of course."

I take a deep breath, and the additional oxygen on top of a great many scotches gives me a brief rush. "Look, I know I'm new to business and all, but I was at that meeting, too. We were a *huge* hit. Gary *Brennan* gave me his card."

6 shrugs. "That doesn't matter."

I say carefully, "Could it be—and this is just a guess—that you're so sure everyone is out to get you that you make it true?" 6's eyes narrow, but I plow ahead. "I mean, you think they're going to be aggressive, so you get aggressive, so you make *them* aggressive."

"I don't think so."

"It's called a self-fulfilling prophesy," I say helpfully. Then I spoil it by being unable to resist adding, "Although you'd know that, having done some psych units."

"You're naive," 6 says shortly.

"Maybe I am," I say, and suddenly I'm in *Days of Our Lives*. "But maybe you shouldn't wait your whole life to find out."

6 rolls her latest cocktail, a Horny Virgin, between her hands.

"Look, how about this: just once, don't assume every person you meet has a personal vendetta against you."

6 frowns at her drink. "That's not a sound strategy."

I reach out and take one of 6's hands. They are warm and smooth and suddenly I have to fight a strong and very stupid urge to lick one. "Please, just don't go after anyone. At least wait until someone comes after us."

6 sighs heavily, then nods. "Fine," she says. "We'll try it your way."

I'm a little taken aback: I have come up with a business strategy, proposed it to 6, and she has accepted it. 6, who is immensely better in business than me, has carefully weighed the merits of my idea and found it worthy of approval. "Gee, thanks."

6 hiccups.

scat opens his eyes

We stagger into the street and I look around for a cab. In response, the street sags dangerously, dipping to the left. "Whoa boy," I say, clutching at what I hope is a lamppost. "I shouldn't have had those last shooters."

6 steps forward and raises her hand at a distant yellow blob, which drifts toward us and begins to look more like a cab. 6 is carrying her drunkenness with immaculate grace; if it wasn't for the overcareful way she is planting each foot, I could take her for sober.

We fall into the backseat of the cab, my face dipping deliciously close to her bare left shoulder. I'm forced back in the seat as the driver accelerates, and when I recover 6 is regarding me with relatively steady eyes.

"You know," she says, "you shouldn't be staying with me tonight. The arrangement is over."

I struggle upward in the seat. "What, you're going to kick me out? Now?"

6 tilts her head, as if she's considering it.

"Oh, come on," I tell her. "You're not kicking me out."

"Why not?"

"Because," I say, pointing at her for no sensible reason, "you don't really want me to go."

6 raises an eyebrow. In contrast to her usual smooth eyebrow moves, this one is a little wobbly, as if it's had a few cocktails itself. "No?"

"No," I say, warming up. Right now everything I do feels suave, so I go with it. "Fact is, you've gotten used to having me around. And as much as you don't want to admit it"—I actually lean closer—"you *like* me."

6 turns away, as if she's disappointed, or maybe hiding a smile. I elect to believe the latter. Then she turns back. Her dark eyes are huge. "Well, let me ask you something, Scat," she says, and her voice is very soft. "Why don't you want to go?"

scat confesses [2]

The answer is so obvious that it's halfway up my throat before I can stop it.

Because I'm in love with you.

It trembles there, caught. And I can't believe I didn't get this before. I can't believe I am only realizing this now, with 6 regarding me with eyes so dark they are like night.

"Well?" she says.

I open my mouth.

almost

"Because I've got nowhere else to go," I say.

6 holds my gaze for a moment longer, then turns away. "Oh," she says.

a new day

I am in love with 6.

"Then *Rod* tells me, 'No way, bitch, you're outa your mind,' " Tina says. "*Un*-believable. Unbelievable." She shakes her head to emphasize, tossing bacon around in the pan. Tina burned another relationship last night, and this morning I'm glad I'm not a bacon rind.

I am in love with 6.

"The problem," she says, "is that men won't admit to their *feelings*. They think they've got to act so fucking *tough* all the time." She throws the pan onto the stovetop and turns to me, hands on hips, her spatula jutting aggressively. "Is it so hard?" she demands. "Is it so hard to just say what you're *feeling?*"

94

"Men," 6 says, not looking up from the *LA Times*. She is wearing a fluffy white dressing gown, her smooth calves peeking through its cotton embrace. She sips coffee between full, pouting lips.

I am in serious, serious trouble.

a chance encounter with

6 spends the bus ride to Coke looking quietly out the window. I spend it trying to hide my sweat patches. Occasionally I break the monotony by mentally reiterating: *I am in serious, serious trouble.* It calms me down a little.

In the elevator I ask, "So, what exactly am I supposed to be doing here?"

"Watching my back," 6 says shortly, frowning at the floor numbers.

"Hey, 6, remember, we're not looking for trouble. We're running the campaign we want. So we're taking it easy, right?"

6 opens her mouth, and I'm fairly sure she's preparing something like, *Actually Scat, I've kind of reconsidered that particular idea and found it to be full of shit.* But then the elevator doors spring open and there's

jamieson

"Mr. Jamieson," 6 says. Her voice is genuinely surprised, which is very unsettling.

"Ah, 6," he says. "I'm glad I caught you. I need to talk to you about the campaign."

6 takes a slow, controlled breath but says nothing. This is a good start.

"The thing is," Jamieson says, punching 12, "it's a damn good campaign. Risky, too. I have to make sure I've got the right people on the job. People I can trust. You understand that, right?"

In case 6 interprets this remark as aggressive and responds in kind, I jump in first. "Of course, Mr. Jamieson. It's critical to get the execution right. We're very concerned about that." I slip in a friendly smile to show Jamieson how we can all be good buddies, and make sure 6 catches it.

Jamieson smiles back. "Excellent! That's just what I wanted to hear."

I can't resist: I throw 6 a smug look. When this is all over, I'm going to sit her down and use the phrase *You see* a lot, and she is going to nod and say, *Well, Scat, I guess you were right.* Which will be a welcome change from right now, with her eyes burning into me as if she can barely contain her fury.

Jamieson says, "As you know, we've been very privileged at Coke to have a new man onboard recently: Sneaky Pete. He's brought a number of very good ideas to the company, including a product we've got great hopes for this summer: Fukk." He nods toward me. "Have Sneaky Pete tell you about it some time, Scat: it's going to be huge."

I say something like: *urk.* It feels a lot like swallowing my own heart.

"The thing is, he's put a case to me to take over the summer campaign," Jamieson says, scratching his ear, "and you know, I'm tempted. I have to match the right people to the job. Right?" He looks at me, and, incredibly, I actually nod. 6 shoots me a gaze so hot I can feel it in my toes.

"Mr. Jamieson," 6 says, stepping forward, "if we can just back up a second here, I think it's too late to talk about bringing someone else in *now.* This is *my* campaign and I'm in the middle of it."

"I appreciate that, 6. I'm not pulling you off it. I just want to meet and discuss how we're going to handle it. Just the three of us—four if you'd like to be involved, Scat."

I open my mouth to agree, then abruptly lose all confidence in my ability to say anything intelligent and close it again.

The elevator dings politely and the doors slide open. "Talk to

Julie about the time and place." Jamieson steps through the doors, then slips us a small, hard smile just before the doors close again. "Thanks for your cooperation."

murder one

6 turns to me slowly, and for a few long seconds, I am pretty sure I'm about to die.

6 makes a call

"So I was wrong," I say. I'm trying hard not to squirm, but I'm finding 6's eyes particularly intimidating right now. "I was very, very wrong."

6 stares at me across the desk for a moment, so intently that I can't help but think she's trying to identify my brain. "Oh, boy," she says finally. She picks up the phone and dials. "Oh, boy."

"I'm a terrible businessman," I grovel. "I will never offer you advice again."

6 abruptly slams the phone down. I notice that the handset has a series of small dents, as if this kind of treatment is fairly common. "Voice mail," she says with disgust.

I am feeling stupid. "Whose?"

"Sneaky Pete."

"Oh."

She dials again but spares the handset by punching for speaker. As it rings she moves over to her personal percolator.

"Julie Stephens."

"Julie, 6." She pushes for a coffee. "I'm glad I caught you."

"Oh, hi, 6." There's that note of caution in her voice again, but it's different this time: there's something else there, too. 6 straightens and frowns at the speaker.

"Julie, do you recall our last conversation?"

"Of course."

"You did transcribe my message for Mr. Jamieson, right?"

"I—I wrote it down," Julie says.

"And you gave it to Mr. Jamieson?"

Julie takes a deep breath, then answers in a voice that's just a little too high-pitched. "Actually no, 6, I thought about what you said and I . . . decided not to."

6's eyes narrow. She walks slowly back to the phone and rests her hands on her desk, either side of the phone. I wince in anticipation of the sizzling accusations 6 is about to sling down the line.

"That's great, Julie. I really appreciate it."

"Oh, you're welcome." Relief gushes from the speaker.

"But that's not what I was calling about. Did Mr. Jamieson tell you about the meeting we're having?"

"Yes . . . does lunch tomorrow work for you?"

"Fine. Which room?"

"It's not in the building. I'll send you the address."

6 pauses. "It's not in the building? Why not?"

"That's just the way it's been arranged," Julie says cautiously.

"Oh," 6 says. "Right. Thanks, Julie."

"You're welcome," Julie says quickly. I get the impression that Julie is particularly looking forward to putting down the phone.

6 says, "Oh, wait."

Pause. Long, reluctant pause. "Yes?"

"I just need to ask one more thing. If you wrote down my message but didn't give it to Mr. Jamieson . . . who did you give it to?"

The speaker is shocked into silence.

"Thank you," 6 says, and kills the call.

"Wow," I say. "6, I have to say, I am *so* impressed."

"We're fucked," 6 says. She pronounces this very clearly. "We are so fucked." She slumps into her ergonomic chair.

"You really think she gave your message to Sneaky Pete? Why would she do that?"

"Politics. He's convinced Julie that it's in her interest to take his side over mine." She sighs. "He's probably right."

"Oh. Shit."

"Yes," 6 says. She leans forward and stares at me morosely, as if maybe this is my fault, too.

"Hey, 6," I say. "It's not over yet. So Sneaky Pete has found out that you were about to resign. Well, big deal. That's irrelevant now. We're just going to go into that meeting and tell Mr. Jamieson why we're right for the job and Sneaky Pete isn't."

"Scat, if Sneaky Pete knows I resigned, he knows why. And in that meeting, he'll tell Jamieson that we nearly killed the company."

I open my mouth but there's nothing to say. In the end I have to settle for: "Ah."

6 leans back in her chair, watching me expressionlessly.

"So that's a *setback*," I say gamely. I'm so game that I stand up. "But this isn't over. I mean, in the end, we came up with a campaign. It all worked out. And if Sneaky Pete wants to talk about what *might* have happened, well, it's all just perception. We just need to position it in a . . . positive light."

6's right eyebrow shoots up.

"It's not impossible. Anyway, what has Sneaky Pete done, really? He's just stolen ideas. Has he actually *produced* anything? *We* have."

6 slowly leans forward in her chair. The gleam is back in her eyes. I lean toward her, resting my hands on her desk.

"Look, Sneaky Pete might have a knack for pulling the strings in the background. Maybe he's brilliant at it. But this meeting will be us and him. No seducing secretaries or stealing trade-marks . . . no tricks. Just us and him. And he's got to beat *you*, 6—he's got to talk you into the ground. I don't think he can do it. I think you'll eat him alive."

6 rises from her chair like she's in slow motion, rises until she is inches from my face. Her intoxicating scent washes over me, and for a moment the office tips dangerously.

"Scat," she says, and her lips are curving into a genuine, authentic smile. It is shocking, stunning. "Sometimes, you—" She stops, licks her lips. I am leaning into them, helpless to stop myself. "You surprise me," 6 says softly.

the eyebrow maneuver

I'll tell you exactly what's required at this precise moment: a raised eyebrow. That's what I need to do. A sardonically raised eyebrow has a good chance of progressing to a brushing of lips, and that could lead to my hand reaching into that dark hair and pulling her close. And after *that*, there could be all kinds of acts that presently defy imagination but I'm sure will be nice.

And I'm pretty sure I can execute an eyebrow raise, too, because I used to be able to do it in high school. Hasn't been much of a calling for it since then, sure, and maybe I'm a little rusty. But some things you never forget, right?

So that's what I need to do, and I am absolutely clear on this as 6's face fills my world, the blossoming smile on her lips suggesting that maybe, just maybe, I am worthy of a little admiration.

My left eyebrow is actually beginning its sojourn upward when I can't help it: I break out in a big, goofy smile.

percolation

Puzzlement flits across 6's face, and then she is pulling away, her gorgeous hair swinging past my goofy, grinning face. That kills my smile pretty fast, but it's too late. 6 heads for the percolator, not looking at me.

"So we have until tomorrow," she says. She frowns at her patient coffee mug. "I want to walk into that meeting with ten reasons why we should manage the campaign and he shouldn't."

"Okay," I say stupidly.

That night, 6 watches *Letterman* in silence and I can't sleep for visions of what should have happened instead.

sixteen reasons

The next morning I stay home, working on the list while 6 goes into Coke. By the time I leave for the meeting, I actually have fifteen reasons why we're going to beat Sneaky Pete today. But even so, I can't help feeling that the real reason is one I haven't written down: Sneaky Pete has made 6 mad.

scat considers some hypotheticals

I arrive at the address 6 gave me a good fifteen minutes early, but already I'm in trouble. Because the address is obviously wrong.

It's a fairly impressive-looking establishment, I'll give it that. Nice trimming on the doorway and modern signage, even if the overall look is a little gloomy. But I can't help but feel the CEO of Coca-Cola wouldn't hold a power meeting in a place that advertises "Hot Live Nude Girls."

I stand on the sidewalk in front of Ludus, the address in my hand and my mouth hanging open, and I enunciate clearly, "Oh, shit."

I can picture, so clearly, 6 pacing in front of some expensive restaurant, frowning at her watch and scanning the street for me. Waiting until the last moment, then going in alone. Already on the defensive as she fields questions from Jamieson: Isn't Scat coming? When do you expect him? Do you even know?

6 is going to kill me. Actually, physically kill me.

I pace the sidewalk in sweaty indecision for ten minutes, and then another scenario occurs to me. In this one, 6 isn't concerned at all. In this scenario, 6 is serenely sitting down to lunch with Jamieson and Sneaky Pete, making a calm apology for my absence. 6 knows very well that I'm not coming, because it was 6 who told me the meeting was here.

This scenario makes a lot more sense than the first one, and suddenly I'm furious. I can't believe she's trying this stunt again. I turn on my heel, ready to storm back to the apartment, maybe even gather my stuff and just leave, and I nearly knock her over. "6!"

She freezes, staring at Ludus.

"Look, we've obviously gotten mixed up. How about you call Julie and find out where we're supposed to be, and we'll grab a cab over there before . . ." I trail off, because 6 is moving toward the building. "6?"

She strides toward the doorway; her eyes narrow. I hurry after her with absolutely no idea what she is doing, and together we enter Ludus.

sim sex

Inside it's dark and they're playing Wham!, which is scary already. Scattered around the tables are maybe a dozen Live Girls—although none of them looks particularly Hot or Nude—bouncing and giggling for young guys in suits. I'm surprised by how disengaged the men are; they talk among themselves or dispassionately survey the women as if browsing a used-car lot for something worth a test drive.

One of the dancers catches my eye and deliberately licks her lips, which is so fake I just feel embarrassed. I turn to 6, who is scanning the crowd, but before I can speak she begins to thread her way through the suits. I push after her, get an elbow in the ribs for my trouble, and by the time I catch up she's forged her way into an adjoining room. "Whoa, 6. What—"

"Scat," 6 says levelly, "shut up."

I snap my mouth shut, wounded, and peer into the room.

And there they are.

laughing with the boys

Three members of the SMT, including Gary Brennan and Jim, are seated around a huge table, drowning in high-back wooden chairs. They are laughing uproariously, empty beer bottles littering the table. Attending each of them is a topless girl.

Gary's girl has fake blond pigtails and fake breasts, and she's sitting quietly on his lap as if vaguely bored. Jim's is short and pale-skinned, grimly massaging his shoulders. As I watch, Jim reaches back and tries to pat the girl's behind, and she scoots away from his hands.

Having left 6's apartment expecting to spend an hour in a classy restaurant exchanging polite, barbed conversation with Sneaky Pete, I now feel just a touch spun out. I feel like I've walked into Hugh Hefner's version of *The Twilight Zone*.

Only one thing makes sense, and I latch on to it: Jamieson's not here. Maybe a couple of boys from the SMT are out for a little lunchtime stress relief, but Jamieson surely wouldn't be so crass as to hold a meeting with 6 here. I scan the table quickly, just to make sure he's not lounging back in one of the chairs. And I'm right: he's not.

But Sneaky Pete is.

welcome back scat

He's wearing shades: deep silver mirrors. I haven't seen them before, so I guess they're a new pair; I guess he splurged with a little of my three million. And some petty cash was obviously invested in his suit, too, because it's immaculate. It's so immaculate I almost expect to see tailors skulking around his feet, straightening a crease here, shooting a cuff there. Sneaky Pete was cool before, but now he's cool and rich. He looks like an advertisement.

As I stare, his head slowly turns to me. I'm momentarily unsure what to do: Wave? Flip him the bird? It's a tough call.

He doesn't let me make it. As I stand in the doorway with 6, seeing myself reflected in his mirrored shades, Sneaky Pete makes a greeting of his own: his lips stretch into a wide, feral grin.

ye who enter here

Jim notices our entrance first. His eyes widen and he almost leaps out of his chair, his eyes fixed on 6. "What—what are *you* doing here?"

I look around the table and see Gary and the other man looking decidedly wary, shooting glances at Sneaky Pete. And suddenly I'm sure that they have no idea what this is about.

Sneaky Pete rises slowly from the table, and for some reason I'm abruptly reminded of Dracula. "Scat . . . 6 . . . thank you for coming." His voice is even softer than I remember, and I have to lean forward to hear him properly. "Please, have a seat."

I'm already starting forward, a little mesmerized by that voice, but 6 stops me. She hasn't moved an inch.

"No." She cocks her head. "I have a meeting with Mr. Jamieson. It obviously isn't here."

Sneaky Pete nods fractionally. "Mr. Jamieson cannot attend in person." He gestures vaguely toward the middle of the table, and

I notice a speakerphone nestling quietly among the beer bottles. "But he will be joining us by phone."

6 considers this for a long moment; so long I'm sure that someone else will have to jump in, or at least clear his throat to break the awkwardness. No one does.

Finally, I have to speak. "Look, there's no way Mr. Jamieson would agree to this." I start to heat up, a little of that post-Fukk rage creeping up my collar. "Whatever scam you're pulling this time—"

"Of course Mr. Jamieson doesn't know about it," 6 says. "It's a stunt. To throw us off-balance. With an audience to see if I can't handle it."

Sneaky Pete's expression doesn't change at all.

"Fine," 6 says. "Watch me."

She steps forward.

As she does, two strippers emerge from the gloom, carrying chairs. They set them down at the table, precisely opposite Sneaky Pete. And they just stand there.

I realize that not just the chairs are for me and 6.

6 is stripped

6 stares at Sneaky Pete, her jaw a hard line, and I actually tense in case I need to prevent her from leaping across the table at him. Then she stalks forward and drops into a chair. I slide in beside her.

"Hi, I'm Candy," one of the girls tells me, and the other says to 6, "Hi, I'm Sugar." I look up at Candy and see that she is smiling brightly, displaying a good set of chompers. I try to avoid looking at her breasts, but they're pretty much in my face and I fail within seconds. They are pointed with large relaxed nipples, and when Candy sees me looking, she gives them a happy little jiggle. "Can I sit on your lap?" she asks politely.

"Uh," I say, but Candy interprets this as an affirmative and swings her legs over mine. It's a fairly confrontational position, and I look across to 6 for support. But 6 is also being accosted, Sugar pushing her rear end into her lap.

Sugar hugs 6 tightly. "*I* like girls, too," Sugar confides.

"Sneaky Pete," 6 says slowly, dangerously, "I don't want this girl on me."

He regards her coolly from behind his mirrored shades. "Why not? As you have made perfectly clear to your colleagues at Coca-Cola . . . you like girls, do you not?"

6's jaw tightens. And I abruptly realize that there is nothing she can say.

mktg case study #9: mktg lies

OCCASIONALLY, JUST OCCASIONALLY, YOUR COMPANY WILL BE CAUGHT IN A LIE. THIS IS NOT GOOD. IF POSSIBLE, IMMEDIATELY FIRE SOMEONE EXPENDABLE AND PUBLICLY APOLOGIZE. IF NOT, YOU MUST STICK TO THE LIE. PERCEPTION IS REALITY.

go

At this moment, the phone rings.

the meeting

Sneaky Pete taps a button. "Mr. Jamieson."

"Hello?" His voice is distant and there's muffled traffic in the background, so I guess he's in his car. "Can you hear me?"

"Loud and clear," Sneaky Pete says, and I actually see him smirk.

"Great. 6?"

"I'm here, Mr. Jamieson."

"Me too," I pipe up, because it would be embarrassing if Jamieson forgot about me.

"Good," Jamieson says. "All right, let's kick this thing off. I don't have much time."

Sneaky Pete folds his hands and rests them on the table.

The speaker says, "We've got a hell of a campaign here, guys. I don't want you to think I've forgotten that. It's great work."

I can't help myself. "Thanks," I say, and I actually grin at Sneaky Pete. "You can count on us for ideas, Mr. Jamieson."

"Yes, Scat. I think I can."

Sneaky Pete says quietly, "But this isn't about ideas."

"That's right," Jamieson says. "This is about execution."

I open my mouth to say *Oh, right,* then realize how stupid that will sound and just frown at the speaker. Candy toys annoyingly with my hair.

"I want this campaign to be driven by whoever will execute it best. It's that simple. This isn't about territory, or who came up with the idea. Do you understand that, Scat?"

"Yes," I say thickly. "But I think—"

"Mr. Jamieson, I see where this is going," 6 interrupts. Her voice is strong and steady, and it startles Sugar into a little jump. "I'm from New Products. I was moved from Fukk before I got involved in implementation. And Scat has no experience, either."

Sugar reaches out to play with 6's hair, and 6 slaps her hand away. The movement is so quick and controlled that my heart leaps: it means that while 6 may be shaken, she is far from beaten.

"But it would be a mistake, Mr. Jamieson, to get caught on that. If you wanted, we could spend all afternoon counting the days I spent in execution and the days he did." She doesn't need to say *Sneaky Pete.* "Maybe he has more—but that's not the point. If you really wanted experience, you wouldn't be talking to either of us. What you're really after is energy. And a determination to get things done. And if I may say so, Mr. Jamieson, this *is* about ideas. You want someone who has enough creativity to find new ways to deliver an extraordinary campaign."

A truck crackles past Jamieson, and he waits until it passes. "Yes, that's partly true. I do want all that."

Sneaky Pete says, "6, you are a very good speaker." He pauses to grin at her, then continues. "May I say so? You present yourself very well. Better than me." Again, he stops to grin, and this is really starting to irritate me. I grit my teeth and push Candy away, who is trying to blow into my ear. "In fact, if you will excuse me, I would suggest that you are . . . more style than substance."

Coming from Sneaky Pete, this is more than I can stomach. "Oh, *please*. Let's talk about substance, huh? We developed Fukk. We developed the summer campaign. What have you done?"

Sneaky Pete says immediately, "Mr. Jamieson, I find this hostile attitude quite inappropriate."

"Yes, Scat," Jamieson says. "Let's keep this professional. Sneaky Pete has been running Fukk for the past two months."

The grin: wide and white. It says: *Thank you, Scat, for getting Jamieson to support me. Please keep it up.* I want to walk around the table and pop him.

"All I'm saying," I say tightly, "is that Sneaky Pete does not have the same credibility as 6 and me."

"Yes, credibility," Sneaky Pete says. He says it so fast that I'm instantly sure I have fucked up. Big time fucked up. He's been waiting for us to raise this, and now he's pounced on it. "Let's talk about credibility."

I glance at 6, but her gaze is fixed on Sneaky Pete. I'm pretty sure she knows what's coming next as well as I do.

"This new campaign: it is remarkable, yes. But I must ask what risk was taken to produce it." He takes a long, slow breath. "It disturbs me to raise such matters . . . but I have reason to believe that 6 and Scat almost failed to produce a summer campaign for Coca-Cola at all. I have reason to believe they allowed the schedule to slip so far behind that this company was in serious jeopardy had the new campaign *not* been developed."

This is serious stuff, and I see eyes widen among the three SMT. No doubt each of these men has a major stock holding plus performance-based bonuses.

The speaker crackles into life again. Jamieson's voice is strained. "What's your justification for thinking that?"

Sneaky Pete sighs. "I didn't want to mention this, Mr. Jamieson . . . but 6 resigned from Coca-Cola last Friday, citing in her resignation her own mismanagement. The following Monday she withdrew her resignation and instead presented her new campaign."

This time, his grin is all for 6.

6 doesn't wait for Jamieson's reaction. "This is what I expected, Mr. Jamieson." She actually sounds a little bored, but her eyes are like fire. "Frankly, I'm a little disappointed."

The speaker allows us to hear Jamieson kill the motor. I guess when you hear that one of your staff took a good shot at fucking up your company, it's worth pulling over to hear more. "Explain."

"What Sneaky Pete says is, of course, a mixture of half truths and fiction. I'm happy to give you a detailed brief on the summer campaign whenever you like. But that's not the point." She sounds so credible; I am truly impressed. "The point, Mr. Jamieson, is that we produced a campaign. We produced a campaign that was better than the one we were given. Let's look at results."

Sneaky Pete says, "No one is disputing the result. The issue is: Can we really trust you?" He is leaning closer, eager. "Are you tough enough to handle this campaign? Do you . . ." The grin, gone as fast as it appears. "Do you have the *balls?*"

I jump in. "Hey, let's get back on track now. Look, if I could just have a minute, I'd like to go through a list of reasons why—"

Jamieson cuts me off. "I want to hear this. He's right: I've got concerns about your ability to handle the pressure at the top, 6. So convince me. Can you handle this campaign?"

"I—" 6 starts, but Sugar reaches out and coyly strokes 6's face. 6 pushes her away, furious, but for a second she is thrown. "Of course I do. I—"

Sneaky Pete cuts in. "And there is something else, Mr. Jamieson. It particularly distresses me to raise this."

"What?" There is a tinge of fear in Jamieson's voice, and that worries me a great deal. If Jamieson is scared, he will choose the safe bet.

"I don't expect this to affect your decision in the slightest," Sneaky Pete says carefully. "I want you to know that I consider this entirely separate." I immediately think: *You don't do business law for the fun of it.* "But I think you should be aware that 6 is pregnant."

I stare at Sneaky Pete in shock, then start to turn toward 6. But I don't make it. Sneaky Pete's grin breaks out again, and I'm instantly positive that 6 is no more pregnant than I am. This is another tactic. A pregnant woman has about as much chance of being given control of a top project as a drunk; they're viewed as equally reliable.

6 is so outraged she can barely speak. "I—am—"

Sneaky Pete says smoothly, "I'm sorry, that was irrelevant. Let's not speak of it."

"I am not pregnant!" 6 screams. Her voice silences everyone; even Jamieson sits quietly in his BMW for long moments.

"I'm sorry," Sneaky Pete says. "That wasn't very sensitive of me. 6, do you need a few moments?"

"Why?" she demands. "Because I'm *female?*"

Sneaky Pete lets her words hang in the air for a few seconds, allowing Jamieson plenty of time to digest them. "That sort of outburst," Sneaky Pete says sadly, "is precisely what I'm concerned about."

6's jaw works uselessly; she stares at Sneaky Pete with wide, outraged eyes.

"I like girls, *too,*" Sugar whispers, and I can't believe her smile isn't malicious.

6 falls. I see it happen. Her face dissolves, and she doesn't hang her head fast enough for her hair to hide it. She pushes Sugar to one side and, before I can rise, flees from the room.

strike three

I break out of Ludus, blinking in the sudden sunlight, and spot 6 just as she slams the cab door. I sprint toward her, but the car peels away from the curb, leaving me staring at the back of 6's head in its rear window. I watch until the traffic engulfs her.

"I love you," I say quietly.

A Brief Interlude with Scat and Tina

CHAPTER 000009

eviction

"I don't know what you did to her," the speaker tells me fiercely, "but it was enough, okay? You leave her alone."

"Tina, you don't understand. I'm on *her* side. She got screwed at Coke today, but I was trying to *help* her. You understand?"

The speaker doesn't answer.

"Tina? Hello?"

Two hours later, the speaker clicks open again. "Are you still there, Scat?"

I struggle up from the sidewalk. "I have no home and you have all my clothes. Yes, I'm still here."

Tina sighs. "Look, you can't stay here. I'll throw your stuff down from the window."

"I know the drill," I say wearily, and I head around to the side street to collect my possessions.

absolutely no idea

So, for the third time, I am homeless.

A New Life

CHAPTER 000010

six months later

When I emerge from the pool, Cindy is by my side with a big fluffy white towel. "Nice workout," she says admiringly. "Mind if I dry you off?"

"Knock yourself out," I tell her generously. I stand with my arms and legs splayed while she gives me a thorough once-over. I can't help but notice her particular attention to my groin. "Hey now, go easy on Mr. William."

"Sorry, Scat," she says coyly, applying a final squeeze.

"Oooh," I say.

"So, any interviews today?"

"Yeah, probably." I roll my eyes. "There's always some show or rag that wants to talk about my success."

"Must get boring," Cindy sympathizes.

"Yeah, well." I shrug. "You gotta give these people what they want."

"Right," Cindy says, vigorously toweling my calves. She pauses. "Except . . ."

"What?"

"Oh, nothing."

"Cindy, what?"

She looks up at me, her blue eyes huge. "Promise you won't get mad?"

"Uh," I say. "Well . . ."

"You don't really have any interviews today."

I gape. "You canceled my interviews?"

"Not . . . exactly," Cindy says. "It's just that you're not really successful. We don't really live in this big house."

"What are you talking about?"

She stands, dropping the towel. "Well, I haven't said anything before, because you seemed so happy. But this is just a dream."

I stare. "A—a—"

Cindy nods.

"You mean—my car? My stock options? God, my invitation to the Academy Awards?"

" 'Fraid not," she says.

I scream.

dawn

° .°° ●. : .°.● °.° .°.:.° °.● .°°. °●

"Are you okay?" Cindy says.

"Uh," I say, clutching the sheets.

"You're all *sweaty.*"

"Sorry. Just a nightmare."

She looks at me sympathetically. "Was it the one with Sneaky Pete again?"

"Ah . . ." I say. "Yes it was."

"Poor baby." She pecks me on the cheek, then swings her legs out of bed.

"Where are you going?"

"It's almost five. I'm going to work out."

"Oh," I say, still a little bewildered from the dream. "Sure."

Cindy frowns at me from the doorway, nude and appealingly

lit by the streetlight leaking past the venetian blinds. "You sure you're okay?"

"Sure," I say. "Sure I am."

a workout

I stare at the ceiling while Cindy puffs and clanks on her workout machines in the next room. When she returns, a thin sheen of sweat on her skin, I haven't moved.

"Hey," she says, a little sharply. "We agreed. No moping over the past."

"Sorry," I say guiltily.

She comes over and sits down on the edge of the bed. "We're doing okay," she tells me. "*You're* doing okay. Okay?"

"Okay."

She pecks me on the cheek again and rises from the bed, tossing her hair, which these days is blond. "So what's on for today?"

"You don't remember?"

"Of *course* I remember," Cindy says. "But I want to hear you say it."

"You've got the Wal-Mart catalog from nine. Your acting class is from four to six. And tonight we're having dinner with a representative of Christian Dior to discuss a signing."

"*Christian Dior,*" Cindy says, her eyes shining.

"Cindy," I warn her, "it's just a first meeting. They're not going to sign you on the spot. You understand?"

"Scat," Cindy says, "you're the best agent in the *world.*"

thank you very much

Cindy leaves at eight, and about ten I drag myself into the bathroom and stare at myself in the mirror for a while. Then I shower, pull on jeans and a T-shirt, and eat breakfast in front of whatever comes up when I turn the TV on, which happens to be an Elvis movie.

A little while later I realize that I'm staring at the screen without really seeing it, so I try to pull myself together by calling a few advertising agencies to see if anyone has a spot for Cindy. One guy asks if Cindy will sleep with him for a spot, and I tell him no but I will.

I do three more calls, then realize that I'm staring pointlessly at my shoes. The phone is dangling from my hand, emitting quiet tones to itself. I hang up quickly, a little frightened by my own listlessness. Five months ago, this stuff was actually fun.

I look at the screen, where Elvis is sitting on a log and strumming thoughtfully at his guitar. A sprightly girl in a bright orange sweater is sitting at his feet with an enraptured expression, like Elvis knows the answer to everything. "Elvis," I say emotionally. "Tell me what's wrong with me."

Elvis says to the girl, "Well, I guess I just love my music. I love making it all up. Some people go through their whole lives without ever getting to create something, you know? If that was me, heck, I'd go crazy."

I stare at the TV, open-mouthed.

"Elvis," I say eventually, "they didn't call you the King for nothing."

relapse

When Cindy arrives home, I'm sitting on the sofa in the dark. She stands in the doorway for a long time.

"Cindy," I say, "I'm having a crisis."

There is a pause. "No," Cindy says tightly. She slaps on the lights. "No, you are not."

"Cindy, I'm sorry," I say, squinting a little, "but I am."

"You are *not* having a crisis," she says, refusing to look at me.

She dumps a bag of clothes on the kitchen bench, her lips tight. "Because tonight we are meeting with Christian Dior."

"Yeah, I don't think I can make that now. You see, I was watching this Elvis movie and it got me thinking: I don't *create* anything anymore. I just—"

"*We are meeting with Christian fucking Dior!*" Cindy screams. I am shocked into silence. She stalks over to me. "We have worked very hard on my modeling career, and tonight we have the opportunity for a dream contract."

I open my mouth to explain my new theories on the importance of creation and the futility of process, then see Cindy's eyes bulge alarmingly and decide this is probably a bad idea.

"*You,*" Cindy spits, "don't *deserve* a crisis. You've had *enough* crises already."

"Hey," I say.

"I've picked you up *twice*." She stabs my chest for emphasis. "It's time you started to think about someone other than yourself. Is that so hard?"

"Uh," I say, starting to feel a little guilty. "Well, I guess not."

"No. It shouldn't be."

I bow my head. "I'm sorry."

Cindy sighs. "It's okay," she says, stroking my hair. "We have a new life now. A *good* life. We've started over, and it's *working*. That's what's important."

"Forgive me?" I ask hopefully.

Cindy looks at me, then smiles. "Sure," she says. "Now go get dressed."

a bolt from the red

The phone rings while I'm trying to decide between a black jacket and a red one, but I let Cindy pick up. I don't hear anything from her for a minute, so I get a start when I turn around and she's in the doorway with the phone.

"Scat," she says carefully, "there's a call for you."

"Okay," I say, equally carefully. "From . . . ?"

"Coke."

an offer

Cindy hands me the phone and I accept it with numb fingers. I try to act as casual as possible, but my eyes have watered over and I feel like I'm blushing furiously. Cindy sits on the bed and watches me.

"Hello?"

"Scat," the phone says, and it is definitely, absolutely, completely not 6. My heart drops out of my mouth and lands somewhere around my feet. "It's Gary Brennan, pal, how you doing?"

"Gary." The fact that Coke's VP of Marketing has chosen to call me is a pretty exciting development on its own, but it's hard to keep the disappointment out of my voice. "I'm doing great. What's new?"

Cindy sniffs. I shoot a glance at her, but she turns and looks out the window.

"Well, that's what I want to talk to you about. I think I've got something that might interest you."

I swallow. Important to stay casual. "Really?"

"It's your kind of scene, all right. Hey, are you on a land line?"

"Yes."

"Good. This is real confidential stuff. You understand?"

"Of course," I say, although I'm not really sure.

"We're starting something big, Scat. Something huge. Maybe the biggest marketing project the world has ever seen."

Something is called for here, but whatever it is I don't have it. I settle for controlling my breathing, which is threatening to get a little out of control.

"It's going to be either a massive success or a total flop. There are asses on the line over it, including mine."

119

I take a deep breath. "And you've called me?"

"I need a creative. I need the best fucking creative I can get. You."

A wind roars past my ears, and I close my eyes and sink on to the bed to ride through it. When I open my eyes, Cindy's blues are boring into me. "That's very nice of you to say, Gary."

"Look, let's not bullshit each other here," he says amiably. "Six months ago, you and 6 got royally screwed. I don't expect you to just forgive and forget. Maybe you don't want anything to do with Coke anymore. Maybe you don't want anything to do with marketing anymore. I could understand that."

"I'm an agent now," I say abruptly. Cindy squeezes my knee.

"Whatever. Here's the deal. I can't tell you any more about this project, but trust me when I say it's big. I'm offering you a position on the team. Do you want it?"

"Gary," I say evenly, "can you hold for just a second?"

"Sure."

I mute the phone and turn to Cindy.

"Well?" she says aggressively. As I watch, little tears form in the corner of each eye. I look at them for a long moment.

I punch off the mute. "Gary?"

"Here."

"No."

en route

In the car, Cindy tells me happily, "You're the best agent in the *world*."

Cindy is wearing an eight-thousand-dollar dress and as we enter the Saville I spot men sneaking her appraising glances. I can't see the representative from Christian Dior, so I get the maître d' to seat us near the window. We end up, I think, at the same table that 6 and I shared ten months ago.

"Do you know this woman?" I ask the maître d', pointing at Cindy.

"I am sorry, sir, I do not," he says. Which is fair enough, given that the only real exposure Cindy has had so far has been in department store catalogs and obscure, unpaid fashion shows.

"Her name is Cindy," I say, "and I'd like every waiter who comes to this table to say, 'Excuse me, but aren't you that model?' "

"Ah, well," he says. "I would love to help you—"

I push fifty dollars across the table.

"And so I will."

"You are most kind," I tell him. He inclines his head modestly.

When he leaves, Cindy leans forward and whispers, "That was *great!* Scat, you are *so* good."

"Uh huh," I say. I am scanning the room for patches of bad lighting. "Stay away from the ferns. You'll look a little flat."

"*Thanks, Scat,*" Cindy says, her eyes shining.

Then I spot him: a short, thin man with the trimmest little mustache I've seen in my life, being led to our table by the maître d'. I nudge Cindy with my foot.

"Hello," the man says genially. "You must be Scat and Cindy. I am Christian."

My mind races. Cindy gasps, "Not Christian *Dior*."

"That is right," Christian says primly. "Not Christian Dior. Christian Summerset." His little mouth smirks.

"Christian, good to meet you," I say, rising and shaking his hand. I learned pretty early in my career as an agent to be friendly to utter jerks; it's an essential skill. "Have a seat."

"Thank you." Christian sits, then runs his gaze critically over

Cindy's body. She smiles back at him hesitantly. "Quite attractive," Christian says thoughtfully. "Yes, quite attractive."

Cindy is a little unsure how to take this and seems to be heading toward the monumental error of giggling when with exquisite timing a passing waiter delivers a truly pathetic double take. "*Hey,*" he says loudly. "Aren't you that *model?*" He breaks into a huge smile, as if he is expecting applause.

His performance is so bad that I'm sure Christian will never fall for it, but I see his thin black eyebrows rise fractionally. *Bang,* I think.

Cindy delivers her performance with much greater skill—maybe her acting classes are starting to pay off. She bats her eyes demurely and murmurs, "Yes, thank you," and Christian's eyebrows rise another tiny notch.

However, this repartee sends the waiter into a slight panic; apparently he hasn't anticipated the dialogue going this far. To prevent him from improvising his way into an attempted kiss or fleeing in panic, I say, "Water for me, thanks."

The waiter grabs his pencil gratefully. "And you, sir?"

"Hmm," Christian says, frowning at the drinks menu. "I think I would like a tall, refreshing glass of Fukk, please."

"One of our most popular brands," the waiter says approvingly. He sounds as if he is smiling brightly, but I can't see through the red haze that has washed over my vision.

Cindy squeezes my hand nervously. Christian and the waiter have fallen silent, and I think they're staring at me. "Scat," Cindy explains quietly, "is the true inventor of Fukk."

I bow my head to the terrible truth of this, and for a moment we are all just sitting around, frozen. Then Christian and the waiter burst out laughing.

"Inventor of Fukk!" Christian giggles, and I see with amazement that there are tears welling in his eyes. "Oh Cindy, you are too much."

"That's a good one, ma'am," the waiter says, pointing his pencil at Cindy. "I tell you what, the guy who invented this drink is laughing all the way to the bank."

It takes a monumental effort, but I do it. "Yes," I say, the smile nearly breaking my jaw. "Yes, I bet he is."

opening moves

After we've ordered, Christian says, "I'm afraid I have to tell you that Christian Dior will not be signing Cindy."

mktg case study #10: mktg negotiations

OPEN VERY, VERY LOW. DURING THE NEGOTIATION, YOU WILL OFFER SOME COMPROMISES AND THEY WILL OFFER SOME COMPROMISES, UNTIL YOU MEET SOMEWHERE IN THE MIDDLE. MAKE SURE THAT THE MIDDLE IS WHERE YOU WANTED TO BE ANYWAY.

own your own

"That is disappointing," I say. "Oh well. Cindy, are you ready to go?"

Cindy stares at me, open-mouthed. Maybe she didn't expect the best agent in the world to give up so easily.

"There's no point in wasting Christian's time any further." I give him a short nod. "Thank you for agreeing to meet us."

I've barely found my feet when Christian says, "Mr. Scat, that doesn't mean there's nothing left for us to talk about."

I let myself sink back into my chair. "No?"

His mouth twitches once, but it's enough to tell me he's annoyed. "Although we cannot sign Cindy as our face, we are interested in retaining her services in some form. We have over a dozen models around the world we use for various product. We would like Cindy to study under one of these, with a view to eventually taking over the position."

"Not interested," I say. Across the table, Cindy appears to have some kind of minor seizure.

Christian's mustache twitches twice. "Pardon me?"

"Well, this is what you say next: since this would be a training position, the pay would be minimal. The real reward would come from the experience and prestige of working as a Christian Dior model. And, of course, the potential for the future."

Christian watches me with narrow eyes.

"The thing is, Christian, Cindy's going to be a top model. She's just starting out, but everyone knows she's going to go big. Now, sure, Christian Dior is a very good name to be associated with, regardless of pay. But whether that's worth turning down the chance to become the Revlon face . . . gee, I just don't think so."

Christian smirks. "I know for a fact that Revlon is not in discussion with you."

"True," I say. That Christian has this kind of information at his fingertips interests me a great deal. "That was just an example. But it will happen. You know it will."

Christian regards me flatly. Which is a good trait in a negotiator, I guess.

"Look, I don't expect you to sign Cindy as your face tonight. She's hot, but to you she's unproven. I can understand that. You need to watch her develop."

"This is true," Christian says.

"So what we need to work out," I continue, "is how you can get both the opportunity to watch Cindy develop as a model, and the ability to sign her if she proves herself. Am I right?"

Christian mulls this over. "Perhaps."

"Okay." Under the table, I wipe my palms on my pants. "So what I propose is—"

"Aren't you that *model?*" a waiter gasps at Cindy.

"Fuck off," I tell him. He throws me a betrayed look and vanishes. "Sorry," I say to Christian.

"Quite all right," Christian says, and his thin lips are actually twisting into a small smile. Christian must enjoy a little bullying now and again.

"Now, I'm proposing," I say, "that you buy an option on Cindy."

I look at Christian.

Christian looks at me.

"What?" he says.

"An option," I say. "I'm suggesting you purchase an option."

"Like for a house?"

"Exactly. You pay us a small amount now for the right to sign Cindy at any time in the next twelve months."

Christian is obviously having a little trouble with this concept. His brow furrows.

"So," I say patiently, "a year from now, if you're impressed with Cindy's development, you get her. With no competitive bidding. Your up-front investment is small, plus you don't risk losing her. You win if she doesn't make it, because you haven't paid a big fee. And you really win if she does, because you get to sign her."

Christian chews this over. "We would need to fix a ceiling price . . . so if we decided to sign her later, you could not simply name a fee too outrageous to meet."

"Of course." This is, in fact, a critical part of the deal. "Given Cindy's potential growth in popularity over the next year, I think it's fair to say that in twelve months' time she could be worth about eight million."

Christian's eyes bulge. "That is ridiculous!"

"That's not per year," I say, acting a little wounded. "That's for a standard three-year deal."

Christian spits, "She is an *unknown*. No model has ever signed her *first contract* for eight million."

"Nevertheless." I wave this away as if it's not important. "I'm not actually asking for eight million. I'm just putting this in some kind of perspective."

"What *are* you asking for?" Christian says, his eyes narrowing.

"Six," I say.

Christian starts the bulging eyes routine again, then seems to realize he's already done that one and settles for snatching at a napkin and wiping his mouth vigorously. "Outrageous," he mutters. "Outrageous."

"Now that's a *ceiling* price," I say. "That's the *maximum* we'll be able to ask if you decide you want to sign her. If she's not worth that much, obviously we'd settle for less. I mean, let's get serious. Over the next year, Cindy could go ballistic. If she's the next supermodel, a three-year contract for six million will be the bargain of the century." I take a sip of my water.

Christian says, "And this option . . . how much?"

"To be honest, not much," I say. "Let's say fifty thousand. I'm not particularly interested in the amount." This is actually true. "What I really want is to be able to call the rags tomorrow and say, 'Cindy has just been signed to Christian Dior in a contract potentially worth six million dollars.' "

"You will use us for your publicity," Christian says, bristling a little. "Use the Christian Dior name to open doors."

"Yes," I tell him. "I'm not trying to hide that. But that publicity will benefit you, too. Because if it helps Cindy's career, you're the one with the option to sign her."

Christian looks at me for a long moment, then turns and stares out the window. He seems to be seriously considering the idea, so I say, "If you'll excuse me, I need to use the bathroom."

Cindy looks up, startled, but I smile reassuringly at her. It's important for Christian to not feel pushed at this moment, and some quiet time alone with Cindy won't do our chances any harm.

I stand and walk away from the table, feeling pretty good. I think I've actually convinced Christian to help me make modeling history. I think the publicity will be like a rocket under Cindy's career, and within six months I'll sign her to Christian Dior for a figure very close to six million dollars.

I find the bathroom, which for some reason looks a lot like an exit, and as I empty my bladder, I think: *This is a special night.*

Then I zip, wash my hands, and on the way out, nearly bowl over 6.

126

salutations

For whole seconds, I can only stare at her. Strong, invisible men grip my arms and legs and someone slides a burly arm down my throat to grab my heart.

She is dressed formally, I am pretty sure, and I think her hair is still the gorgeous dark waterfall it was six months ago. Her shoes are probably black and high, and there could be some kind of handbag slung around her shoulder. But I can't tell for sure, because I can't take my eyes off her face.

"Scat," she says, and I never knew my name sounded so good.

scat and 6 catch up

"6," I say. This relieves me greatly, because for a few moments the tiny part of brain still functioning was leaping headlong into *Marry me.* Not such a good opening line, that. A touch too intense. "You look great. How are you?"

"Very well," 6 says cautiously. She pauses, then adds, "You look good, too."

"Thanks," I say, and to demonstrate how utterly unimportant I consider this remark, I grin like an idiot. 6 looks away. "What have you been doing? Since . . ."

"Consulting," she says, still not looking at me.

"Hey, that's great. That's really good."

6 shrugs fractionally, shifting her weight to her other foot. I am momentarily sure she is about to say, *Well, it was good to see you,* and I panic. "Are you doing well?"

Stupid, stupid question. "Yes," 6 says.

"Oh. That's great."

"Well," she says, "it was good to see you, Scat."

Her eyes rest on me for a second, then she turns and walks away.

I'm desperate. I'm as desperate as I've ever been in my life. I open my mouth and grant it full executive authority to say whatever the hell it wants. "I got a call from Coke."

6 stops.

restaurant revelations

"I mean, I don't know if you're interested. I guess you don't really care what happens there anymore."

6 studies my face for a moment, then walks back. "I know there's no place for me there now."

"Oh." She stares at me until I realize that she wants to hear it anyway. "Gary Brennan called me up this morning. Said he wanted to talk about a big new project."

She sniffs dismissively. "I know about it."

I blink. "Gary wouldn't tell what it was."

"Well," 6 says, frowning at the floor, and suddenly this feels so familiar that I get a warm shiver. "I don't know what the project actually is. But Sneaky Pete is running it."

This is a surprise. "Really? From what Gary was telling me, it didn't sound like his kind of thing at all. It sounded like . . . well, *our* kind of thing."

6 looks up, frowning. I struggle mightily against the urge to lean over and kiss her eyebrows.

"Creative. Gary said the project needed creatives. And he said, 'asses are on the line.' Which I guess reminded him of our little project. I turned him down, though, because . . ."

Then I stop, because something amazing is happening to 6. First her eyes widen, then they narrow. Her lips part, then tighten. It's a little scary, and a lot exciting.

"What? You're surprised I don't want to work at Coke anymore? Well, I have a new life now. I—"

6 takes a step closer, brushing my words away. "Are you telling me that *Sneaky Pete* has his ass on the line at Coke?"

"Uh, well, if you say he's running this project . . . then I guess, yeah. I didn't really—"

6 says slowly, "Sneaky Pete has his ass on the line over a *creative* project?"

Now that 6 mentions this, it seems a little strange. "Yeah . . . although creative was never his strong suit . . ."

"No," 6 says, and now there is a strange glint in her eyes. It takes me a moment to realize what this glint is: revenge. "No," she says again. "No, it was not."

a plan

6 hands me her card, and I read that she is now Director of Marketing at some firm I've never heard of, which probably means she is the only employee. "Tomorrow, call Brennan. Then call me."

"You got it."

6 studies me, then turns and walks away. They *are* high heels.

I wander dazedly back to my table, where Cindy is laughing fetchingly at some remark of Christian's.

"Mr. Scat," Christian says warmly, "I have decided to accept your proposal."

where scat proves to all and sundry that he is indeed a great fuckwit

"You are *magnificent*," Cindy says breathlessly. "You are *unbelievable*."

"Uh, Cindy," I say, "it's kind of hard to drive with your hands in my pants."

"I have a *contract*. I can't believe I have a *contract* with *Christian Dior*."

"You have an option," I remind her. "They may never sign you."

"Oh, *Scat*," Cindy says. "I know you just don't want me to get my hopes up. This is *fantastic!* This is the best night of my *life!*"

Her mood is a little infectious, and I grin. "Well . . ."

"You're the best agent in the *world*. I can't believe you *wasted* all that time at Coke."

"Hey," I say, "speaking of which, you'll never guess who I ran into tonight."

feminine wiles

° . °° • •. : . •° • °.° °° .°.:° ° ° .° •°• °• °• •°

"You *son of a bitch!*" Cindy screams.

I stumble after her, trying to tuck myself in and run at the same time. "Cindy, wait!" A truck roars past, whipping my tie into my face. "Wait!"

"You *bastard!*" She rounds on me, lit by the headlights of the cars rushing past. Behind her, there's a huge billboard of the ad 6 and I developed for Coke six months ago. "I can't believe you did this *tonight!*"

"Cindy, hang on." I reach out but she slaps my hands away viciously. "I didn't *do* anything. I just *met* her. We just *talked*."

"Oh, sure," Cindy says, her eyes roving wildly. "I know how *that* goes. Next you don't want to stay with *me* anymore and you're living with *her*."

"Cindy, that's crazy. That's not true at all."

"Do you have her number?" she says suddenly. "Are you going to see her again?"

I hesitate.

"Taxi!" Cindy shouts.

"Cindy! Come on, give me a chance here! We're just exploring a business opportunity!"

"You're supposed to be exploring *my* business opportunities!" Cindy yells, and although kind of a weird thing to say, this is true and I'm not sure how to respond. "Fucking *agents,*" she says, starting to cry.

"Come on, Cindy . . ." This time, she lets me put my arms around her. "It's okay. It's all okay."

She sniffles for a minute and I stroke her hair.

"Just tell me it's over between you two," Cindy says. "Just tell me it's over."

here, have a shovel

"Cindy, it's over." I kiss her forehead. "I'm pretty sure it's over."

wandering wilshire

Cindy takes the car.

Which is fair enough, I guess, since if one of us has to be wandering the streets of West LA at midnight (and I'm pretty sure one of us does), it's probably safer that it be the man in the suit than the woman in the body-hugging dress.

It takes me almost an hour to walk back along Wilshire to Cindy's apartment in Santa Monica, waving at uninterested cabs all the while. On the way, I realize that I don't have a set of keys, and I deliberate the merits of waking Cindy up to let me in versus spending the night on the street, not sure which is more dangerous. Eventually I ring the doorbell, but it's a tough call.

"Yes?" Cindy says. Her voice is hard, as if she is expecting people seeking donations, or me.

"Uh, hi. Can I come in?"

There is a long pause before the security door buzzes. A long, relationship-reviewing pause.

When I get upstairs the door is ajar and all the lights are off. This is disturbing. "Cindy?"

I'm reaching for the light switch when she says, "Scat."

I peer into the darkness and eventually spot her sitting upright on the sofa, silhouetted by the venetian blinds.

"Oh," I say. "There you are."

"Do you want to know your problem?" Cindy says.

scat's problem

I screw up my face, but she probably can't see it, "Aw, Cindy—"

"Your problem is that reality isn't good enough for you," she says levelly. "You need a fantasy."

"Cindy, that's not true."

"Yes it is," she says. "I'm sorry, but it is. And right now I'm not your fantasy."

I start to protest that she is a fantasy, then realize this might not be a good thing either and end up just standing there with my mouth open.

"I mean, I'm a *model*. Living with me should be enough of a fantasy for anyone. But no, you're hooked on this girl who won't even look at you straight."

"Cindy—"

"So I've decided," Cindy says abruptly. "If I'm your reality and you need a fantasy, I'm not going to be your reality anymore."

I'm slow, but I get it. "Are you breaking up with me?"

"Why wait? For you to dump me?"

"Cindy," I say, alarmed. "I'm not dumping anybody."

"Well, I'm dumping you," Cindy says. "Get out of my apartment."

I reel against the door frame. "What—"

"You heard me!" she shouts.

"Cindy, it's not even all your apartment. It's partly mine."

"Fifteen percent of it," Cindy says scathingly. "Sure, your commission. *I* really earned that money."

I gape.

"Go on!" she shouts. "I thought you liked it when girls treat you mean!"

Suddenly this whole scene begins to make sense. "Oh . . . I get it."

"What?"

"That's very good. Those acting classes are really working."

Cindy's eyes widen. "You think I'm *acting?*"

I hold up my hands. "Okay, look, you've made your point. Now can we talk about this in bed? I'm really beat. I actually had to walk back from—"

Cindy rises from the sofa like a guided missile.

"Uh—"

She punches me hard in the jaw, eight months of weight training behind her, and spills me out into the hallway. Before I can pick myself off the floor, she slams the apartment door so hard the entire stairwell shudders.

I look at the closed door for a long time. Then, slowly, I get to my feet, and that's when I realize that there's an old man across the hallway peering at me through his chain lock.

"I don't think she was acting," he tells me. He looks at Cindy's closed door, then back at me. "I don't think she was acting at all."

on the road again

This time, Cindy doesn't even throw down my stuff.

new plans

I spend the night on the stairs of Cindy's apartment complex.

I'm so exhausted that I wake at nine the next morning only when an old woman steps on my hand. I almost grab her leg and send her tumbling to the floor out of pure reflex, and when she shoots me a contemptuous look and no apology, I almost do it deliberately.

I take a few moments to stretch the stiffness out of my limbs, then climb the stairs to Cindy's apartment. I take a deep breath and knock. I'm not completely sure how serious Cindy was last night—or, more important, how serious she is this morning. But there's only one way to find out.

Cindy takes a long time to answer, and when she does she's wearing only a thin dressing gown. "Good morning."

"Morning," I say, pretty happy with the way this conversation has opened. I had suspected I might have to conduct it through the closed door. "Cindy, I'm really sorry about last night—"

"And good-bye," she says sweetly, gently closing the door in my face. I stare at it for a second, but it's still a closed door.

So I guess Cindy is serious.

contemplation

Obviously, it would be wrong to call 6.

First, it would be wrong because that's exactly what Cindy said I was going to do: call 6 and try to move in with her. Proving her right on this point might suggest she is also right about her more recent theories.

Second, I've only just met 6 again. She's going to think I do this kind of thing on a regular basis. And while the desperate, homeless image might be cute for a while, I don't think it's a good image to cultivate in the long term. Because in the end, gorgeous, independent women like 6 don't go for desperate, homeless types. No, I'm pretty sure that intriguing, unmanning, devastatingly beautiful women like 6—

I call 6.

She answers the phone herself, further confirming my suspicions that her consulting firm is a one-woman shop. "Synergy."

"6!" I say warmly. I'm sitting on a park bench with my cellphone, which is now my largest asset in the world. "It's Scat. How are you?"

"How was Brennan?"

"Ah," I say. "Well, I haven't actually called him yet. I've hit a small snag."

There is a pause. "A snag," 6 says heavily.

"Ah, yeah." I throw in a little chuckle, to show 6 that really, this is quite amusing. "You won't believe what's happened." I leave a pause, wide open for 6 to fill with a *Really?* or an *Uh-huh* or even an *I sincerely doubt that,* but she just waits. "I'm homeless."

Pause.

"It's crazy, I know." I laugh at exactly how crazy it really is. A girl walking a German shepherd glances at me warily. "But—"

"Don't even bother. You're not staying with me."

"6," I say, injecting a little hurt into my voice as I backpedal furiously. "I wasn't going to ask *that.*"

"Uh-huh," 6 says, almost sounding interested.

"It's just that if I call Gary and he wants to see us, I've got no clothes. I don't even have anywhere to change into the clothes I don't have."

6 sighs. "Call Brennan. If he wants to see us, we'll work something out."

This isn't a genuine offer, but I grab it anyway. "Hey, *thanks,* 6. I knew you'd come through."

She hangs up.

commitment

I get put through to four different secretaries, but eventually I get Gary. "I've changed my mind."

"Hey, Scat, I'm really glad," Gary says. He sounds harried, and in the background I can hear someone yelling, "No, *players*, we need *players*." "I could really use you. Can you see me today?"

"You bet," I say, and when I hang up I call 6 to find out if this is true.

scat freshens up

6 sighs.

"6, look," I say. "I'm not asking for much. I just want to shower and get dressed. I'll be in and out in half an hour." My cellphone beeps twice, complaining about weak batteries. Given that Cindy has my charger, this is a real problem, and I start to panic. "6, come on, just let me visit, okay? I'll buy some clothes, I'll wash and shave, and we'll go see Brennan. Then when this is all over, we can go back and do the whole bit where I beg you for favors and you frown and tell me you don't think so. But right now, I just want a shower and I don't have time for a debate! Okay?"

I stop, a little taken aback at my own aggressiveness. I am positive 6 is already putting down the phone, and I wince in anticipation of the tone.

"Okay," 6 says, and although I could be mistaken, it sounds as if 6 is smiling.

synergy

She *is* the only employee.

Even so, I'm impressed by how well she's established herself. The office is on Lincoln in central Venice and in dire need of refurbishment, but it has a kind of old-world charm that contrasts nicely with 6's new-world complete lack of it. There are a few strategically placed ferns straining to cover horrific cracks in the plaster, a percolator and a huge wooden desk. It's very similar to 6's office at Coke, but with more cracks, no view and no Elle Macpherson. I suspect 6 misses Coke more than she is ever going to admit.

"Hey, I like this place. You've done well."

6 shrugs fractionally, regarding me from behind the desk. Her chair is almost a throne: a hulking great black thing doing a pretty good imitation of leather. It allows 6 to lean right back into it, her arms resting commandingly on either side, making her look a little like Captain Kirk.

"Well." I look at my watch. "I'd better get moving."

"You can change in there," 6 says, pointing to a shaky-looking wooden door. "There's a shower."

"Right." I push through the door, carrying my new suit. I'm halfway through when I realize why this office has a shower: it's not an office, it's a tiny house. There are four rooms back here, and I'd bet my thin remaining credit card limit that one of them is 6's bedroom. I turn back to ask her, but she reads my face and beats me to it.

"So?" she says aggressively.

"No problem," I say, and close the door.

memory lane

Since neither of us owns a car, I have a reluctant reunion with the LA bus system. The route actually takes us past Tina and 6's old apartment, and without thinking I turn to her and say, "We had some times, huh?"

6's head slowly turns toward me, and before I can even see her face I know she's going to blast me with one of her looks.

"Forget it," I say quickly.

137

I watch 6 carefully as we enter the lobby. She's playing it very cool, and to the casual observer she probably appears to be fairly unconcerned about the whole deal of returning to her old workplace. But I'm not a casual observer. I'm a highly motivated, full-time observer, and I think 6 could be a little scared.

"Scat and 6," I tell the receptionist, to spare 6 from having to do it. "To see Gary Brennan."

The receptionist (who is possibly the same person as before but probably just another blandly good-looking woman) hands me a couple of visitor passes. With world-weary experience, I clip mine onto my tie, but 6 just stares at hers balefully and pockets it.

Mere minutes later, Gary springs from one of the elevators, smiling broadly and extending his hand. "Scat! So glad you could make it." He pumps my hand three times fast. Then he spots 6. For a second, his grin slips down to his toes. Then it's back up, flashing away as if 6's presence is the greatest thing ever. "6! I wasn't expecting you."

"Is it a problem, Gary?" 6 says.

"Of course not," he says, shaking her hand vigorously. "It's good to have you back, 6." He straightens. "Here, I've booked a meeting room."

He leads us down a short hallway into a truly enormous room. I see 6's eyebrows shoot up and guess that Gary is laying on something special today.

"Please, sit," he says, dropping into one of the leather chairs. I follow suit and immediately decide I'm never going to stand again. "Or do you want a coffee?" He straightens, ready to leap up again. "I can have them sent in."

"Uh," I say, unsure as to whether it's a good business move to ask your potential employer to fetch for you. I decide to go with my thirst. "Okay."

Gary stops. "Scat, if you're going to work for Coca-Cola, you will never use that word again."

"What word? *'Okay'?*"

"*Okay* is the most widely known word in the English language. Number two is *Coke*. We're trying for top spot. Get it?"

"Got it," I say, avoiding an embarrassing *okay* just in time.

"You need to know this stuff, since you're going to be part of Coke history. And you are going to be part of history. You know that, don't you?"

6 leans forward. "Gary, let's cut the spiel, okay? I know you too well for the sales pitch. Just tell me what you've got."

Gary pauses, then his smile drops. "Fine," he says quietly, and leans forward. Despite myself, I lean forward too. It occurs to me that Gary's overjovial opening may have been designed to precisely this end.

"Some of it you know already. We're planning one of the biggest marketing projects in history. We're doing something that's never been done before."

"Budget?" 6 asks.

Gary pauses. If it's anything over ten million, I'm going to be impressed. Ten million buys you a series of cutting-edge TV ads and enough spots to show them to half the country.

"Sixty," Gary says.

There is a long moment of silence. Somewhere around the start of it, I quietly swallow my tongue.

6 says, "Sixty *million?*"

"Coca-Cola is funding sixty million," Gary says, "but our partner in this venture is supplying another eighty. So I guess to answer your question, the project has a budget of one hundred forty million dollars."

Suddenly I have to fight against the urge to laugh. But that would be a bad move, because Gary is obviously very, very serious.

"Gary," I say unsteadily. "Pardon me, but what the fuck are you buying for one hundred forty million dollars?"

A smile twitches at the corner of Gary's mouth. "We're making a

Hollywood

CHAPTER 000011

movie," Gary says.

scat ponders the developments

"Holy *shit*," I say. I look across at 6 and see that she looks as dazed as I feel. "Holy *shit*."

"It's been a long time coming," he says, leaning back in his chair. "Pepsi's been doing its fucking product placements for years. Now it's our turn."

mktg case study #11: mktg product placement

GET YOUR PRODUCT INTO THE HANDS OF THE HERO AND THE PROD-UCT BECOMES A HERO, TOO, ASSOCIATED WITH THE ADMIRABLE QUALITIES OF THE CHARACTERS. IT'S NOT COINCIDENCE WHEN THEY SHOOT A PEPSI OFF A SPACESHIP OR USE AN ERICSSON AS A SECRET WEAPON: IT'S TENS OF MILLIONS OF DOLLARS.

the new paradigm

"We're not fucking around with the hero kicking cans here," Gary says. "I want you to be clear about that. Having our product as some incidental prop isn't worth shit in sales. Coke will be an integral part of this film."

"You're making an ad," I say suddenly. "An ad that people will pay seven bucks to see."

"Yeah," Gary says, smiling broadly. "Yeah, you got it."

flicks

"Now this is going to be a damn good movie." He pokes the top of the table for emphasis. "This is going to redefine what advertising is all about. We're buying the best scripts and the best people. Trust me, we're very concerned about making a good movie, not just a good ad. And our partner is Universal, by the way, and they're even more concerned about it than we are."

Gary stops and looks at us. I should probably throw a comment in at this point, but I'm feeling a little stunned. I came in here expecting to talk about giveaways and TV spots, and Gary is talking Hollywood.

"So what do you think?" His gaze swaps from me to 6, then back. "Do you want to be part of this?"

I take a breath. "Gary, it's amazing. You know any marketer would kill to be in on a project like this."

Gary smiles.

"But there's a problem," I say. "Isn't there?"

Gary sighs, as if this is an annoying diversion. "Yes, there's a problem. The problem is Jamieson's goddamned golden boy."

"Sneaky Pete?" I ask, hardly daring to hope.

"Yeah," Gary says. "You got it."

"I knew it." I smack the table. "He's just not a creative, right? I mean, a project like this needs someone who can come up with ideas."

"Uh, right," Gary says.

"This is *great*." I turn to 6 excitedly. "It's our turn, 6. This is our time."

She regards me blankly, then turns back to Gary. "Gary, what problems is the project presently experiencing?"

"Well," Gary says, blowing out his cheeks, "like Scat says, I think it's a general lack of ideas. I just don't think he's got the . . . creativity to handle it." He nods emphatically. "Just not creative enough."

6 takes a moment to digest this. "Are you on schedule?"

"Oh . . . technically," Gary says, waving dismissively.

"Are you on budget?"

"Ah." Gary frowns at the table. "It's hard to say." He looks up at 6 hopefully, but she declines to accept this as an answer. "Yes."

"I see," 6 says. "So what you're saying is that Sneaky Pete's lack of creativity is causing the project to run on schedule and within budget."

Gary blinks at 6, but she simply stares back at him. "Uh, well," Gary says uncertainly, "I suppose the problems haven't begun to really manifest themselves yet."

6 waits for this comment to sink quietly into the carpet. Then she says simply, "He's after your job, isn't he?"

Gary sighs. "Yes," he says.

gary's plan

"Jamieson thinks Sneaky Pete is God's gift to the carbonated beverages industry," Gary says, "and so does everyone who has Jamieson's ear. If you look at what he's really done, there's nothing. But he's got the perception."

"Gary," I interrupt, "I have to know this. Whose project is it? Do you control it, or does Sneaky Pete?"

Gary sighs. "Well, technically it's mine. I'm at the top of the tree. But he's been delegated all the real responsibility; he allocates the funds. Practically speaking, it's his." I see 6 nod grimly. "If it succeeds, he's going to reap the kudos. And probably get VP Marketing in the bargain."

I am shocked. "*Vice president?* He's twenty-seven years old!"

Gary looks at me, and I suddenly see that he is furious. "You don't have to tell me that," he says slowly, "and I don't have to tell you how good he is."

I am humbled. "Sorry, Gary."

6 leans forward. "Gary, this scenario doesn't seem to have much room for us."

He straightens. "Trust me. There's room."

the alternative

"I don't want this project to succeed," Gary says. "Frankly speaking, I hope it dies in the ass."

I struggle to keep a poker face and fail. "You're going to write off sixty million dollars?"

"No, not at all. I hope *Sneaky Pete's* project fails. I very much want the *movie* to succeed."

"You're proposing," 6 says slowly, "a second movie."

Gary nods.

I look at him, then at 6, then back at Gary. "Huh?"

"I want to do what Sneaky Pete's doing, but do it better, faster and cheaper. Much cheaper. I want to rough cut a few scenes within a month, to demonstrate what we can do. And then I'll make a case to take back the whole project."

"And get rid of Sneaky Pete."

"Yes," Gary says. "Oh yes."

"Right . . ." A thought occurs to me. "Will Jamieson really let you produce two separate movies at once?"

Gary lets out a short bark of laughter. "*Shit,* no. *Jamieson's* not going to know about this." He shoots a glance at 6. "I'm sure you understand this."

"Of course," 6 says.

I'm starting to feel like the dumb one in the class, but I open my mouth, anyway. "So how are we going to get some of that one hundred forty million?"

Gary clears his throat.

"We won't," 6 says. "Will we?"

He hesitates, then shakes his head. "It's already been signed off. I'll have to fund you out of miscellaneous."

"Ah," I say. I look at 6, but she doesn't seem about to ask. "You don't happen to have another one hundred forty million in miscellaneous, do you?"

"No," Gary says.

"How much do you have?"

"Well," Gary says, "you have to understand that I'm not talking about making a whole new movie out of this. I only need you to do a few scenes."

"Gary," 6 says relentlessly. "Budget."

Gary hesitates, and I see 6 wince. "Ten thousand."

10k

I burst out laughing.

I can't help myself: I just spray laughter across the table like

144

champagne. Neither Gary nor 6 seems particularly impressed, or particularly jovial for that matter. "So what you're saying," I tell Gary, trying to regain sobriety, "is that you want us to take your ten thousand and go head to head with Sneaky Pete and his one hundred forty million." Another snigger slips out. "Have I got that right?"

"Yes," Gary says, not embarrassed at all. "That's right."

"We'll do it," 6 and I say simultaneously.

searching for a story

When Gary leaves to collect the scripts, I jump out of my chair and start pacing. "It's not much," I tell 6. "I mean, boy, we're really up against it. But I think we can do this. Don't you?"

6 shrugs.

"Oh, come on," I say. "I know you're playing it cool, but you're just as excited about this as I am. You *jumped* at the chance. I mean, a movie! We're going to make something special, 6, I just know it."

6 says carefully, "Scat, we're not going to beat Sneaky Pete."

I blink. I run her words back through my mind, but can't get rid of her *not*. "What?"

"Gary's dreaming. He might as well pack up his desk now."

I gape. "But—but you just agreed to—"

"If he's willing to spend ten thousand trying to keep his job, I'll take his money." She sniffs and looks out the window. "And we'll make a good attempt. But it won't be good enough."

"6," I say, "that's not very positive."

"Scat, you just don't get it," she says, exasperated. "You can't make a film for ten thousand—even part of a film—and expect to compare it to one with a budget of one hundred forty million. It just can't be done."

"But—" I begin, but Gary returns, cradling a mass of scripts.

"Here they are," he says, dumping them onto the table. One

145

conveniently skids straight into my hands, and, feeling a little serendipitous, I pick it up. Printed on the cover in neat twelve-point Courier is: BACKLASH. "These are just the good ones. We started with about a thousand."

"Can we take these with us?" 6 asks.

"Sure, I'll get them delivered today. What's your address?"

6 is halfway through Synergy's address when I look up. "You won't need to do that," I say steadily. "I've found our script."

6 and Gary look at me.

I hand Gary the script. "Now I've only read the first few pages," I say, "but this is *fantastic*. Look this action! And wow! What a concept!"

Gary frowns at the script, then looks up. "Uh, Scat . . . this is the movie Sneaky Pete is making."

scat and 6 go home

On the bus ride back to Synergy, 6 shakes her head. "The movie Sneaky Pete is making," she says, and though I can't really see her face through her hair, it sounds as if 6 is grinning.

playing hard to get

6 unlocks the office and I enter, carrying the stack of scripts that have actually beaten us back here. We should have caught a ride with the messenger.

The answering machine light is staring back at us unblinkingly, so I'm guessing that Synergy isn't exactly overflowing with business. "Where do you want these?"

6 waves her hand vaguely, so I just dump them in the middle of the office floor. They spill across the snappy blue carpet and 6 frowns at them. I smile at her uncertainly and she tosses her hair

and starts rifling through her desk, leaving me unsure of what the hell I should do. I'm fairly sure that at some point in the near future 6 is going to say, *Well, time for you to hit the street.*

"So," I say, "we've got some job ahead of us, huh?"

6 stares at me, then sighs. "Scat, just get it over with."

"Huh?"

6 heads toward the percolator. "You're homeless and desperate. You need a place to stay. You want to stay here." She punches a red button and the machine purrs happily.

"Well," I say, "it's a little depressing to be summed up like that . . . but yeah, I do."

"Well, forget it," she says, turning back to her coffee.

I open my mouth to protest, then catch myself. All of a sudden, 6's words sound a lot like: *I'm afraid I have to tell you that Christian Dior will not be signing Cindy.* I stare at her, but she is ignoring me to push percolator buttons. I take a deep breath. "Fine. I'll take the scripts and go. You obviously don't believe in this project, anyway."

6 stops so fast that I could swear there's sugar hanging in midair. By the time she turns around, I'm scooping runaway scripts off the floor.

"Scat—"

"No, I understand completely," I say, really laying it on now. "I imposed on you too much last time, and it's not fair to do that again. I'll just tell Brennan I'm working alone. After all, he called me, not you."

I have one hand on the doorknob when 6 says again, "Scat." Only this time she's not protesting; she's commanding. It's so many octaves lower it's like a growl. Despite myself, I turn.

There is a small approving smile playing on 6's lips. "You're getting better at this."

scat stays

I even get a bedroom.

the morning after

I wake to the sound of 6 in the shower, which is so much like a dream that it takes me long minutes to work out I'm actually awake. Then I start thinking about what I'm doing here.

I'm not completely sure how I feel about 6. And even if I was, I have no idea what I'd do about it. I mean, sure, she's intriguing, gorgeous and treats me like shit, but despite these attractive qualities I don't know if I'm ready for a relationship based on manipulation.

It's all too hard for this time of the morning, so I drag myself out of bed and start dressing. Since I have exactly two outfits— the clothes I was wearing when I met 6 at the Saville and the suit I bought yesterday—there's not a whole lot of decision making required. I toy briefly with the idea of walking out in only underwear, then realize I never want to be that vulnerable around 6.

There's not much space behind the office: just two tiny bedrooms (although 6's is bigger than mine), a kitchen from the 1960s, and a bathroom so small you have to stand in the bath to brush your teeth. I head into the kitchen, vaguely hoping 6 has some good toasting bread, and become locked in a struggle with one of the cupboards. I don't realize that 6 has come up behind me until she speaks.

"It's fake."

I start. 6 is standing in the doorway, one fluffy white towel around her torso and one around her head. Her calves coyly call out to me, naked and dripping. "What?"

"That. It's not a cupboard."

"Oh," I say. "Well, I'll quit trying to open it, then."

6 gives me a searching look and vanishes into her bedroom.

I make a decent attempt at a plate of toast, given that the toaster appears to be powered by a single cigarette lighter wedged down the bottom, and when 6 emerges in a figure-hugging sweater and stretch pants, I have food waiting for her. She takes a piece without speaking and pulls up a chair at the counter. I join her and we munch together for a few moments in what I would like to call a companionable silence, but is, in fact, more of a wary silence.

"You know," I say eventually, "I think I'm going to have to become a partner in Synergy."

6 finishes her mouthful before replying, even teasingly sucking some errant crumbs from one finger. I studiously ignore her tactics. "Partner?"

"Sure. After all, Brennan's probably going to write checks to the firm, not us personally. So it would make sense for me to have equal control over how we spend that money."

6 is silent.

"6," I say gently, "you can't change my mind on this."

"Fine," she says irritably.

I bite into the toast to hide my grin, and we sign ten minutes later.

scat and 6 get romantic

"Hey," I say, "this is a good one."

6 looks up wearily, and I abruptly realize that she is wearing glasses: thin black frames that make her dark eyes look amazingly sexy. She frowns at me, sitting cross-legged in a sea of paper. "What?"

"It's a sci-fi action thriller. You see, there's this spaceship crew who pick up some weird, contagious virus and it mutates them into pulsating, yogurtlike—"

"Scat," 6 says testily, "we cannot make a special-effects movie for ten thousand dollars."

"Oh," I say, disappointed. "Oh yeah."

6 shoots me a dark look and returns to her script. I toss "The Spreading" into our growing reject pile and pick up "Strafe." "Hey, a cool action flick," I say. I snicker. "Man, he actually drives a *tank* through the White House."

6 sighs and puts down her script. "Scat, we need to focus."

I blink. "Okay."

"What are we trying to do here?"

"I don't know," I say honestly. "I'm not even sure if you really want to be doing this."

6's eyebrows descend. "I've signed on to this project, Scat. Don't question my commitment."

"Sorry," I say meekly. "Okay. We're trying to make a movie."

"Why?"

"To beat Sneaky Pete."

"So we are, in fact, trying to make a *better* movie than Sneaky Pete. Am I right?"

"Yes you are," I say generously.

"Now, what is Sneaky Pete's great advantage?"

"Fashion sense," I say quickly. When 6 doesn't smile, I say, "Uh, I guess he has one hundred forty million and we don't."

"Correct." She takes a breath. "So, obviously, we need to minimize that advantage."

I wait for 6 to explain how we do this, but she doesn't. "How, exactly?"

"We need to make a movie that doesn't depend on a huge budget for its success."

I get it. "So no special effects."

"No science fiction," 6 says. "No action. No horror."

"Aw," I say, tossing "Strafe" into the reject pile. "What does that even leave?"

6 holds up a script. "Diet Life" is printed across the middle of the page. "Romantic comedy."

"Ugh," I say.

There's a '50s-style diner around the corner named Fishtail, and we go there for lunch. 6 and I both get huge vanilla milkshakes with kooky curly straws, but somehow 6 still manages to look cool.

"Look, I have to say, I'm not really taken by this idea of doing a romantic comedy."

6 ignores me, sucking milk through daring acrobatic feats.

"Sure, *When Harry Met Sally . . . ,*" I say. "*Jerry Maguire.* I know where you're coming from. But I just don't see us being especially good at making a feel-good movie, you know? How about a courtroom drama?"

6 sniffs. "No one's making courtroom dramas anymore. They're all Grishamed out."

"Okay," I say, "what about a screwball comedy?"

"*Weekend at Bernie's II. Kingpin.*"

"There's no need for that," I tell her, hurt. "Man, but romantic comedy."

"Scat, you haven't even read the script," 6 says, a little exasperated. "It's not syrupy, too-cute fluff. It's good."

I stir my shake with my loopy straw, unconvinced.

"It's about a girl trying to break into advertising. She has all these great ideas for ads but can't get a job."

"Really?" My eyes narrow. "How is this a romantic comedy?"

"There's a love interest who works for the ad agency," 6 explains. "He helps the girl. Guides her through the politics."

"Interesting concept," I muse.

6 looks at me.

"Okay," I grumble. "I'll read the script."

diet life

It takes me a while to get into it, because it's full of weird script formatting, but by page 8 I'm hooked. I laugh out loud first on page 12 and by page 30 I'm sniggering so often that 6 leaves the kitchen to get away from me.

When I finally put down the script, I literally have to wipe tears from my eyes. I reach for my coffee, then realize I haven't touched it since 6 made it an hour ago. I wander out to the office, where 6 is going over some notes in her Captain Kirk chair. She looks up as I enter.

"Well?"

"It's great," I say. "Let's do it."

developments

We get Brennan on speaker. "Gary!" I say. "We've got ourselves a script."

"Hey, great," Gary crackles. I sneak a look at 6, remembering our last shared experience with a speakerphone, but she's staring at it impassively. "Which one?"

" 'Diet Life.' You know it?"

"Don't think I read that one. Which genre?"

"It's a . . . well, a romantic comedy, I guess," I say, "but it's really good."

"Romantic comedy?"

"It's actually really good," I say.

"Right . . ." Gary says dubiously.

"So we're ready to start hiring a director and a crew. It's going to be tough to do this within a month, Gary, but I think we can do it."

"Ah," Gary says.

I look at 6, puzzled, and she frowns. "Is there a problem?"

"No, no. Well, a small one. But nothing you should worry about."

6's eyes widen fractionally. Even I know it's a bad idea to tell 6 that there's a problem but she shouldn't worry about it. "How about you fill me in anyway?"

Gary sighs. "Well, Sneaky Pete might be ahead of schedule."

6 doesn't hesitate. "How far ahead? How long do we have?"

Another sigh from the speaker. 6 clenches her jaw. "I've heard that he might be ready to present a rough cut at the next board meeting. And if that happens, and it's well received . . . there's no point in trying to stop him."

"When's the board meeting, Gary?" I ask.

Gary ignores me. "Now, I'm not sure that he really has finished. I don't want you to panic."

"Gary," I say, as calmly as I can, "you need to tell me when the board meeting is."

There's a long pause. "Tomorrow," he says.

throwing in the towel

"So, like I said, there's no point in worrying about it. If he's ready for tomorrow, that's just too bad. There's nothing we can do."

For a moment, neither 6 nor I speak. The disappointment is so thick I can taste it, and it tastes bad.

"Well," 6 says, "you're right. We can't do anything about it. Not by tomorrow."

"Yeah, well," Gary says miserably, and I am suddenly reminded that his job is in the balance here. "I'm sorry. I want to get this prick as much as you do."

"I doubt that," 6 says, and kills the speaker.

a fishtail

We spend a listless afternoon making storyboards (me), reading up on film production (6), and making lots of coffee (mainly 6, since she drinks much more than me). It's hard to get motivated when everything we do could be wasted effort by this time tomorrow.

When 6 finally calls a break for dinner, I'm so relieved I leap up from the floor. "Fishtail?"

6 shrugs. "Whatever."

It's drizzling outside, so we huddle under 6's umbrella. Fishtail is bright, warm and so far away from Sneaky Pete that it feels like paradise. We slip into a booth and both order burgers.

I'm happily stirring my milkshake with my loopy straw when I realize what we're doing. I put down my shake and look at 6.

She meets my eyes. "What?"

"We're letting him beat us," I say. "We're giving up."

6 looks away. "I don't want to talk about it."

"But it's true."

"I know it's true," she says, annoyed. "But there's nothing we can do about it. We came in too late. End of story."

Another long pause. I keep watching 6.

"What?" she says finally.

"Well . . ."

"Oh," she says, "I'm disappointing you, is that it? Well, sometimes you just can't win. Understand? We've done everything we can."

"We haven't actually—"

"Oh, sure," 6 says. "Obviously we haven't decided to spend the next twenty-four hours in a doomed, frantic rush to make some scenes from a movie which inevitably turn out to be not as good as the one that's been filmed over several months with a colossal budget. Yes, Scat, you're right. We could have done that. So, fine, we're giving up."

I'm tempted to argue, but I don't. I just look at her until she's mad enough to speak again.

"Damn it, Scat, this is *stupid*. Do you want to kill yourself over the next day, so when Sneaky Pete wins it hurts even more? Is that what you want?"

I consider. "Yes."

"Fine," 6 says. A waiter appears with our food, smiling broadly. "Bag it," she tells him. "We'll take away."

action

I call Gary on the mobile while 6 holds the umbrella. "Gary!" I shout over the rain. Another couple, huddled together, walk past us in the opposite direction and 6 nearly impales the girl with her spokes. I assume it's accidental. "It's Scat. We're making the movie."

"Scat, I know that."

"No," I say, "I mean for tomorrow."

"Holy Christ," Gary says.

"When's the board meeting? We need to know exactly how long we've got."

"It's at three. But Scat, I can't get you money that quickly."

"What?"

"There are processes," Gary says patiently. "I can give you a purchase order today, then you need to invoice us. And then ninety days later Credit will pay you."

"*Ninety days?* Gary, we need the cash *now*."

"Scat, we just don't operate with cash. Look, I can lean on our people. But we're looking at a couple of weeks, minimum."

I begin to protest, then quit. "Look, Gary, you do what you have to do. We're going to make a movie."

"We need a crew," I say, taking a bite from my rain-soaked burger, "and a cast. Oh, and a director, too."

6 closes the door, shutting out what is becoming very bad-tempered weather. "But we can't pay them."

"No. At least, not up front." I sigh and drop onto the sofa. "Well, I guess a lot of colleges would have a film school—or at least a film club. Maybe we could call some."

6 is shaking her head. "Not good enough. No one's going to commit resource to help someone they don't know. We'd spend a day just trying to prove our credibility."

"Right . . ." I think while 6 attends to her percolator. "So I guess a professional crew or actors definitely wouldn't help us."

"No," 6 says, not turning.

"So what does that leave? What sort of people would work with us without any sort of guarantee that they'll get paid?" 6 brings me over a coffee, and the act is so sweet that for a moment I forget all about films and Coke and money, and smile at her gratefully.

6's eyes shift uncomfortably. "People you know."

I'm momentarily thrown. "Huh?"

"People you know," she repeats. "They're the only ones who will help you out of kindness. Contacts."

"Oh," I say. "You mean friends?"

"Sure," 6 says uncertainly. "Friends."

I eye her for a moment, then decide to let it ride. "Except I don't know anyone in film."

"Oh," 6 says, disappointed. She retires to her Captain Kirk chair.

"You know, 6," I say, a little annoyed despite the coffee. "You don't have to wait for me to come up with all the ideas. Feel free to throw in your own any time."

"Ideas aren't my strength. They're yours."

"That doesn't mean I have to come up with every idea, does

156

it?" She regards me expressionlessly. "Go on, just hit me with one little idea. Just one."

6 looks at me for a long time, then sighs soulfully. "Fine." She looks around the office, perhaps seeking inspiration. "Maybe," she frowns, "we could make it all ourselves."

"Okay . . ." I don't want to dissuade 6 from ever suggesting another idea. "Of course, we'd do a total hack job, having never done it before. And we'd still need help—we can't do everything. We still need actors."

"Maybe Tina would act," 6 suggests.

"Hey," I say, brightening. "Good idea. She's at UCLA, right? Maybe she'd even have a few ideas for us. What's her major?"

6 stares at me.

"What?"

6 frowns at the table for a moment, then looks up at me. Her expression is curious: a mixture of embarrassment and excitement. "Film."

idle chitchat

"Wow," Tina says, flashing her green eyes at me. They really are startling, even though they're partially obscured by lank black hair. She puts her hands on her hips, her tiny frame blocking the doorway. "I didn't think I'd see you two again."

"Uh," I say, looking around 6's old apartment, "well, you never know, huh?" There's a boy sitting on the sofa, flicking through cable and studiously ignoring us. Tina is also studiously avoiding introducing us to him, so I guess it's just a typical Tina relationship.

"And how are *you*, 6?" Tina asks pointedly.

"Fine," 6 says, looking away.

"Did 6 tell you why she left?" Tina asks me.

"For Christ's sake," 6 breathes.

"She didn't like *William*," Tina says accusingly. "*Normal*

157

people live together all the time, but 6 didn't want to share the apartment with a *man*."

"So this must be William," I say heartily, sincerely hoping we can avoid opening our request for Tina's help with a fight.

Tina stops. "No, that's Kevin. William and I broke up."

"Imagine that," 6 mutters.

Tina's eyes narrow, but I get in before she can speak. "Tina, 6 and I really need your help."

Tina looks at me for a moment, then at 6. "Really?" She smiles. "Well, come in then."

briefing tina

"Holy *shit*," Tina says. "This is so *cool*."

"But the problem is," I say carefully, "unless we can produce a few scenes by three o'clock tomorrow, we're screwed."

"Sure."

"So I need to ask if you know anyone—"

"No," Tina says, "I mean: sure, I'll do it for you."

I look at 6, who just blinks, then back at Tina. "Are you saying you can organize a shoot for us? Where are you going to get a crew?"

"I have a crew," Tina says. "For my film. It's my third-year project."

"Shit," I say, stunned.

"I have a camera, too," Tina says helpfully.

artistic intent

Tina settles down on the sofa with "Diet Life," and as soon as she does, Kevin gets up and disappears into the bedroom.

"Boy," I say. "Kind of moody, isn't he?"

Tina doesn't respond, and I realize that she's lost in the script. She's making notes alongside the dialogue with a little red pencil and looking so much like she knows what she's doing that I'm buoyed with hope.

She finishes about nine, and over pizza we argue about which scenes we should film. Tina's particularly taken with a bit where the main character sits alone on a sofa and toys with her hair, which concerns me deeply, but 6 and I argue the merits of two humorous scenes.

"So *explicit*," Tina says, wrinkling her nose.

"Tina," I say carefully, "we're pitching to a room full of executives. They're not going to appreciate all the artistic subtleties of your work."

Tina sniffs. "Like I care what *they* think. If they can't appreciate—"

"Tina, *we* care. That's why we're doing this."

Tina's eyes flick between me and 6.

6 says, "Tina, please."

Tina sighs. "Okay, okay. But I'm not putting my name on this."

whereby scat and 6 sleep together

Tina's shoot is at ten tomorrow morning, which is not great but much better than having no shoot. We decide we'll film until twelve, edit until two and get to Coke in time for the three o'clock board meeting. We all agree on this schedule and no one says anything about how insane it is.

"Well, I'll see you guys in the morning," Tina says.

"Which bedroom is mine?" 6 asks.

Tina stops. She says slowly, "You'll have to sleep out here."

6 takes a moment to answer, and when she does it's through clenched teeth. "But you have two bedrooms."

"Yes, but *Kevin's* in one of them."

159

"Tina," 6 says with obvious restraint, "you're *sleeping* with him."

"Not tonight I'm not," Tina says. For Kevin's benefit she adds loudly, "Not with him in *that* mood."

6 takes a deep breath. "Tina—"

"Oh, come on, Scat's okay. Just snuggle up on the sofa."

"Okay," I say quickly.

"I'm not snuggling with Scat anywhere," 6 says emphatically.

"We could go top and tail," I suggest helpfully. 6 turns and glares at me.

"Look, you're both smart people," Tina says. "I'm tired and I have to shoot a film tomorrow. You work it out."

"Tina—" 6 says again, but she has already shut the door. 6 stares at it for a long moment.

"I don't snore," I offer.

"I'm sleeping on the sofa," 6 says, and she stalks over to it to emphasize her point. "You can find somewhere on the floor."

"There's only one blanket," I point out.

"So?" she says aggressively.

"6," I say patiently. "Let's be reasonable. No one wants to catch cold here."

"Scat, I'm going to be very clear," 6 says. "There is no way in hell you're sleeping on that sofa with me."

"Well, that makes for an interesting situation," I say, firing up, "because there's no way in hell I'm sleeping without a blanket."

"*Fine,*" 6 says, her dark eyes flashing, "then I'll sleep on the sofa and let the blanket hang over onto the floor, where you can sleep."

I open my mouth to send back a sizzling rejoinder, which will no doubt inflame 6 even further and maybe our passions will rise so much that I'll even grab her and just kiss her hard, but then I realize that 6's idea actually makes sense. "Oh," I say. "Okay."

Neither 6 nor myself envisioned spending the night at Tina's, so we're without pajamas. This doesn't particularly worry me, but 6 is keen to rectify the situation and she risks Tina's wrath to borrow some nightwear. When she pads back in, she's wearing a set of shiny blue satins that are probably a loose fit on Tina's tiny frame but cling to 6 in very distracting ways.

"What?" 6 says, catching me staring. She puts her hands on her hips, which only makes the situation worse, and I begin to realize the danger of wearing only boxers.

"Nothing," I say quickly.

6 steps over me onto the sofa and slips under the blanket. We have a brief, lovely moment where we both tug the blanket for position, then settle on a mutually suspicious position with our backs to each other.

I lie there, listening to 6 breathe, until I get the feeling that 6 is also listening to my breathing. I try to breathe quietly for a while, but then I run out of air and let out a gasp.

"What are you doing?" 6 says sharply.

"Nothing."

Silence. I count to a hundred, concentrating on breathing steadily. I'm up to eighty-six when 6 rolls over and something flops down onto my chest.

I look up but can't see anything except her sheet of hair. I carefully lift up the blanket and peer under it to see that, amazingly, 6's arm is resting on my chest. One immaculate hand extends from Tina's blue satin top and rests, black nails and all, on my chest.

I wait for a minute, hoping that maybe this is some clever seduction ploy, then I carefully rest my left arm on top of 6's.

No reaction. I can't believe it. I just can't believe it.

It takes me half an hour to pick up enough courage to intertwine my fingers with 6's, and when I do, it feels like heaven. I can't understand how it can feel so good to just hold her hand.

I lie like that in the darkness for two hours, and by the time I fall asleep I'm pretty sure I'm in love with her again.

the psychology of business

When I wake up, Kevin is sitting above my head, watching a hockey game. 6 is gone.

"Wa," I say, which I never do except first thing in the morning. "Where is everyone?" Kevin doesn't look at me. "Kevin?"

"My name is Steve."

"Oh. Sorry." I'm pretty sure that Tina said he was Kevin. Maybe this is why he's so pissed at her.

I extract myself from the blanket and wander into the kitchen. Tina is eating toast and jam. "Hey there."

"Hey," Tina says distractedly, and I see she is rereading the script.

"You know, Tina, I want to thank you for this. It really means a lot to me and 6."

"That's okay," Tina says, smiling brightly. "I'm not really pissed at 6."

"That's good."

"She's such a bitch," Tina says, which I find a little contradictory, but overall quite true. "She's got to be in charge of everything."

I sit next to her. "Well, I guess. But in business, that's leadership."

Tina stares at me for a second. "I can't believe you consider that a positive trait. How about her inability to accept other points of view? Is it good leadership to be narrow, too?"

"Focus," I say. "They call that focus."

Tina stares at me. "Her paranoia?"

"Business savvy."

"Compulsive need to have everything just how she wants it?"

"Organizational skills."

"Aggressiveness?"

162

"Aggressiveness," I say, "is already a good thing."

"Jesus Christ," Tina says, her eyebrow ring glinting in the morning sun. "Sometimes I worry about this country."

the shoot

I don't realize that we have a major problem until we arrive at the shoot.

Right up until then everything's fine. We leave on time and Tina even has a beat-up Chrysler to take us. The front left tire vibrates alarmingly around corners, but it's definitely faster and probably safer than LA public transport.

Both the 10 and the 405 are pretty clear, and we arrive at UCLA a full half hour before the crew and cast are due. Tina has the keys to a big Gothic building on the campus's east side, and she leads us through to her studio. While she inspects all kinds of weird equipment I don't even recognize, 6 and I check out the set.

"We can get rid of these," I say, pointing to a bizarre collection of tiny cardboard beds, "and bring around that desk. There's enough here to pass for an office."

6 nods. "This is professional. Tina has a good shoot."

People start drifting in over the next thirty minutes, and soon we have almost a dozen people standing around the set in groups, smoking and talking. Tina makes her way over to me. "Okay, we're starting."

"Where's the cast?" I ask, looking around. I'm pretty eager to find out who these people are and hoping like crazy they'll be good enough to carry this off.

"Well, James is over there," she says, pointing out a lanky blond guy who is smoking and staring at his feet. He actually looks like a movie star: I'm extremely impressed. "I thought he could play the love interest. And the guy next to him is playing the executive."

"Wow, Tina, these guys look great. Can they really act?"

"Oh, sure," Tina says. "I'm lucky to have them, especially James. He's doing a pilot for NBC."

"Wow," I say again. "And who's going to play Jane?"

"Ah," Tina says. "Well."

I am struck with absolute terror. Jane is the central character. "What? Tina? Do we have a Jane?"

"The thing is," Tina says, "I thought I could play her."

I look at Tina for a very long time. "Uh . . . 6?"

tina's debut

"Tina, you are not playing this role."

"*6,*" Tina protests. "I'll be *good.* Let me play her."

"Not going to happen," 6 says shortly. "Tina, I know you're a good director, but you've never acted. We need solid talent."

"*Well,*" Tina says, her eyes narrowing, "unless *you're* going to play Jane, I don't see what choice you have."

I look hopefully at 6. Her eyes widen with alarm. "*I'm* not doing it."

"Well, there you go," Tina says smugly.

6 stares at her. "You little bitch."

Tina sniffs and looks away.

"Look," I say, trying to play peacemaker. "Let's give it a try. Okay? If Tina can't . . . if Tina's not suitable, then we'll work out what to do. But let's not create problems where there might not be any, okay?"

Tina and 6 are silent for a moment. Then 6 sighs heavily. "Fine. We'll test Tina."

they test tina

Tina is crap. She is really, really crap.

a new jane

"Okay, fine," Tina says irritably. "So get someone else."

"Tina, it's nothing personal," I say. "It's just that your skills are in direction, not acting. I mean, *I'm* no actor."

"Yeah, whatever." She calls out to the group. "Okay, let's take a break! Back in fifteen!"

6 has been pacing out wide, furious circles, but now she strides over. "I can't *believe* you didn't tell us we don't have an actress," she hisses. Her eyes are dark slits. "What the hell were you thinking?"

"Do you want my help?" Tina yells suddenly. "Because I don't have to be here!"

6's lips tighten until they are white. I quickly take her arm and lead her away from Tina before she destroys our slim remaining chances of making a film. "6, it's just a setback. We've been through setbacks before."

"We have four and a half hours," 6 says, "and we need an actress. Do you have one?"

"Well, no," I admit, and then I close my eyes. "Oh."

"What?"

I take a deep, unsteady breath and open my eyes. "I know an actress."

cindy [2]

I take 6's cellphone and find myself a nice open space on campus, far away from where anyone might hear me. Because I'm reasonably

165

sure that there's going to be a fairly embarrassing amount of prostration and begging on my part.

She picks up on the fifth ring. "Hello?"

"Hi, Cindy!" I say heartily. "How are you doing?"

There's a long, somehow satisfied pause. "Well, how about that. Scat."

"Uh, yeah," I say.

"What has it been?" Cindy asks, as if she is truly interested. "Two days? Three?"

"Three, I guess," I say, a little surprised that so much time has passed so quickly. I'm tempted to slide straight into a description of what I've been doing, which would lead easily into a plea for help, but I can't escape the fact that some serious rapport building is required first. "Are you doing okay?"

"Oh, I'm good," Cindy says. "I'm *great.*"

"Really?" I ask, genuinely surprised, then immediately curse myself.

"Sure," Cindy says smugly. "You know, I was at this industry party last night, and people told me I've never looked happier."

"Great," I say, dismayed at the turn this conversation is taking.

"So in all, I think I'm a lot better off for having dumped you. My career's taking off, I've got my freedom and I don't have to waste time supporting you through your periodic neuroses. In fact, I almost think you did me a favor by being such an egotistical, self-obsessive asshole."

I swallow. "Well, Cindy," I say, and in this moment I don't like myself at all, "now you can do me a favor."

negotiations

Cindy laughs for a long time. "Oh, Scat," she says, and I can just tell she's wiping away tears. "You're too much."

"I know you probably don't feel like helping me right—"

"You know the best part?" she says suddenly. "The best part is that you don't even see it. I dumped you because you can't see past your own needs, and now you call me up to ask a favor. Doesn't that seem funny to you?"

"Cindy—"

"I mean, do you really expect me to do it? Do you?"

"I don't *expect* you to do anything," I say carefully. "I'm *asking* you because I'm desperate."

"Is 6 there, too?" Cindy asks.

I hesitate. "Yes."

Cindy breaks into laughter again. I wait her out, shifting from one foot to the other. "Too much," Cindy says.

"Look, I know I wasn't great to you. You've given me much more than I've ever repaid. I acknowledge that."

"Go on."

"But I did help you, Cindy, when you needed it. I helped you to get your modeling career off the ground, and I suggested you start those acting classes."

"*Career,*" Cindy says scathingly. "What about some personal feeling, huh? What about some emotional commitment? Where was that?"

"Cindy, I'm sorry. What can I say? You win. I was the bastard. You can hang me out to dry if you want."

There's a pause, then Cindy sighs. "The thing is, if I helped you now, it would be just the same. You obviously haven't changed at all. Once I've done enough to help you through your latest crisis, you'll go away again. Won't you?"

I freeze.

"You didn't even think about that, did you?" she asks sadly. "You haven't even thought past how you're going to get out of your immediate dilemma, have you?"

I think about this for a long moment, and Cindy waits while I do it. Finally, I confess, "No."

"So you've called me," Cindy says, and I get the terrible feeling that she's winding up, "to say you're sorry for only being around me when it suits your career, and, by the way, will I do it again?"

I choke, but force the words out. "Yes," I say miserably, "you're right." After having it phrased like this, I can't believe I actually called her. "Cindy, I'm really sorry. I'll just go—"

"Well," Cindy says with satisfaction, "as long as you realize that, I'll help you."

I nearly cry.

scat scores

I take a couple of minutes to compose myself, then stride back inside with my most casual expression. Tina and 6 turn to face me at exactly the same moment.

"Well?" 6 demands.

"I got her," I say nonchalantly, then sneak a glance at 6.

Both her eyebrows shoot up and her lips even part in a tiny ring of surprise. There is no doubt: 6 is genuinely impressed.

"*Very* good," she murmurs.

art for fun and profit

Despite actually living on Wilshire in Santa Monica, Cindy manages to get lost en route to UCLA, showing up only after I place three increasingly desperate cellphone calls. By now it's almost one, which is exactly one hour after we expected to finish shooting and two hours before the board meeting. We exchange quick, reserved greetings, then Tina whisks her away to discuss motivations. I wander over to 6, who has started pacing between a couple of halogen lights.

"It's not going to work," she says. "We're too late."

"It'll work," I tell her. "We're still in this."

"Why don't they *start?*" she demands, staring at Tina and the talent.

"Artists," I offer apologetically.

"Students," 6 mutters.

It's another half hour before Tina is satisfied that the cast is ready, then she sends them outside to do breathing exercises while she orders the lights all over the place. When it's getting toward two, 6 and I can't take it anymore and we grab her.

"Hi, guys," Tina says. "You know, Cindy's pretty good. She'll do well." She pauses to shout at a skinny boy wearing a Lakers cap. "No, back! Back!"

"Gee, that's great," I say, not really listening. "Tina, we're running extremely short on time here. When are we going to actually film something?"

Tina turns to me, hands on hips. "Do you want to do this right?"

6 says, "We just want to *do* it, Tina. If it's not done by three, it's useless."

"I can't do a half-rate effort just to meet a deadline," Tina says, as if this is obvious.

6 freezes. "Tina, I don't think you really understand what we're trying to do here."

"Oh, I understand what *you're* trying to do," Tina says. "I don't think you understand what *I'm* trying to do."

"Which is?" I ask.

"Shoot a good scene."

I choke. "Tina, we're—"

"Fine," 6 says.

"What?" I say. *"Fine?"*

"I need to talk to you," 6 tells me, pulling me aside.

"6," I complain, "we need this thing done by three. And that's *done:* filmed, edited, everything." 6 stares at me until I blush. "Okay. You know that."

6 says, "We can't rush Tina, or she won't do her job. You'll have to stall the board."

I stare at her. "You know, it sounded like you said—"

"Stall the board," 6 says impatiently. "It can be done."

She says this like the method is obvious, so I think for a moment to see if it will present itself. It doesn't. "How?"

6 looks at me. "You'll think of something."

to stall a board

With no car and just two dollars cash, I'm forced to resort to public transport again. I stand at the bus stop for twenty minutes, staring vainly down Wilshire, before giving up and running. I actually run. Bag ladies, dealers and wandering freaks turn and stare at me in amazement.

I run for what feels like an hour, and by the time I arrive at Coke it's five to three, I'm swimming in my own sweat, and I can't breathe. But I'm here.

I stagger to reception and gasp, "Brennan." The receptionist is keen to get rid of me, and within seconds Gary pops from one of the elevators.

"Christ, Scat, you look terrible. Do you want to sit down?"

"I'm fine," I whisper, leaning against the wall of the elevator. Gary punches for the 20th.

"Right," he says, eyeing me. "So how did it go? Did you do it?"

I don't have the breath to explain, so I just nod.

Gary stares at me. "Amazing."

I try a modest smile but it turns into a repulsive bout of coughing. Gary takes a small step back and waits until I recover.

"We just need to stall the board," I wheeze, "until the film gets here. 'Kay?"

Gary starts. "You don't have the film?"

"No."

"Have you *seen* the film?"

"Uh, no." I swallow. "But I'm sure it will be good."

the opening

There's a projector and a huge screen set up in the boardroom, and both the board and the SMT are gathered around them, talking loudly and excitedly. It seems kind of cute to me that all these important men, who control billions of dollars, get a little giggly over the idea of a private movie.

I hang back near the door. "Is Sneaky Pete here?"

"No," Gary says. "He'll come in when the preview's over. Make an entrance. Now I have to schmooze, but you stay near the door. When our film arrives, you run down and grab it. Got it?"

Without warning, the lights go out and the projector starts. Two dozen men grope in the semidarkness for their chairs, and Sneaky Pete's movie starts.

artificial sweetener

The first thing that comes up is Sneaky Pete, which is alarming. His face fills the huge screen, his sunglasses glinting. I shift uncomfortably.

"Welcome," Sneaky Pete says softly, "to history. Hollywood has never seen anything like this. The soda industry has never seen anything like this. Marketing has never seen anything like this.

"This film is a collaboration between the Coca-Cola Company and Universal Pictures. We are not completely finished, but we can show you this thirty-minute rough cut.

"Gentlemen, welcome to *Backlash*."

And it starts.

fair credit

The first thing that hits me is the sound. Someone has hidden half a dozen very large speakers around the boardroom, and abruptly the room explodes into music. Onscreen, the word *Backlash* forms out of a cloud of shrapnel, and just as I'm gasping at the special effects, the opening credits come up.

Tom Cruise.

Winona Ryder.

Gwyneth Paltrow.

I stand up and walk out.

whitewash

I walk briskly to the bathroom and I scream, *"Fuck! Fuck!"*

When I'm tired of that, I kick the wall, and when that doesn't make me feel better either, I try a combination of the two. For variety, I turn the faucet on full blast and splash my face with cold water.

Suddenly everything that 6 and I have been doing over the last twenty-four hours seems childish. I realize that I've been holding on to the belief that somehow Sneaky Pete's one hundred forty million dollars wouldn't really matter, and now I've been shown how pathetically naive that idea was. One hundred and forty million dollars buys a computer graphics studio and A-list talent.

It's a long time before I can go back.

window dressing

The sound effects reverberate down the hall, and when I open the boardroom doors they almost buffet me. I've walked into the middle of a full-on action sequence, and all eyes are glued to the screen.

I attach myself to the side wall and watch as Tom Cruise leaps out of a bizarre-looking hovercraft and tumbles to the icy ground, the vehicle exploding behind him. By the look of the special effects, this is a science-fiction blockbuster: there are laser guns, minimalist fashion, and truly gross-looking aliens zipping by in sleek blue flying machines. The sheer volume of special effects on the screen is stunning, overwhelming.

Winona Ryder is some kind of alien overlord, all scales and blue tongue but strangely exciting. We cut back to Tom, and he's running through a dark tunnel with Gwyneth, who is apparently consigned to a screaming-and-covering-face role, but carrying it off with aplomb.

And it's flawless. It's simply flawless.

three cheers

The final scene of the rough cut is chosen for its audience: Tom and Gwyneth are lost inside the alien base and they burst into a huge hall. The hall is filled with aliens, all drinking from Coke cans, and they turn at once to face the humans. From what I've been able to work out, these aliens have a real weakness for Coke: I think it's been offered up as the reason they invaded Earth.

Everyone loves this shot of Tom and Gwyneth, stricken, facing dozens of Coke-drinking aliens, and the applause is thunderous even before the lights come up. There is shouting and whistling, and several of the SMT close to Gary Brennan clap him on the back. Gary's face is white.

When Sneaky Pete enters, the applause goes up a decibel, and even a few board members break into smiles. He regards us all coolly, nodding fractionally to a couple of key players. Then he sees me, and stiffens. I stare back at him expressionlessly, hoping that if nothing else I can afflict him with a vague sense of unease.

"Gentlemen," he says softly, and the room quietens. "Thank you very much for your appreciation. We have worked hard on this project, and it is gratifying to finally see some results." He sweeps the room with his gaze. "Now, I open the floor. I welcome all comments, suggestions and criticism."

The SMT lead off, and the first six men fall over themselves to heap praise on *Backlash* and Sneaky Pete. By the time it's Brennan's turn, I'm feeling vaguely nauseous. But at least the tide turns here.

Brennan swallows. "I'm extremely pleased with our progress to date."

et tu

I wait for more, but that's it. The next SMT member starts gushing praise, and Gary just sits there, stiff-backed, refusing to look at me.

Gary has betrayed me. He's decided that we can't win, and he's not going to risk trying. Before I realize what I'm doing, I take a few steps forward. A couple of men on the opposite side of the room raise their eyebrows. I even see Sneaky Pete's head turn slightly.

But I have nothing to say. Without support from Gary, I don't even have a reason to be here.

I step back to the wall and try not to imagine what 6 is going to do to me.

juggernaut

"I know it's been said before," another anonymous suit says, "but those special effects really were amazing. Wow! I thought it was just great."

I need to get out of here. Eleven men have declared their undying love for *Backlash*, and I don't know how much more I can stomach before I start screaming.

"I have a criticism," someone says. Despite myself, my hopes rise. The room falls silent. "That Gwyneth Paltrow. Can't we see more of her legs? She has really good legs."

The man to his left roars with laughter and claps him on the back. I have to restrain myself from going over and slapping the both of them.

The board is considerably more reserved than the SMT but just as impressed. The first makes a totally absurd plot suggestion, which Sneaky Pete fields with a short, noncommittal nod, and the next two say that they can't fault the film at all. I've decided that I really am going to make a break out of here, when the chairman speaks.

"I agree, it's very hard to fault this movie," he says, his voice low and rumbling. "Mr. Pete, you've certainly done a very good job." He takes a breath. "But—"

hark

I swear, I actually hear angels.

rally

"There's something missing," the chairman says, dipping his enormous white eyebrows into a frown. "I'm not sure what, but I just feel like . . . something's missing."

The room is utterly silent, shocked at this unexpected salvo. Sneaky Pete doesn't flinch, but I lived with this guy and I think he is stunned. It is long seconds before he responds. "Missing?"

"I'm sorry to be so ambiguous, Mr. Pete, but I'm trying to

explain the feeling that the film has left me with. And that feeling is . . . something is missing."

I see the muscles in Sneaky Pete's jaw clench. "Missing," he says again.

The chairman nods slowly. "I don't know what, exactly—"

"I do," I say.

mktg case study #12: mktg appliances

MAKE SURE THE CASING AND BUTTONS LOOK VERY, VERY GOOD. USE CHEAP COMPONENTS; CUSTOMERS CAN'T SEE THEM.

scat makes an impassioned plea

Boy, does that get a reaction.

Sneaky Pete is talking almost before I've got the two words out, asking that I be removed from the room. Gary Brennan, apparently expecting something like this from me, is on his feet, telling me I'm no longer required. When Jim and another man suddenly remember me from our glory days at Ludus, it seems like suddenly everyone's trying to rush me from the room.

I ignore them all, waiting until the chairman silences them. "Mr. Scat, isn't it?" he says slowly. "From Fukk?"

I'm surprised at his memory. "Yes, sir."

"What do you have to say about this film, Mr. Scat?"

I take a deep breath and peel myself from the wall, moving in front of the screen until I'm standing next to Sneaky Pete. "Sir, this film is very well made. As several people said, its technical quality is flawless. And in that sense, I agree that it's very hard to find anything wrong with this film." I swallow. "However, you are absolutely right, sir, when you say there's something missing. I think a couple of critical concerns have been overlooked."

"Mr. Croft," Sneaky Pete interjects, "I must object to this person's presence. He is not an employee of Coca-Cola, nor—"

"The first thing missing," I interrupt, "is a sense of fun. This film takes itself too seriously, and that, sir, is not something our customers like. Nor is it something Coca-Cola likes. We sell a lot of cans on the premise that we have a fun product, sir, and I don't believe this film helps that."

Three dozen faces stare at me impassively. I was at least hoping for a nod or two. "But there's something even more important missing," I say, forcing the waver out of my voice, "and that's identification. None of the characters in that film are really likable." Possible exception of Winona Ryder's alien, but it's not the time to raise that now. "This is a major concern, sir, because if I understand it correctly, that's the reason we're making this film. If we just wanted to show a bunch of people drinking Coke, we'd make a thirty-second TV spot. This film is meant to develop characters that our target market identify with and wish to emulate. It doesn't do that."

The chairman stares at me wordlessly, and I'm suddenly thrown into a panic. If he says, *No, that's not what I meant at all,* I'm completely, utterly screwed. I toss up hopefully, "Is that what you meant, sir?"

There's an achingly long pause. Then the chairman lifts his head. "Exactly."

the cavalry

There is utter, bewildered silence. I can see all those men who spoke about how good the film is silently resolving to sit on the opposite side of the chairman in future. Then Sneaky Pete speaks. His voice is low and surprisingly hostile; right now I could believe he is preparing to do me some real physical harm.

"Mr. Scat," he says, barely containing his fury, "I appreciate

177

your suggestions, but I dislike the way you have expressed them. Certainly those issues that you have mentioned will be given our attention. However, it is not as easy as simply standing up and saying, 'All the characters should be identifiable.' In practice, accomplishing this is extremely difficult."

The boardroom door opens a crack behind Sneaky Pete but he doesn't see it. Abruptly, a plan so beautiful that it comes with its own top ten soundtrack drops into my head. "Excuse me, but I don't see why."

He takes a moment to swallow his first retort. "I would suggest this is because you have never tried it. I don't suppose you can actually *demonstrate* how you would create identifiable characters?"

I take a moment to smile at 6, who is standing uncertainly near the door with a can of film in her arms. "Actually," I say, "yes, I can."

duping sneaky pete

For a moment, I honestly think he's going to hit me. I really do.

id

6 hands the reel over to someone from Facilities and the room takes a ten-minute break while the projector is being set up. There are a lot of people who suddenly want to talk to me, so 6 and I escape to the only safe refuge: the women's toilet.

"So is it good?" I'm actually chewing on a fingernail. "How did it turn out? Is it okay?"

"It's pretty good," 6 says distractedly. "How was Sneaky Pete's film?"

"It was fantastic," I say, and I brief her on the drama. By the end, her eyes are shining.

"Identification and emulation," she murmurs. "*Very* good."

"Does our film have identification? Because I'm going to look pretty stupid if it doesn't."

6 considers. "Yes," she says thoughtfully. "I think it does."

the showing

Our rough cut runs for only six minutes, but it feels like an hour. I sit at the back with 6 and gnaw my fingernails down to stubs. My only consolation is that Sneaky Pete looks just as nervous.

Tina has done a superb job. Technically, it's not even close to *Backlash*, but when Cindy corners the ad agency's creative director in the men's room, a ripple of laughter spreads across the room. I look across at the chairman, and, impossibly, he is nodding slowly.

conquest

When the lights come back up, I see a room full of smiling faces. In fact, the only people in the room who aren't smiling are 6, who I have seen smile exactly once, and Sneaky Pete, who looks murderous.

The chairman calls for a ten-minute break so that the board can consider "these new developments" privately. But everyone knows what's happening here. As the SMT file out, they shoot me awed, nervous glances.

As soon as we're out, 6 takes my hand and pulls me down a corridor. Before I can be surprised, she leads me into a small meeting room and shuts the door behind me.

"Uh . . . 6?"

She stares at me for a moment. Then she steps forward, grabs my face and kisses me hard.

The first time 6 kissed me, six months ago in the elevator, it was fast.

This isn't. This is passionate, desperate and very, very long.

scat says it

I guess we break before ten minutes, but I can't tell. I've lost all sense of time. I've lost all sense of everything except what it feels like to be with 6.

"We have to go," she says. Her face is excited and flushed. She's never looked so beautiful.

I can't stop myself. "I love you."

"I know," 6 says.

Scat and 6 in Love

CHAPTER 000012

changing of the guard

With my whole body tingling, I make my way back inside. The chairman waits until everyone is seated, which is an agonizingly long time due to the ineptitude of one of the SMT in locating his chair. While he paces back and forth and shoots the chairman embarrassed glances, 6 and I grip hands under the table.

"Gentlemen and Ms. 6," the chairman says, "thank you for returning so promptly. My colleagues and I believe that Mr. Scat has raised valid concerns about our project. We further believe that he and his team have demonstrated a capacity to satisfy those concerns, and we therefore feel that his input will contribute to our own success."

The whole room is staring at me. I feel like staring at me myself.

"The Coca-Cola Company and its partner, Universal Pictures, have invested a considerable sum in this film, and we do not intend to jeopardize that. We will complete *Backlash*. However, we would like to do so under Mr. Scat's direction." The chairman pauses for a moment. "Is this acceptable to you, Mr. Scat?"

I open my mouth to say something like *You betcha,* but my vocal cords have frozen. I gulp air for a few seconds before 6 rescues me. "It would be an honor, Mr. Croft."

"Good." He shuffles paper for a moment, and I take the opportunity to glance at Sneaky Pete. He is utterly rigid. "I would like to make clear that in no way do we think the work of Mr. Pete is substandard. The film is technically flawless, and we highly value the skill he has shown to make it so. In fact, we feel those skills are more appropriate to management, rather than operations."

"Hello," 6 murmurs.

"It is disappointing," the chairman says, frowning, "that the same cannot be said for Mr. Brennan. It appears obvious to us that Mr. Brennan brought in an external team—Mr. Scat and Ms. 6—to subvert the work of his own employees. Despite the result, such methods are deplorable. Behavior such as this leads to disharmony within the company and will not be tolerated. It is not the board's place to dictate the termination of employees, but we recommend that Mr. Jamieson consider Mr. Brennan's position very carefully."

Brennan is in shock. His mouth works uselessly, and his eyes rove from the chairman to Jamieson, back and forth. There is no sympathy in either face.

"Should Mr. Brennan's position become vacant," the chairman continues, "we would suggest that Mr. Pete would fill the role perfectly. Does anyone wish to comment?"

I am numb. It's impossible: Sneaky Pete is Vice President of Marketing. 6 shakes her head slowly.

"Good," the chairman says. "Then I look forward to the completion of *Backlash.* I am sure that under Mr. Pete's vigilance, Mr. Scat and Ms. 6 will produce a resounding success."

I look at Sneaky Pete. Very slowly, the corners of his lips curl upward. Across the room, he grins at me.

"Oh fuck," I say. I can't seem to stop saying it. "Oh, *fuck.*"

"Scat," 6 says, peering down the street for a cab, "we won. We set out to wedge ourselves into the project, and we've done it." A cab roars past us and 6 glares at it. I almost expect the car to explode right there. "You should be happy."

"Happy?" I choke. "I'm working for *Sneaky Pete.*"

"So?"

"He'll eat me alive," I say. I look over my shoulder, just in case. 6 sighs, watching the street.

"Well, I never picked *you* for the optimist," I tell her, aggrieved. "How can you be so calm?"

"We accomplished our objective," 6 says blandly. "Therefore I'm happy."

I study 6 for signs of happiness.

"Fucking cabs," she mutters. She turns back to me. "Look, we'll deal with it. Right now we're just going to go back to Tina's and celebrate."

"Celebrate?"

"They're waiting to find out how it went. Tina and the crew. And the cast, I guess."

"Oh. Cindy too?"

6 shrugs.

"Oh." I'm about to add something noncommittal when 6 nudges me. I am leaning in for an embrace before I realize she's just trying to get my attention.

"Brennan," she murmurs.

I turn and see Gary heading vaguely in our direction. He is holding his car keys, but in a way that suggests he's forgotten what to do with them. When I call out, his head slowly comes up and he looks around, confused, before spotting me.

"Scat," he says, shambling over. "6."

"Gary, shit," I say. "I'm really sorry."

"Yeah," Gary says.

There's an awkward pause where I'm expecting 6 to add to the condolences, but she declines to do so. I add lamely, "It's a real bitch."

"I'm fifty-one," he says dazedly, and suddenly he sounds frighteningly close to tears. "I've got four kids."

"I'm sorry, Gary," I say again, and when it comes down to it, that's all I can do.

the true merit of internal competition

"That's bullshit," 6 says in the cab. "What Croft said about Brennan."

"What? That his behavior was unacceptable?"

6 nods. "He said that in the long run, Brennan's behavior was detrimental to the company's performance."

"Isn't that right? Employees should work together, not stab each other in the back."

6 is shaking her head. "Not true. In the long run, internal competition benefits the company. Even when it's insidious."

"How can that be?"

"Because it's a marketplace. Competition forces the weaker players out, leaving the stronger product. Brennan gives way to a stronger player in Sneaky Pete, and the company benefits."

"Huh."

"Of course," 6 adds, "it can't be explicit. If the company openly encourages it, it gets out of hand. When someone makes it too obvious that they're playing politics, like Brennan, they make an example out of him. Even though he's doing what they want."

I think about this. "That's a little scary."

"That's business," 6 says.

I'm not looking forward to this at all. What I am looking forward to is spending some quality time alone with 6, and being stuck in a room with a bunch of strangers, her ex-roommate and my ex-girlfriend is not even close.

6 pushes the buzzer. "So?" Tina says eagerly.

"We did it," 6 tells the speaker, and it distorts with a dozen cheering voices. The door clicks open and we make our way up the sagging stairs.

When we reach the top, Tina pulls 6 in for a hug. "You're the best!" she yells.

"Okay," 6 says, alarmed.

"So come in—everyone wants to know what happened."

We squeeze into Tina's apartment, where she's somehow managed to fit about twenty people. There's lots of smoke, beer and '70s fashion, and it's hard to believe that 6 ever lived here.

I spot Cindy engrossed in conversation with James, who acted in our scenes, and decide I should really go over and thank them. It takes me a while to force my way through the crush, during which time a girl accidentally sticks her cigarette into my arm, another drops her drink on my foot and some guy, I swear, pinches my butt.

"Hi, Scat," Cindy says happily. "You know James, of course?"

"Of course," I say, shaking hands. "Hey, I want to thank you both for your help today. You really saved us."

"Yeah, well," Cindy says. "Let's not go into that."

I smile at her. "That would be good."

"Oh, hey," she says suddenly. "I brought you a present. You know, you left all your things at our apartment, and I thought maybe—"

"You brought my *things?*" I ask, pathetically grateful. "You brought my *clothes?*"

"Um, no," she says, almost apologetic. "I brought your phone charger." She reaches into her purse and hands it across, a sad little bundle of wire.

"Oh," I say. I stare at it for a moment, then look up at her. She shrugs and looks at the carpet. "Well," I say slowly, "thanks again, Cindy."

mktg art

I'm expecting that 6 will want to stay at this party for roughly five minutes, but three hours later, she's sipping neat vodka and guarding a prime position on the sofa. The closest I can get to her is a tight group with Tina, so I strike up a conversation.

"So," I say, "you're okay with the fact that your artwork was actually liked by a corporation?"

Tina sips at her beer. "I didn't produce art."

"I mean the film. Art, right?"

"No," Tina says. "Not."

I'm lost. "What?"

"Art and marketing can't coexist," Tina says. "It's either one or the other."

"Not this again," 6 says from the sofa.

Tina ignores her. "I made the film for you with the intention of appealing to a bunch of corporate suits. That I used artistic techniques to do it is irrelevant."

"Just because it's aimed at a particular market means it's not art?" I say.

Tina nods once. "Exactly."

I frown. "What if I take a work of art and market it? It's still art, right?"

"You can't take artwork and just tweak it to be more commercially appealing." She sips at her beer. "Not without destroying its artistic merit."

"Tina, this is so crap," 6 says, standing up. "If I showed you a painting but didn't tell you whether it was created by a starving artist or an agency commissioned to produce it, you couldn't tell me whether it was art or not."

"Oh, I think I'd be able to tell," Tina says.

6 shifts impatiently. "Who cares what the intent was? It's the *result* that matters."

"The intent is not divorceable from the result," Tina says. "I know you people don't want to face that, but it's true."

"*You* don't want to face the fact that marketing is the greatest producer of art on the planet. There's packaging, copy, TV advertising—can you tell me why that's not art?"

"If you can't make that distinction yourself, I won't be able to explain it to you."

"Oh, right," 6 says, "you think some hack's poems that no one ever reads are more important than a movie half the world sees? A lot more people have seen a Coke can than a van Gogh."

"I've noticed you corporate people do this," Tina says. "Confuse popularity with quality."

"It's a democratic society, Tina," 6 says. "Your opinion of what's quality is no more valid than mine. Popularity *is* quality. And so marketers *are* today's real artists."

"Drink, anyone?" I say.

scat gets clueless

Most people—including Cindy—leave by midnight, but a lot stay on until about one. A few hang around until two, when Tina disappears into her bedroom with James, and a few obnoxious assholes don't leave until it's three A.M. and I open the door and point to it.

6 has spent the last hour watching *Clueless*, which Tina has on tape, and I can't work out whether it's weirder that Tina has this or that 6 is watching it. "Well," I say. "That's the last of them."

6 ignores me. Alicia Silverstone says, "As *if.*"

"So," I say carefully, sliding onto the sofa next to 6, "I guess it's just you and me."

6 frowns slightly but doesn't take her eyes off the screen. This

is a little disconcerting, and I bite my lip for a second, then shuffle a little closer. 6's frown deepens, but again that's the limit of her reaction.

I'm not sure if she's deliberately brushing me off or just really absorbed in the movie. I struggle between the two for a moment before realizing I should just find out.

So I do.

a stolen kiss

I lean in fast, but even so she beats me easily. With my lips puckered and heading for her cheek, she whirls and slaps both hands on my cheeks, catching me smack in mid-descent.

"God *damn!*" I yell. I pull my head free and jump up from the sofa, my cheeks burning. "God *damn!* What was *that?*"

6 rises from the sofa, her eyes like black flames. Her voice is low and murderous. "What do you think you're doing?"

"I'm *kissing* you! What do you *think* I'm doing?"

"We need to get something straight," 6 says. "Whatever might have happened between us at Coke, I am *not* your little woman."

I gape. "Little—?"

"You think it's all over," 6 says, as if she is amazed. "You think because of what happened at Coke, it's over. Well it's not. Do you understand that?"

"6, I just wanted a *kiss.*" I rub my cheeks. "*You've* kissed *me* twice."

"What's your point?"

"My *point* is that you're a control freak." 6's eyes widen. "You want to keep me on a leash, so every time—"

"This is *so* not true," 6 says.

"Is so," I say, a little sullenly. Doesn't really match the rest of my argument to date.

"You need to realize something, Scat," 6 tells me, leaning

close. I try to act nonchalant, but don't even get close. "You can't *ever* take me for granted."

a stolen kiss [2]

When the credits roll on *Clueless*, we make up our sofa-floor bedding combination in silence. We plant our backs to one another and, feeling resentful, I don't even try to modulate my breathing.

I'm annoyed with 6. Now, I know I have a long tradition of being wrong, but here I'm fairly sure I'm right. If 6's behavior doesn't qualify as mixed signals, I'm giving up on relationships.

Growing steadily more righteous, I start running through a few revised arguments in my head, making my points clearly and effectively in all of them. However, they all seem to end up with 6 apologizing profusely, and that's just too implausible to swallow.

Despite this, I eventually slip into a light doze and dream something weird involving Sneaky Pete and a cactus. It's one of those dreams where everything is spinning out of control, and there's so much going on in my head that a vague rustling from the sofa takes a long time to pierce my consciousness. It could be minutes before I become aware that 6 is leaning over me.

I concentrate on not moving, which is a little difficult since my heart and lungs immediately shift into fourth. 6's scent teases my nostrils, and I even feel her hair tickling my chest. I have no idea what she's doing, but I'm willing to take the risk that it's good.

Then she moves, and with dismay I realize she's leaving. But she's not. Like a brush from angel wings, I feel the unmistakable contact of 6's lips on mine.

action and reaction

At this point, I'm very, very lucky.

You see, my reaction is instinctive. The kiss is so unexpected that I have no chance of controlling my body's response. A few of the less appealing possibilities include snorting, gasping, and sitting bolt upright and screaming.

Fortunately, I do none of these. Instead, my entire body, maybe figuring that this display of affection from 6 must be a dream, shuts down. I don't freeze, I *relax*. I've never felt so relaxed in my life. It's like her lips have drugged me.

6 hovers above me for a few more moments: I feel her there. Then, perhaps satisfied, she rolls over and resumes her position on the sofa, her back to mine. I slip back to sleep like it's the easiest thing in the world, and I don't dream at all.

welcome to the weekend

We're woken by Tina snapping a Polaroid of us, which ensures that 6 starts the day in a foul mood. She mutters about privacy and Tina mutters about whose apartment it is and in the end I have to cook breakfast and talk inanely about the weather.

The whole morning feels very strange until I realize that for the first time in a long while, 6 and I don't have anything to do. We have the whole weekend to kill: no deadlines, no last-minute struggles, no panic. It almost feels illegal.

Midmorning, 6 takes me shopping for new clothes. I try to tell her that unless my new clothes cost less than sixteen dollars, I can't buy anything, but she produces her credit card. "We'll get a budget from Coke. Trust me, if we're successful, we can charge whatever we like."

"Really?" I say. "Wow. What if we're not successful?"

"Then," she says, "it will be the least of our problems."

6 is a dynamo: she stalks through shops like a commando, her eyes flicking from one rack to another. Occasionally she rests her hand on a jacket or a pair of pants, which is my signal to go try it on. Then she studies me, which is pretty unnerving but also pretty exciting, and makes the final decision. We buy everything I try on, and by the time we get back to Tina's, we've totaled up just over five thousand dollars' worth of purchases.

In the afternoon, Tina drags us to an all-day film festival in Santa Monica, which turns out to be such an astounding bore that I vow to never see an independent film again. After fidgeting through a thirty-minute epic about a man who wanders around Hollywood telling people, "Bluebird," 6 and I walk out. That night, Tina tries to explain that it was a heartfelt examination of mankind's failure to acknowledge nature as the precept of civilization, and I nearly throw my takeout at her.

Around seven I ask 6 if she wants to go for a couple of drinks down by the beach, and she actually agrees. We take Tina's car and watch the sun set over the Rollerblades and bikinis.

By the time we get home, it's eleven o'clock and we're both tanked. In the bathroom, I boldly peck 6 on the cheek and she glances at me in a way that I could swear is affectionate. When we go to bed, she lets one forearm dangle off the sofa so that her fingers graze my arm but acts like she doesn't know she's doing it, and I could believe that this is the best night of my life.

mktg case study #13: mktg magazines

GIVE AWAY FREE CRAP (PREFERABLY ADVERTISER-SUPPLIED FREE CRAP). DOESN'T MATTER HOW WORTHLESS OR USELESS IT IS: SALES WILL RISE. STRANGE BUT TRUE.

a day of rest

I wake on Sunday and spend ten minutes just looking at 6. She is splayed out across the sofa, her face hidden in a mass of midnight hair, and with the soft orange sun teasing at her it's like I'm looking at a vision. I don't notice that Tina has emerged from the bedroom until she speaks.

"Hey," she says quietly. I look up, startled, but she's smiling. "Coffee?"

love and success

"Have you told her?" We're sitting on the steps outside, nursing coffees while bums and kids in baggy jeans trawl the street.

I feign confusion. "Told her . . . ?"

Tina rolls her eyes. "That you're in love with her."

I splutter into my coffee. "Hey, I never said anything about—"

"Scat," Tina says. "It's obvious."

I search Tina's eyes for a way out and fail to find one. I sigh. "Yes, I told her."

Tina snickers.

"What?"

"You're screwed." She takes an impressive swig of her coffee.

"Pardon me?"

"She didn't say it back, did she?"

"Uh," I say. "Well, you know, not everything is said in so many words . . ." Tina's green eyes bore into me. "No."

"Oh, *brother*," Tina says, shaking her head.

"So help me." For a moment, the irony of asking Tina for relationship advice is dizzying. "What should I do?"

"Look for a new girl," Tina says shortly.

"Tina, that's not very helpful."

"Okay, fine. You want 6? Be a bastard."

"I don't want to be a bastard."

"Oh, sure you do," Tina says airily.

"Tina," I say levelly, "I'm not every man you've ever dated, okay?"

"Ooooh," Tina says. "Look, it's true. It's how she is. She won't respect you unless you don't let her control you. And that means you have to fight her."

I boggle. "She'd whip my butt."

"So, like I said," Tina says, growing bored of the conversation, "find another girl."

I watch the street for a moment. "Can't I just win her admiration and affection by proving to be a spectacular public success?"

"Yeah, well," Tina says, "whichever you think is easier."

the end of innocence

6 is showered and prowling the kitchen in Tina's pajamas when we come back up, and she regards us both suspiciously. "Hi, 6," Tina says flippantly, and 6's eyes narrow even further.

"So," I say, a little too heartily. "What do you want to do today? Go see a movie? A real one?"

"We're going home," 6 says. "We need to prepare for tomorrow."

"What? Prepare how?"

"We need to anticipate Sneaky Pete's attack," she says, sawing through a loaf of bread. "And prepare our response."

"Aw, 6 . . ." After a whole day of not having to worry about any of this stuff, I'm reluctant to give up my chance at another. "Can't we leave it until tonight? It's a beautiful day out there."

6 doesn't even bother to answer. I gloomily start getting my stuff together, and by one we're on the bus.

last rites

It feels very different at Synergy. At Tina's, it was possible to ignore the fact that Sneaky Pete is waiting for us on Monday. Here, it's not. Here, it feels like Sneaky Pete is oozing out of the walls.

6 settles into her Captain Kirk with a huge notepad. I pace the room and occasionally kick around the crumpled-up bits of paper that 6 throws onto the floor. "So what do you think he's going to do?"

6 frowns, still writing. "Sabotage the project."

"What?" I say, genuinely surprised. "But it's still his movie. He's VP Marketing."

6 sighs and runs her fingers through her hair, unexpectedly exposing an expanse of soft, gleaming neck. It's so abruptly erogenous that I feel a little dizzy. "Sneaky Pete's already proved himself. If it crashes now, after we start making changes, who do you think will be blamed?"

"Shit," I say reflectively.

"He'll disown himself from the movie now. Find something to take him away from it. That way its failure will be entirely our responsibility."

"Failure? How can it fail?"

6 sighs, not answering.

night moves

I cook up some fettuccine in 6's tiny kitchen while she scribbles late into the night. By the time we're ready for bed, it's nearly midnight and Sneaky Pete is just eight hours away.

I'm cleaning my teeth with a brush I stole from Tina's, ready to retire to my closet space for the night, when 6 pauses outside the door. I look up at her expectantly, but she just hovers there, her red satin pajamas shimmering at me. I stare at her for a second, caught between the pros and cons of trying to speak through a mouthful of paste.

"Scat," 6 says hesitantly. "We're partners, right?"

I nod. "Mmm-hmm."

She nods. "So—we're in this together." She nods again.

I wonder if it would be bad etiquette to spit at this juncture, and decide probably yes.

"It's cold," 6 says suddenly, apparently deciding to change tack. "Isn't it? This place gets cold at night."

"Mmm," I say noncommittally.

6 stares at me for a moment and she really seems caught up in something. Her brow furrows. "If you wanted," she begins reluctantly, and it looks as if the words are killing her. "If it made sense to you—" She stops.

I raise my eyebrows encouragingly.

"Oh, fuck it," 6 says. "You can sleep with me tonight."

I spit.

sex

Imagine that a huge new billboard is erected along Sunset Drive. And this billboard, instead of carrying an advertisement for Pepsi or American Express or Ray•Ban, sports a naked woman. A very naked woman. Naked, smiling, reclining. A *Playboy* centerfold, splashed across one of the most famous streets in the world.

On the day this billboard went up, massive crowds would surround it. People would hear about it, go, "No way," and zip down for a look. Protesters would gather within hours. Traffic would back up for five miles (or, at least, five miles further than usual).

Imagine that, for whatever reason, this billboard stays exactly where it is. Congress misfiled the Decency Act 1991 and now they just can't find it anywhere. That naked woman just stays there.

For the next month, men all over the city would be making unnecessary detours past it. They'd be gathering in groups, saying, "Hey, want to go down to the picture of the naked babe?" A nightclub would immediately spring up on the opposite side of the road.

But it wouldn't last. It would take a while, but, eventually, no one would notice the billboard at all.

Because sex isn't sex at all.

It's marketing.

sex, sex, sex

If you have a men's magazine in the vicinity, I'd like you to flip to the "model profile" section. You know, the part where the mag quits pretending it's in the business of producing high-brow fiction and informative reports on the decline of efficient manufacturing processes in America and gets down to the business of showing pictures of naked women.

There will be a few models, so you'll have to pick one. Stacy. Fine. You'll notice that the first page shows a picture of Stacy's face. Just her face. There will be a little text, like: "Stacy is a dental assistant, but wants to travel the world. Her interests include opera, white-water rafting and men with hard cocks." (Incidentally, I can't help but wonder if the magazine adds that last bit themselves. I see Stacy at home three weeks later, flipping through her advance copy, going, " 'Men with hard cocks'? I just said opera and rafting! Man, that changes the whole context!")

On the next page, you'll see Stacy's face and Stacy's buttocks. You will probably also see a hint of breast, but only a hint. Stacy will be half out of four different outfits, as if she's the world's sloppiest dresser. Then, on the next page, Stacy's breasts will pop free. You'll see them from the side and you'll see them from the front, and there's a fair bet you'll also see Stacy cupping them with an expression of utter surprise, as if she's never noticed them there before.

In one of the pictures, you'll see a few strands of Stacy's pubic hair, but you have to turn the page again to get any further. And there it will be: Stacy completely naked, saying, "Okay, I've got nothing left now. All my clothes are gone. Go on, you might as well take a look."

Now, my point is this: What are all the previous pictures for? If you want to see Stacy's breasts, well, there they are, on the last page. There is, in fact, everything that was peeking out from behind this and half hidden behind that in all the other pictures.

The answer is marketing. Stacy has been marketed to you.

You could produce a magazine with page after page of naked women, just standing there. But it wouldn't be right. It wouldn't even be erotic. It would be like those articles in *Cosmo* ("Are Your Breasts Normal?") where six average girls decide to expose themselves to the nation—but even worse, because at least with *Cosmo* there's the clandestine satisfaction of knowing they didn't *mean* to be perved at.

What it comes down to, you see, is that a naked body is just a naked body.

But the *possibility* of a naked body is something special.

sex and 6

"You stay on that side," 6 warns me, gesturing. Her pajamas ripple like a deep, mysterious pool.

"Okay," I say, slipping under the covers. I discover that 6 has an electric blanket and the bed is like a little furnace.

"And don't *fidget*," 6 says, frowning at me. "You tend to fidget. Don't do that."

"Okay," I say again, wiggling my toes. So warm.

"Good," she says, pulling up the covers.

We lie there together on our backs. 6's Barbie lamp fills the room with soft yellow light, illuminating her miniature TV and vast collection of pop culture posters. Gillian Anderson in particular seems to be eyeing me suspiciously.

"This is really cozy," I say to the ceiling.

6 says nothing.

"Much warmer than my room. Thanks for letting me move in here." I glance across, but she's biting her lip and staring at the ceiling. I sigh. "You know, 6, I understand that right now you're having some doubts about me being here. Suddenly I'm all over your personal space, and you're wondering if maybe you made a mistake."

She turns and regards me. The lamp is behind her, so her face is mostly in darkness. Her eyes are big black lagoons.

"I want you to know that I'm cool with your mixed signals," I say. "In fact, I'm kind of getting used to it. So don't worry. I can take it."

6 is silent.

"I love you." It's a little risky, but it comes out okay: casual but sincere. I leave a pause, just in case 6 is inspired to do some declaring of her own, but to tell the truth, I'm never very hopeful. When it's obvious there will be no new developments tonight, I lean over to kiss her cheek. I go in slowly, in case she's in a retaliatory mood, but she doesn't move at all. I plant a gentle kiss, kind of amazed that she's allowing me to do it, then I roll over so my back is to her. I feel very satisfied.

6 lies there for a long time, maybe five minutes. Then I hear her lean over and flick off the lamp. We both lie awake in the darkness for a while, and when I fall asleep I haven't once thought about Sneaky Pete.

Backlash

CHAPTER 000013

it begins

So it's Monday morning.

For some reason this phrase sticks in my head. When I wake, a good thirty minutes before the six A.M. alarm, it's the first thing that enters my brain. As I lie in the darkness, it's like an annoying pop song, going around and around. When the radio kicks into the LA traffic report and 6 slowly raises her head from the pillow, her hair like a brewing storm, I see it in her face.

There's not much conversation: we just get up and get ready. It's a very still morning, and while we wait for the bus—me in a navy jacket and cream pants, 6 in a truly stunning deep red suit—it's so quiet that I could almost swear Venice is deserted.

You can see the hulking Coke building from the 10 a good five minutes before we actually get there, and 6 grips my hand. I turn to her, surprised. Her face set in a hard mask.

"We can do this," she says grimly. "Whatever he tries, we are going to do this."

Coke is busy and cheerful when we arrive, which is a bit of a clash with our tense moods. A couple of suits catch us in the elevator and enthusiastically congratulate us on last Friday, and 6 fields them with short nods until they get out on the 10th.

The elevator doors slide open on the 14th, and, as if we're expecting Sneaky Pete to be hiding around the corner, neither of us moves. Finally, 6 takes a deep breath and strides out.

Of course, everything looks normal. There are people gathered around the coffee machine, talking about the Lakers, and the ubiquitous chatter of keyboards is almost mundane. It looks exactly the same as when I was here last, until 6 nods toward an empty office. "Brennan's. Now Sneaky Pete's."

I peer inside. "He's not here yet?"

"No," she says, frowning. This obviously bothers her, and that it bothers her scares the hell out of me.

She leads me toward a secretary, a tiny wide-eyed woman with huge golden earrings. "Hi, Pam," 6 says distractedly. "Where's my new office?"

"Oh, I haven't been told," Pam says, and I abruptly realize that this is the woman who sounds like my mother. Seeing her in the flesh is something of a relief: she doesn't look like Mom at all. I have closure. "Maybe Mr. Pete will tell you at the meeting."

6's eyebrows rise. "Meeting?"

"Oh, yes," Pam says. "He's called a meeting at nine, in the boardroom. To introduce himself."

"I see," 6 says slowly. "Thanks."

"No problem," Pam says, sinking back to her monitor. "And, 6—welcome back."

6 ignores her, staring at the carpet. "A *meeting*."

gathering

To save us from having to hang around the coffee machine, 6 se-
cures a meeting room and we burn the forty-five minutes by pacing, staring out at the cubicles and drinking coffee. I have to also
make a pit stop, but 6 displays impressive bladder control by
sinking three coffees without leaving the room.

A couple of minutes before nine, a visible ripple sweeps the
floor. I suddenly see heads turning, phones being put down, people leaning together.

"It's time," 6 says, standing. "Let's go."

@

The troops are chatting bravely en route to the boardroom,
but there's nervous tension in the air. I guess that's inevitable
when the VP of your department gets sacked, and I also guess
that when his replacement is someone like Sneaky Pete, a lot of
people start wondering about job security.

We file into the boardroom, and I wonder about the coincidence of meeting here so soon after Friday's triumph. Maybe it's
nothing; maybe Sneaky Pete was late getting onto the room
booking system and this was all there was left. But I don't think
so. I think he's trying to tell us something.

He's already seated at the head of the table, sprawled out in his
three-thousand-dollar suit. He looks relaxed, prepared. His dark
sunglasses regard me blankly.

Then my eye is caught by the person sitting next to him. It's a
girl, and she is the blondest person I've seen in my life. Her skin
is virgin snow and matched by hair so white it seems to glow, the
effect is slightly blinding. From an exquisitely manufactured face,
eyes like blue pilot lights watch me coolly.

People bump around looking for chairs, but the girl doesn't

wait for them. "Ladies and gentlemen," she says, "thank you for coming."

I look at Sneaky Pete in surprise, but apparently the girl is now doing his speaking for him. He is looking only at me.

"My name is @," the girl says, "and I am Mr. Pete's personal assistant." Her eyes sweep the room, and nobody even sniggers. "Let's talk about change."

6 fumes

°•.°°°•. : •°•°•°•.° .°°.°°•°•° .°•° •°°•° •°

There's a coffee break at 10:30, and 6 and I take the opportunity to talk in an adjoining meeting room. "You should be flattered," I say. "It's really a compliment."

"It's a *copy*," 6 spits. She's actually pacing. "He's *stolen* me."

"Well," I start, then suddenly I can't really think of anything to say. I stretch. "You'll always be the original."

6 stares at me.

"Hey, 6," I say, trying to comfort, "it shows he's worried. It shows he's so impressed by you that he had to make a copy."

"I'm surprised he didn't call her *5*," 6 mutters.

a smattering of mktg

°•.°°°•. : •°•°•°•.° .°°.°°•°•° .°•° •°°•° •°

Until the break, it's all been routine. Sneaky Pete wants updates on a half dozen projects, @ tells us; he's nominating coffee as a Tier Two competitor to Coke (which for one thing means the communal coffee machine has to go), and he wants to see a cost-benefit analysis from Sponsorship. But nobody loses their jobs and @ never once mentions *Backlash*.

When we arrive back, the pace changes. "Many of you will have heard," @ says, raking the room with her baby blues, "that the project *Backlash* has been taken out of Mr. Pete's direct responsibility. Given the demands of his new role, he will not be able to continue personal involvement. The new project leaders, Mr. Scat and Miss 6, will carry it through to completion."

This is precisely what 6 anticipated. I glance at her, but her eyes are fixed on @.

"We would like to make it clear to Scat and 6 that if any difficulties arise, Mr. Pete and myself will immediately make ourselves available. But he relies on you to alert him."

I almost snort. I'm no master of politics, but even I can see that the only reason to announce this in public is so there are witnesses later.

"In the interim," @ announces, "Mr. Pete has formed a crossfunctional management committee to serve as an advisory body and clearinghouse for *Backlash*. At least one manager from each department is serving on this committee, to ensure that Scat and 6 have the support of the entire organization."

"Excuse me," 6 says slowly, "but did you say this committee is a *clearinghouse?*"

"Yes," @ says, eyeing 6 warily.

"And what does that mean, exactly?"

"It means that the committee will approve or reject your suggestions, depending on their suitability. Given you have only just returned to Coca-Cola, it is appropriate that experienced staff be able to guide you where necessary."

6 grits her teeth. "Are you telling me that we need to have our every move *approved?* By a committee of accountants, engineers and administrators?"

"Each person on the team," @ says, a little hostility creeping into her tone, "has at least some marketing knowledge."

6 freezes.

"I don't get it," I say in the elevator.

"You will," 6 says morosely.

"So we have to get everything approved by this committee? How bad is that? They'll probably be a great help. And you know, if things go wrong, it's almost like we've got someone else to blame."

"It's all responsibility and no control," 6 says. "The classic path to failure."

"Oh, I get it," I say as the elevator doors slide open. "You don't like losing control."

6 turns and stares at me. "Scat," she says testily, "I know that you enjoy psychoanalyzing me, but not everything I say is evidence of some deep personality trait. Sometimes I'm just telling you what's going on. Got it?"

"Oh," I say, a bit taken aback.

"We're being measured on the success of the movie," 6 says, stepping into the corridor, "but the committee has the power to prevent us from making it a success. We therefore lose control of our own destiny. This is not a good thing."

"Oh," I say, catching up. "So we avoid the committee? Go around them?"

"It won't be that easy," 6 says. "They're signing the checks. But we'll do what we have to." She stops and stares at the office coffee machine for a moment, perhaps bidding it a silent farewell.

"Hey," I say. "How bad can this committee be? I mean, most of the time they'll just have to go on our say-so. Right?"

6 sighs.

"In here," Pam says, holding the door open for us.

I'm stunned, staring open-mouthed at the vast space, the indoor fernery, the tremendous views.

"We have to share?" 6 says, sounding faintly disgusted.

"I'm really sorry, 6," Pam gushes. "We're short on office space. We're converting some meeting rooms next month."

"Wow," I say, fingering a fern.

"Does @ get her own office?" 6 demands.

"Uh, I don't know," Pam squeaks unconvincingly.

6 sighs.

"I'll leave you to it," Pam says, escaping. She shuts the door behind her.

"This is *fantastic*." I walk over and press my face against the floor-to-ceiling window. "Look how small the *people* are down there."

6 ignores me, and I hear her pushing buttons on her personal percolator. I bet there will be some fiery words when they try to pry that away from her.

"Wow," I say again.

"Scat," 6 says tersely, "if we're going to share an office, we need to establish some ground rules."

"Oh," I say. "Okay."

"For one, don't gawk out the window. You look like a six-year-old."

"Sorry."

"And if you have a meeting with someone in here, don't lean right back in the chair, even though they tilt."

"They do?" I ask, interested. I reach over and swing one, just to check.

"Don't do it," 6 warns. "You feel confident, but you look pompous."

"Ah." I let the chair spring back.

"Make sure that the desk is always clean, but keep the In tray piled right up," 6 says. "You're busy, but efficient."

"Got it."

"Don't put any personal effects on the desk—no family photos, no cute little quotes, nothing."

"How come?"

"It emphasizes your personal side," 6 says, "and therefore your vulnerability."

I frown. "What are these? The rules of engagement?"

"Just do it," 6 says wearily.

fiscal salvation

We spend our first morning running through status reports. Brennan has been commissioning reports from everyone even remotely connected to the film, and we plow through four months' worth before realizing that they all say the same thing: things are going just fine.

In the afternoon, 6 goes through the schedules and I try to study the expense reports. At 7:30, she catches me staring out the window. "Something you need?"

"6," I say, pained, "can we take a break? There's only so much I can read about budgets."

"Fine," 6 says, closing her folder. I notice that she doesn't appear tired at all. 6 looks like she always does: alert and wary. "Let's call it a night."

"We should hurry. There's a 7:42 bus." Although I'm not particularly looking forward to half an hour in a freezing tin can trying to avoid eye contact with potential psychopaths.

"We're not taking the bus anymore," 6 says. She pulls open a drawer and removes an envelope. "Coke pays the bills now." From the envelope, she pulls out a credit card–sized object and slides it across the desk to me. I realize, hardly daring to believe it, that this credit card–sized object, its face glinting gold in the evening sun, is, in fact, a gold credit card.

"Corporate cards," 6 says. "Charge everything on them."

"Oh," I say, feeling close to tears. The end of my poverty rises before me like a big gold credit card. "Okay."

the schedule

6 unlocks and I go into the kitchen to scrounge up dinner while she pokes hopefully at the answering machine. The sum total of 6's larder is a half dozen eggs, a Mr. Goodbar hidden underneath a box of cereal, and an old, old bagel, but I manage to get a couple of omelets out of it anyway. 6 is impressed but tries not to show it.

We meet in the bathroom and eye each other while brushing our teeth, then have a small face-off over who is going to leave so the other can go to the toilet, which ends up being me. When I finally make it to bed, I am stunned to see 6 sitting up with a report, the manila folder illuminated by her Barbie lamp. "You've got to be kidding me. You're not seriously going to keep working."

"According to this," 6 says, not looking up from her folder, "we have two months to finish this thing."

"Sounds like plenty of time," I say, hoping to induce 6 to put down her folder.

"Mmm," 6 says distractedly, and flips the page.

review

"I don't know," Tom Cruise whispers. "I've never seen anything like it before."

"Let's junk it," I say. "Sounds like every other alien flick I've ever seen."

6 flicks the remote, freezing Tom just as he is reaching one gloved hand toward the alien spacecraft. "Scat, this is kind of important to the plot."

I sigh heavily.

"What?" 6 says.

"Well," I say, a little annoyed, "we've been here for three hours and you've knocked down every one of my ideas. I mean, do you want to fix this thing or not?"

"Yes, I do," 6 says, her lips tightening, "but preferably not by removing all sense from the plot."

"6, who cares if the plot's shaky? It's an ad."

"Scat, you obviously have no comprehension—" 6 begins, then stops. She stares at me for so long I shift in my chair.

"What?"

"You're right. You're absolutely right. I've been approaching this from the wrong angle." I gape, waiting for the thunderbolt to strike in retribution for such blasphemy. "I've been treating this like a movie. That's what Sneaky Pete did, too: he made a good movie. Now we need to make it into a good ad."

"So you want to hear my ideas again?"

"Scat," 6 says, "I want you to trash this thing. We're going to rebuild it from the ground up."

the new ad

"This whole deal with the aliens being all scary? No good. They should be cool. They should have personality. They should have one-liners."

6 scribbles on her notepad.

"And when they drink a Coke, they have to look like they're loving it. Everything else should stop. None of this just gulping it down and tossing the can away."

"Right," 6 says, writing.

"Speaking of which, how they've invaded Earth because they're addicted to Coke's secret ingredients—let's face it, that's never going to be plausible. We should acknowledge it's not plausible and just have fun with it."

"Mmm," 6 says. "Good thinking."

"As for the characters," I say, warming up, "if they were any stiffer, they'd be my dad. Everyone takes themselves way too seriously."

"You're right. There's no self-deprecating sense of humor."

"Uh, yeah." I glance across to see if she finds any irony in talking about a lack of humor, but apparently she doesn't. "For one, Winona is too totally evil. I like her evil, but she needs some kind of counterpoint, a contrast. I'd like her to get drunk on Coke, maybe even a little giggly. And then when she gets vicious, it's even nastier."

"Good," 6 says, writing this down.

"Oh, which reminds me," I say. "Can Winona have double layers of teeth? Just at the end, when she pulls back her lips?"

6 looks at me.

"Go on," I say. "It'll be cool."

She frowns, but writes it down.

"Gwyneth's character is total cardboard. She doesn't do anything but scream. She's gotta blast a few aliens of her own. And she should save Tom's ass at some point, too. As for Tom, we've got to change that first scene with him entering the space academy. It's so keen on making him out to be macho, it's just pathetic. I think we'd like him more if he got beaten in that first fight. Hey, how about *Gwyneth* beats him up?"

"Mmm," 6 says. "Intriguing."

"Just some ideas," I say modestly. "Just throwing them out there."

"I like it." She sits back. "Now, this is where things get tough. We need to push all this through the committee."

"Oh, right," I say. "The committee. When do we actually meet those guys?"

"Tomorrow," 6 says, a grimace flickering across her face. "Wednesday. Our first review meeting."

I frown. "You keep hinting how bad this committee is going to be. Are you going to tell me why?"

6 sighs heavily. "If there's anything worse than dealing with someone who knows nothing about marketing," she says wearily, "it's dealing with someone who knows a little."

"Ms. 6! Mr. Scat!" the financial controller says, grinning. He's a little man with small watery eyes and tight-bunched teeth. "How nice to finally meet you!"

"Hi," I say, and shake his paw. 6 just frowns.

"Come on in," he says. "Everyone's looking forward to meeting you." He ushers us into the boardroom, where perhaps ten men and women are scattered around the huge table. Abruptly—and very disconcertingly—all conversation dies and ten pairs of eyes swivel onto us.

"Take a seat, please," Finances says, moving to his own chair at the head of the table. "I must say, we're raring to go, Ms. 6 and Mr. Scat. I'm sure you'll find us full of bright ideas." He chuckles modestly. 6's face darkens.

"Well," 6 says, as we slide into the two spare chairs, "we have a few ideas at this point. But they're all quite minor. In fact, we probably shouldn't waste your valuable time discussing them. Perhaps we can just move on to—"

"Not at all," a portly man interrupts. According to his ID tag, he's from Logistics. "We're here to get our hands dirty." He smiles at her reassuringly.

"We all have a little marketing experience," a woman pipes up. Jean from Credit. "I did a half-day course, once."

"That's . . ." 6 says, then struggles to come up with something positive to finish with. ". . . fine. Then I'd like to gain your approval for the set of plot changes that Scat and I have developed. You should have all received a hard copy of these this morning. Did anyone not get that?" There is no hard copy, of course, and abruptly the room is filled with people frowning and complaining about the mail room. "Never mind. I'll just summarize them for you."

She almost gets through our entire list of changes before Logistics interrupts. "Let me add something to that," he says. "Everyone here has seen that *Diet Life* film that these guys created, right? Well, the actress in that was sensational. I think we should grab her for *Backlash*."

My jaw drops. "Cindy?"

Heads nod wisely all around me. "Agreed," Credit says. "I loved that bathroom scene. And she's so pretty."

"She has real presence," Finances says. "We'd be fools not to use her. Fools."

"Well," 6 says, shooting me a glance, "I'm sure we can use her as an extra somewhere. Now, my second proposal—"

"*I* think," Finances interrupts, "we should consider her for a *serious* role."

"Could we put an unknown into a large role with all those big stars?" a woman muses. I can't read her tag, but I'm guessing from her tight brown suit and hair that she's a bigwig in Accounting. "It might seem strange."

"Then maybe," Logistics says ominously, leaning forward, "we should *market* her."

Silence, as the room digests this.

"Could you explain that remark, please?" 6 says.

"*Apparently,*" Logistics says, sharing a secret, "Hollywood studios have been renaming stars for years. To make them more appealing to the public. Big stars, like Kirk Douglas and even *John Wayne*"—his eyes sweep the room—"used to have stupid, hard-to-remember names. But with a new name, they became famous." He tips a wink in my direction. "Perception is reality."

I struggle mightily against the urge to lean across the table and smack him. Saying *Perception is reality* to a marketer as if you're handing out clever advice is grossly insulting. It's like saying to an accountant: *Now make sure those numbers add up;* or to a new mother: *You know, you have to feed them or they die.* Never, never do it.

"So we should rename Cindy?" Accounting muses. "To make her more appealing to the audience?"

"*Cindy* is pretty easy to remember," I say.

"Let's call her something *special,*" Personnel says eagerly. "Something that really stands out. Like . . . um . . . Cindy Cindy."

" 'Cindy Cindy'?" I say, appalled.

"How about Cindy Star?" Accounting offers. "Since she's going to be one?"

"Cindy Hollywood," someone else says. Kelvin, Manufacturing.

"Holly Hollywood," Logistics says, his eyes lighting up.

"Cindy Starholly, maybe. No, Starry Cindwood."

"Cindy Star."

"I *said* that," Accounting says scathingly.

"Let's call her," Manufacturing says with relish, "Babe-A-Licious."

The room falls silent. I, too, am stunned at the utter gall of Manufacturing to brazenly throw up such a truly pathetic suggestion.

"That's *brilliant*," Personnel says admiringly.

"Good job," Logistics says. "I like it."

"*Excuse* me," I say, "but we're not calling her Babe-A-Licious."

"Now, let's give this some consideration," Finances says. "Babe-A-Licious. Intriguing."

"You wouldn't forget that in a hurry," Manufacturing says, sitting back in satisfaction.

"I'm *sorry*," I say. "But it's ridiculous."

Eyes widen around the room. 6 says quickly, "What Scat is trying to say is that it may not be appropriate. It may lack . . . credibility."

"*I* think it's *innovative*," Accounting says. "Very . . . uh . . . top-of-mind." There is a murmur of appreciation at her successful employment of a marketing term. "*Very* top-of-mind," Accounting confirms, nodding.

"Our customers would really go for it," Credit says. "You know, young, hip . . . Babe-A-Licious. It suits our, uh, demographic."

Another marketing term, and now Credit earns a ripple of approval. This is starting to resemble a particular recurring dream I have where the entire world goes insane.

"Is it agreed, then?" Finances asks, pleased with the committee's productivity.

"It certainly is *not*," I say.

Finances turns to me, frowning. "Then perhaps, Mr. Scat," he says, "you can tell us why."

I open my mouth to tell them it's goddamned stupid, then realize I already said that. Then I start to say it's cheap and tacky and realize 6 covered that with her credibility comment.

"Well?"

"It will detract from the impact of the movie," I throw in desperately. "Distract the market from the movie itself."

This sends the room into a moment of introspection, but only a moment. Then Accounting says, "If you're referring to *split focus,* Mr. Scat, I'm sorry, but I don't agree. I think Babe-A-Licious would actually be an added feature."

I start to protest, but Accounting's cunning use of more marketing-speak has won the room. "Then it's settled," Finances says. "Babe-A-Licious it is."

damage assessment

"Oh boy," I say. "Oh boy. Oh, *boy.*"

6 stares at me from across her desk. Or rather, our desk, except somehow only 6 seems to be sitting on the right side of it. "This is going to be difficult."

"Oh?" Stupid sarcasm rises in my throat. "You think so? You know, I thought maybe things were going along just fine. I mean, sure, our film now stars Tom Cruise, Winona Ryder and *Babe-A-Licious,* but—"

"Scat, shut up," 6 says tiredly.

"Fine," I say, a little hysterically. "I'll just sit here and wait for you to come up with an idea that will save us. Okay? Because we know *you're* full of great ideas."

6 stares at me impassively. "Scat, you're embarrassing yourself."

"I won't do it," I say suddenly. "I'll just refuse to do what they say. What can they do?"

"Fire you."

"Assholes."

"Yes," 6 says, "but we are forced to bow to the wishes of those assholes. We need to find a solution that satisfies both their requirements and ours."

"Seeing as their requirements are to bugger the film with a barge pole," I say aggressively, "that could be difficult. You know?"

"Scat, you're too emotionally involved," 6 tells me, frowning. "It's impairing your performance."

"*They're* impairing my performance!" I shout dramatically. I stand up and start pacing. "Can't we go over their heads?"

"To Sneaky Pete?" 6 says, raising an eyebrow.

"Then let's go over *Sneaky Pete's* head."

"To *Jamieson?* You can try."

"Okay," I say, "I will. I'll tell Jamieson that I can't do my job because of that stupid committee."

"Fine." 6 actually picks up the phone and punches in an extension. "Talk to him." She holds the handset out to me.

For a second I stare at her. She stares back. "All right," I say, taking the phone. "Fine."

"Jamieson."

"Mr. Jamieson. It's Scat. How are you?"

He sounds distracted. "Great, Scat. What's up?"

"Look," I say. "We're having a small problem here. I'm hoping you can straighten it out."

There is a pause. "What problem?"

"You brought us onboard to improve this film, right? Well, we're trying to do that. But we're getting blocked."

"By who?"

"Well, there's this committee—"

"I know about it. What's the problem?"

"They're an obstacle," I say. "We have to get them to approve everything. And they're . . . difficult to deal with." I glance at 6, who is regarding me steadily.

"Scat, let's get something straight," Jamieson says. "You've been with the company two days. You're involved in the most significant marketing project this company has ever initiated. I'm not going to entrust the whole damn thing to you with no checks and balances."

I swallow. "Sure. But if I'm going to do this—"

"Scat, I'm in a bit of a hurry here. Is there some reason you can't sort this out with Sneaky Pete?"

"Well," I say, "he's . . ." I struggle for an explanation that won't get me fired. "Hard to get hold of."

"He's your boss. Talk to him. We don't have a chain of command for nothing."

"I—"

"Thanks for calling, Scat," Jamieson says, and hangs up.

I stare at the handset for a moment.

"Well," 6 says. "Feel better?"

"I should have told him about Sneaky Pete," I say. "Told him how he's trying to ruin the movie just to discredit us."

"That's a serious accusation," 6 says, flipping through her desk calendar. "Got proof?"

"Uh," I say.

"Then maybe you should just threaten to quit," 6 says. She looks up. "You want to do that? Since things are so tough? Just bail out of the biggest marketing project in history?"

She waits me out.

"No," I say.

subliminal buy messages popcorn

"Now we need to work the committee very carefully," 6 says. "It was a mistake to try to bulldoze them. We need to feed them suggestions, so they come up with the ideas we want them to. We need to guide them without letting them know we're doing it."

"Huh," I say. "Nice theory."

"It can be done," 6 says. "I'll give you an example."

"Look, 6," I say impatiently, "I know you're a very good negotiator and all that. But we're dealing with a pack of utter

215

morons. We can't rely on them to do anything except come up with the most stupid solution to any given problem."

"Hmm," 6 muses. "That's a good point."

I blink. "Well, thanks."

"So are you saying," 6 says, frowning, "that there is some kind of method in their madness?"

"Well, they obviously *think* they know what marketing's about."

"I see. So you mean, if a proposal makes sense to their warped idea of marketing, they'd go for it?"

"Uh," I say. "Well yeah, I guess they would."

"That's a great idea," 6 says approvingly. "So we couch our suggestions in terms that will appeal to their basic, misinformed beliefs. Good thinking."

"Uh, thanks," I say. "Huh, you know I didn't actually mean—" I trail off as I realize that 6 is staring at me in disbelief.

"I was *demonstrating,* you moron," she says. "*That's* how you feed someone a suggestion."

some direction

It's after eight, but neither of us suggests heading home. 6 is chewing through a stack of manila folders on crew logistics and I'm on the phone to *Backlash*'s director, trying to impart my ideas about identification.

"Yeah, look, I was told about all this," the director says. I think his name is Kline, but he is speaking with the short, impatient tone of one forced to deal with an idiot and I didn't quite catch it. "You think you have a lot of smart ideas."

"Hey, I'm not trying to tell you how to do your job," I say. "You're still the director here."

"You are damn right," Kline says.

"I do have a bunch of ideas. But I don't know how to make

them work on film. You know how to do that best." I bite my tongue, hoping that this is enough to soothe his ego.

"You go fuck yourself," Kline tells me, so I guess not. "I don't have to deal with you. I am busy here."

"I'm sorry but you do have to deal with me, you dumb shit," I say before he can hang up. It works: I hear his heavy breathing snuffling down the line. Across the desk, 6 looks up. "Maybe I didn't make this clear, but I'm holding the purse strings here. We can work together to make these changes, or you can get the fuck off my set."

There is a long, silent moment. Then Kline bursts out laughing. I smile reassuringly at 6, to let her know that Kline and I have just been through one of those little macho standoffs and emerged with a healthy, male respect for one another. 6 frowns.

"You must be a dumb ass," Kline says, startling me. "You are in charge of jack shit. Now you get off my phone. I have to call Mr. Pete."

"He isn't running this show any—"

Kline snorts. "You think what you like," he says, and the line goes dead.

scat gets obnoxious

"Now *that's* it," I say, slamming down the phone. "I'm going back to Jamieson."

"Sit *down*," 6 says.

"I'll get him to *make* Sneaky Pete tell Kline that we're in charge," I fume. "We can sit there and watch him make the call."

"Then what happens when we leave the room?" 6 asks. "He calls Kline back. Do you want to watch him twenty-four hours a day?"

"I can't believe this," I say. "He can't keep blocking us like this."

"Of course he can," 6 says irritably.

"If Jamieson knew what he was doing—"

"Scat, you're really beginning to bore me," 6 says. "You can stomp around and complain that the rules aren't fair, or you can grow up and start playing the game. Now what's it going to be?"

"Well," I say, a little sulkily. "Well, if you're going to be like that."

a tussle

We work until ten, which is the point where my head actually hits the desk. I snort and sit up to see 6 eyeing me. "Uh," I say. "Tired. Just a little tired."

"That's enough," 6 says. "Let's go."

"If you think so," I say lamely.

When we get back to Synergy, I'm so exhausted that I just brush, flush, and fall into bed. By the time 6 finishes in the bathroom, I'm already asleep, still in my suit. Then I become vaguely aware of her tugging at my feet. "Wa," I say, which I guess proves it's not just in the mornings that I get so eloquent. I eventually realize she's taking my shoes off, so I decide to fall asleep again.

"Roll over," 6 says, a million miles away.

"Wa," I mutter again, but I manage to roll. My face is enveloped by one of 6's soft pillows, and that's enough to put me out again. I fall into a dream where I'm fighting 6 for the world heavyweight boxing championship, and 6 is whipping my ass. Every time I swing at her, she ducks under my punch and lands a couple of body blows, her mouthguard grinning whitely at me. When I finally crash to the canvas in the fourth round, 6 has hardly worked up a sweat, and when I wake up the next morning I'm only wearing my boxers.

talent

"So," I say, taking a big bite of my toast, "you think we're still in this thing, or what?"

"Of course," 6 says, distaste flickering across her face at my table manners.

I swallow. "So what do we do today?"

"We go on location," 6 says, sipping at her coffee. "I'm going to talk to Kline and the assistant directors. You need to handle the talent. And when you've done that, get in touch with our post-production house and tell them what's going on."

"Mmm," I say, thinking of Winona Ryder. "Handle the talent."

"Which includes," 6 says, a little testily, "telling Cindy about her new name."

"Ah," I say.

on location

I'm surprised by how small it is. Obviously this isn't Universal's main lot, but even so: they've bought themselves an ancient, dust-blown airport halfway to Nevada and called it a studio. I can't believe that something as impressive as *Backlash* actually came out of here.

There's a single guard, who seems to have the backbreaking responsibility of protecting a vast amount of sand, and he ushers us straight through as soon as we identify ourselves. "Studio One," he tells us. I seriously doubt there's a Studio Two.

We find the entrance to the building, which is an old aircraft hangar, and step inside. And that's when I realize that this really is a movie set, and it really is serious, because there are maybe sixty people and twenty tons of equipment in here, and Gwyneth Paltrow is heading in my direction.

"Excuse me," she says, and pushes at the door 6 and I have just come through. It sticks in the sand. "God *damn*," Gwyneth says.

"Where is Gwyneth going with her *hair?*" a small man demands loudly, and from the voice this must be Kline. He is sitting in a huge mechanical contraption that looks like an antiaircraft gun, but I guess is just a big camera.

"I'm getting some *air,*" Gwyneth shouts.

"Air?" Kline shouts back. "There's plenty of air in here."

"Mr. Kline?" 6 says. He stops and peers at her, and Gwyneth takes the opportunity to slip outside.

"Damn it," Kline shouts. "Somebody go get Gwyneth."

"Mr. Kline, my name is 6," she says, striding toward him. "This is Scat. We're from Coke."

Kline stares at her for a moment, then sighs hugely, perhaps to show the crew exactly how tired he is of corporate interference from suits who wouldn't recognize a good film if it was projected on their butts in 70mm. "I'm on a schedule here. Can't it wait?"

"Of course it can," 6 says, which surprises me. "Don't let me get in your way, Mr. Kline. Just let me know when you have a free minute."

This obviously surprises Kline, too, because he blinks and is momentarily silent. I think he's almost disappointed that he doesn't get to have a public argument with his corporate backers. "Fine," Kline says. "I will let you know." He turns back to his antiaircraft gun and a short brunette with a clipboard.

"Now what?" I ask, looking around to see if I can spot Winona. "We twiddle our thumbs all day waiting for him?"

"He won't keep me waiting," 6 says, and she is also scanning the hangar, although I presume not for Winona. "When he sees me talking to a few of his key staff, he'll worry about what I'm doing and come see me."

"Oh." By now I'm no longer surprised by 6's business acumen. "So we've got a few minutes?" I am now thinking about wandering outside and accidentally bumping into Gwyneth.

"You," 6 says, "are making a call. Remember?"

"Oh yeah," I say, disappointed. "Cindy." I pull out my cellphone, then pause as a particularly sneaky idea occurs to me. "I'll go outside. For the reception."

6 looks at me.

"Reception," I say again, a little more desperately.

"Whatever," 6 says, and heads toward the first assistant director.

a conversation with babe-a-licious

I step out into a blast of desert sun, which makes it momentarily difficult to get a bead on Gwyneth. Then I spot her leaning against the hangar a bit further down and wander in her direction without trying to make it look too obvious. When I sneak a look, she's staring out at the desert, oblivious to my presence.

I dial Cindy and do a little desert-staring myself while it rings. Gwyneth notices me and squints in my direction, and I give her a smooth little eyebrow-raise just as Cindy picks up. I can't speak for Gwyneth, but I'm fairly impressed with me.

"Hello?"

"Hi, Cindy. How you doing?"

"Oh, *great,* Scat," she says, laying on the cheerfulness in thick, barbed slabs. "What do you need?"

"Now, you *see,*" I say obnoxiously, "you just *assume* I need something. As it happens, I've got an offer for you."

Cindy's silence oozes suspicion.

"Coke was very impressed with your work on *Diet Life.* We want to offer you a small part in *Backlash.*"

"Really?" Cindy says excitedly. "A real part?"

"Probably only a small one," I say. I glance at Gwyneth, who has turned her attention back to the desert. "But still, it's a great opportunity."

"It's *fantastic,*" Cindy enthuses. "Wow, thanks a lot, Scat. You're the—" She stops herself. "Thanks a lot."

"You're welcome." I take a breath. "There's just a teensy little catch."

Pause. "Oh?"

"There's this committee. They're kind of in charge, and they want to . . . change your name."

"My name? What to?" Only surprised so far. Not yet outraged.

"To . . ." I have to swallow before I can say it. "Babe-A-Licious." I rush on to beat her objections. "Now, I know it sounds terrible. I know you won't want to perform under that name. But—" Then it abruptly occurs to me that if Cindy really does refuse, it's no skin off my nose. In fact, it's the obvious solution to this particular problem, and I can't believe I didn't think of it before. "So I want you to know that if you hate it, I'll just go back and tell the committee you won't stand for it. I mean, you have your credibility to protect, right?"

"Are you kidding? Like I'd risk a shot like this because of a *name*."

"Uh," I say, which is, apparently, my submission to Great Rebuttals.

"I mean, I've heard better," Cindy says. "Geez, Babe-A-Licious. But I was actually thinking of changing it, anyway. Maybe something short and snappy, you know. But that's okay."

"Uh," I say, my brain racing for a solution.

"When do I start?"

"Uh," I say.

"Wow," Cindy says. "A *movie* role!"

scat makes an impression

When I kill the call, I realize that Gwyneth is staring at me. There is an expression of incredulity on her face.

"*Babe-A-Licious?*" she says.

deadline management

6 is standing just inside the door, hands on hips, surveying the hangar. She turns as I approach. "I just talked to Kline. It's going to be difficult, but he'll shoot our changes."

"Hey," I say, brightening, "that's great. How long?"

"He wanted five weeks. I talked him down to three. We'll have to squeeze post-production, but I think we can have this finished within the two-month deadline."

"Should I talk Kline through my changes?"

6's mouth tightens. "No, Scat, you should not. You should not talk with Kline about anything. He doesn't like you."

"Oh," I say.

She softens. "Look, your ideas are great. They're going to transform this thing. But let me handle the politics."

"Okay," I say, mollified.

"Here's a script," 6 says, handing me a manila folder. I am becoming very, very sick of manila folders. "The writer is over there." She points out an old lost-looking guy in a dirty T-shirt. "Now I want you to work with him to rewrite the scenes we talked about, and do it without offending him. Can you do that?"

I take a breath. "I promise not to offend him."

6 stares at me for a moment, weighing this up, then takes a step closer to me. "That's right," she says, her dark eyes glinting at me. "You won't."

I'm very careful with the writer.

silver screen

On Friday we start shooting the changes, which is pretty exciting. In the morning, Tom Cruise appears beside me without warning, and I nearly leap backward with fright. He looks calm—even

223

vaguely bored—and somehow manages to look nothing like he does in the movies while being unmistakably, incomparably, Tom Cruise.

The day's shoot starts slowly, with Kline devoting a full hour to a shot of Tom turning his head, but then things start to pick up. It's particularly gratifying to see the scene where Tom and Gwyneth meet reshot, where instead of wrestling a male partner at the academy to the ground, he goes up against Gwyneth and gets rubbed into the dirt. When it's done, Gwyneth shoots me a happy grin and I get warm shivers.

Cindy arrives on the lot about ten, is swept into makeup and emerges two hours later looking like a goddess. She is playing Gwyneth's roommate at the academy and has only two lines ("What was that?" and "Wait here. I'll go check") before being blasted by aliens. But she's palpably excited about the whole deal and it shines through in her performance. Inexperienced as I am, I can't help but feel that things are going well.

I'm supposed to be getting in touch with post-production, but instead I catch Cindy between scenes. "You were *great*," I tell her. "Cindy, I'm really impressed."

"Thank you," she murmurs, lowering huge eyelashes.

"You look fantastic. What is that, silver mascara? And boy, that uniform—it really fits you well."

"Oh, Scat," Cindy sighs happily. "I'm so grateful for all this. This really means a lot to me."

"Aw, it's not as if you don't deserve it. For putting up with me, if nothing else."

"Oh," she says coyly, taking a step toward me. "You weren't so bad."

"No, I think I was," I admit.

"You were worth it." There's a little smile tugging at her lips, and I don't really know what that means. "You're a special guy, Scat."

I shrug, a little embarrassed. When I look up, she is still smiling at me. "You want to get a coffee?"

There's a tiny coffee room at the back of the hangar, and it takes us ten minutes to coax a respectable cup of coffee from the ancient Beanmaster 2000. It takes us another twenty to drink it, and somehow another thirty minutes or so slips in there, too, so I guess we've been gone a pretty long time when 6 appears in the doorway.

"It was *nothing* like that in high school," Cindy is shrieking. "*You* were chasing *me*—"

"Scat," 6 says. Her voice is low and dangerous.

"Oh," Cindy says. "Hi, 6."

6's eyes never leave me.

"Can I help you?" I say awkwardly. It comes out all wrong.

6's eyes burn into me for long moments. Then her gaze flicks to Cindy. "You," she says, "are needed on the set."

"Oh," Cindy says, flustered. She puts down her polystyrene cup. "Okay. Sorry." She shoots me an apologetic glance as she squeezes past 6. "Bye, Scat."

"Bye," I say, and then it's just me and 6. Her stare is unnerving. "We were just talking," I tell her, defensive for no reason. "Just catching up." That doesn't make any impression, so, stupidly, I switch to aggressiveness. "Is that okay with you?"

"I *trusted* you," 6 says.

This is not a good start. "Hey, now—"

"I thought you were *different.*" She shakes her head, slowly, but her eyes never lose their intensity. "I can't *believe* I fell for that."

"6, please. Don't get—"

"*Don't* you tell me what to do."

"6," I say carefully. Calm but forceful. Like handling a snake. Or so I would imagine. "There's no reason to be jealous. We were just—"

Her eyes bulge alarmingly. "You think I'm *jealous?*"

I stop. "Well—uh, aren't you?"

"You obviously have *no* idea about me."

I'm starting to think she's right. "6, let's just talk about this."

"I need some space," she says. Her eyes narrow. "You're crowding me." My jaw drops. "I don't think you should stay with me tonight."

She turns on her heel, leaving me standing stupidly in the coffee room.

"Oh boy," I say to myself. "Oh, *boy.*"

I can't believe I'm homeless again.

corporate nights

I actually consider getting a room at the Beverly Wilshire, just to rack up expenses, and get so far as raising the phone to my ear, already imagining late-night room service and wide-screen TVs. But then a better idea occurs to me: I can go to Coke. Then, when this is all over and 6 asks me what I did, I can say, "Well, 6, I spent the weekend at work."

The security guard lets me in without comment, as if it's not uncommon for Coke executives to head back to work on a Friday night. I catch the elevator to the 14th, wander around the deserted office reading the cartoons taped up on the cubicle walls, then settle down in my office.

For a while I feel pretty cool, putting my feet up on the desk and staring out at the city. I feel like I'm a high-flying, hardworking marketing executive, rather than a penniless, homeless chump, and frankly, the former feels much better.

When I can't sustain the fantasy any longer, I boot up the computer and hunt around for Minesweeper. To my disgust, 6 has already deleted it in favor of some corporate messaging utility, so I have to roam the cubicles for a more entertaining PC. I discover a disturbing dearth of games on all machines until I come across one guy's computer that seems to have nothing else. Then I get embroiled into a bizarre game called Death Clowns, which has me blasting away until four in the morning.

When I can't keep my eyes open any longer, I wander back into my office and settle into the big chair. I fall asleep immediately and dream, alas, not of 6, but of giant menacing clowns.

a close encounter

I have a feeling when I wake up that it's pretty late, but it's not until I crane my neck around to peer at the wall clock that I see that it's almost seven P.M. I've slept through almost the whole of Saturday.

My first thought is to call 6. She hasn't heard from me for more than twenty-four hours, and she won't like having me out of her control like that. I reach for the phone.

Then I stop. I mean, I'm not the bad guy here. Cindy and I were just talking; 6 is the one who overreacted and threw me out. If she can't deal with her own feelings, then maybe she's learning something now. I lean back in the chair, bathing in the yellow evening sunshine, and look out over the city. I don't think I will call 6.

When I'm through feeling smug, I raid the office fridge for food. There's only a block of chocolate and a bowl of fruit salad, but I make do with it: for some reason I don't feel like leaving Coke today. I feel like staying in my corporate tower, playing computer games and feeling superior. So I do.

Two hours later, I'm so wrapped up in Death Clowns I don't even notice @.

execution

"Hi," @ says.

I yelp and literally jump an inch in the air. On the screen, maniacally grinning clowns fall on me and start bludgeoning me with sausage dogs. "@!"

She is so white: I am surprised all over again. It's hard to tell where her skin stops and the peroxide begins. She shifts from one foot to the other, her men's business suit creasing attractively. "Scat," she says softly.

The "Scat" tells me that something is going on. It's not a *Shit-what-are-you-doing-here Scat,* or a *I'm-going-to-wipe-the-floor-*

with-your-ass Scat. It's just *Scat.* "Uh," I say, turning off the clowns, "how are you?"

"I'm good," @ says. She pauses. "How are you?"

"Good. I mean, busy. With the film and all."

"Yes," @ says. "I'm sure."

There's a long pause. @ just stands there, searching me with her glowing blue eyes. "So," I say eventually, "is there anything I can do for you?"

@ thinks about this for a while, although I'm pretty sure she already knows the answer. "Yes," she says finally. "Yes, there is."

the last seduction

"You're wasting yourself," @ says sadly, leaning forward. I'm in the leather chair, gripping the sides so I don't flip over backward. "6 is a lost cause."

"6 is okay," I say carefully.

"No," @ says, shaking her head. Her blond hair ripples like a sheet of sunshine. "No, she's not. She's not up to *Backlash*. It'll swallow her."

A little laugh pops out of me. "Uh, @, have you even *seen* 6? If anyone on this *planet* is up to *Backlash*, it's her."

"She has an act, and that's all." She shrugs lightly. "It's not enough."

"Hey, look," I say, nettled. "Let's not bad-mouth 6, okay? She's my partner."

@ regards me sadly. "No, she's not. You just think she is."

"Oh," I say. "Oh, right. You want to tell me what that's supposed to mean?"

"She's not on your side," @ says simply. "You must already know this. 6 is looking out for 6. You're expendable." Her eyes search me. "Do you really trust her?"

I open my mouth, then stop. Finally I say, "Sure I do." But even I hear the uncertainty.

"She's dragging you down, Scat," @ tells me, leaning across the desk. And I have to say, in this moment, she is gorgeous. I'm not sure if any part of her is real, but I'm also struggling to remember why that's important. "She's not good enough to win, and she's going to take you down with her. Is that what you want?"

"Without 6, I wouldn't even be on *Backlash*. She's helped me more than you know."

"Has she?" @ says, and I see with amazement that @ even has a little eyebrow movement of her own. It's not as good as 6's—not as practiced, maybe—but in its own way it's quite funky. "Who did Brennan invite into the project: you or 6?"

"Well, me. But—"

"Who comes up with the ideas? The summer campaign, Fukk cola, the changes to *Backlash*—whose ideas are those?"

I stare at @ for a moment. "6 does the . . . management. Ideas aren't . . . just aren't her strength."

@ rises from her chair and walks around the desk, her eyes pinning me. "Scat," she says quietly. She slips her behind onto the desk and rests a hand on my shoulder. "I know you like her. I know it's hard to get past that. But you have to."

"And what?" It's meant to come out aggressive, but somehow it gets tangled up in @'s perfume and ends up low and forced. "Help you and Sneaky Pete instead?"

"Let's not worry about Sneaky Pete," @ says. She is leaning in to me, her white hair falling around her face, filling my world. "Let's just worry about you . . ."

"Wait," I say, and that's not aggressive at all. That's just a croak.

"And me," @ says, her hand snaking around the back of my head. Her lips are slightly parted, leaning in to mine.

I hesitate, but it's just for a second. To be honest, it's not a *Should-I-or-shouldn't-I*. It's just a *Yes-I-think-I'm-going-to*.

@'s fingers release her top shirt button and move down to the next. "If you want," she says, her breath coming a little fast, "you can call me 6."

229

The Partnership

CHAPTER 000014

no

"Get out."

Her breath catches in her throat. I see it happen. "What?"

"You heard me." I push her hand away from my face. "Get out of my office."

"Scat," @ says, "wait. I'm sorry. Okay?"

"Save it," I say. I push away from the desk and stand up so I can point to the door with a little more authority.

"You're making a mistake. You don't—"

"No, I *almost* made a mistake," I say.

@ stares at me for a moment. Then she slowly rises from the desk, open hostility spreading across her face. Suddenly I'm not finding her nearly as attractive. "You have *no idea* how bad your position is." There is real venom in her voice. "He is going to *destroy* you."

"Sneaky Pete?" I try to act like I don't care. "I doubt—"

"He will do *anything* to beat you," @ says. "He will do *anything*. Do you understand?"

"Just get out."

"You've already lost," @ says, "and you don't even know it."

"Get *out*," I say, and now my voice even scares me. @ wheels and strides out, slamming the door behind her. I watch her through the blinds until she's disappeared down the hallway to the elevators, then sink back into my chair.

When I'm sure it's safe, I exhale.

scat sleeps on it

As soon as I'm confident of avoiding @, I leave Coke and catch a cab back to Synergy. I knock and wait expectantly, rubbing my hands against the night's chill, and in the few seconds before 6 opens the door, I go over exactly how I'm going to tell her about this.

But 6 doesn't open the door. Oh so gradually, it dawns on me that 6 isn't home. "No way," I say. "Oh, no way."

I search around the building for a while, looking for a way to break in, but only succeed in attracting quick, scared glances from passersby. So I guess I should now get a cab to a nice hotel for the night and meet 6 tomorrow morning. This makes a lot of sense: a hell of a lot more than sleeping on the streets of central Venice. But I don't do it: I don't want to risk missing 6. So I stuff my wallet through the mail slot, curl up in the doorway, and try to look derelict.

Despite the cold and the fact that I've been awake for something like five hours today, I get drowsy pretty quickly. I'm looking up at the streetlights and wondering, for some reason, how many shopping days there are until Christmas, and the next thing I know, it's morning and 6 is prodding me with her foot.

caffeine

"Here," 6 says, handing me a coffee. I take it and start slurping gratefully. "You look terrible."

"Cold," I gasp between sips. "Dirty. Hungry."

6 settles into her Captain Kirk, smoothing her black pants. It abruptly occurs to me that I've never seen 6 slop around in old clothes: I can't even imagine her in a tracksuit.

"I came around last night. You weren't home." I take a long slurp. "Where were you?"

"I do have a life of my own," 6 says.

"Oh." I think for a second. "Were you at Tina's?"

6 frowns irritably, so I know I'm right. "I'm going to bring her on set next week, to help us out. Where were you?"

"Ah." The coffee is working wonders: I feel stronger already. "Well, that's something I need to talk to you about."

the slipup

"Son of a bitch," 6 says. She picks up a pen and starts tapping it fast against the desk. "That son of a bitch."

"@?" I ask, wondering if 6 is engaging in a little non-gender-specific wordplay.

6 sniffs. "@'s a pawn. Trust me, this is all Sneaky Pete."

"Oh."

"She said, 'You don't know how bad your position is'? That we'd already lost but didn't know it?"

"That's pretty much it."

"Son of a bitch," 6 says again.

"I mean, I assume she was just blowing smoke. Trying to scare us."

"I don't think so," 6 says. "No, we've missed something. Something big."

I put down the coffee. "What?"

"I don't know," she says, her jaw tightening. "We've started shooting the new scenes, and we'll get them done inside a month. We had a bad start with the committee, but we'll get back on track. I've reviewed the budgets. I've reviewed the schedule." She looks up. "Are the post-production people ready for us?"

"Uh," I say. I clear my throat. "Actually, I haven't got around to talking to them yet."

6's razor eyebrows descend.

"Monday," I promise. "First thing Monday, I'll talk to them."

"Scat," 6 says grimly, "we can't afford slipups. If post-production needs more than a month, we're in real trouble. Talk to them."

"Got it," I say, trying to inject a note of reliability into my voice.

"There's a committee review meeting tomorrow. I'll be on set, but you have to go. Check the post-production with them. And double-check our schedule."

"Right," I say. "Will do."

6 stares at the desk. "I don't like this."

a scare

6 catches a cab at five to be on the lot early, but that's just a little too extreme for me and I stumble out of bed around seven. According to 6's note, the committee meeting is at one, so I've got the morning to spend at the post-production house. I have a quick breakfast, get lured into a slow coffee and an even slower shower, then grab a cab over to West LA and Visuality.

It's nestled among a coven of computer firms, and the first time I walk into an Apple dealership by mistake. When I work out the right entrance, I find myself face-to-face with a kid younger than myself, flipping through a copy of *Wired*. He is wearing horn-rimmed glasses. "Can I help you?"

"I'm Scat," I say. "From Coke."

"Yeah?" the kid says.

"Yes," I say.

I wait, but I don't appear to have galvanized any action on his part. I try to be a little blunter. "I'm in charge of *Backlash*."

"Oh!" His eyes widen behind the horn-rims. "Right! Pleased to meet you! I'm Jerry."

"Sure thing," I say, my gaze passing over art deco furniture and *Star Trek* memorabilia. "Can I talk to someone in charge?"

"Well," Jerry says, "that's probably me."

I blink.

"I mean, I'm only part owner of Visuality," Jerry says. "But I'm the project leader on BL."

"BL?" I say, embarrassingly slow.

"*Backlash*." Jerry smirks. "We're doing great things with your movie, Scat."

"Well," I say, feeling a little dazed. "That's good."

"Hey, why don't you come down back? I'll show you what we've got."

"Great," I say, and I am beginning to realize just how obnoxious youthful success can be.

I follow Jerry down a dingy corridor into a little room that looks almost exactly like my college dormitory. Except, of course, I never had a million dollars' worth of computer gear lining the walls. Or a Bill Gates dartboard. The three guys lounging around in flannel shirts look about right though.

"This is the Dungeon," Jerry says, grinning at me. "That's what we call it. Our workroom."

"You must be very proud," I murmur. One of the monitors has an animated Pamela Anderson running along in her *Baywatch* outfit, and although it's hard to be sure, I think the boys have been playing around with digital enhancements. "So you're working on *Backlash* here?"

Jerry lets out a little laugh, his eyes flicking to his workmates. "Uh, well, we've *done Backlash* here."

I start. "What? You think you've *finished?*"

"Of course. You guys called up and canceled the rest of your booking."

I gape. "Who did? Sneaky Pete?"

"Yeah," Jerry says. "He's the guy we've been dealing with from the start. He called us a week ago."

"Jerry." I'm feeling a little dizzy. "We haven't finished. We still need you."

Jerry stares at me. "But Scat, you *canceled*. Next week we start work on a Columbia picture." His face falls. "It's not as good as yours. I mean, it doesn't have, you know, aliens and Gwyneth Paltrow." He sighs heavily. "It's some *women's* flick."

"But we *need* you," I say, appalled. "We can't wait for you to finish some other—some—" I tug at my tie.

"Hey, look," Jerry says, a little alarmed. "What sort of footage are you shooting? Because if you want, you know, Winona to eat someone else, that's a big job."

I think fast. "No, there's no major special effects. We just need some color and lightness work, I guess a little sound mixing . . ."

"Oh, well," Jerry says. "That stuff is easy. You're only talking about a week's work."

I blink. "I . . . thought it would take months."

Jerry barks out a laugh. "Months? No way. We've already spent months on *Backlash*. We'd only need to work on your new stuff." He leans forward. "Look, Scat, we know how these things sometimes run over. If you need some more work, we'll fit you in. When we start the Columbia picture, you'll be second priority, but we'll help you out. Okay?"

"Are you sure? Are you sure you can do that? Because—"

"I'm sure," Jerry says.

"Okay," I say, trying to calm down. "Thanks. Thanks a lot."

"You're welcome," he says, beaming. "So, you want to see what we've done?"

I sit through all the post-edit *Backlash* footage, but there are no surprises: it's virtually a copy of the stuff 6 and I have already seen at Coke. It seems incredible, but if Kline can shoot our changes in three weeks, I'm beginning to think we could have this movie finished in a little over a month.

I catch a cab to Coke and have time for a quick sandwich and a call to 6 before the afternoon committee meeting.

"They've been working in parallel with production?" 6 asks, surprised. "They don't need months?"

"No way," I say through an unattractive mouthful of beef. "We just need to give them our new footage and tell them what to do with it. They said about a week, maybe longer if we have to share them with Columbia." I wash down my beef with a gulp of Fukk. "So I guess Sneaky Pete's plan failed, huh? He thought we'd lose post-production."

"Mmm," 6 says.

"How are things on the set? Is everything okay with Kline?"

"We're getting what we need."

"Great," I say. "Hey, things are looking up."

mktg case study #14: mktg film

FILMS LIVE OR DIE BY WORD OF MOUTH. IF YOU HAVE A BAD FILM, SUPPRESS WOM UTTERLY: NO PREVIEWS, NO REVIEWS AND BUCKET-LOADS OF ADVERTISING. IF YOU HAVE A GOOD FILM, PULL IN AS MANY OPINION LEADERS—CRITICS, CELEBRITIES AND HOLLYWOOD HEAVYWEIGHTS—TO SEE IT AS SOON AS POSSIBLE.

then

I arrive ten minutes late for the committee meeting, which provokes a round of furrowed eyebrows and obvious glances at watches. But I'm feeling pretty good about securing post-production and I confidently ignore them all.

"Mr. Scat," Finances says, with just the tiniest peevish tinge, "thank you for coming."

"Pleasure," I say, settling into a chair. "6 can't make it, unfortunately. She's on location. She . . . sends her apologies."

"Duly noted," Finances says, satisfied, making a little note. "Perhaps you can open, Mr. Scat, with an update on the action items as identified in our last meeting."

It takes me a moment to work out what "action items" are, but I get there in time. "Right. Well, Cindy is on location and performing extremely well." I abruptly recall 6's tips for dealing with the committee. "If I may, I'd like to say that her inclusion was a brilliant idea on this committee's part."

Astoundingly, false modesty breaks out across the room. "We're all just trying to do our part," Accounting blushes.

"Your comment is duly noted," Finances says, and he's not even kidding. He beams at me. "Well, it certainly sounds as if things are on track for the premiere."

say what

Imagine you are walking down a street.

Any street. It doesn't matter. You are happily strolling along, observing the birds in the sky, the trees lining the road, the litter on the sidewalk. You are very comfortable walking along this street, because it all makes sense. Everything is how it should be.

Then a trash can leans toward you and says, "Nice day, isn't it?"

This is very much what it feels like to hear the words *the premiere.*

ticketed

"What?" I say. My voice is low and strained.

"The premiere." Finances' head is buried back into his notepad, transcribing my praise. "I was just remarking that everything seems ready for it."

"Of *course* we're ready," Logistics says dismissively. "You're practically finished, aren't you, Scat?"

"Uh, well, kind of," I say. "But pardon me, did—"

"Can't we *go?*" a girl pipes up from the back. I have no idea who she is and at this moment I really don't care. "Please?"

"Unfortunately, no," Finances says sadly. "Only top management are going."

"I heard *Brad Pitt* is going to be there," the girl says, her eyes shining.

"*All* the stars will be there," Logistics says importantly. "This is a very big night."

The girl pouts. "I want to *go.*"

"Madeleine, we'd all like to go." Finances turns to me, eyes wide with hope. "Mr. Scat, if there is any chance at all of procuring some spare tickets—"

I say evenly, "When is the premiere?"

panic

A long pause.

" '*When?*' " Finances says. His voice is hoarse and shocked. "You mean you don't know?"

As steadily as I can manage, I say, "No one told me about any premiere."

238

"But it was announced more than a week ago," Finances protests. "The same time you and Ms. 6 came onboard. Everyone knows about it." His eyes plead me to confess knowledge of it. "It's been in the *papers*."

"This is the first I've heard of it."

"Oh my God," Logistics says.

"You must be ready in time," Accounting says. "You *must!*"

Perhaps it's just Accounting, but I'm getting very close to punching someone. "Will somebody please tell me when the premiere is?"

Uncomfortable looks shoot back and forth. Finances loses. "Ah, well," he says. "You see, it's, ah, Saturday. This Saturday night."

the gray moment

I think about this.

It is now Monday afternoon. Saturday is five days away. *Backlash* still needs three weeks of filming and at least one week of post-production. And although I'm having trouble focusing at this particular moment, I'm pretty sure that makes it impossible for us to be ready in five days.

I consider this carefully, approaching it from a couple of different angles, and every time it comes out the same: it just can't be done.

When I look up, pale committee faces are staring at me. "Mr. Scat," Finances says. He swallows. "Please tell me that when the Coca-Cola Company unveils its history-making marketing project before the most influential people in Hollywood, we will have something to unveil."

I say nothing.

"Mr. Scat. *Please.*"

"Excuse me," I say, and I stand and walk out of the room.

I stride out of Coke and head for the street. When I switch on my cellphone, it informs me that in the last half hour there have been nine unsuccessful attempts to call me. So I guess 6 has found out about the premiere, too.

She picks up on the first ring. "Scat."

"Yes."

Her voice is hard. "I got a call from Coke's Event Marketing. They wanted to talk about the seating arrangement. For the premiere."

"I know." I wave at a cab, to no avail. "The committee just asked if I could get them tickets for it. Apparently everyone knew about this thing but us."

"This is the setup," 6 says grimly. "A deadline we can't meet."

"We've got to go straight to Jamieson."

6 is silent for a moment. "Did you tell the committee that we can't be ready in time?"

"Uh, no, not exactly. But they realize something's wrong." Another cab sails toward me and this one responds to my wave. "Why?"

"We could, as you say, go talk to Jamieson. We could tell him we won't be finished by this weekend because we didn't know we had to be."

I get into the cab and give the driver directions to Synergy. "We have to do that, right?"

"No."

I blink. "Why not?"

"Because we did know about the premiere."

I'm speechless. "*I* didn't know about it! 6, what the—"

6's voice is perfectly level. "After I got off the phone to Event Marketing, I called Pam. I had her go through my In tray, voice mail, drawers, everything. She finally found it in my e-mail."

"What? Found what?"

"A copy of the message we sent to Sneaky Pete. Confirming a

previous meeting with him that ended in a joint decision to move the date of the premiere forward."

"6! I didn't—"

She sighs down the line. "E-mails can be faked, Scat. They're just electronic. @ probably just sat down in our office and wrote it."

I'm reeling. "But this is—it's—"

"It's business."

"No, wait. He can't prove we wrote that e-mail. It'll be our word against his."

"This isn't a court of law, Scat," 6 says, irritated. "Everything in business comes down to somebody's word. And he's VP Marketing. He'll say we're lying because we screwed up and now can't meet the deadline."

I hate to say this, because it's so obvious it can't be right. "But that's not true. None of this is *true*."

"Whatever," 6 says. "Look, Scat, we are deep in this thing. It's a bomb that goes off as soon as we start shouting about it. The second Jamieson finds out there's a problem, we've lost this. Do you understand?"

"So what can we do? Actually try to finish this by Saturday? You know we can't do that."

"We have to. If we don't, he wins."

"Hey, wait a minute. 6, we can't do it. We just can't. Let's try and work out some compromise, okay? Maybe we can postpone the premiere or—"

"Scat, *Spielberg* is attending. This thing is *booked.* Come Saturday night it will be like the Academy Awards at Mann's Chinese Theatre, and we have to show them something." I hear Kline shouting something about Winona's extra teeth in the background and 6 says, "Scat, I have to go. I'll meet you home around nine and we'll talk. Got it?"

"Got it," I say, but 6 has already killed the call.

scat gets serious

At Synergy I change into jeans and a T-shirt, fix a snack out of scraps from 6's fridge and start work. I find a notepad in 6's desk and cover the first three pages with all the things I need to do between now and Saturday. I come up with thirty-two tasks, which sends me into a panic, so then I concentrate on condensing them into broader categories. By the time 6 arrives home, I have a much smaller list, and even though each item is a major challenge in itself, at least I can start to comprehend what needs to be done.

the deceptively short list

1. Film
2. Edit
3. Present

6 gets serious

"Good," 6 says, shrugging off her jacket. She studies my notes critically. "Shows focus."

"Aw," I say modestly.

"I've done some planning, too," she says, and from her giant black folder she pulls another notepad. She flicks quickly through twenty or thirty densely covered pages, then stops at one labeled PANIC PLAN. "Kline said the changes would take three weeks to film. Obviously we don't have that anymore. I just talked him down to four days."

"So we finish shooting on Friday—the day before the premiere? What about post-production?"

"Scat, if we can get the filming done in four days, it's a miracle," 6 says shortly. "This is as good as it gets."

"Oh," I say. "Well, in that case, fine."

"We'll send the rushes to post-production every day, so they can work on it simultaneously. And they'll work continuously from Friday until it's finished on Saturday."

"They've agreed to this?" I ask, surprised.

"No," 6 says. "You're going to talk them into it."

"Ah," I say. I scribble this down on my pad. When I look up, 6 is studying me. "What?"

"Scat," she says carefully, "I want you to realize what we're getting into. So you don't freak out later."

"I understand what we're doing. We're trying to finish a movie. I don't know if we can actually do it, but I understand that we have to try."

6 eyes me for a moment, then says carefully, "On Saturday night, we're going to stand in front of some of the most powerful men and women in Hollywood, and we're either going to show them the best piece of marketing cinema they've ever seen, or we're going to apologize to them for having nothing to show. Do you get that?"

I think about this for a moment, just to make sure I really do. "It would be pretty embarrassing if we had nothing to show."

"It would be a humiliation," 6 says. "We wouldn't work in this country again."

6 confronts her true feelings

Lying in bed, waiting for 6, I actually start to feel excited. I know I'm deeply, deeply enmeshed in Sneaky Pete's trap, but nevertheless it's exhilarating to be in there with 6.

When she slips under the covers, I give her a little grin. It's meant to be kind of encouraging, but I guess I didn't really think about what a young man in pajamas grinning at a young woman from bed actually looks like, and 6's eyes widen alarmingly. "No, hey," I say quickly. "Sorry. I'm just a little worked up."

"Save it for tomorrow," she says, turning her back to me. "You'll need it."

"Right." I pause. Weighing my chances. Evaluating the odds. "I love you," I say hopefully.

"Night," 6 says, and flicks off her Barbie lamp.

I lie there in darkness for a while, maybe five minutes, thinking about 6. I should just roll over and go to sleep, I know. But I don't. "You still awake?"

A long sigh.

"Look, I was just thinking," I say. "I've told you I'm in love with you a few times now, right?"

Silence.

"Well, I have. And, you know, I don't want to put any pressure on you. If you're not ready to, well, commit in the same way, that's okay. Right?"

Still no reply. I suddenly get a little paranoid that maybe 6 really is still asleep and I'm pouring my heart out to her pillow, so I give her a hesitant little poke.

"*What?*"

"Sorry," I whisper. "Just checking."

"Scat," 6 says wearily. "What's your point?"

"It's just that, well, you know how I feel about you, right? But I don't know how you feel about me."

Silence from 6's back. I resist the urge to poke her again.

"I mean, do you feel *anything?*" I say, a little strained.

6 sighs. "Scat . . ."

"Well?" I say, a bit more aggressively than I mean to. "Do I mean something to you? Or am I just some naive moron you're using to get what you want?"

"I . . ." 6 says, then stops. She sounds as if she's really reaching for words, so I force myself to wait for her. "Scat . . ."

"Yes?"

"You are—" She takes a breath. Then she abruptly rolls over so that she's looking straight at me. It's night, we're in bed together, and we're sustaining eye contact. It's possibly the most intimate moment we've ever shared. "Scat," 6 says tenderly, "you're more than a naive moron to me."

the shakes

Tuesday starts well. We're both up and dressed by five, on the lot by six. Of course, there's nothing we can do until everyone arrives, but 6 is adamant that we need to make the right impression. We're depending on a lot of people to throw themselves behind this project, and 6 wants our commitment to set an example.

The first assistant director arrives at seven, and 6 immediately snares her into conversation. I hang around until the rest of the crew begin arriving on set, and then I go around and meet them one by one. Most of them are wary about talking to me, just like I'd be in their position, so I have to work pretty hard to get them talking about their roles and their opinions. I listen carefully and tell them honestly about the deadline and what that means in terms of the work required, but everyone surprises me with their enthusiasm for the film. By the time Kline starts things moving around eight, I'm actually feeling pretty positive.

Tina turns up at ten, hugely excited about being here but trying not to show it. I'm showing her around the set when 6 catches my arm. "Cindy's not here."

I blink. "Not . . . ?"

"Find her," 6 says.

starlet

The phone rings maybe twenty times before Cindy picks it up. "Hello?" Her voice is low and shaky.

"Cindy? It's Scat."

"Oh, hi Scat." A sigh turns into a cough. "What time is it?"

"Time for you to get your butt down here. You should have been in makeup two hours ago."

Cindy breathes into the phone for a bit. "Oh, Scat, I had such a wild time last night. There was this party, and I swear, everyone there was from the industry. You won't believe who I got talking to—"

"That's sweet, Cindy, but we need you here. Now."

"Well I'm not feeling so good," she says, turning petulant. "Maybe I can't make it in today." She softens, maybe seeking sympathy. "I only got home, like, two hours ago, and—"

"Look, I don't care," I say, exasperated. "Whatever you've done, however you feel, I really don't care. Right now I care about this film, and I care that there is an aircraft hangar full of people standing around waiting for you. Understand?"

"Don't talk to me like that," Cindy says sulkily.

I open my mouth, then shut it with great effort. Everything I want to say will guarantee that Cindy doesn't show up today. Instead I silently grind my teeth and wait.

"Can't you shoot without me today?"

"No," I say shortly.

A long sigh. Again, I force myself to wait it out. "Okay," she says finally. "I'll be there."

cruise control

I spot 6 speaking into her cellphone and head over. "Wait," she is saying. "It's not—" She stops, listening, and I can tell by the furious line of her jaw that something is very wrong. "You can't *do* this. You can't—" Abruptly she lowers the phone. "Son of a *bitch*."

"What?"

"Tom Cruise has pulled out."

"*What?*"

"That was his agent. He's denying us further access to Tom."

"He can't do that. Isn't there a contract?"

"Oh, there's a contract," 6 says. "Apparently we broke it."

"*We* broke it?"

"Cruise is committed to *Backlash*, but he's got an out clause if we substantially alter the film's content. If the film changes, he gets to reevaluate if he wants to be in it." She shoves the phone into her pants pocket. "Obviously, the clause is never meant to be invoked this late in the project. It's there to allow him to commit to a script early on but back out if it's developed in a direction he doesn't like."

"Tom doesn't like my changes?" I ask, aghast.

"No, the changes are fine," 6 says, scowling. "That's just the excuse. What he doesn't like—or rather, what his agent doesn't like—is Babe-A-Licious. She doesn't want Tom in a film with a girl called Babe-A-Licious. Thinks it harms his credibility."

I blink. "Well, that's actually understandable."

"That's not the *point*. The point is that the committee ordered Cindy to be billed as Babe-A-Licious, and we don't have the power to overrule them."

"Who does?"

"Sneaky Pete."

"Oh." I think for a second. "Okay, so let's just ignore the committee. What can they do to us? If we get this thing done, we'll apologize. Big deal."

"That's not what I'm concerned about. The problem is that if we directly contravene the committee, we could get Jamieson down here asking us why."

I consider. "We'll just have to be sneaky. We change Cindy's name back, but we don't tell them."

6 shakes her head. "There's a better way."

"Ah," Finances says. He doesn't sound particularly happy to hear from me. "Mr. Scat."

"Hi," I say cheerfully. The wind is starting to pick up, swirling dust around me, and I move around the side of the hangar to shield the phone. "Look, I just need to check something with you."

"Well," Finances says, "perhaps you should have raised it at our scheduled meeting yesterday."

"Uh, yes, if I'd known about it, I should have," I say, "but I didn't. So I'd like to raise it now."

There's a pause from Finances, which starts to raise my suspicions. But maybe I've just been around 6 too long. "Yes . . ."

"I know the committee wanted to bill Cindy as Babe-A-Licious, but Tom Cruise's agent has objected. He won't comply with our changes unless we ditch the name."

"What's your question, Mr. Scat?"

"I want an unofficial green light from you to just call Cindy 'Cindy.' "

"No," Finances says.

This is a surprise. "I'm sorry, I obviously didn't explain the situation properly. You see—"

"Actually, Mr. Scat," Finances cuts in, "I'm quite busy now. Can we talk later?"

"Well, no. We have a situation here and I need a quick answer."

"Does the committee hold enough scheduled meetings for you, Mr. Scat?" Finances inquires.

"More than enough," I say truthfully.

"Then I suggest that you organize yourself and present your concerns at the next meeting."

"Look," I say, wondering why Finances is being so obtuse. "I can't wait until then. Get it? I need to run it by you now."

"I can't make that decision," Finances says. "It needs to be considered by the committee."

"Well, fine," I say. "But you're the chairman, right? I want you to say that, unofficially, in principle, you think it would be okay for 6 and me to do what's necessary to complete this film. Then the committee can ratify it. Look, we're not allowed to make decisions without your approval. I'm just trying to do this by the book."

"I'm sorry, but I can't help you."

"Oh for fuck's sake," I breathe.

"Good-bye, Mr. Scat."

"Hold it," I say. "Just wait a goddamned minute. What's with you people? I'm not asking for your kidneys here. I just want your green light."

"Mr. Scat," Finances says tightly, "let me make this clear for you. I don't want to have anything more to do with *Backlash* than I absolutely have to. This disaster is all yours."

Slowly, it dawns. "You're covering your ass. Suddenly we're in trouble and you want to disown us. Well, thanks for the support."

"We did what we were supposed to," Finances hisses. "We arranged meetings and made suggestions to help you. This isn't our fault."

"You did what you were supposed to, all right," I say, heating up. "You stalled us and you threw up obstacles. That's what you were chosen for."

"I'm going straight to Mr. Pete," Finances says tightly, "and reporting that the committee no longer wishes to act in a supervisory capacity for you."

"That's beautiful," I say. "That's just what I wanted to hear."

"This is on your head, Mr. Scat. Yours alone. I want you to be clear on that."

"Sure," I say. "It's duly noted."

committeeless

When I reenter the hangar, Kline is wrapping up a shot of Gwyneth doing a military drill. She slaps around a big laser gun in her hands and snaps to attention and, all in all, looks pretty cute. 6 is talking with Tina, but when she spots me she heads over. "How'd it go? Did you get around the committee?"

"The committee is no longer an issue."

6 nods, impressed. "Good work."

I shrug modestly.

a stumble

Cindy finally turns up at three and is finished with makeup at five. While Kline and the first assistant director run the shoot like a hyperactive army camp, I sit with the writer and we work on my ideas, making them as shoot-friendly as possible. When we work out we can save three days by relocating a scene from Earth to the alien spacecraft—and use an existing set—we whoop with excitement, and the overworked crew glare at us.

Kline shoots for a long, frustrating four hours before he's happy with a few shots of Tom and Gwyneth running down corridors, and when we break at nine the whole crew is grumpy and tired. We're already way behind schedule, but 6 and I aren't stupid enough to try and keep them back any later.

6 and Tina hang back to talk to Kline for a while, and since I'm not allowed near Kline, I spend my time wandering around the set and playing with cool props. When Kline finally leaves, 6 is looking pale and drawn.

"So?" I say.

She shakes her head. "This is tight. Too tight."

We don't get back to Synergy until midnight, then we eat and get ready for bed in silence. Just before 6 switches off the Barbie lamp, I say, "Hey. We're still okay, right?"

6 looks at me for a long moment, then kills the lamp.

Wednesday is a total disaster.

We do well at first: 6 gets hold of Tom Cruise's agent and tells him we've caved on the Babe-A-Licious issue, and by lunch we have Tom again. We have Cindy from eight, mainly because I make a point of calling her at six to get her out of bed. Event Marketing leaves a message for me, volunteering their resources to help organize the premiere. And Kline is skilled and efficient, tearing through the shots and making up a little of the time we lost yesterday.

Then we can't find the rushes.

I'm on the phone to Visuality, checking that Jerry isn't having any problems with the film, and he says, "What film?"

"Uh, Jerry," I say. "The rushes we couriered to you yesterday. Everything we've shot from halfway through last week."

"I haven't got any rushes," Jerry says.

I force him to put down the phone and talk to everyone at Visuality to make sure no one's received our rushes, and I pace back and forth across the sand while he does it. "Sorry, no rushes. You'd better check with your courier."

It takes me an hour to find the person who organized the courier and learn which company they used. By the time I get on to them, it's midafternoon and I'm seriously panicking.

The couriers are prompt and helpful, but they can't get in contact with the right driver for two hours. When they finally inform me that they've found my film and will deliver it within the hour, I just about fall over with relief. Then I get angry and demand to know where the hell my rushes were all this time. The woman says, "I'm not allowed to tell you that, sir."

I'm able to breathe again, but I've burned a day. I haven't got back in touch with Event Marketing and I've completely forgotten to ask Jerry if we can hire them for twenty-four hours straight starting Friday afternoon.

I'm not feeling so excited anymore.

more meetings

On the way home we stop at a Mexican restaurant, deserted at this hour, and eat burritos in silence. I want very badly to ask 6 if she thinks we'll finish in time, but I'm scared of what her answer might be.

"Apparently we have a meeting," she says, almost offhand. Her eyes scan the drinks menu. "At Coke tomorrow morning."

I wipe away a rogue blob of salsa. "Oh? Who with?"

"I don't know." Her eyes rest on me. "Pam left me a 'reminder.' This is the first I've heard of it." She shrugs. "By the time I called her back, she'd gone for the day."

"So who's going? You or me?"

6 frowns at her burrito. "Both of us."

I blink. "Can we afford to spend that time—"

"I don't know what this meeting is about, or who it's with. But if it's been kept secret from us, it's important. We're both going."

"Oh." I wonder how I can possibly fit everything I've got to do, plus this meeting, into Thursday, Friday, and half of Saturday. "If you say so."

6 bites into the burrito. "I do."

thursday

We're at Coke by seven-thirty, to give ourselves time to find out about this meeting before it starts at eight. Except the first thing we find out is that it doesn't start at eight. We sit alone in the meeting room as instructed until quarter past, then 6 stalks out to see what's going on. I amuse myself by spinning my pen around my knuckles until she returns.

I pick the pen off the floor. "What's going on?"

"A 'mix-up,' " 6 says. Her face is dark. "We're an hour early. It starts at nine."

"Oh." I consider. "Do we know who it's with?"

6 looks at me. "According to Pam," she says, "it's with Sneaky Pete."

we love sneaky pete

Naturally, @ is there, too. She's wearing a startling red jacket across a body-hugging black top, which nicely offsets the muted tones of Sneaky Pete's suit. She's seated by his side and as 6 and I enter, she turns to watch me. I look for any special gesture—maybe not a wink and a smile, but at least a scowl—but there's nothing. Like Sneaky Pete, her expression is unreadable.

Pam is there, too, taking the minutes. Her chair is against the wall, away from the table, as if to remind everyone that she is of no importance here. The players are all seated at the table.

Jamieson sits at the head.

When 6 sees him, I hear her exhale slowly. She sounds almost satisfied, as if this is finally starting to make sense. I hope that's a good thing.

We take our positions at the table's foot, greeting Jamieson and nodding perfunctorily to Sneaky Pete and @. @ says warmly, "6, Scat—how are you?"

I'm ready to give her the cold shoulder, but 6 surprises me by responding, "Very well, thank you @. And yourself?" She actually sounds friendly, and again I am impressed by 6's talent for deception.

"Thanks for coming," Jamieson says, leaning forward. "I suppose you know what this is about."

"Actually, no," 6 says carefully. "We only found out about this meeting last night."

Jamieson glances at Sneaky Pete, who cocks his head. I have no idea what that gesture means, but I get the impression that Jamieson does. And if that's true, it implies that Jamieson and Sneaky Pete have had a conversation about us before now, and that scares me a great deal.

6 is on it immediately. "As I'm sure you'll appreciate, we've been completely consumed by *Backlash*. It's probably hard to reach us at the moment."

I don't know what 6 is trying to imply, but Jamieson nods. "Of course."

"We've tried very hard to keep the lines of communication open," @ interjects. Her face is pure sincerity, hangdog honesty. Except, of course, she's lying through her teeth. "I hope you haven't had any problem getting in touch with us when you've needed support. Although, of course, you've had the committee for support, as well."

"Oh, sure," I start. This is the perfect opportunity to tell Jamieson exactly what sort of support we've been getting from Sneaky Pete and his committee. "They've been *very* helpful. They've excelled at getting in our w—"

"We have received total support from Sneaky Pete and the committee," 6 interrupts. "Everyone has shown complete commitment to *Backlash*."

I choke, but Jamieson is nodding again, and @'s eyes narrow. I am therefore forced to confront the possibility that 6 knows what she is doing.

"We have had a couple of communication breakdowns," 6 admits, "and these have been our fault as much as anyone's. We do need to work harder to make sure that everyone involved in *Backlash* is fully informed of what's going on."

"I see," Jamieson says slowly. "So your working relationship with Sneaky Pete is satisfactory?"

"Absolutely," 6 says, as if she is surprised by the question.

"I see," Jamieson says again. He frowns, then turns to me. "Would you agree, Mr. Scat?"

hmm

An interesting question.

My immediate reaction is to say, "Actually, I'd say Sneaky Pete has been about as helpful as salt at a slug convention." As well as not being particularly good at lying, I'm also kind of petty. It's difficult for me to suppress my immediate reaction.

But I do. Because, in the end, I trust 6.

and so

"Yes, I agree completely," I say. "In fact, I think it would be hard to find a more supportive, encouraging, honest—"

The sarcasm is starting to leak through, so 6 jumps in. "We're very happy with Mr. Pete," she says, and under the table she steps on my foot with her heel.

"Good," Jamieson says, and there's no doubt: he is surprised. It seems that Sneaky Pete has told him we would rant and sling accusations, and instead we're singing his praises. "That's very good to hear. I was concerned that you may have been having difficulties."

"We're very busy," 6 says, frowning, "but I wouldn't say we've had difficulties."

"Well," Jamieson says, blinking. "Excellent."

Sneaky Pete glances across at @, and as if on cue, she asks us, "Are you confident, then, that the premiere will be a success?"

"Will be a . . . ?" 6 says, looking flabbergasted. "Well of . . ." She looks at me for a second, weighing me up. "Would you like to answer that, Scat?"

"Mr. Jamieson," I say, spreading my palms, "with our skills and determination, plus all the support that Sneaky Pete has thrown behind us, how could it not?"

a momentary reprieve

"Okay," I say, when we're safely in the cab, "you want to tell me what the hell all that was about?"

"You did good, Scat," 6 says. "You laid it on a little thick, but it was good enough."

"Well, great. So why didn't we tell Jamieson what's really going on? Now we've promised him that the film will be ready for Saturday and made it clear that if it's not, it's all our fault. Is that about right?"

"Yes," 6 says. "That's all we could do." She turns in her seat. "Nothing's changed, Scat. Complaining about Sneaky Pete now—which Jamieson clearly expected us to do—makes it look as if we're trying to blame someone else for our screwup."

I bite my lip, unconvinced. "I still feel like we're being backed into a corner on this."

6 frowns. "Well," she says, "of course we are."

on set

I can't believe it's Thursday.

In fact, it's not just Thursday, it's Thursday lunchtime. We have today and tomorrow to finish the filming, then less than a day to get everything finalized for the premiere. This is starting to look very, very bad.

With some help from Tina, 6 and Kline are struggling to bring the filming under control. Although it's going to be difficult, it's almost conceivable that when everyone walks off the set Friday night, we will have everything we need. But I'm way, way behind.

The first thing I do is get myself a coffee and hunt for a place in the hangar where I can phone undisturbed. I eventually find an unused spaceship stacked up against one wall, and I carefully clamber up onto it. While Kline orders his shoot around in front of me, I call Coke and ask for Event Marketing, finally getting put through to a girl named California. She sounds about sixteen years old, and the fact that she's in charge of making sure the nuts and bolts of the premiere run smoothly scares me a little. But when we get into the logistics, her organizational skills become obvious. Petty details like how to seal off the city block take an hour, then the serious issue of where to seat each celebrity takes two more.

I jump down from my spaceship to go refill my coffee, passing Tina on the way. "Look, I know Kline just asked for fog around their ankles," she is saying. "But trust me, when he sees it really swirling, he'll love it."

Back on my perch, I call Visuality. "Jerry, hi! It's Scat. How you doing?"

"Hey, *great,* Scat. You won't believe what we're doing with your film here."

I brighten. "That's great. Hey, Jerry, I need to ask you a big favor."

"Sure, Scat. Name it."

I like the way this conversation is going. "You know how you said you'd try to fit us into your schedule over the next few weeks, even though you're booked for something else?"

"Yeah, that's right. Although, you know, we won't be able to be ultra-responsive—"

"Well, we won't need you after this week."

Jerry's voice lifts. "Hey, that's great! Because, you know, we were really going out on a limb for you there. And Columbia wouldn't have liked it if they found out."

"I really appreciate you being prepared to help us, Jerry. And I need to ask for your help in another way."

Pause. "Oh?"

"We need to have this film finished, ready to present, by this Saturday," I keep my voice calm and chatty, as if this is actually pretty reasonable. "So I really need you. This is a hell of an ask, but I want you to work through Friday night until it's done on Saturday."

There is a long pause. "Work through the night?"

"That's right." Kline has started shouting even louder than usual, and I block my other ear. "Now look, we will make this up to you. We can—"

"Scat, I'm sorry, but we can't do that. We have commitments."

My stomach falls about six feet. "Uh, I'm sure you do, but—"

"Look, if I could help you, I'd do it. But we can't. We just can't."

I swallow. "Jerry, let me make this clear. I will pay you whatever—"

"Money isn't the issue, Scat," Jerry says, sounding offended. "All of us here have personal commitments."

"To?"

"Well," Jerry says huffily, "if you must know, we're playing Warlords."

I swallow again, and when that doesn't help, I swallow once more. But there's still nothing coming out of my mouth.

"We're in a tournament," Jerry says, "and tomorrow night the final is being held here." He rushes on before I can object. "Now I know a lot of people don't get behind conquest games, but there's a big group of guys coming around here with their maps and castles and it's very important to them. We've even got Dwarven Marauder pieces."

"But—"

"So you see, I have commitments," Jerry says. "I mean, you're calling me on Thursday night, Scat. I just can't do it."

"Whatever you want," I tell him desperately. "I'll get it for you."

"See you, Scat," Jerry says sadly, and hangs up.

kline and tina

I'm staring at the phone in shock when Kline roars, "That is it! That is the end!" I look up and see him shaking his fists at Tina.

258

Tina looks ready to have a piece of him and 6 is standing between them both. I drop to the ground and hurry over.

"I do not have to put up with this constant nagging!" Kline is shouting. "Criticizing and complaining all day! I want her off the set!"

"You pompous asshole—" Tina starts.

"Tina, get off the set," 6 tells her coldly. "I appreciate your help, but right now I need you to leave the set."

"You wouldn't even *have* a film without me!" Tina shrieks.

"Hey, now," I say soothingly. "What's going on here?"

"*You,*" Kline says, his eyes bulging.

"Hack," Tina spits at Kline. "It's people like you that turn film into a commercial wastela—"

"Enough!" Kline roars. "We are finished for today!"

"Kline, please," 6 says, but Kline pushes past her. "End for today! Go home!"

To my horror, the crew and cast begin dissipating. "Wait!" I shout, but apparently I carry a lot less weight than Kline. The hangar empties and then it's just me, 6 and a whole lot of silence.

6's eyes are wide and staring. "No," she whispers. "This cannot happen." Her eyes search my face, seeking answers.

I try to find something to say. "I . . . lost Visuality."

descent

6 unlocks Synergy and slowly walks inside. She's really starting to scare me, so I put my arms around her and hug her tightly. She just stands there, as if I don't even exist. "I love you," I say hopefully, but I get no reaction.

I fix a quick and tasteless dinner while 6 sits in her Captain Kirk and stares at the wall. She hardly touches the meal, and I have to prompt her to get ready for bed.

When we're under the sheets, I hug her and say firmly, "We

are not going to lose. Tomorrow we can fix everything." I really don't know if this is true, but it's important to say.

6 is silent. I hold her tight, trying to offer as much comfort as I can, and I can feel her trembling.

a symbolic dream

I dream that 6 and I are in a car together, some kind of convertible, driving out in the desert. 6 is smoking a cigar and throwing playing cards out the window, all Jacks, and every time I reach over to stop her, the car lurches across the road and startles the cacti, which, I notice, are drinking from cans of Fukk.

I'm leaning over for the umpteenth time when there's a thump on the roof of the car and a hand punches clear through the vinyl and grabs my throat. I look up and see Sneaky Pete perched above me, grinning, his black shades glinting. "You lose," he says.

I wrench the wheel and the car careens off the road, bumps over the sand and hits a cola-drinking cactus. Sneaky Pete is thrown clear and lands in a particularly thick bunch of cacti, which I realize are actually movie stars in cactus suits, and then he starts advancing on us. I tug at the door handle, but it's jammed fast. Sneaky Pete gets closer, growing, towering above the vehicle, and, knowing that the end is near, I reach out for 6 so that in the final, despairing moments we can at least be together. She looks at my hand as if she doesn't know what to do with it, and as Sneaky Pete tears the door from the car and reaches in for us, her brow furrows. "Actually," she says, "only one of us has to lose."

the black moment

I wake and 6 is not in bed with me.

I ponder this development for a few minutes, long enough to

establish that she isn't just making a midnight toilet run. When I'm clear on this, I pull back the covers and get out of bed.

For some reason, I don't turn on the light. And this doesn't make sense, because I'm looking for 6 and the light would help me find her. The only reason I wouldn't turn on the light would be if I wanted to sneak up on her. And I can't think why I'd want to do that.

I open the bedroom door carefully, too, making sure it doesn't creak. Again, I have no reason. I step out into the hallway and see from the light leaking under the office door that 6 is inside. I stand there for a moment, considering, and then I move up to the door.

I put my hand on the door and pause, listening. I can faintly hear 6 talking but can't make out her words. For a moment I think she must be on the phone—maybe ordering a late-night pizza—then it clicks: 6 is talking to herself.

I turn the handle very, very carefully. A shaft of light springs from the crack, and suddenly I can see 6. She's in her chair, staring at the desk. Her face is totally bleak.

"No," she murmurs. "Obviously we were specifically entrusted with delivering the film. That won't work." She sighs, closing her eyes. "Which leaves . . . sacrificing Scat."

but

I don't know if I let the handle go on purpose or out of shock. But either way, the door slowly swings open.

6's head jerks up. Her eyes are wide and shocked. She stares at me for a long moment, and I stare back at her.

"Scat," she says, and her voice is low and earnest, "I love you so much."

261

Coquette

CHAPTER 000015

severance

I leave, then.

direction

It's raining outside: the type of annoying drizzle that keeps LA cab companies in business. Although I've got my Coca-Cola credit card, I stalk along on foot and steadily soak through my jeans and sweater.

It takes me an hour to work out where I'm going.

shelter

"Scat!" Cindy says through the speaker. "Is that really you?"

"Yes," I say. "It's really me."

The door buzzes and I push it open. Cindy meets me halfway down the stairs, wearing, I notice, the same cotton dressing gown as the morning she shut me out. "You're soaked *through,* you poor thing." She wraps her thin arms around me endearingly. "Come up and get out of those wet things."

"Okay," I say.

consolation

Cindy still has all my old clothes in a cardboard box, and while I towel off in the bathroom, she selects a few of my favorites and leaves them outside the door. By the time I'm dressed and snuggled up in front of the living room heater, it feels like I never left this place.

I tell Cindy why I was wandering the streets at one in the morning, and she responds appropriately. "I *knew* 6 was trouble. I'm sorry, Scat, but she's just wrong for you. Everyone can see that but you."

"I know."

"She's just using you," Cindy says, shifting a little closer to me on the sofa. "She can't see past the needs of her own ego."

"I know," I say again.

"You need someone *giving,*" Cindy tells me earnestly. "The exact *opposite* of 6."

I turn to her. "Someone like you?"

"Well," she says, looking down. Maybe she's a little embarrassed, but I think mostly she's pleased. "I was always there for you, Scat. You know that."

I stare at the heater again. "You said I was no good for you."

"Well . . ." She loops her arm around mine. "You have your flaws." She smiles. "Sometimes you get a little self-obsessed. You can have trouble seeing past—" She stops.

"Seeing past my own ego?" My eyes narrow. "Like 6?"

"No," Cindy says firmly. "Not like 6. Scat, you're nothing like 6."

"Maybe I am," I say, despairing.

"Scat, look at me." She takes my face in both hands and physically turns my head. She *has* been working out. "You are a good person. I believe you have a good heart."

"Then why did you kick me out? Unless I was—"

"I realize now that I need to accept you for who you are," she tells me. She sounds so sure of herself that I can't help but wonder if this is rehearsed. "If you didn't do stupid things sometimes, you wouldn't be Scat."

I stare at her. "And if 6 wasn't ruthless, she wouldn't be 6."

Cindy's smile drops about ten floors. "Scat, that's completely different."

"How?"

For a moment Cindy just stares at me. Then she laughs. "You know what this is? This is like a movie, where the hero is chasing this elusive, fantasy girl. And the whole time, the girl he *really* belongs with is right there with him, being his friend, supporting him when he needs it. Only he doesn't realize, until right at the end, when they finally get together."

"I can't believe you're using *movie* logic," I say.

"Scat," Cindy says, exasperated. "Look at what's happened to you since you left. You're two days away from being fired at Coke. The girl you moved in with has betrayed you." She looks deeply into my eyes. "This is not a healthy lifestyle."

"Hmf," I say.

"You can move back in with me," she offers gently. "Leave 6 and Coke behind. It'll be just like it used to be." Her eyes implore me. "My career could really use your help. And . . . so could I."

And, strangely, it sounds tempting. It sounds really tempting. Could I just step out of all this? I think maybe I could. At worst, Coke would sue me, but unless they're willing to accept my underwear as damages, they might as well not bother. I actually think it can be done: I can just walk away from all this, from Sneaky Pete and 6 and Jamieson and meetings in strip bars, and go back to managing Cindy's modeling career. I'd even be good at it.

Of course, I'd never work in marketing again. I'd never rub shoulders with film stars. And I'd never be famous.

"No," I say.

rebuff

"Oh," Cindy says. "Oh, I see. Nothing's changed. You're exactly the same." She pulls her arm away from me, climbing to her feet.

"Cindy," I say, "I just can't. It's not who I am."

"Sure," she says, slightly hysterical. "Who you are. Of course. Don't let me get in the way of your almighty goddamned quest to find yourself, or whatever the fuck it is."

I blink. "What happened to accepting me as I am?"

"Yeah, whatever," Cindy says.

"Cindy—" I start, but then her buzzer sounds. We both stare at it for a second.

"Oh, this is just great," Cindy says.

"Do you, uh, want me to get that?"

"Why not?" she says, really starting to steam up now. "Since we both know who it is."

"Are you sure?" I say, and I think I'm actually biting my lip.

"Sure," Cindy says. Her arms are swinging dangerously. "Why don't you invite her upstairs and I'll just wait quietly in the kitchen while you two—"

"I'll meet her downstairs," I say quickly.

"You worthless *shit!*" Cindy yells.

I practically run out the door, shutting it hard behind me. Across the hall, the same old man who saw Cindy send me sprawling a few weeks ago is peering around his door. "Hi," I say.

He doesn't react. I run down the stairs to where 6 is waiting in the rain.

reparation

The skies have opened up and 6, standing on the street in her red pajamas, is soaked through. She peers through the glass door at me, her hair hanging in thick, bedraggled locks, and she is absolutely gorgeous. She's not wearing makeup, her hair is a disaster and she isn't dressed, and she's just beautiful.

I open the door but she doesn't move. She just stands there as the rain dumps down and looks at me.

"Come in," I say. "Come out of the rain."

She shakes her head, biting her lip.

"Fine," I say, and step out onto the street.

The door closes behind me, stranding us in the downpour, but I hardly notice. I only notice 6.

"I'm sorry," she says. Although it's hard to tell, I think there are tears mixed with the rain on her face. "I'm sorry, Scat."

I consider. "Are you?"

She turns away, and for a second I think she's going to run away. Then, so quietly I hardly hear her over the rain, she says, "Yes." She turns back to me. "I don't want to hurt you." She takes a step closer, her eyes searching my face. "But I can't lose now, Scat. I've worked too hard to get to this point to lose now."

I nod. "I know."

We stare at each other. And I just can't help but wonder: Is this real? If 6 needs my trust so she can sell me out, could this be an act? It's a cold, heartless thought, but I've been around 6 too long to avoid it.

She looks down at the road for a second, then up at me. "Am I too late for you, Scat?" Her face is pure misery. "Am I?"

"Come here," I say, and she does; she practically falls into my arms. We hug tightly: two wet, soggy bodies clinging to each other. "I love you."

"Yes."

I have to ask. "Do you love me?"

"I—" 6 says. "I—really—" She buries her face in my shoulder. It's enough for me. It's real.

resolution

"So," I say. It's four in the morning. The light from 6's Barbie lamp plays across her face. "Are we going to finish this damn film?"

She regards me across the bed. "Oh yes."

The Panic Plan

CHAPTER 000016

friday

We sleep until seven. This is pretty late, even though it's only three hours' sleep, but we have a sleepless night in front of us. When I wake up, I almost feel refreshed.

Then we start.

tina

I'm carrying bowls of cereal through to the office, so we can work and eat at the same time, when I hear 6 in the shower. I pause for a moment, listening, because it sounds very much as if 6 is on the phone.

"Tina, you have been amazing," 6 is saying. The shower slips into one of its brief pipe-shuddering fits, and she takes a second to fix it. "Scat and I know how much you've done for us. And when Hollywood producers want to talk to us about how we did this and what we want to do next, we're going to tell them all about you." Pause. "Thanks, Tina. You know it's just to get around Kline. I'd have you on location the whole time."

I head through to the office.

kline

° • ° • ° • • ° • •

"Of course," 6 says into the cellphone, then swallows a mouthful of corn flakes. I'm impressed by her dexterity. "Kline, this is your baby. We know what we want to achieve, but you know which shots will get us there. We've always said that."

I nod approval, pulling on my jacket.

"No, Tina won't be there. You don't want her on set, she's not on set." She listens. "No, I don't think you were harsh. You're the director. If you find her distracting, then she goes." She rolls her eyes at me. "Well, that's very kind, and I'll tell her that. Thank you. No, really, thank you."

visuality

° • ° • ° • • ° • •

"Scat, I'm sorry," Jerry says firmly, "but I told you before. No can do. I mean it."

"I understand that," I say. Sitting on my spaceship in the hangar, I'm Mr. Reasonable. Reasonable wouldn't melt in my mouth. "But there must be something that means more to you than your game. Come *on*, Jerry. There must be something I can do for you that will change your mind."

"Scat," Jerry says wearily. "There's not. Tonight's our only opportunity to play the final. I can't let down the guys. Understand?"

I sigh. "Okay. But I'll call you later. When I think of something."

"Whatever," Jerry says, and hangs up.

talent

I head off for a coffee before trying California, and on the way I almost bump into Winona Ryder. I'm a bit of a Winona fan, so I take a moment to stop and gape. Her eyes flick over me and she keeps walking, carrying her scaled tail in her hands. It's a beautiful moment.

While I'm standing there staring after her, I nearly get clobbered by a stage light. "Sorry, bud," says the kid carrying it, and I hurry out of the way. There's a lot of people working very hard today, courtesy of a rev-up speech Kline made while I was on the phone. I still don't know if we're going to make it, but everyone here is going to try.

I get a coffee for 6, too, and find her standing behind Kline. "Here."

She glances at me, takes the coffee, then peers back at the stage. It's set up for the final confrontation between Tom and Winona, and there's weird mechanical junk strewn over the floor, alien goo oozing from the walls and a couple of battered Coke machines. "Thanks."

"How are we doing?"

6 considers. "We're doing okay."

"Is that good enough?"

"I don't know," she says. "But it'll be close."

california

"California, you gorgeous thing." I haven't even met this girl but feel compelled to flirt with her. It must be the name. "How you doing?"

"It's *madness* here," she tells me. "You wouldn't believe how much hand-holding the LAPD need to block off a few streets."

"I'm going to give you lots more work," I tell her. "Okay?"

"Aw, *Scat*."

"But in return," I say generously, "I will personally introduce you to Tom Cruise."

"Hey," California says brightly. "Deal. Anything for a celebrity."

I freeze. "Oh, shit."

chasing gwyneth

"Scat," Gwyneth says, putting down her script. The makeup artist is doing something to her eyes, and bathed in the wattage of a dozen light bulbs she looks almost angelic. "I'm kind of busy. Can't this wait?"

"Gwyneth," I say seriously, "I'm about to ask you for a huge favor. It will be a major pain in the ass. You won't want to do it."

"Sounds tempting," Gwyneth says.

"But I really need your help. I'm desperate."

"Uh-huh," Gwyneth says, as the makeup guy traces around her lips. "And why do I want to do this huge favor?" The makeup guy frowns at her.

I drop into the chair beside her. "You have to admit, your role has become a lot more interesting since 6 and I beefed it up. Strong female roles must be so hard to find—"

She eyes me suspiciously. "You didn't do that for me."

"Well, true. But—"

"Sorry," she says, picking up her script.

"Oh," I say, "so maybe you're not interested in strong roles. Maybe next time I'm making a film and I need a female lead, I should just call up Julia Roberts and say—"

"You might never make another film."

"True," I admit. "But then again . . ."

Gwyneth looks at me for a long time. Finally she sighs. "What is it you want me to do?"

"Scat," Jerry says tiredly, "it's kind of hard to work with you interrupting all the time."

"Jerry, I have an offer."

"Save it, all right? I've already—"

"You don't want to let down your buddies, right? With Warlords tonight?"

"That's right."

"Well," I say, "the thing is, Gwyneth Paltrow is a bit of a Warlords fan, too."

Silence. "Really?"

"Sure. I was talking over our little situation with her, and she said she'd love to play. If it's all right with you."

A long pause. "You'd let her play with us? Even though we can't do your film?"

"Well, that's the thing," I say. "See, you only get Gwyneth if you do the film. Tonight."

"Oh," Jerry says, "oh, I see. You're blackmailing me. Is that it?"

"Well," I say, "yeah."

"Oh." He thinks for a second. "So while I'm working on *Backlash*, Gwyneth is playing Warlords with my friends?"

"That's right," I say. When he hesitates, I add, "You've got to think they'd be impressed."

"Boy," Jerry says, "you don't have to tell *me*." He pauses, and I can almost hear him biting his fingernails. "Gwyneth *Paltrow*."

"So," I say, hardly daring to hope, "do we have a deal?"

A long sigh from Jerry. "Okay," he says finally. "I'll finish your damn film."

it's a wrap

We're meant to finish at six, and if anyone wanted to be difficult, they could walk off the set right then. But they don't. We go until ten, and no one, not even our multimillion-dollar talent, says a word.

Finally, Kline says, "Okay. That is it. We are done."

It's strange: a hush falls over the hangar. There's no cheering, no slapping of backs, or even mutterings of *Thank God for that.* Everyone just falls silent.

"I would like to thank every one of you," Kline says. He stands up in his crane, looking over the sixty or so people present. "You have all performed exceptionally well under considerable pressure. This could not have been done without you."

Then they cheer.

post

When 6, Gwyneth and I arrive at Visuality, there are a half dozen young, sweaty men in the lobby. When Gwyneth enters, a low *ahhhh* emanates from them.

"Oh, God," Gwyneth says.

I take charge. "Hi guys. Is Jerry here?"

"Here," Jerry says, emerging from the hallway. I notice he's freshly shaved.

I nudge Gwyneth. She takes a deep breath, then says, "Uh, hi, Jerry."

"Ohhh," Jerry says.

workload

So we do it: Gwyneth sits down with a coven of war gamers to a table laden with miniature ogres and dragons and aliens or whatever the hell they're meant to be, and 6, Jerry and I get to work on *Backlash*. Every time Gwyneth tries to make a move, guys rush to explain why that's not legal, but despite this, she seems to be doing pretty well. I'm not sure if this is because she has innate Warlords talent or because all the other players are trying to ally with her.

Around one, we order a couple of monster pizzas and sit around on the floor—there's no disturbing the table, of course—and munch them down. Revitalized, we work solidly on *Backlash* until dawn: coloring laser flashes, painting aliens, tweaking Winona's extra teeth. The warlords don't last so long: they're all done by two. Gwyneth is on the winning side: a skinny guy with a big grin and a propensity for declaring "Now is the time of the Orcish clan" has struck down anyone who dared attack her. Everyone tells Gwyneth how good she is for a beginner, and they're genuinely sad when she calls a cab. Gwyneth just looks exhausted.

When the sunlight starts leaking through Jerry's *Star Wars* blinds, it's a surprise. We blink and look at one another for a second, trying to remember what we were doing before we were consumed by a world of Coke-drinking aliens.

"Hey," 6 says. "It's Saturday."

we'll be right back after these important messages

"That's it," Jerry says. The screen reads: *Compiling Movie: Pass 1 of 17016.* "It's rendering."

"We've done it," I say wonderingly. "We've really done it." I look at my watch. "And with twelve hours to spare."

"No." Jerry is shaking his head. "Scat, I told you about this. It's rendering. We can't lay it onto film until the computer finishes rendering."

"Yes," I say slowly. Irritably, too. "But it's rendering *now*."

Jerry sighs, rubbing his eyes. "Rendering takes a long time, Scat. Even with computers like this."

"How long?" 6 says.

"Can't tell. Some parts take awhile, some render real quick." Jerry points to the screen, just as it clicks over to *Pass 2 of 17016*. "But it's got to do *that* another seventeen thousand times."

"Holy shit," I say.

"Jerry," 6 says tightly. "How long?"

Jerry shrugs. "Twelve hours."

6 loses control

6's eyes widen. "Jerry, that's not good enough."

"Hey, guys, there's nothing we can do. It has to render."

"Don't tell me there's nothing we can do," 6 says. "There's always something we can do. How can we make it go faster?"

"Look," Jerry says, starting to lose it, "this is it. This computer is fully maxed out doing the rendering. And it's a fast computer. Unless you want to go buy yourselves a Hewlett-Packard V-class, this is it."

"How much?" 6 demands. "For a, uh—"

"A million," Jerry says. "Okay? A million. And even if we had one, we'd need days to get it loaded and running. Look, it can't be done faster."

6 takes a couple of deep breaths. "Okay," she says. "Okay. What's the worst-case scenario?"

Jerry rubs his eyes. "Well, if we're lucky, it'll take nine hours. It'll *probably* take ten to twelve. If we're not lucky . . ." He shrugs. "Fifteen."

"Fifteen," 6 breathes.

I force myself through the addition. "That's eleven at night. We're scheduled to screen at eight."

"That's unacceptable," 6 says. "We can't stall a hall full of celebrities for three hours."

Jerry looks like he's about to scream, or cry, or maybe both, so I say, "Okay, let's calm down. We'll probably finish in time. 6, I know this is difficult, but you just need to face the fact that this is out of your control."

6 stares at me, and for a moment I'm sure she's going to argue. Then she takes a deep breath. "Fine," she says. "I can do that."

begrudgingly

In the cab, 6 mutters, "I can't believe we just have to *wait*."

zipping along

We're showered, changed and at Mann's Chinese Theatre by ten. 6 has slipped into something less comfortable but a hell of a lot more attractive: a long, sheer black dress, killer heels and tiny ear studs. She's also wearing her glasses, and I can't believe how sexy she looks.

"6," I say again, "you look gorgeous. Really." I tug at my collar. "How do I look?"

6 frowns at my suit. "Aggressive."

"Aggressive? Really?" I'm a little taken aback; it's just a suit and red jacket. Okay, the jacket is pretty sharp. And the tie has little pictures of Uncle Sam, scowling and pointing. But they're pretty small pictures.

Despite myself, I'm awed at being here. I've never visited Mann's before, not even to gape at celebrity handprints: the only time I've ever seen this place has been on TV. Today there are already a lot of people around, sweeping the sidewalk, arranging signs, roping off areas. 6 spots California in the lobby and we head over.

"California," 6 says, "this is Scat."

She's young, blond, and even wearing a Coca-Cola T-shirt. "*Hi,* Scat. You excited?"

"Just a little," I lie.

"You should be," she says, grinning. "This is going to be the biggest film of the zips!"

"What?"

"The *zips,*" California says, tossing her hair happily. "You know, two thousand and zip. The '80s, the '90s, the zips."

"Oh, right."

"So, are you here to help?"

"We sure are," I say. "Although you look like you've got everything under control."

"Ha," California says, grinning. "Looks are deceiving. I really need you guys."

completion

At three, I break to call Jerry. "It's doing pass 12,020," he tells me.

"Is that good?"

"Well, if it was linear, it'd be finished by five."

"Hey, great!"

"But it's not," Jerry continues. "The end is loaded up with special effects, so that'll take longer."

"How much longer?"

Jerry sucks in his breath. "Maybe another two hours. But probably no more than that."

"So . . . ?"

"My guess is . . . you'll have this thing by seven."

I whoop. I can't help it: I let out a big, good old whoop. 6's eyes shine.

"It'll take half an hour to dump onto film. I'll do it fast and dirty, but you won't notice the quality loss in a standard cinema projection. I'll courier it to you by eight."

"No, no couriers. I'll pick it up personally. Just call me when it's time, okay?"

"You got it," Jerry says, and hangs up.

I turn to 6. "It'll be finished." The words sound like magic. "It's not definite, but he thinks it'll be finished."

6 nods slowly. I think she is trying to keep a smile under control. "Good boy."

mktg case study #15: mktg the channel

LAUNCH AN INCENTIVE PROGRAM FOR THE STORES THAT SELL YOUR BRAND; SO THAT, FOR EXAMPLE, EVERY SALES ASSISTANT WHO SELLS A NUMBER OF YOUR STEREOS GETS A FREE STEREO THEMSELVES. FOR THIS, THEY WILL PERSUADE, DECEIVE, AND CAJOLE IGNORANT CUSTOMERS INTO BUYING YOUR PRODUCT OVER YOUR COMPETITORS'. PRACTICE THE LINE: "OUR COMPANY CANNOT BE RESPONSIBLE FOR THE UNSCRUPULOUS ACTIONS OF A FEW RETAILERS."

enter

Jamieson arrives at five.

Sneaky Pete is with him, as is @. They stroll down the red carpet that's still being brushed down, resplendent in their tailored suits. I think even their sunglasses match. They pass 6 and me in the lobby without even noticing us and head straight into the main theater. We watch them all the way in.

"He needs to decide if we're going to make it or not," 6 says.

I look at her. "Huh?"

"Sneaky Pete has to make a decision." She turns to me. "If he thinks we're going to make it, he has to claim the glory. But if he thinks we're not going to make it, he'll disown himself."

I stare at her. "But as soon as he sees us here attending to all the details, he'll know. We wouldn't be here if we didn't have a film to show."

6 sniffs. "Sure we would. We'd be here trying to make him think we'd finished, to trick him into claiming ownership of the project."

I blink. "We're pretty smart."

6 shrugs. "It's what I would have done."

"So now . . ."

"Now we can't let him know we've finished." She steps closer, her eyes dark. "Do you understand this? If he finds out we've done it, he'll stand up tonight and call *Backlash* his baby. He'll take all the credit."

"No way," I say. "Oh, no way."

"So you see," 6 says, just a touch menacingly, "it's critical that we let him continue to believe we're not going to make it."

"Uh," I say, "and how are we going to do that?"

"By *lying*."

"Oh," I say. "Of course."

"Not to Jamieson. Sneaky Pete expects us to tell Jamieson everything's okay regardless of whether we've actually finished or not, so that's exactly what we'll do. But when Sneaky Pete wants a private chat—and he will—we let him force it out of us that we haven't made it." She eyes me. "And we do this convincingly."

"Right," I say slowly. "Well, I can try."

"You'll do better than that," 6 says darkly. "We've worked too hard to lose it to your conscience now."

Jerry calls at six, just as night is falling. The streetlights are warming up, the traffic cops are moving the barricades into position and the early stargazers have already turned up for the best positions.

"We're done," he tells me. He sounds in desperate need of sleep. "I'm dumping it to film now. Be here by seven."

"Count on it," I say. "And, Jerry? If anyone else from Coke asks you about our progress, you say we haven't finished yet, okay?"

He pauses. "Should I ask why?"

"No."

"Okay," Jerry says.

I find 6 with California in a corner of the lobby and relay the news. "Good," 6 says. "That'll give us time to finish with Jamieson."

I start. "Jamieson?"

"He wants to see us. To make sure everything's under control." She shrugs. "He's still worried, of course. So we'll sit down and reassure him. We'll be finished in time for me to go collect the film from Jerry."

"You?" I say, surprised. "Don't you want me to go? So you can stay and, uh, keep things under control?"

"No," 6 says, "you stay here. I can't control everything, right?"

"Uh, 6," I say, "you don't have to begin your journey of self-discovery right now, okay? How about I go get the film?"

"Why?"

"Well . . ." I swallow, then lean close to 6. "What if Sneaky Pete wants to talk to me?"

"He probably will. You just do what we talked about."

"Right . . ." I shift from one foot to the other. "You know, 6, I don't feel real comfortable about this. What if I can't fool him?"

"Then we're fucked," 6 says. "But that won't happen. Right?"

"Yeah," I say, not feeling sure about this at all. "Right."

Jamieson gathers us inside the actual cinema, strung along the front row like late patrons. He separates 6 and me from @ and Sneaky Pete as if it was intentional.

"Team," Jamieson says, "I want to say what a great job you've all done to get us to this point. This is going to be a sensational event. It's a credit to all of you."

I blush modestly. 6 says, "You're too kind, Mr. Jamieson."

"Not at all," he says, then pauses. Not for long. It's a tiny, tiny pause. But it's long enough to telegraph that he's about to get to the real reason he wanted to see us. "So how does the film look? In its finished form?"

The question isn't directed squarely, but I think it's fair to assume that it's meant for 6 and me. It's interesting, then, that @ jumps in first. "We haven't actually seen the finished product," she says, arching an eyebrow at us. Definitely not as good as 6's. "I understand that Scat and 6 were too busy to send us a copy. And we haven't been able to get in contact with either of them for the past two days, which is why, regrettably, we weren't able to show you a preview as we originally intended. But I'm sure Scat and 6 would have reached us if there was any problem?"

"Of course," 6 says. "The film is . . . finished. Of course."

I glance at 6, surprised at her pause, then realize that this is part of the trap. She's being deliberately unconvincing.

"So you have reviewed it?" Jamieson presses. "The entire product?"

"Yes," 6 says, more firmly now. "We've seen it. It's fine. It will be a credit to the organization."

"Right," Jamieson says slowly. "Good." He almost leaves it at that, but can't quite do it. "Are you sure? I don't mean to go on about it, but . . ." He smirks. "This is quite important."

"Mr. Jamieson," 6 says, looking shocked, "it would be humiliating for this company if we didn't have a film to present tonight.

I wouldn't expect to put the company in that situation and keep my job."

"No," Jamieson says. "Of course not. Good." He favors us with a smile, but his lingering doubts leak through. I anticipate an urgent exchange with Sneaky Pete as soon as we leave. "Then let's do it, team. We've got Hollywood arriving here tonight."

6 leaves

"Are you *sure* you don't want me to go?" I ask her anxiously.

"Scat," 6 says, exasperated. She slides into the cab. "I'll be back before you know it."

"Okay," I say nervously. I watch the cab until it's lost in traffic.

stargazing

"Hey!" someone in the crowd shouts. "There's Bruce Willis!"

The Premiere

CHAPTER 000017

fear

I just know he's going to find me.

It's not that I'm scared of him. I mean, okay, maybe a little. But I've gone up against him before, and even beaten him once. This, however, is different. Back then, I had the truth on my side. Now I have to lie.

I don't know if I can do it.

I mean, I don't have a moral problem with it. If there's one person in the world I wouldn't mind lying to right now, it's Sneaky Pete. But the thing is, I'm not very good at lying. I've never been good at it. It's like acting, and, like I said, I'm a terrible actor.

I can't believe Sneaky Pete won't see through me in an instant. So I hide.

show business

I ask California what I can do to help, and out of the long list of
possible jobs, I pick the one that takes me up into the projection
room. The projectionist, a little bald man named Harold, is already there, checking over the equipment, so I engage him in a
long and slightly inane conversation about the history of film
media. I figure I only have to hide for an hour, and then I can go
downstairs and find 6 and we can tackle Sneaky Pete together.

As the minutes tick by, the rising noise level signals the growing accumulation of stars, press and Hollywood powermongers.
At a quarter to eight, I can't stand not knowing who's out there
any longer, and, figuring 6 should be back by now, I escape my
conversation with Harold to head back down to the lobby. The
band—which is actually a mini-orchestra—is playing the theme
song from *Backlash*, and the bass reverberates through the staircase, mixing with four dozen Hollywood conversations. It sounds
really exciting, and I probably hurry down the staircase just a little
too quickly.

He catches me halfway down.

lies

I freeze.

For a long moment, he just stares at me. His sunglasses glint
dangerously. "Scat," he says softly. "How are you?"

Again, I have forgotten his voice. It's like an oiled massage. It's
a voice to open your soul to. If he wasn't already worth upward of
three million dollars, I'd suggest he consider a career as a tele-
phone counselor.

"I'm good," I say. My first lie! I'm off to a great start. I'd feel
pretty pleased, if I wasn't nervous enough to wet myself.

He cocks his head at me.

"No, really," I say. "I am good. Very good. Really." And that's just pathetic. Ruined all my early work. "How are you?"

"I am concerned," Sneaky Pete says, "that we may not have a film to show tonight."

"Oh!" I say, in a truly humiliating attempt at surprise. "Really?" And already I'm in trouble, because I've forgotten what I'm meant to lie about. Was I meant to tell him that we haven't finished it? Or was I meant to say that we have, and then, when he presses me, admit we haven't? Yes, I think that was it. But the long seconds it's taken me to get this straight haven't done wonders for my credibility. "We've done it," I say, a little breathlessly. "Yes. Film finished."

"Where is it?" It's a kind question. I could almost believe he just wants to help.

"It's—" I say, but a blond model in a shiny pink dress abruptly pushes past us. She looks around uncertainly. "Bathroom?"

Sneaky Pete regards her expressionlessly, so I say helpfully, "Down the stairs, corridor on your right."

"Thanks," she says, patting my behind as she passes.

"Hoo," I say, startled.

"Scat," Sneaky Pete says. "I need to go out in front of these people tonight and tell them whether or not we have a film for them."

"Yes," I say. This much I understand.

"If there is no film, I need to know now. I need to apologize to them."

"Yes," I say.

"So," he says. He takes a step toward me, and then, to my horror, removes his sunglasses. This is the first time I have ever seen Sneaky Pete's eyes, and I am stunned to discover that they are beautiful. They are mesmerizing. They pierce me. "Is *Backlash* completed?"

no

"Yes," I say convincingly.

no, no, no

It sounds very much as if this comes out of my mouth.

repercussions

He stares at me for long moments. I literally feel the blood drain from my face. I have fucked up, and Sneaky Pete can see it.

"Thank you," he says softly.

He turns, snaps his shades back on and descends the stairs.

calamity

"Oh my God," I say weakly. I suddenly need very much to sit down. So I do. I sit on the stairs and hold my head in my hands.

"Hi, Scat," someone says, and ruffles my hair.

I look up, startled, and see 6. She is balancing a stack of film cans. "6—"

"I'm taking the film up to the projection room." Her face is flushed with success. "We're about to start. This is it, Scat!"

"Wait—" I say, but Jamieson's voice booms out across the lobby.

"Ladies and gentlemen," he says, a little too theatrically. "The Coca-Cola Company and Universal Pictures are proud to welcome you . . . to *Backlash*."

"Scat, get down there," 6 says. "Here come your ideas. I'll meet you in the cinema." I open my mouth to protest, but at that moment the lights die and aliens burst into the lobby.

get ready

° ° °° ●. ⦂ °●°● °.° ●° °.●⦂● °. ●°● ° ●°● °.● °

They look a little corny, I admit, but this is Hollywood. When a dozen guys in rubber alien suits from the movie pour inside, firing their fake laser guns, everyone cheers.

A couple of the aliens set up atmosphere-inducing lamps, shedding filtered, complimentary light on the celebrities, and others zip through the crowd handing out cans of Coke. The rest of the aliens spend a few minutes shouting and firing, just long enough to keep everyone entertained while press photographers take shot after shot of film stars holding Cokes. This is one of my ideas, and I guess it's worth maybe five to ten million in free advertising. But I'm having trouble feeling good about that right now.

Before anyone can get cynical about the photographers, the aliens begin herding the crowd into the cinema. They overcome the inevitable objections about seating arrangements by leveling their rifles and shouting incomprehensible threats, and, amazingly, this seems to get people seated much more efficiently than trying to engage them in a reasonable dialogue.

I find my way to the front of the theater, where the Coke entourage is gathered. Sneaky Pete, @, Jamieson, and California are all here, while key members of the board and the SMT are precisely seated throughout the theater next to key producers and potential business partners. I look around for 6 but can't find her: maybe she's having trouble tearing herself away from Harold's fascinating opinions on the benefits of celluloid over digital video.

Jamieson gives the crowd a few minutes to settle, then stands and brushes down his suit. "Okay," he says, I think to himself. "Let's do it."

He strides to the microphone, set up neatly in the middle of the floor between the front row and the screen. A spotlight springs onto him, and the entire theater, revved up to high pitch by the aliens, claps and cheers.

I hunch miserably into my seat, searching for 6. Instead, my gaze stops on Sneaky Pete, sitting directly behind me. He is staring straight at me. I look away quickly, but not quickly enough: I see him nod slowly, and the grin starts to spread across his face.

hollow

"But enough from me," Jamieson says. "I'd like to hand over to the man responsible for all this: our Vice President of Marketing, Mr. Sneaky Pete."

More cheers and applause, even a few whistles. I feel physically ill. The movie is going to be a roaring success, and I don't think I've got the stomach to watch Sneaky Pete take the credit for it.

He stands and strolls across to the microphone, @ trailing at one shoulder. "Thank you," he tells the crowd softly.

"Scat," 6 whispers, dropping into the seat beside me. "How's it going?"

"6," I say miserably. "I—I don't know how to tell you this. He knows. He knows we've finished it." I wait for realization to spread across 6's face—for her to blast me off the face of the planet—but there's nothing. Her expression doesn't even change. "I mean," I say, "he's going to take credit for it. It's all been for nothing."

"Mmm," 6 says. "I don't think so."

She doesn't understand what's going on, and suddenly I'm furious. "I *told* you not to leave me alone," I hiss at her. "He cornered me and he got it out of me. He *knows*."

"Scat," 6 says, looking at me oddly. "He'll assume you lied to him."

I gape.

"I mean, *really*," she says. She shifts in her seat to get a better view. "As if he'd expect us to tell him the *truth*."

For long moments, I can't speak. I stare at 6 and make pathetic little *caw* noises in my throat. Then, finally, I spit out, "You *knew*. You *knew* I'd tell the truth." I can't believe she'd do this. "You *used* me."

"Whatever," 6 says, and she actually shoots me a quick grin.

sneaky pete speaks

"Ladies and gentlemen," Sneaky Pete says. He speaks softly, but his voice pours out of the speakers like syrup, spreading through the hall. "I'm afraid I have some bad news." Beside him, Jamieson stiffens. "Unfortunately, I have just discovered that we will not be able to show you *Backlash* tonight after all."

A woman in the crowd gasps. I feel like hugging her.

"This is extremely embarrassing," Sneaky Pete says, and he actually hangs his head for a second. "And I extend my humblest apologies to all concerned. But it is beyond our control. Mr. Jamieson and myself spoke to the persons responsible for delivering the film to us just a few hours ago, and we were assured that it would be ready. However, I now discover that this is not the case." His face darkens impressively. "I assure you that we will take action to reprimand the individuals concerned. In fact, I would like you to hear their apology in person."

He turns and points a long finger straight at us. "Ms. 6? Mr. Scat?"

backlash

The spotlight swings onto us immediately, so I guess Sneaky Pete prepped the operator. There is a long moment where we sit there in its magnesium glare, two hundred pairs of celebrity eyes on us.

Then 6 says clearly, "I'm sorry, but I don't know what you're talking about." She doesn't have a microphone, but in the silent theater her voice is perfectly clear.

Sneaky Pete answers quickly, as if he is expecting a response like this. "You are responsible for the final delivery of *Backlash*, are you not?" His voice is quiet and somber, as if he really doesn't want to get us into trouble but there's no other way.

"Yes, of course," 6 says. She glances at me. "Scat and I are primarily responsible for the entire *Backlash* project."

Sneaky Pete hesitates. Obviously this isn't quite what he was expecting: there's no squirming denial of responsibility. "Then . . . please apologize to our guests for your failure to produce the film."

I stand up, slowly. The light is blinding, but I can see him perfectly. "But as I told you . . . *Backlash* is ready."

oops

Sneaky Pete opens his mouth, closes it, then opens it again. But before he can get a word out, Jamieson grabs the microphone. His face is purple. "Then let's see it!"

The spotlight dies immediately, and a few moments later the projector begins to whir. It is a beautiful, beautiful sound.

Backlash begins.

fallout

Sneaky Pete is ashen-faced. Jamieson sits ramrod-straight beside him, refusing to look in his direction. I think it's a fairly safe bet that, as of now, Sneaky Pete is only technically an employee of Coca-Cola.

6 and I just enjoy the movie.

ovation

The applause begins even before the lights come up. It rolls up and down the theater like a bass drum, and when people start getting to their feet, it crashes around my ears.

Jamieson stands slowly, as if he can't believe what's happening, and stares at the rows of Hollywood faces cheering our success. Then he reaches down and pulls 6 and me to our feet, and the applause becomes deafening.

Sneaky Pete takes the opportunity to leave discreetly through a side exit. At least I assume he does: I don't actually see him go. I just realize he's not around anymore.

schmooze

The tide of celebrities flows around us like a river, and en route to the lobby I get separated from 6. "*Great* stuff," a man suddenly tells me, and I actually think it's George Lucas. "Winona's teeth at the end? I loved it. Let's catch lunch sometime, okay?"

"That would be great," I say, but I'm distracted, scanning the crowd for 6. I catch a glimpse of her talking to someone who looks very much like Tom Hanks.

"Mr. *Scat*," Winona Ryder says, catching my arm. Her eyes are shining. "I never got a chance to speak to you on set, but—wow! That was fantastic! Those changes of yours—"

"Great!" I say. "Hey, I need to catch up with 6 right now, but thanks very much for—"

"You!" someone shouts and I turn just as Kline wraps his thick arms around me. He hugs me tight for just a little too long. "You are a big man," Kline says. "I work with you again."

"Gee, I'd love to—"

"Got time for your old friends anymore?" Tina says, snaring me from Kline. She breaks into a huge smile. "Look, I dressed up 'specially for your corporate buddies. No eye-rings!"

"Hey, Tina," I say, pleased. "Look, I need to talk to 6 right now. You understand?"

"I think I do," Tina says, flashing me a grin. "Go boy! Go!"

I push forward, accepting slaps on the back, handshakes and congratulatory kisses, trying to get to 6. Then a tall, stunning blonde says, "Well, hello," and I abruptly realize it's Cindy. "Looks like you're quite the success."

"Cindy, hi," I say awkwardly. "Uh, I—"

"I was just telling Brad about you," she says, gesturing to the man beside her. I blink, and it's still Brad Pitt. "How much you helped me."

"Oh," I say. "Well—"

"I won't keep you," Cindy says. "I'm sure you've got important people to hobnob with. But congratulations, sweetheart." I open my mouth to thank her, but she's already deep in conversation with Brad. "It's the never-ending schedule that kills me," she is saying.

I turn and take a deep breath, ready for a final plunge into the mass for 6, and suddenly, terrifyingly, I'm face-to-face with Sneaky Pete. I take an involuntary step backward.

"You." He stares at me for a second, then shakes his head. "You told me the truth."

I don't know what to say. "Yeah."

"Scat," he says, a pained expression on his face, "haven't you learned *anything?*"

I blink, but someone bumps into me from behind. I turn and it's 6. "Hello," she says.

"Hi!" Suddenly she's here and I have no idea what to do. "How are you?"

"I'm fine," she says, nodding. "Yes, I'm good." She pauses. "We did well."

"Yes," I agree. "Yeah, we did."

She nods again, looking at the floor.

"So," I say.

She looks up. "Yes?"

I take a breath. "I think that now is a good time for us to be straight with each other. So I want to tell you . . ."

"Yes?"

"I think you're sensational. I'm completely, utterly in love with you."

"Mmm," 6 says. She considers. "This is good to know."

I wait.

"Very good to know," 6 says.

"6," I say sternly.

She looks up. "Yes?"

"Well," I say, a little exasperated, "I just think that, you know, if you wanted to tell me something, now would be a good time."

"Tell you?" 6 says, smirking.

"Oh, forget it," I tell her. "You're obviously in love with me but just can't admit it."

6 shakes her head, and just for a moment I have the terrible feeling that maybe I'm on completely the wrong track. Then she looks up, and I see that she is smiling. She is actually, physically smiling at me.

"You moron," she tells me. "I've been in love with you from the start."

epilogue

"You know," I tell her that night, "I always suspected that." I kindly pull the covers over her exposed shoulder.

"Yeah," 6 says. "Whatever."

variety

This Issue's Star Bio

Scat

Born 1977. Graduated from California State University with marketing major. Produced "Backlash," considered the first successful feature cinema advertisement. Later produced and starred in sequel, "Backlash II," followed by "Diet Life." Co-owns Synergy, global marketing consultancy firm, with partner, 6 (see Star Bio 34-2). Upcoming film rumored to be "Soda," starring Brad and Cindy Pitt.

**Read on for the first chapter from
Max Barry's novel, _LEXICON_,
available from The Penguin Press.**

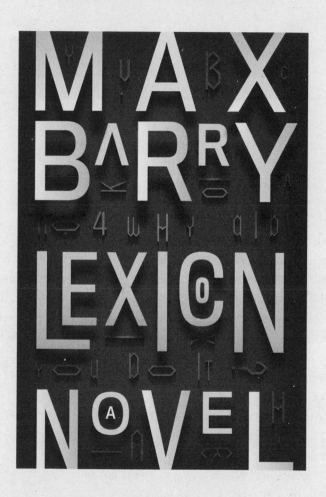

[O N E]

"He's coming around."

"Their eyes always do that."

The world was blurry. There was a pressure in his right eye. He said, *Urk*.

"Fuck!"

"Get the—"

"It's too late, forget it. Take it out."

"It's not too late. Hold him." A shape grew in his vision. He smelled alcohol and stale urine. "Wil? Can you hear me?"

He reached for his face, to brush away whatever was pressing there.

"Get his—" Fingers closed around his wrist. "Wil, it's important that you not touch your face."

"Why is he conscious?"

"I don't know."

"You fucked something up."

"I didn't. Give me that."

A rustling. He said, *Hnnn. Hnnnn.*

"Stop moving." He felt breath in his ear, hot and intimate. "There is a needle in your eyeball. Do not move."

He did not move. Something trilled, something electronic. "Ah, shit, shit."

"What?"

"They're here."

"Already?"

"Two of them, it says. We have to go."

"I'm already in."

"You can't do it while he's conscious. You'll fry his brain."

"I probably won't."

He said, "Pubbaleeese doo nut kill mee."

An unsnapping of clasps. "I'm doing it."

"You can't do it while he's conscious, and we're out of time, and he probably isn't even the guy."

"If you're not helping, move out of the way."

Wil said, "I . . . need . . . to . . . sneeze."

"Sneezing would be a bad move at this point, Wil." Weight descended on his chest. His vision darkened. His eyeball moved slightly. "This may hurt."

A *snick*. A low electronic whine. A rail spike drove into his brain. He screamed.

"You're toasting him."

"You're okay, Wil. You're okay."

"He's . . . aw, he's bleeding from his eye."

"Wil, I need you to answer a few questions. It's important that you answer truthfully. Do you understand?"

No no no—

"First question. Would you describe yourself as more of a dog person or cat person?"

What—

"Come on, Wil. Dog or cat?"

"I can't read this. This is why we don't do it when they're conscious."

"Answer the question. The pain stops when you answer the questions."

Dog! he screamed. *Dog please dog!*

"Was that dog?"

"Yeah. He tried to say dog."

"Good. Very good. One down. What's your favorite color?"

Something chimed. "Fuck! Oh, fuck me!"

"What?"

"Wolf's here!"

"That can't be right."

"It says it right fucking here!"

"Show me."

Blue! he screamed into silence.

"He responded. You see?"

"Yes, I saw! Who cares? We have to leave. We have to *leave.*"

"Wil, I want you to think of a number between one and a hundred."

"Oh, Jesus."

"Any number you like. Go on."

I don't know—

"Concentrate, Wil."

"Wolf is coming and you're dicking around with a live probe on the wrong guy. Think about what you're doing."

Four I choose four—

"Four."

"I saw it."

"That's good, Wil. Only two questions left. Do you love your family?"

Yes no what kind of a—

"He's all over the place."

I don't have—I guess yes I mean yes everybody loves—

"Wait, wait. Okay. I see it. Christ, that's weird."

"One more question. Why did you do it?"

What—I don't—

"Simple question, Wil. Why'd you do it?"

Do what do what what what—

"Borderline. As in, borderline on about eight different segments. I'd be guessing."

I don't know what you mean I didn't do anything I swear I've never done anything to anyone except except I once knew a girl—

"There."

"Yeah. Yeah, okay."

A hand closed over his mouth. The pressure in his eyeball intensified, became a sucking. They were pulling out his eyeball. No: It was the needle, withdrawing. He shrieked, possibly. Then the pain was gone. Hands pulled him upward. He couldn't see. He wept for his poor abused eyeball. But it was still there. It was there.

Blurry shapes loomed in fog. "What," Wil said.

"*Coarg medicity nighten comense*," said the taller shape. "Hop on one foot."

Wil squinted, confused.

"Huh," said the shorter shape. "Maybe it *is* him."

They filled a sink with water and pushed his face into it. He surfaced, gasping. "Don't soak his clothes," said the tall man.

He was in a restroom. An airport. He had come off the 3:05 P.M. from Chicago, where the aisle seat had been occupied by a large man in a Hawaiian shirt Wil couldn't bear to wake. At first, the restroom had appeared closed for cleaning, but the janitor had removed the sign and Wil had jagged toward it gratefully. He had reached the urinal, unzipped, experienced relief.

The door had opened. A tall man in a beige coat had come in. There were half a dozen free urinals, Wil at one end, but the man chose the one beside him. Moments passed and the tall man did not pee. Wil, emptying at high velocity, felt a twinge of compassion. He had been there. The door had opened again. A second man entered and locked the door.

Wil had put himself back in his pants. He had looked at the man beside him, thinking—this was funny, in retrospect—that whatever was happening here, whatever specific danger was implied by a man entering a public restroom and fucking *locking* it, at least Wil and the tall man were in it together. At least it was two against one. Then he had realized Shy Bladder Guy's eyes were calm and deep and kind of beautiful, actually, but the key point being *calm as in unsurprised*, and Shy Bladder Guy had seized his head and propelled him into the wall.

Then the pain, and questions.

"Have to get this blood out of his hair," said the short man. He attacked Wil's face with paper towels. "His eye looks terrible."

"If they get close enough to see his eyes, we have bigger problems." The tall man was wiping his hands with a small white cloth, giving attention to each finger. He was thin and dark-skinned and Wil was no longer finding his eyes quite so beautiful. He was getting more of a cold, soulless kind of vibe. Like those eyes could watch terrible things and not look away. "So, Wil, you with us? You can walk and talk?"

"Fuck," he said, "orrffff." It didn't come out like he meant. His head felt loose.

"Good," said the tall man. "So here's the deal. We need to get out of this airport in minimum time with minimum fuss. I want your cooperation with that. If I fail to receive it, I'm going to make things bad for you. Not because I have anything against you, particularly, but I need you motivated. Do you understand?"

"I'm not . . ." He searched for the word. *Rich? Kidnappable?* "Anybody. I'm a carpenter. I make decks. Balconies. Gazebos."

"Yes, that's why we're here, your inimitable work with gazebos. You can forget the act. We know who you are. And *they* know who you are, and they're *here*, so let's get the fuck out while we can."

He took a moment to choose his words, because he had the feeling he would get only one more shot at this. "My name is Wil Parke. I'm a carpenter. I have a girlfriend and she's waiting out front to pick me up. I don't know who you think I am, or why you stuck a . . . a thing in my eye, but I'm nobody. I promise you I'm nobody."

The short man had been packing equipment into a brown satchel, and now he slung it around one shoulder and peered into Wil's face.

He had thinning hair and anxious brows. Wil might have pegged him for an accountant, ordinarily.

"I tell you what," Wil said. "I'll go into a stall and close the door. Twenty minutes. I'll wait twenty minutes. It'll be like we never met."

The short man glanced at the tall man.

"I'm not the guy," Wil said. "I am not the guy."

"The problem with that little plan, Wil," said the tall man, "is that if you stay here, in twenty minutes you'll be dead. If you go to your girlfriend, who I'm sorry to say you can no longer trust, you'll also be dead. If you do anything other than come with us now, quickly and cooperatively, again, I'm afraid, dead. It may not seem like it, but we are the only people who can save you from that." His eyes searched Wil's. "I can see, though, that you're not finding this very persuasive, so let me switch to a more direct method." He held open his coat. Nestled against his side, nose down in a thigh holster, was a short, wide shotgun. It made no sense, because they were in an airport. "Come or I will shoot you through the fucking kidneys."

"Yes," Wil said. "Okay, you make a good point. I'll cooperate." The key was to get out of the restroom. The airport was full of security. Once he was out, a push, a yell, some running: This was how he would escape.

"Nope," said the short man.

"No," agreed the tall man. "I see it. Dope him up."

A door opened. On the other side of it was a world of stunted color and muted sound, as if something was stuck in Wil's ears, and eyes, and possibly brain. He shook his head to clear it, but the world grew dark and angry and would not stay upright. The world did not like to be shaken. He understood that now. He wouldn't shake it again. He felt his feet sliding away from him on silent roller skates and reached for a wall for support. The wall cursed and dug its fingers into his arm, and was probably not a wall. It was probably a person.

"You gave him too much," said the person.

"Safe than sorry," said another person. They were bad persons, Wil recalled. They were kidnapping him. He felt angry about this, although in a technical kind of way, like taking a stand on principle. He tried to reel in his roller skate feet.

"Jesus," muttered a person, the tall one with calm eyes. Wil didn't like this person. He'd forgotten why. No. It was the kidnapping. "Walk."

He walked, resentfully. There were important facts in his brain but he couldn't find them. Everything was moving. A stream of airport people broke around him. Everyone going somewhere. Wil had been going somewhere. Meeting someone. To his left, a bird twittered. Or a phone. The short man squinted at a screen. "Rain."

"Where?"

"Domestic Arrivals. Right ahead." Wil found this idea amusing: rain in the terminal. "Do we know a Rain?"

"Yeah. Girl. New."

"Shit," said the short man. "I hate shooting girls."

"You get used to it," said the tall man.

A young couple passed, gripping hands. Lovers. The concept seemed familiar. "This way," said the tall man, steering Wil into a bookstore. He came face-to-face with a shelf that said NEW RELEASES. Wil's feet kept skating and he put out a hand to catch himself and felt a sharp pain.

"Problem?"

"Possibly nothing," murmured the tall man, "or possibly Rain, passing behind us now, in a blue summer dress."

In glossy covers, a reflection skipped by. Wil was trying to figure out what had stabbed him. It was a loose wire in the NEW RELEASES sign. The interesting thing was that being stabbed had helped to clear the fog in his head.

"Busiest part of any store, always the new releases," said the tall man. "That's what attracts people. Not the best. The new. Why is that, Wil, do you think?"

Wil pricked himself with the wire. He was too tentative, could hardly feel it, and so tried again, harder. This time a blade of pain swept through his mind. He remembered needles and questions. His girlfriend, Cecilia, was out front in a white SUV. She would be in a two-minute parking bay; they had arranged that carefully. He was late, because of these guys.

"I think we're good," said the short man.

"Make sure." The short man moved away. "All right, Wil," said the tall man. "In a few moments, we're going to cross the hall and walk down some stairs. There will be a little circumnavigating of passenger jets, then we'll board a nice, comfortable twelve-seater. There will be snacks. Drinks, if you're thirsty." The tall man glanced at him. "Still with me?"

Wil grabbed the man's face. He had no plan for what to do next, so wound up just hanging on to the guy's head and staggering backward until he tripped over a cardboard display. The two of them went down in a tangle of beige coat and scattered books. *Run*, Wil thought, and yes, that was a solid idea. He found his feet and ran for the exit. In the glass he saw a wild-eyed man and realized it was him. He heard yelps and alarmed voices, possibly the tall man getting up, who had a shotgun, Wil recalled now, *a shotgun*, which was not the kind of thing you would think could slip your memory.

He stumbled out into an ocean of bright frightened faces and open mouths. It was hard to remember what he was doing. His legs threatened treachery but the motion was good, helping to clear his head. He saw escalators and forged toward them. His back sang with potential shotgun impacts, but the airport people were being very good about moving out of his way, practically *throwing* themselves aside, for which he was grateful. He reached the escalators but his roller skate feet kept going and he fell flat on his back. The ceiling moved slowly by. The tiles up there were filthy. They were seriously disgusting.

He sat up, remembering Cecilia. Also the shotgun. And, now he thought about it, how about some security? Where were they? Because it was an airport. It was an *airport*. He grabbed the handrail, intending to pull himself up to look for security, but his knees went in opposite directions and he tumbled down the rest of the way. Body parts telegraphed complaints from faraway places. He rose. Sweat ran into his eyes. Because the head fog wasn't confusing enough; he needed *blurred vision*. But he could see light, which meant *exit*, which meant *Cecilia*, so he ran on. Someone shouted. The light grew. Frigid air burst around him as if he'd plunged into a mountain lake and he sucked it into his lungs. Snow, he saw. It was snowing. Flakes like tiny stars.

"Help, guy with gun," he said to a man who looked like a cop but on reflection was probably directing cabs. Orange buses. Parking bays. The two-minute spaces were just a little farther. He almost collided with a trolley-laden family and the man tried to grab his jacket but he kept running and it was starting to make sense, now, running; he was starting to remember how to coordinate the various pieces of his body, and he threw a glance over his shoulder and a pole ran into him.

He tasted blood. Someone asked if he was okay, some kid pulling earbuds out of his hair. Wil stared. He didn't understand the question. He had run into a pole and all his thoughts had fallen out. He groped for them and found Cecilia. He raised his body like a wreck from the deep and shoved aside the kid and rode forward on a crest of the kid's abuse. He finally saw it, Cecilia's car, a white fortress on wheels with VIRGINIA IS FOR LOVERS on the rear window. Joy drove his steps. He wrenched open the handle and fell inside. He had never been so proud. "Made it," he gasped. He closed his eyes.

"Wil?"

He looked at Cecilia. "What?" He began to feel unsure, because her face was strange. And then it came to him, in a fountain of dread that began somewhere unidentifiable and ended in his testicles: He should not be here. He should not have led men with guns to his girlfriend. That was a stupid thing to do. He felt furious with himself, and dismayed, because it had been so hard to get here, and now he had to run again.

"Wil, what's wrong?" Her fingers came at him. "Your nose is bleeding." There was a tiny furrow in her brow, which he knew very well and was sad to leave.

"I ran into a pole." He reached for the latch. The longer he sat here, the closer the fog pressed.

"Wait! Where are you going?"

"Away. Have to—"

"Sit down!"

"Have to go."

"Then I'll drive you somewhere! Stay in your seat!"

That was an idea. Driving. "Yes."

"You'll stay if I drive?"

"Yes."

She reached for the ignition. "Okay. Just . . . stay. I'll take you to a hospital or something. All right?"

"Yes." He felt relief. Weight stole through his body. He wondered if it was okay to slide into unconsciousness. It seemed out of his hands now. Cecilia would drive to safety. This car was a tank; he had mocked it before, because it was so big and she was so tiny but they were equally aggressive, and now it would save them. He might as well close his eyes a moment.

When he opened them, Cecilia was looking at him. He blinked. He had the feeling he'd fallen asleep. "Why . . ." He sat up.

"Shhh."

"Are we moving?" They were not moving. "Why aren't we moving?"

"Just stay in your seat, until they get here," Cecilia said. "That's the important thing."

He turned in his seat. The glass was fogged over. He couldn't see what was out there. "Cecilia. Drive. Now."

She tucked a wisp of hair behind one ear. She did that when she was remembering something. He could see her across a room, talking to somebody, and know she was relating a memory. "Remember the

11.

day you met my parents? You were freaking out because you thought we were going to be late. But we weren't. We weren't late, Wil."

He rubbed condensation from the window. Through the whiteout, men in brown suits jogged toward him. "Drive! Cil! *Drive!*"

"This is just like then," she said. "Everything's going to be fine."

He lunged across her, groping for the ignition. "*Where are the keys?*"

"I don't have them."

"What?"

"I don't have them anymore." She put a hand on his thigh. "Just sit with me a minute. Isn't the snow beautiful?"

"Cil," he said. "Cil."

There was a flash of dark movement and the door opened. Hands seized him. He fought the hands, but they were irresistible, and pulled him into the cold. He threw fists in all directions until something hard exploded across the back of his head, and then he was being borne on broad shoulders. Some time seemed to have passed in between, because it was darker. Pain rolled through his head in waves. He saw blacktop and a flapping coattail. "Fuck," said someone, with frustration. "Forget the plane. They can't wait for us any longer."

"Forget the plane? Then what?"

"Other side of those buildings, there's a fire path, take us to the freeway."

"We drive? Are you kidding? They'll close the freeway."

"Not if we're fast."

"Not if we're . . . ?" said the shorter man. "This is fucked! It's fucked because you wouldn't leave when I said!"

"Shush," said the tall man. They stopped moving. The wind blew awhile. Then there was some running, and Wil heard an engine, a car stopping. "Out," said the tall man, and Wil was manhandled into a small vehicle. The short man came in behind him. A disco ball dangled from the mirror. A row of stuffed animals with enormous black eyes smiled at him from the dash. A blue rabbit held a flag on a stick, championing some country Wil didn't recognize. He thought he might be able to stab that into somebody's face. He reached for it but the short man got there first. "No," said the short man, confiscating the rabbit.

The engine revved. "How'd it go with the girlfriend, Wil?" the tall man said. He steered the car around a pillar marked D3, which Wil recognized as belonging to the parking garage. "Are you ready to consider that we know what we're doing?"

"This is a mistake," said the short man. "We should stay on foot."

"The car is fine."

"It's not fine. Nothing is fine." He had a short, angry-looking submachine gun in his lap. Wil had somehow not noticed that. "Wolf was on us from the start. They knew."

"They didn't."

"Brontë—"

"Shut up."

"Brontë fucked us!" said the short man. "She's fucked us and you won't see it!"

The tall man aimed the car at a collection of low hangars and warehouse-like buildings. As they drew nearer, the wind picked up, spitting ice down the funnels made by their walls. The car shook. Wil, jammed between the two men, leaned on one, then the other.

"This car sucks," said the short man.

A small figure loomed out of the gloom ahead. A girl, wearing a blue dress. Her hair danced in the wind, but she was standing very still.

The short man leaned forward. "Is that Rain?"

"I think so."

"Hit her."

The engine whined. The girl grew in the windshield. Flowers on her dress, Wil saw. Yellow flowers.

"*Hit her!*"

"Ah, fuck," said the tall man, almost too quietly to hear, and the car began to scream. The world shifted. Weight forced Wil sideways. Things moved beyond the glass. A creature, a behemoth with searing eyes and silver teeth, fell upon them. The car bent and turned. The teeth were a grille, Wil realized, and the eyes headlights, because the creature was an SUV. It chewed the front of the car and bellowed and shook and ran into the brick wall. Wil put his arms around his head, because everything was breaking.

He heard groans. Shuffling. The tick of the engine cooling. He raised his head. The tall man's shoes were disappearing through a jagged hole where the windshield had been. The short man was fumbling with his door latch, but in a way that suggested to Wil that he was having trouble making his hands do what he wanted. The interior of the car was oddly shaped. He tried to push something off his shoulder but it was the roof.

The short man's door squealed and jammed. The tall man appeared on the other side and wrenched it open. The short man crawled out and looked back at Wil. "Come on."

Wil shook his head.

The short man breathed a curse. He went away and the tall man's face dipped into view. "Hey. Wil. Wil. Take a look to your right there. Lean forward a little. That's it. Can you see?"

The side window was a half-peeled spiderweb, but beyond that he could see the vehicle that had attacked them. It was a white SUV. Its front was crumpled against the wall. Steam issued from around its bent front wheels. The sticker on the rear window said: VIRGINIA IS FOR LOVERS.

"Your girlfriend just tried to kill us, Wil. She drove right at us. And I'm not sure if you can see from there, but she didn't even stop to put on a seat belt. That's how focused she was. Can you see her, Wil?"

"No," he said. But he could.

"Yes, and you need to get out of the car, because there are more where she came from. There are always more."

He got out of the car. He was intending to punch the man in the jaw, knock him down and maybe choke the life out of him, watch those eyes go dim, but something snared his wrists. By the time he realized the short man was handcuffing him in white plastic, it was done. The tall man pushed him forward. "Walk."

"*No! No! Cecilia!*"

"She's dead," said the tall man. "Faster."

"I'll kill you," Wil said.

The short man jogged ahead of them, cradling his submachine gun. His head moved from side to side. He was probably looking for that girl, the one they'd called Rain. The girl who had stood like she was nailed to the blacktop, like she could stare down a car. "Utility van in the hangar there," said the short man. "May have keys."

Some men in hard hats and overalls approached. The short man screamed at them to lie down and not fucking move. The tall man pulled open the door of a white van and put Wil in it. Wil swung around so that when the tall man followed him in, Wil could kick his teeth down his throat, but a flash of blue in the side mirror caught his eye. He peered at it. There was something blue crouched under a refueling truck. A blue dress.

The van's side door was pulled open and the short man came in. He looked at Wil. "What?"

Wil said nothing. The tall man started the engine. He had slid into the van without Wil noticing.

"Wait up," said the short man. "He's seen something."

The tall man glanced at him. "Did you?"

"No," he said.

"Shit," said the short man, and tumbled out of the van. Wil heard his footsteps. He didn't want to look at the side mirror, because the tall man was watching, but he glanced once and there was nothing there anymore. A few moments passed. There was a noise. The girl in the blue dress burst past Wil's window, startling him, her blond hair streaming. There was a hammer of gunfire. She fell bonelessly to the concrete.

"Don't move," the tall man said to Wil.

The short man came around the van and looked at them. The barrel of his gun was smoking. He looked at the girl and gave a short, barking laugh. "I got her!"

Wil could see the girl's eyes. She was sprawled on her stomach, hair sprayed across her face, but he could still see that her eyes were the same blue as her dress. Dark blood stole across the concrete.

"Fucking *got* her!" said the short man. "Holy shit! I nailed a poet!"

The tall man revved the engine. "Let's go."

The short man gestured: *Wait.* He moved closer to the girl, keeping his gun trained on her, as if there was some chance she might get up. She didn't move. He reached her and proddel her with his shoe.

The girl's eyes shifted. "*Contrex helo siq rattrak*," she said, or something similar. "Shoot yourself."

The short man brought the tip of his gun to his chin and pulled the trigger. His head snapped back. The tall man kicked open the van door and raised his shotgun to his shoulder. He discharged it at the girl. Her body jerked. The tall man walked forward, ejected the spent cartridge, and fired again. Thunder rolled around the hangar.

By the time the tall man returned to the van, Wil was halfway out the door. "Back," said the tall man. His eyes were full of death and Wil saw clearly that they were now dealing in absolutes. This knowledge passed between them. Wil got back in the van. His bound hands pressed into his back. The tall man put the van into reverse, navigated around the two bodies, and accelerated into the night. He did not speak or look in Wil's direction. Wil watched buildings flit by without hope: He might have had a chance to escape, but that was over now.